A part of Lucas wondered if they'd ever be finished.

He looked into her eyes and saw the passion-glazed stare of a woman completely undone and should have felt a jolt of satisfaction for a plan that was coming together all too well.

Instead, all he felt was more want. More need.

Her blue eyes were shining with every ounce of passion that was flaring inside him. The smoldering fire between them leaped to life like an inferno.

Heartbeat pounding, he took her mouth again. And then Lucas did the only thing he could. He moved inside her again and heard her groan of satisfaction as his reward.

This wasn't seduction anymore.

This was *need.* Crashing, burning desperation— and it wouldn't be denied.

* * *

Dear Reader,

Writing a continuing family series, like the Kings of California, is as much fun for the writer as it is for the reader. We all love revisiting earlier characters. It's like having a nice long chat with an old friend you haven't seen for a while. I especially enjoy doing groups of two or three at a time that are more connected than just by their family name.

In *Ready for King's Seduction,* Lucas King gets his heroine. Not too long ago, he stood on the sidelines, snickering at his brother Rafe as he fell in love with Katie Charles, the Cookie Queen. Now, it's Rafe's turn to chuckle.

Lucas meets Rose Clancy, the younger sister of his ex-friend, and concocts a plan. He's determined to get back at Rose's brother for betraying the King brothers.

Rose Clancy, though, isn't the wide-eyed innocent that Lucas remembers. She's had a hard time of it, but she's survived and rebuilt her life. Now she teaches people how to cook in their own homes. When Lucas hires her, Rose agrees because she can use all the clients she can get.

But while Rose teaches cooking, Lucas is teaching her passion, and neither of them is prepared for what they find.

I really hope you enjoy *Ready for King's Seduction!* Next up is Sean King's book, *The Temporary Mrs. King,* and I hope you'll watch for it! Follow me on Facebook and Twitter and let me know what you think!

Happy reading,

Maureen

MAUREEN CHILD

READY FOR KING'S SEDUCTION

ISBN-13: 978-0-373-73126-8

READY FOR KING'S SEDUCTION

MAUREEN CHILD

is a California native who loves to travel. Every chance they get, she and her husband are taking off on another research trip. The author of more than sixty books, Maureen loves a happy ending and still swears that she has the best job in the world. She lives in Southern California with her husband, two children and a golden retriever with delusions of grandeur. Visit Maureen's website, www.maureenchild.com.

To my mother-in-law, Mary Ann Child,
for years of laughter and love and adventures.
I couldn't love you more.

One

"There's something you don't see every day."

"What are you talking about?" Lucas King stepped through his front door onto the wide porch and handed his younger brother a beer. Just for a second, he took the time to admire the view of the Pacific Ocean, across the street. The sun was setting, staining the dark blue water deep shades of crimson and gold. He settled into the closest chair and took a sip of his beer.

Sean grinned and pointed. "That. Look what just pulled up outside your neighbor's house."

Lucas shifted his gaze to Ocean Boulevard and his eyes widened. A dark blue minivan was parked in front of the house next door. Ordinarily, no big deal—except for the giant covered skillet on the roof.

"What the—"

"Check out the sign on the side," Sean said, laughing.

"'Home cooking taught at home,'" Lucas recited,

shaking his head. "So the sign on the side of the car in bright yellow paint wasn't enough? They had to stick a pan on top?"

Sean was still laughing as he took a sip of his beer. "Not exactly aerodynamic."

"It looks ridiculous," Lucas said, wondering what kind of person would have so little pride they'd be willing to drive the thing. "Who the hell runs a business like that, anyway?"

"Mmm…" Sean's tone changed as the minivan's door opened and the driver stepped out into the street. "Whoever she is, she can teach me whatever she wants to."

Lucas rolled his eyes even as he shifted his gaze back to the ocean. Big surprise. Sean was always willing and eager for the next woman to roll into his life. Give him five minutes with Pan-on-the-Car Woman, Lucas told himself, and Sean would have a weekend getaway scheduled. Well, Sean was welcome to the stream of women entering and exiting his life. Lucas liked his life a little more orderly.

Only half listening to Sean's running commentary, Lucas ignored the woman and the car and focused on the stretch of water sliding toward the horizon. This is what he loved about where he lived. Every night after work, he could come out to the porch, have a beer, stare out at the water and let the world slip away for a while. Usually though, he thought—Sean's voice an annoying buzz of sound in the background—he was alone.

Here, he didn't have to be on top of King Construction. Here, no one was hounding him for a meeting or to fix something gone wrong with permits. There were no needy customers to placate and no hurry to accomplish a damn thing.

Oh, he liked his work. He and his brothers Rafe and Sean had built King Construction into the biggest firm of its kind on the west coast. But damned if it didn't feel good to come home and let it all go for a while.

"Always did like a blonde," Sean was saying. "And a tall one, too."

Lucas snorted. "Blondes, redheads, brunettes. Your problem is you like 'em all."

"Yeah? Your problem is you're too damn picky. When was the last time you called a woman who wasn't a customer?" Sean kicked back in his chair, setting his feet on the stone porch-balcony rail in front of them.

"None of your business," Lucas muttered.

"Hell. That long? No wonder you're such a pain in the ass lately." Sean took another drink of his beer. "What you need is a little female attention and if you've got eyes in your head, one look at this blonde and you'll be ready to go."

Lucas sighed and surrendered to the inevitable. Sean wasn't going to shut up about the woman, so Lucas might as well get a good look at her for himself. "No way," he muttered.

"Huh?" Sean glanced at him.

"I don't believe this," Lucas said, more to himself than to his brother. He stood up, eyes locked on the tall, curvy blonde hurrying around the front of her car. Her long hair was pulled into a ponytail at the base of her neck, the wind whipping her hair into a frenzy. Her skin was pale and, he knew, dusted with freckles across her nose and cheeks. He couldn't see her eyes from here, but he knew they were a deep summer blue. Her mouth was wide and curved easily into a smile, and her laugh was infectious as hell.

He hadn't seen her in two years and seeing her *now* sent a near electric current sizzling through him. Lucas watched her open the sliding side door, then bend over to reach inside.

Instantly, he shifted his gaze to the curve of her behind, defined by the tight black jeans she wore. That buzz of something inside him heightened into a crackling, pulsing energy.

"What's going on?" Sean pushed out of his chair to stand beside his brother. "You know her?"

"I used to," Lucas admitted. Not as well as he had wanted to at the time, of course. A guy just didn't make moves on his friend's sister.

"Great. How about you introduce me to tall, blonde and luscious—"

Lucas glared at him.

Sean nodded and held up both hands. "Okay then, never mind. So who is she?"

"Rose Clancy."

Sean's eyebrows went up high enough that the shock of black hair falling across his forehead completely hid them. Then he turned and looked at the blonde, still fishing around inside her van. "*That's* Dave Clancy's little sister?"

"That's her."

"The one he always claimed was practically a saint? Good? Sweet? Pure as the driven snow?"

"The very one," Lucas muttered, his gaze now narrowed on her as he remembered all the times he had listened to his ex-friend Dave brag about his baby sister.

The Clancy family ran a rival construction company.

Well, rivals in the sense that they were all in the same business. In Lucas's mind, there had never really been a contest between them. King Construction was the best firm in the state, but Clancy came in a close second.

He and Dave had met at a chamber-of-commerce meeting and had immediately hit it off. They'd been friends as well as friendly competitors. Until the day two years ago when Lucas finally figured out that Dave Clancy was a liar and a thief.

"Didn't I hear that Rose got a divorce last year from that ass she married?"

"Yeah," Lucas said, still watching as Rose hurried back to her van for more supplies. "I heard she divorced him. Weren't married long, either."

Long enough, though, Lucas thought, to discover her husband was a cheating dog that should have been neutered for the good of humanity. Funny that her so protective older brother hadn't bothered to save her from a bad marriage.

Rose gathered up a few more things, then slid the door closed, beeped the lock and headed for the house again. She never once glanced at her surroundings, so she didn't notice Lucas and Sean standing on the porch staring at her.

"What're you planning?" Sean asked and Lucas turned his head to look at him.

"Not planning a thing," he lied as his mind raced with sudden possibilities.

"Right. Sell that to somebody who doesn't know you."

"Don't you have a date tonight?" Lucas asked.

"Yeah, I do."

"Then maybe you should go."

"Translation," Sean said wryly, "you don't want to tell me what you're thinking about doing."

Lucas grinned. "Smart man."

Shaking his head, Sean set his half-empty bottle of beer down onto the stone rail and headed for the steps. He paused, though, to look over his shoulder at his brother. "You know, it was *Dave* who cheated us. Not his sister."

Lucas met Sean's gaze evenly, his eyes giving away nothing he was feeling. "Did I say anything about Dave?"

"No," Sean admitted. "But I know how your mind works."

"Is that a fact?"

"It is." Sean tipped his head to one side and studied him for a long minute. "Kings don't like getting screwed. But Lucas King takes betrayal as a personal insult."

"Isn't it?" Lucas looked away from his brother, back to his neighbor's empty front yard and Rose's ridiculous van.

Dave Clancy had been a friend. Someone Lucas trusted. And he didn't trust many people. Having that friend turn on him had cut deep and damned if he'd apologize for still being angry.

"Dave cheated all of us," Lucas reminded his brother. "He paid one of our employees to give him insider information and then he went out and undercut our bids on four different projects. I call that pretty damn personal."

"We never found any proof of that."

"Yeah? I got my proof when Lane Thomas left us to go to work for Dave's outfit and suddenly the undercutting stopped. Coincidence?"

"Fine." Sean pushed one hand through his hair and

shrugged. "All I'm saying is taking your anger out on Rose won't do a damn thing to settle up with Dave."

"Who says I'm taking anything out on anybody?" Lucas asked.

"So you're not planning on a little payback?"

"I'll see you at work tomorrow, Sean."

"No way does this end well," Sean told him, then turned and headed down the front walk to his car.

Lucas dismissed his brother in the next minute. "It won't end well for the Clancys," he murmured thoughtfully. "That's for damn sure."

Rose waved goodbye to the woman standing in the doorway and didn't let her smile fade until the front door was closed. The sidewalk was brightly lit and the streetlights on Ocean Boulevard gave off a soft, yellow glow, so she didn't mind the darkness. It was actually a relief to get out into the cold, crisp night and away from the lingering smell of burned onions.

Kathy Robertson was determined to become a good cook—which made her an excellent client—but it wasn't going to be easy. Still, that meant Mrs. Robertson was going to be a long-term project, and that meant solvency for Rose's burgeoning business. A good thing. Smiling to herself, Rose stacked her supplies back in her van, slid the door closed and then jumped when a man's voice spoke up from behind her.

"Been a while."

She spun around, hand to her chest, and looked up at a man she hadn't seen in two years. Not since he and her older brother had cut off all communication. As soon as her heart slid out of her throat, it started pounding in excitement. "Lucas?"

He was leaning against her van. How had he walked

up without her being aware of it? Now that she knew he was there, her skin was prickling and her nerve endings were standing up straight, dancing in appreciation. He was wearing a pullover red sweater over a white T-shirt and black jeans. His boots were scuffed and his black hair was ruffled by the wind. His jaw boasted the shadow of a beard and his blue eyes were fixed on her.

"You scared me to death," she admitted when she could find her voice again.

"Sorry," he said, but didn't sound apologetic at all. "Didn't mean to startle you. But I wanted to talk to you before you left."

"Where'd you come from?" She glanced up and down the street, idly noting the steady stream of traffic.

"I live next door," he told her, jerking his thumb toward the two-story house boasting a wide, stone front porch.

"I didn't know," she said, which was a good thing. Because she might not have taken the Robertsons on as customers if she had known Lucas King lived right beside them.

A few years ago, she had spent a lot of time daydreaming about this man. It hadn't gone any further than that, of course, because her brother, Dave, had made sure to keep Lucas at a distance from her. Still, it hadn't been easy to put Lucas out of her mind. He continued to sneak back in at unexpected moments. Seeing him again was only going to refuel those old daydreams and make *not* thinking about him even more difficult.

But he'd made himself very clear three years ago. He hadn't been interested in her enough then to go against her brother's interference and there was no reason to think that had changed. Besides, she'd been through a lot in the past few years. She wasn't the easily charmed or foolishly romantic girl she had been.

Sure, her mind taunted slyly, *that's why your heart's still pounding and your palms are damp. Because you're so cool and controlled.*

Frowning at her own inner turmoil, she missed what Lucas said and was forced to ask, "What?"

He pushed away from the car, stuffed his hands into his back pockets and repeated, "I said, I'm glad to see you're teaching Kathy to cook. I've been to dinner at their place. Not pretty."

Wryly, Rose was forced to admit, "She is…challenging. But she's determined to improve, and that's good for all of us."

Nodding his head, he glanced at the skillet on top of her car. "Interesting advertisement."

She knew what he must be thinking, but Rose liked her skillet. An artist friend had made it for her and attached it to the roof of the van. "I think it's quirky."

"That's one word for it," he said.

Instantly, her back went up. She'd had to defend her new business to her older brother, and she wasn't going to do the same with Dave's ex-friend. Which reminded her of the fact that Dave and Lucas weren't even speaking anymore. So why was Lucas talking to her now?

She pushed windblown hair off her face and asked, "Was there something you wanted, Lucas?"

He looked at her for a long, silent moment, those blue eyes of his shadowed in the dim light. But his stare was just as powerful as it had once been, and Rose felt her heartbeat quicken again in response. It was an involuntary reaction, she told herself firmly, and refused to acknowledge it further.

"Actually," he said, "there is. You teach cooking classes in people's homes, right?"

"Yeah…"

"Then I want to hire you."

She hadn't expected that and wasn't entirely sure what to make of it. Lucas King was one of the wealthiest men in America. He could employ a dozen chefs and never once have to enter his own kitchen if he didn't want to. So why learn to cook for himself?

"Why?"

He pulled his hands free of his pockets and folded his arms across his broad chest. "I should think that would be self-evident. I want to know how to cook."

"Yeah, I get that," she said, still not willing to believe that he was serious. "What I don't understand is why you want to hire me."

"Because I don't want to have to go out to take classes. You coming to my home is more convenient."

"Uh-huh." She was thinking fast and trying to see the trap in what he was saying, but she just couldn't. Maybe he was being sincere. Maybe he really did want to learn how to cook for himself and seeing her here tonight had just been a happy accident.

But even as she thought it, Rose told herself there had to be more to it than that. As far as she knew, Lucas and her brother hadn't spoken in a couple of years. Though she had tried to find out from Dave what had gone wrong in their friendship, her brother hadn't told her a thing.

All he'd been willing to say was that Lucas King was out of their lives and she had better leave it that way.

If Lucas felt the same, and she had no reason to think he didn't, why was he trying to hire her?

"How much do you charge?" Lucas asked, splintering her thoughts.

She told him and he nodded. "I'll pay you twice your usual rate."

"What? Why would you do that?"

"For your undivided attention," he told her. "I'd want you here every night. Teaching me."

She took a quick breath and tried to put out the flickering flames in the pit of her stomach. Every night. Teaching him. It sounded way more sexual than it should have.

"I have other clients," she told him, though the truth was, her new business was barely up and sputtering. Besides Kathy Robertson, there were only three other women who had hired her so far and they were only once-a-month commitments.

"Three times your usual rate," he countered, his gaze fixed on her, his expression unreadable.

Rose blew out a breath she hadn't realized she'd been holding. With that kind of money, she could get a running start on building her business. Yes, she didn't *have* to struggle. She was a Clancy after all, and if she was in deep trouble, she would only have to tell Dave she needed money.

But she really didn't want to go to her brother. And she'd already invested everything she had into her business. So it was sink or swim. Lucas's offer would make it much easier to stay afloat.

"You're not making it easy to say no," she admitted.

"Glad to hear it," Lucas said.

She took a deep breath and, shaking her head slowly, heard herself say, "I don't know, Lucas. If Dave found out about this—"

"So," he interrupted, "you're still letting your older brother run your life, is that it?"

Her head snapped up, her gaze locked with his and a fast spurt of anger shot through her. "Dave has never run my life."

"Not how he saw it."

"Things change."

"Do they?" Lucas prodded. "Then take my offer."

Frowning to herself, Rose knew she was being manipulated and she didn't like it. But she also didn't like the fact that Lucas had a point. If she turned his offer down, she was kowtowing to the older brother who already thought he had a right to run her life.

Well, times had changed and so had Rose. She was a grown-up. She had survived the loss of her father, the disintegration of a bad marriage and the bossiness of a brother who thought he knew best. She could handle Lucas King and the still-sizzling attraction she felt for him.

"All right," she said, holding out her right hand, "it's a deal."

His hand enveloped hers in a warm shake that sent tendrils of something deliciously wicked streaming through her system. He gave her a half smile and said, "Great. We'll start tomorrow. Six work for you?"

He let her go but her skin was still buzzing from his touch when she mumbled, "Yeah. Six is fine."

"See you then." Lucas turned and headed back to his house and Rose watched him go.

Leaning against her car, she ordered her heartbeat to slow down and told her stomach to stop spinning.

Neither of those commands had the slightest effect on her.

When he disappeared into his house, Rose shook her head slowly and whispered, "I'm in *so* much trouble."

Two

"Real men don't eat mushrooms," Lucas pointed out the next night as he sliced into the tiny white buttons. "They're not even vegetables. Aren't they a fungus?"

Rose laughed, and Lucas stilled for a second, listening to the sound of it. Just as he remembered, that laugh of hers was damned infectious. Made a man want to smile in response, then pull her in close for a long, deep, wet kiss that would end in—

"Technically, yes," she said, when she'd stopped laughing at him long enough to speak. "They are fungi. For a long time, they were considered vegetables, but then researchers discovered they weren't plant or animal, but their own species."

"Great. And I'm going to eat them, why?"

Lucas waited for it and wasn't disappointed. She laughed again and something inside him shifted, expanded.

Their first cooking lesson was going more smoothly than he'd expected. Sure, there had been some tension when she first arrived, but that had dissipated quickly enough when she got a look at his kitchen. He smiled to himself when he realized that she was the first woman to be seduced by his subzero fridge and Viking stove.

Hell, when he remodeled the house after buying it five years ago, he had insisted on top-of-the-line, and the designer had been given free rein in the kitchen. From the bamboo flooring to the glass-fronted cabinets, the granite counters and workstations and the island sink, the kitchen was the kind of room every cook dreamed of.

And the most Lucas had ever made in it himself was the occasional plate of bacon and eggs.

Now, though, he thought as he watched Rose moving through the room, he would always see her here. He would hear the echoes of her laughter. See the way she practically danced around the room with a sort of balletic grace. She cooed over the copper pots and pans and sighed deeply when she first opened the nearly empty butler's pantry.

She might have been a little nervous when she'd first arrived, but in his kitchen, she was right at home.

"We're using button mushrooms because they're the most common. You can find them in any grocery store and they add just enough flavor to any dish to give it a hint of something…more."

"More fungus. Great." He shook his head, reminded himself that he wasn't here to enjoy himself—or her. He had set this up as a way of paying back a friend for the kind of betrayal that Lucas never forgave. Rose wasn't a date.

She was a tool.

Grimly, he went back to the task of slicing mushrooms while Rose gathered up the supplies she'd brought along and set them out on the cooking island.

"I brought enough with me for tonight's lesson," she said, "because this was all so sudden I figured you wouldn't have the right ingredients."

"Good call," he said, his knife sliding through button after button.

"But it's just a crime that you have this amazing kitchen and nothing in it," she said with a long sigh. Shaking her head, she looked around the room as if studying an abandoned puppy and wondering how to find it a good home. "I'm going to leave a list of supplies for you to pick up. With a well-stocked pantry and refrigerator, you'll always have options."

He lifted his head to look at her, and their eyes locked. A second or two of pulsing tension passed before he said, "Until I learn how to cook, being well-stocked really isn't necessary, is it?"

She plopped one hand on her hip. "How am I supposed to teach you how to cook if there's nothing in your house to cook *with?*"

"Good point again," he muttered, then rallied. "Okay, leave your list. I'll have my secretary take care of getting whatever you think I need."

"Your secretary."

He frowned at her. "Something wrong with that?"

"Oh, no," she said, lifting both hands in surrender. "Just typical, that's all."

"Typical of what?"

"Men like you. And Dave."

"Excuse me?" He stiffened. "I'm nothing like your brother, let's get that straight right now."

Now it was her turn to stiffen up, and Lucas noted

the flash of emotion in her eyes. "Look, I know you and Dave don't speak anymore—"

"That's right, we don't," he said, cutting her off before she could try to do something as fruitless as attempt to salvage a friendship that was dead to him.

It was good that she'd brought him up, though. Good to reinforce the fact that Rose was the sister of his enemy. A man he had once trusted. And the only reason Rose was standing here, driving him insane with her soft scent of lemons, was that Lucas was going to use her to get back at the man who had betrayed him. Revenge. Pure. Simple.

Sweet.

A minute or two of strained silence passed before she said, "All I meant was that men like *you* most often delegate work to your secretaries—even when it's not something that's really part of their job descriptions."

He looked at her, the knife in his hand still. "My secretary's job description includes pretty much whatever I say it does."

"Uh-huh. Even grocery shopping?"

"There's something wrong with that?"

She leaned both hands on the cooking island's cool granite surface. Her skin looked even paler against the gleaming black stone. "How will you know what to get in the future? You plan to always have your secretary do the work for you?"

Actually, it sounded like a good plan to Lucas. If he wanted to grocery shop, there would be actual food in his house right now. But why would he when there was a great diner just a half block away and enough restaurants in the city of Long Beach that a man wouldn't have to eat at the same place twice during a six-month span?

Rose shook her head. "Maybe I should be giving your secretary the lessons."

Okay, that was a little insulting. "Fine," he said. "I'll get the groceries. Make a list, and I'll take care of it before tomorrow night."

Smiling, she said, "How about we do it together tomorrow? We'll call it part of the lesson. I'll show you how to choose your produce and what to look for at the meat counter."

Lucas nodded, and she smiled even wider. Grocery shopping. Not exactly a high-end kind of date, he told himself, but then he wasn't dating her, either. This was a planned seduction. What he wanted to do was get her off guard and keep her there. Then, when she was relaxed enough, he'd tumble her into bed. Once that was done, Lucas would tell her brother just how good she had been, and he'd have the kind of revenge that would tear at Dave Clancy for the rest of his life.

"But for now," Rose was saying, "you finish slicing the mushrooms, then I want you to chop three table-spoons of fresh parsley."

He paused and frowned. "Isn't parsley the decoration on plates that no one ever eats?"

"Some of us actually do eat it."

"Amazing," he muttered, but went back to his task. While he worked, he managed to keep one eye on Rose as she explored his kitchen. She drew down plates and wineglasses from the cupboards, opened up the fridge and grabbed the sour cream, cheese and butter she'd brought with her for tonight's recipe.

In a few minutes, they were working together amiably. But when she turned on the radio and soft jazz spilled from the speakers, Lucas began to worry.

He was actually enjoying himself.

And that wasn't part of the plan.

"So?" Rose asked an hour later, "what do you think?"

She was sitting opposite him at the glass-topped table at the far end of the kitchen. Beside them was a bay window that overlooked a wide backyard. The garden lights were on, spilling small circles of golden radiance across the grass and neatly tended flowerbeds. The winter garden was sparse, but even in the dimly lit darkness, Rose could imagine how beautiful it all was in daylight.

She didn't usually stay after the lesson and join her students for the meal they had created, but Lucas had insisted and frankly, Rose thought with an inner sigh, she hadn't wanted to leave. Probably not a good idea to start getting attached, she warned herself sternly, but then she had always had a soft spot for Lucas King. She couldn't explain it. It just...*was*.

Still, after two hours of working closely together in his amazingly wonderful kitchen, Rose still couldn't have said that she knew Lucas any better than she once had. Oh, he seemed friendly enough, despite the thin thread of distance he insisted on keeping between them.

But then, she reminded herself as she looked back at her memories, Lucas had always been a little closed off. That's probably what had drawn her to him in the first place, Rose realized. In her own family, the men had been outgoing, gregarious. Whatever they were thinking, they didn't keep to themselves. They were loud and emotional and easy to read.

Meeting Lucas had been like brushing up against a gorgeous mystery. His blue eyes held secrets, his almost unreadable expressions tempted her to delve deeper and his quiet self-assurance had been a welcome difference from her brother and father.

He'd attracted her with his quiet thoughtfulness and, apparently, that hadn't changed.

"Earth to Rose," he said, snapping his fingers in front of her face.

She came up out of her thoughts fast and gave herself a shake. "Sorry. What?"

Lucas gave her a half smile. "You zoned out. Was it the sparkling conversation or the slightly charred chicken breast?"

She laughed a little. "The chicken is just a little well done," she said, glancing down at the salsa-covered meat on her plate. "Not bad at all for a first try."

"So the conversation put you to sleep?"

"No," she said, taking a bite of the mushroom au gratin casserole. "But the lack of it might. You haven't had a lot to say in the last hour or so, Lucas."

"Cooking takes concentration," he said with a shrug.

"Is that all it is?"

He looked at her. "What else would it be?"

"I don't know," she mused, taking a small sip of the chardonnay he had poured for both of them. "Maybe you're regretting hiring me? After the way you and Dave left things, I'm still not sure why you hired me in the first place."

His features tightened briefly at the mention of her brother, and, once again, Rose really wished she knew what had come between the two men. One day, their friendship was just…over. Lucas hadn't come around anymore, and Dave had refused to talk about it with her. Unfortunately, that hadn't changed two years later. Neither of them seemed willing to satisfy her curiosity.

"Dave's got nothing to do with this," Lucas murmured. "You teach cooking, I need to learn, end of story."

"If you say so." She didn't believe him. Sure, there had been the coincidence of him seeing her at his neighbor's house. But what had moved him to ask her to help him learn to cook? Why would he suddenly be willing to talk to the sister of the man he hadn't spoken to in years? There was more here and she'd eventually get to the bottom of it. But for now, she was willing to let it go.

"So what did you think of the mushrooms au gratin?"

He grinned and took a big bite of the casserole side dish in question. Once he'd chewed and swallowed, he said, "It proves that with enough sour cream and cheese, anything is edible. Even fungi and parsley."

"A lovely compliment," she said, chuckling. "But you have to admit, the first meal you cooked turned out pretty well."

"Better than Kathy Robertson's?"

"Why are men so competitive?"

"It's a gift. So?"

"Yes," she reluctantly admitted. "I don't really like to talk about my clients, but yours was way better. Kathy burned the onions so badly, I had to throw one of my favorite pans away."

He shuddered. "Hope she kept the name of the last caterer she used."

Laughing, Rose said, "That was just mean. She's going to get the hang of it."

He studied her for so long, Rose began to shift uneasily in her chair. "What?"

"Nothing," he said with a shake of his head. "But you

really are a positive, glass-is-half-full kind of woman, aren't you?"

Rose tensed briefly. For most of her life, she had pretty much been the Pollyanna type. She looked for the good around her and generally found it. Until, of course, her ex-husband had not only snatched off her rose-colored glasses, but also ground them to dust under his heel.

After that, she'd had to fight to regain her sense of well-being. She'd had to force herself to smile until, eventually, it had become real. And now, she wasn't going to go back to the dark side again. She wasn't going to apologize because she liked rainbows and puppies and laughing children.

"Seeing the empty half doesn't make you more mature or more intelligent," she said softly. "It only means you're looking for what you don't have. How is that a good thing?"

"I didn't mean—"

"It's okay," she said, folding her napkin and standing up. "I like a half-full glass. And if yours is half-empty, then I'm sorry."

He stiffened as if she'd hit a sore spot. Instantly, Rose regretted the fact that their semipleasant evening had deteriorated somehow. But maybe it was better this way. Keep the distance of teacher and student between them. Because he hadn't hired her to be his friend—or anything else. This was a job. A good-paying job at that, and she wasn't willing to risk it by opening up doors that should probably remain closed.

"My glass is just fine, thanks," he said, his voice hardly more than a low rumble of sound.

"Glad to hear it." Rose looked at him, and, in spite of knowing that she should just keep her mouth shut and protect this very well-paying job, she just had to say, "Maybe your glass is full, but if it's holding the wrong things, what difference does it make?"

"*What?*"

"Never mind. Dumb analogy anyway. Look, why don't I help you clean this up? Then we'll make out a menu and a grocery list for tomorrow."

She left him sitting at the table and even though she didn't look around, Rose knew he was still watching her when she started loading the dishwasher.

"That's it, you're paying my dues at Weight Watchers."

"Hmm?" Lucas looked up from the sheaf of papers he had been staring at for an hour without really reading any of it and looked at his secretary. "Evelyn, what're you talking about?"

"This." She held up an oversize frosted cookie and shook it at him. "Ever since Rafe married Katie, we've got these amazing cookies in the break room every day."

"That's a bad thing?" he asked, smiling.

Evelyn was in her late fifties with a rounded figure and short, graying brown hair. She was smart, efficient and knew as much as Lucas did about running crews and the customer base. She'd been with him for five years and had long since let go of her polite, businesslike tone with him.

"I've gained five pounds," she muttered and gave the cookie a glare before taking a bite and nearly groaning in pleasure.

"Don't eat them," he said with a shrug.

"Excellent advice," she muttered with a dark look. "Why didn't I think of that?"

"Evelyn, was there a point to this?"

She sighed in defeat, took another nibble of the

cookie and said, "There's trouble on the Johnson site. The crew started digging for the new gas line before the WeDig people came out to clear the site and they hit the water line."

"Perfect." Anger churned his guts. His crews were more professional than that. They knew damn well that any digging had to be cleared by the city guys who came out to tell them where gas, water and cable lines were, giving them specific areas to avoid. "Who's in charge of that site?"

She rolled her eyes. "Warren."

"Damn it."

"Exactly," Evelyn said. "He's on line two right now, wanting to talk to you."

"Good. I've got a few things to say to him, too." He waved one hand at his secretary, who backed out of his office chewing on her cookie and moaning like a woman having sex.

Oh, now there was an image he didn't need in his head. Evelyn. Having sex.

He snatched up the phone, pushed line two and snapped, "Warren, what the hell is going on? You dug before getting the go-ahead?"

"Not me, boss. It was Rick. The new guy. Got impatient, I guess. I was making a run to a supply shop for more pipe. When I got back, it was like the Great Flood out there."

"You're in charge, Warren," Lucas told him, tired of the man's excuses. Whenever anything went wrong on one of his sites, he was never around. Always off doing something else. "You give the orders on this project, and you take your orders from *me*. You damn well know better than to dig before WeDig comes out to clear it and the guys should know it, too."

"Yeah, but—"

"No more buts. I'll be at the site in a half hour. For now, get some pumps in there to clear the yard and get that water pipe capped off."

"Already done."

"That's something anyway…" Shaking his head, he added, "Keep the guys on site until I get there."

"Right, boss."

When he hung up, Lucas was still furious, but almost grateful for the shift in his thoughts. If not for Warren's ineptitude, he'd have nothing on his mind but Rose Clancy. And he'd already done nothing but think about her since the night before.

She had haunted his dreams, making sleep nearly impossible, and then this morning over his cup of coffee, he'd smelled her in his kitchen. It was as if she was imprinting herself on his consciousness.

Now, Lucas thought back to how Dave had always described his sister. Younger, softer, easily hurt and scared of her own shadow. She hadn't sounded all that appealing to him until the day he first met her. Then, her looks had bowled him over first and her laughter had hit him hard. There was something about a woman who knew how to laugh, he thought now. Maybe it was because growing up, he'd never heard his own mother laugh at a damn thing. Whining on the other hand… she had been very good at that.

As soon as that thought entered his mind, Lucas deliberately shut it down. It had sounded bad— disloyal—even to himself. His mom had done the best she could. She had just been too…alone.

Hell. Memories from his childhood weren't going to make this situation any easier to deal with. Disgusted with himself and his lack of concentration, Lucas pushed aside all thoughts but those related to work. For most of his life, work had been his sanctuary. The place in the world where everything was as it should be. Where the rules were well-defined and always followed. Here, Lucas kept his finger on the pulse of the company. Here, he wasn't questioned, just obeyed. Here, he was—

"How'd it go last night?"

"What?" He looked up as Sean strolled into his office and plopped himself down into one of the three chairs in front of Lucas's desk. He was chewing on one of the frosted cookies.

"Did you know we've got cookies in the break room now?" He held one hand to his heart and bowed his head. "Thank you, sister Katie…."

"Yeah, I heard," Lucas muttered. "Apparently a Weight Watchers class is in the offing."

"Not for me," Sean said with a laugh as he licked the last bit of frosting from his finger.

Lucas sighed. "Is there a reason you're here?"

"Yep. Curiosity. How did it go last night? You know. With Rose?"

"How did you know about that?"

"Your secretary told my secretary, who told me and…" He shrugged and grinned. "Here I am. Seriously? Cooking lessons?"

Frowning, Lucas leafed through a pile of papers on his desk. He didn't want to talk about this with Sean. Hadn't he just been focusing on *not* thinking about her? For all the good it had done him.

In spite of his best efforts, she kept popping back into his mind. Her smile. The way light flashed on her long blond hair. The sound of her laugh and the fresh, lemony scent of her. It was all right there whether he wanted it to be or not.

"Nothing to say?" Sean whistled low and long. "Must be even more interesting than I figured."

Glaring at his brother, Lucas demanded, "Don't you have something to do?"

"Actually, yeah. I'm headed out to look into a new service provider. With the way the company's expanding, our old one just isn't keeping up."

Lucas didn't even have to pretend disinterest. Sean was enamored of all the technological aspects of the business, but once he started talking about it, Lucas's eyes glazed over. "Good," he said. "Go do it."

"In a sec." Sean leaned forward, bracing his elbows on his knees. "So tell me."

"Tell you what?" He dropped the papers on his desk and sighed as he figured the fastest way to get rid of his brother was to answer his questions. "You already know I hired her."

Sean laughed. "For cooking lessons."

"Why is that so hard to understand?"

"Seriously?" Sean shook his head and stood up. "*You*, cooking? I should have been more impressed with her. Blonde, beautiful and a miracle worker. Teaching *you* to cook? Does she get hazard pay?"

Frowning, Lucas thought of the triple-her-usual-salary offer he'd made and realized that she *was* getting hazard pay. His scowl deepened as he snapped, "I've cooked for you before and you're still breathing."

"Only because of my excellent digestive system. It can withstand all sorts of toxins."

"Get out, Sean."

"Going, Lucas," he said amiably.

"Oh—" Lucas stopped him with a single word. "There's trouble at the Johnson site."

"Warren again?" Sean frowned.

"Yeah, they dug without the okay and hit a water pipe. Apparently the home owner can now dock a boat off the patio."

Shaking his head, Sean said, "I know the crews are your department, but if you want my opinion, we ought to get rid of Warren. We spend more time cleaning up after him than anything else. He's more trouble than he's worth."

"Agreed." Lucas nodded. "We'll talk about it at the weekly meeting."

"Right." Sean headed for the door, but before he left, he asked, "On the Rose front, I hope cooking lessons are all you're really up to."

"What?"

"I hope you're not still planning on using her for payback on Dave. Because, my man, that way lies misery."

Lucas didn't say anything, just stared at his younger brother until Sean shrugged and walked out. But long after he was gone, the man's words were still ringing in the air.

Was he right? Was Lucas just asking for trouble by using Rose to get back at Dave?

Standing up, he turned his back on the work waiting for him and stared out the window at the world beyond the glass. Long Beach was shivering under gray skies and a cold rain driven by an icy ocean wind. Oak trees rattled bare limbs, and the tall pines swayed with each gust.

Truth be told, Lucas didn't much like the idea of using Rose, either, though damned if he'd admit that to Sean. But the bottom line was, she was the sister of a man who had cheated him. Lied to him. And Lucas couldn't let that slide.

Liars deserved what they got, he told himself as his hands fisted at his sides. Hadn't he grown up watching his mother's heart broken again and again by the very men she had trusted to keep her safe? First, it was his father, Ben King—though to give Ben his due, he hadn't promised Lucas's mother any more than he had the mothers of any of his sons.

But Lucas's mother had pinned her hopes on love. Time and again, she'd gone searching for it, only to have whatever man she was pining over use her up and let her go. Her trust shaken, her heart shattered more times than he could even count, she'd finally given up. Destroyed by the very emotion she'd so longed to feel.

No, betrayal couldn't be forgiven. Or forgotten. And he'd do whatever he had to do to make sure that Dave Clancy finally understood that.

Three

"How's Rafe doing?"

"What?"

As Rose followed him down the wide aisle in the grocery store, Lucas heard her sigh heavily. "Your brother? Rafe? Didn't he get married a few months ago?"

"Oh. Yeah. He did." Lucas frowned at the seemingly endless selection of products. He'd spent most of his life avoiding grocery stores. When he needed food in a hurry, he stopped in at a deli or something. He hadn't been raised around a kitchen and, as a King, if he wanted someone cooking in his house, he could hire a damn chef. So why learn?

Now, he felt like a stranger in a strange land. The brilliant fluorescent lighting gave him a headache. There was a screaming child a few aisles over and an old woman had just crashed her cart into his and then had the guts to blame *him*. Seriously, men just didn't belong in grocery stores.

He was actually starting to rethink his whole plan. He hadn't really considered at the beginning just what all this would entail. And his interest in cooking was about as low as it could get. Then he reminded himself sternly that getting back at Dave would be worth all the hassles he was going through at the moment. Nobody betrayed a King and walked away.

Nobody.

"And?" Rose prompted. "How's he doing?"

"Rafe?" He dragged his mind back to the conversation. "He's good. Seems happy enough."

"What a touching testimony for marriage," she mused and reached over to pick up a box of bread crumbs.

"Bread crumbs aren't on the list," Lucas said, checking just to make sure.

"I know, but it's good to have them in the house. They come in handy in all kinds of ways. These are the best," she said, handing him the blue box. "Low in sodium and carbs, plus they're crispier than ordinary bread crumbs."

"Crispier is better. Right." If he did inadvertently learn how to cook during this process, he promised himself, he'd hire somebody to shop for him.

"So, you don't like Rafe's wife?"

He blinked at her. "Where did that come from? Of course I like her."

"Well, you don't seem thrilled that he got married," she said with a shrug. "So I assumed you didn't like his wife."

"So if I didn't like Christmas that would mean I hated somebody else's present?" What was it with women? A man makes a simple statement and they take it and run in the exact opposite direction.

"You don't like Christmas?" she countered.

"I didn't say that." Shaking his head, he continued down the baking aisle. "Have you ever heard the word *logic?*"

"I don't know," she said on a laugh. "I may have heard a vague reference at some point. Sounds like Latin."

"Naturally," he muttered, ignoring her smile, because frankly he didn't like the buzz of interest he felt lighting up his insides. He had a plan here, and he wasn't about to be distracted from it. Yes, he was going to seduce her. But that didn't mean he was going to do something stupid like come to care for her.

Keeping his voice lighter than the tension filling him would ordinarily warrant, he said, "I like Katie fine. She's way too good for Rafe, if you ask me."

"So it's just marriage in general you're against?"

"Pretty much." He stopped dead, and she crashed into him.

"Sorry."

He ignored the increased buzzing in his blood and told himself to get a grip on the situation. To get his mind off what his body was clamoring for, he scanned the shelves of spices and was instantly irritated. "How can there be so many?"

"Ah," she said with an understanding grin, "life outside the narrow confines of garlic, salt and pepper."

He frowned. "Nothing wrong with salt and pepper. It's basic. Classic."

"Boring."

"Fine," he said. Anything to get out of here that much sooner. "What do we need? I mean, what do *I* need?"

"It's all there on the list," she urged and stood by, deliberately letting him find his way through the spice racks.

He squinted at labels and hissed at the elevated prices of some of the more esoteric spices. Who knew this stuff was so expensive? Thoughts rolled through his mind even as he continued to read labels. The Kings should look into this. If they could set up suppliers, they could move into the spice industry and really take it over. *King Spice,* he thought with a half smile. It could work.

Now here was where he felt comfortable, Lucas thought. Planning, focusing on business and growing the ever-expanding King empire. Get him the hell out of a grocery store and there was nothing that could stop him once his mind was set on something. He slid a glance in Rose's direction. Her big blue eyes were fixed on him, a quiet smile tugging at her lips. Even in this hideous lighting, her skin was like porcelain and the long ponytail she habitually wore spilled across one shoulder, her thick blond hair a tempting mass of waves and loose curls.

She was enough to make any red-blooded male take a long, second look. Hell, he'd looked plenty himself when he had first met her. But Dave had practically wrapped her up in barbed wire and posted a No Trespassing sign over her head. So Lucas had kept his distance out of respect for his friend.

That respect was long dead, though, and soon he'd have this luscious-looking woman right where he wanted her. In his bed. *Under him.*

Until then, he'd just focus on the task at hand, he told himself, as he shifted his gaze back to the damned racks of spices.

* * *

Rose couldn't seem to tear her gaze off of Lucas. His black leather jacket was open to reveal the plain white T-shirt beneath. Black jeans clung to his long, muscular legs and he was wearing the same scuffed boots she had noticed the day before. What was it, she wondered, about a gorgeous man in jeans and cowboy boots? Was it instinctive? Did it pull at something primal in a woman?

Or was it simply that Lucas King would look too good in absolutely anything? Sadly, she thought, the latter was probably closer to the truth.

"I don't see peppercorns," he muttered, "and why can't I just use ground-up pepper? Why do I have to grind it myself? Haven't we come further than that as a society?"

"Funny," she said and reached out to tap one fingernail against the peppercorns. Right in front of him. Somehow, she found that thought comforting. Lucas was so…formidable, that finding out he was like other men in the can't-find-something-directly-in-front-of-him way made him seem…not ordinary by any means. But more *touchable*.

Not that she was thinking about touching him. All right, she was. But what woman wouldn't when she was standing right beside Lucas King? Still, if there was one thing Rose had learned in the last year or so, it was that she didn't want anything to do with another alpha male.

Lucas picked up the bottle of peppercorns, tossed it into the cart then consulted his list again. "Kosher salt? I'm not Jewish. You know that, right?"

Was he trying to be charming, she wondered, or was it just part of who he was? And if he was trying, *why?* Three years ago, when they first met, he had never made a move on her. And back then, she would definitely have been interested.

"Kosher salt is pure," she said, still studying him, trying to figure him out. "No chemicals. It's better for you."

"Fine."

"So why do you hate marriage?" she asked, returning to their earlier conversation.

"Didn't say I hated it," he told her, not even bothering to glance her way.

"Really didn't have to," she pointed out.

"Why are you such a fan?" He straightened up, turned his head and gave her a flat stare. "Didn't you get divorced yourself only last year?"

His eyes were sharp and cool and distant. There was accusation in their depths, and she frowned to herself at the justice in it. He was right, after all. She wasn't exactly a stellar example of a good marriage. "Fine, you're right. I did get divorced last year. But how did you know about it? You and Dave never talk and oh... never mind. Gossip columns. I know I made all the papers and even a few of the tabloids when I divorced Henry."

"Please. I don't read that crap. But word does get around." He looked at her for a moment or two longer before he said, "Never did understand why you married that guy in the first place, if you don't mind my saying."

"Nope, don't mind," she said with a sigh. Henry Porter had been a mistake from the jump. But the real mistake had been in allowing her father and brother to talk her into marrying the jerk for the sake of the family. Henry's business had aligned nicely with theirs, since he was an architect with a string of successful upscale housing developments in his portfolio. Dave had figured that by working with Porter's Palaces—idiotic name for a company, in Rose's opinion—Clancy Construction would take the next step up the proverbial ladder.

Of course, then her father died, Henry showed his true colors and Rose had reclaimed her life, leaving Dave fuming.

"So?" he asked again, his voice quiet beneath the Muzak constantly pumped through the store. "Why'd you do it? And don't try to tell me you actually loved that pompous twit Porter."

"No," she said with a rueful smile. "That's one mistake I didn't make."

When she didn't elaborate further, Lucas shrugged and grabbed a tiny plastic jar of cloves. He tossed it into the cart before searching for the next one on his list. "Don't want to talk about it?"

"Not particularly," she admitted.

She knew all too well what he'd heard about the end of her marriage. Rose shifted uncomfortably, remembering the humiliation of her marriage and the horrific ending of it. She'd married the wrong man for all the wrong reasons. She'd gone along with her family because that's who she had always been.

The pleaser. That was Rose. Always going out of her way to make sure everyone around her was happy. She'd subjugated her own wants and needs in favor of everyone else's. Well, those days were gone. She'd learned her lesson the hard way, but now, she was determined to make *herself* happy.

He tore his gaze away from the spice shelf and shot a quick look at her. If she hadn't known better, she would have thought she saw a quick flash of regret in his eyes. But it was gone almost immediately, so she dismissed it as a trick of the overhead lights. "I didn't mean—"

"Sure you did," Rose interrupted, then pointed. "There's the rosemary. Get the big bottle."

As he did, she watched him. "You wanted to point out that I was being a sunshine-and-rainbow girl with nothing to back it up."

He nodded, then turned his head to look at her. His black hair fell across his forehead and his eyes narrowed on her. "I suppose I did."

"Thanks for admitting it, anyway," she told him. "And you're right. I absolutely don't have any personal experience with a happy marriage." Reaching out, she picked up a box of blueberry muffin mix, read the back and wrinkled her nose before setting it back down. "Look, my marriage was a disaster, but I went into it for all the wrong reasons—"

"What were they?"

She looked at him. "None of your business. The point is," she continued, "just because my marriage didn't work, doesn't mean there's something wrong with the whole institution."

"Institution," he muttered. "That word says it all."

"Is that how Rafe sees it?"

He laughed shortly, checked his list again and glanced at her. The amusement in his eyes was real this time and the curve of his lips did something amazing to the pit of her stomach. "He's too crazy about Katie to think anything at this point. And my brother Sean is ecstatic because now he's related to the cookie queen and has all kinds of expectations for free food."

"What about you? Any expectations?"

He stilled, looked her up and down and, in that blink of time, Rose felt her skin begin to hum and sizzle. "Not where Katie's concerned, no."

They had really veered into what could quickly

become uncomfortable territory. Funny, to be having such a deep conversation in the middle of the baking aisle, with Muzak pouring down from overhead and a child still screaming in fury somewhere in the distance.

Seconds ticked past and neither of them looked away. Rose felt the searing heat of his gaze licking at her skin and in another minute or two, she might just melt into a puddle.

Thankfully, she was spared that humiliation when Lucas spoke up.

"I've got all the spices. What's next?"

Spices. Spicy. Sexy. Sex...

"What? Oh. Right." She shook her head hard, ridding herself of the images rushing through her mind. Images of Lucas, bending down, kissing her, holding her, leaning her back onto a bed and... "First we'll get some olive oil, then we'll head to the butcher department."

She walked farther down the aisle, silently lecturing herself about hormonal surges and inappropriate behavior with a client and anything else she could think of to take her mind off of Lucas. Naked.

God.

He followed behind her with the cart and stopped when she did. Staring at the long shelf crowded with dozens of types of oils, Lucas looked about as lost as a man could get. "Why do we need so many different kinds of oil? How're you supposed to know what to get?"

"Always get the extra virgin," she said.

His eyebrows lifted and his mouth quirked. "There's *extra* virgin?"

He was amused again. Perfect. She was simmering, he was chuckling. Oh, this was going just fabulously well.

"Just get this one," she said and reached for a bottle on the top shelf.

He went for it at the same time and their hands brushed over the heavy plastic bottle. That one instant of contact was all she needed to kick that smoldering fire inside her into an inferno. Rose was really tempted to take him down the ice cream aisle. At least there, the frigid air might do something to help quash the heat threatening to engulf her. Instead, she led him to the butcher department and tried to keep her mind on cuts of beef and pork loins.

A half hour later, they were finishing up in the produce section. Lucas couldn't have been less interested as she explained what to look for in fresh broccoli. "You want dark green florets and thinnish stalks."

"Thinnish?"

"Yes. Not too skinny, not too fat."

His gaze raked her up and down again, and Rose had to take a deep breath. She was beginning to think he was deliberately trying to get her all jangled up. He was making her nervous and clearly enjoying himself at the same time.

"You know, not *everything* I say is intended as a come-on of some kind."

"Just a happy accident, then?" he inquired.

"Lucas?" A high-pitched, completely surprised feminine voice stopped whatever Rose might have said in return. Instead, she turned to watch a voluptuous redhead in skin-tight jeans and three-inch black heels scurrying toward them, a beaming smile on her gorgeous face. The woman was made up as if she were going to an opera. Yet, she had a small basket tucked over her arm, the single tomato and avocado inside rolling from one side to the other in her agitation.

"Marsha," Lucas said stiffly. "Nice to see you."

The words were right, Rose thought, but the tone in his voice should have warned the redhead off.

"I can't believe you're in a grocery store, of all places," the redhead crooned, leaning in to brush an air kiss in the vicinity of his cheek.

Rose took a step backward, sliding away to give the two of them a minute alone. Maybe Lucas didn't seem happy about running into the woman, but she doubted that Marsha would miss her presence. Rose had every intention of hiding behind the bin of Vidalia onions, but Lucas stopped her cold with one hand on her arm. His grip tightened as she tried to squirm free, but the redhead never noticed. Her big green eyes were fixed on Lucas as if he were a Prada bag on a seventy-five-percent-off table.

"Imagine, running into you here, of all places."

"Yeah," he said, "you said that already. Not really surprising, Marsha, I do eat."

"Yes," she agreed on a seductive chuckle, "but you forget, I've seen your refrigerator for myself."

Perfect, Rose thought. Nothing like standing here witnessing one of Lucas's bedmates trying to meta-phorically lick him in the produce aisle. And could she have looked any more hideous, Rose wondered furiously. Why was her hair in a ponytail, of all things? And why hadn't she worn her *new* jeans...instead of her favorite, often-washed, faded pair?

And *why,* she demanded silently, did she *care?*

She wasn't on a date, for heaven's sake. She and Lucas weren't a couple. He was a client. A customer. She was his cooking teacher, nothing more.

Which should have made her feel better but it *so* didn't.

"You look wonderful, Lucas," Marsha said, her voice dropping to a low purr of interest.

Behind Lucas, Rose rolled her eyes and willed herself to sink into the floor. Nothing happened.

"Thanks, you, too," Lucas said brusquely. Then he added, "You'll have to excuse us, though, we've got to finish shopping and get home."

"We?" For the first time, Marsha's gaze slid past Lucas to notice Rose. Surprise flickered across her eyes briefly.

"Marsha Hancock, this is Rose Clancy. Rose, Marsha."

"Hi. Nice to meet you," Rose said when she couldn't avoid it.

"Uh-huh," Marsha murmured, then turned her renewed interest on Lucas. "Like I was saying, you look wonderful and if you're not busy this Friday, I'm having a small, intimate party at my place and—"

"We'll be busy," Lucas told her, then looked at Rose. "What do you think, honey, we done here?"

Honey? He'd called her *honey?* Rose's mouth opened and closed a few times while she tried to think of something clever—heck, *anything* to say. Then Lucas dropped one arm around her shoulders and gave her a hard hug. Keeping her tucked in close to his side, he looked at the redhead and said, "Yep, guess we're done. Good seeing you, Marsha."

He pushed the laden cart one-handed, still keeping one arm draped around Rose. She walked right beside him, trying to figure out what had just happened. Risking a quick glance backward, she could see that the beautiful Marsha was trying to understand the same thing.

Rose stood beside him while he paid for the groceries,

then followed him out to the parking lot and his car when he was finished. A cold night wind blew in off the ocean, and, overhead, the stars were glittering.

She turned her face into the wind as he loaded up the trunk of his SUV and didn't say a word until he'd finished and closed the lid again with a solid *thunk*.

"What was that about? Inside there, with Marsha?"

He shrugged, and pushed the shopping cart into the area set aside for them. "Marsha's annoying. Letting her believe you and I were together was the easiest way of getting rid of her."

He might think she was annoying now, but the redhead had made it all too clear that at one point in the not so distant past, Lucas had found her much more interesting.

"And you had to call me 'honey' to get that point across?"

"Seemed like a good idea at the time." He tilted his head and looked at her as one corner of his mouth turned up. He took a few steps closer and with every step, he asked, "You object to 'honey'? How about 'babe'? 'Darlin''? 'Sweetie'?"

Her insides were shaking, and her mouth was dry. Rose looked up into those blue eyes of his and couldn't read what he was thinking. Not enough lights in this parking lot. Too many shadows in his eyes, on his features.

"But I'm not any of those things to you, Lucas," she pointed out and backed up until she bumped into his SUV. "What if she starts telling people that she saw us together? That you called me 'honey'? That we looked like a couple?"

"That would be bad?" he asked.

"It wouldn't be honest."

"And you're always honest."

"Try to be."

"Fine," he said, leaning into her and bracing both hands on his car at either side of her, "answer me this, then. And try to be honest. What would you do right now if I kissed you?"

Her knees went weak.

This was just ridiculous.

She was a grown woman. A divorced woman. She was no shy virgin sighing with eagerness because the captain of the football team happened to notice she was alive.

She was still looking up into his eyes, and he was still waiting for an answer to his question. His scent swirled around her, something spicy and all too male. His face was just a breath away from hers. The heat of his body seeped into hers and she felt that smoldering fire inside her erupt into something a lot more volcanic.

Rose had a choice here. She could be completely professional, and tell him that she didn't want him to kiss her. But that would be a big, fat lie. *Or,* she could be honest and tell him that if he kissed her, she'd probably explode with all of the banked sexual energy she was feeling at the moment.

So what was it going to be?

He licked his lips and just like that, her decision was made. Three years ago, when she had first met him, she'd daydreamed about being kissed by Lucas King.

Now, she was about to find out if her fantasies were as good as the reality.

"Well, Rose?"

"You want honest?" she asked.

"Yeah."

"Okay then." She grabbed the lapels of his black leather jacket and yanked him down to her.

His mouth closed over hers and what felt like an electrical charge blasted them both.

Rose wrapped her arms around his neck and held on while his tongue parted her lips and slipped into the heat of her mouth. She sighed into him and instantly tangled her tongue with his, as eager and hungry for him as he seemed to be for her.

Her stomach flipped, her heartbeat staggered in heavy beats and the knees that had been weak before turned to water under the onslaught of too many sensations to count.

He pulled her close, pressing her to his length, and she felt every hard, muscled inch of him imprinting itself on her body. A throbbing ache settled between her thighs as he swept his hands up and down her back, caressing her behind.

She couldn't breathe. Could hardly stand.

But at least, she thought idly, she had her answer.

The reality of kissing Lucas King was *way* better than the fantasy.

Four

Lucas was hanging on to his common sense by a quickly unraveling thread.

She felt so...*good* in his arms. He hadn't expected that. Hadn't expected her taste to enflame him or for the scent of lemons that clung to her to drive into his mind and cloud up his thoughts. The feel of her body pressed against his only made him harder. He pulled her closer, to let her know what he was feeling, and when she moaned, it almost pushed him over the edge and down a very slippery slope.

He had thought time would have muted the attraction that drew him to her. But it hadn't. One taste and all he could think was...he wanted more.

One kiss, that's all this was supposed to have been. A small preview of things to come. To get her thinking about him. Dreaming about him.

But it was so much more.

Rose Clancy.

Her name lit up in his mind like a shock of neon and that was enough to have him ending the kiss, however reluctantly. Lucas pulled away, though his every instinct clamored at him to hold her even tighter. He took one long breath and then another, hoping to steady himself.

This wasn't the time for instincts. Or urges. This was a time for logic and cool thinking, and damned if he'd risk his plan by seducing her in the parking lot of a damn grocery store.

Somewhere close by, a car's engine fired up, and Lucas took a step back from her, deliberately putting some distance between them. He could still taste her. Feel her.

Shoving one hand through his hair, Lucas thought that maybe Sean had been right. It *had* been too long since he'd been with a woman. That's why Rose had gotten to him so completely. Hell, he was practically a starving man. Was it any wonder that a tender steak looked good to him?

His gaze was locked on her. She leaned against his car, lifting one hand to her mouth and holding the other hand up as if to warn him to stay away. Not really necessary, Lucas thought, but he got the message.

She was as shaken as he.

And that was a good thing, he told himself. At least he knew now that she would be thinking about him. Remembering this kiss, just as—he hated to admit it— he would.

"That was—"

"Rose—"

"—not something that's going to happen again," she finished, surprising him.

She straightened up, smoothed her hair and took

another breath. After a second or two, she met his eyes and gave him a smile that was so forced it was more of a grimace.

"I can't say I didn't enjoy it, but Lucas, you should know that I'm not looking for a relationship."

Stunned, he could only stare at her. *She* was giving *him* the don't-expect-anything-from-me speech? Had the world gone completely crazy? Her eyes were soft, her expression kind but remote, and Lucas was at a loss for something to say. This kind of thing didn't happen to him.

Women didn't turn away from Lucas King. They generally chased him down and did whatever they could to hang on to him.

"Excuse me?" he finally managed to say.

"Look, I'm sorry. I should have said something the minute I agreed to work for you." She inhaled and rushed on before he could speak. "I noticed right away that there was an...*attraction* between us, but I didn't think anything of it. It's my own fault, I should have said something sooner. But the truth is, I'm not looking for another man in my life—"

She wasn't—

"I don't remember offering," he said, his voice tightly controlled. Anger and disbelief warred in the pit of his stomach, kicking up an ugly brew as he felt the sting of rejection for the first time in his life.

She ignored that jibe. "And if I were considering getting involved with someone," Rose continued, "it wouldn't be with you."

Completely shocked now, he just stared at her, too amazed to speak for a moment. This was not how he'd seen this little chat going. He'd expected to have to talk her down from their passionate kiss. To ease her gently into the seduction he had planned. What he *hadn't* counted on was being insulted.

"What do you mean it wouldn't be me? What the hell is wrong with *me?*" he finally shouted.

Rose winced and looked past him at the brightly lit grocery store as if checking to make sure no one else had come out and was listening.

Then she turned her gaze back to him. "Nothing's wrong with you, Lucas. You're just…not my type."

"Type?" he echoed. This was not happening, he told himself sternly. No way was he standing in a grocery store parking lot looking at a beautiful woman and hearing her tell him to buzz off. This was so far out of his universe, he didn't have a clue how to handle it. But his temper was on the rise and a sudden, pounding headache erupted behind his eyes.

Crossing his arms over his chest, he glared at her. "What type am I then?"

"Bossy."

"Bossy isn't a type," he argued, because he couldn't argue with the word itself. Sure he was bossy, but he preferred to think of that trait as confidence. All of the Kings were confident in themselves and their abilities, and they didn't suffer fools, either. They took charge, got things done and steamrolled over whomever might be dumb enough to stand in their way.

Lucas was no different.

Yeah, he'd been called arrogant before. And unrelenting. And even, on occasion, egotistical. But it was a small price to pay for getting what he wanted when he wanted it. And he wasn't about to apologize to Rose Clancy—or anyone else for that matter—for being the man he was.

"Just when exactly have I bossed you around?" he challenged, his eyes locked with hers.

She sighed. "You haven't, in so many words. Not yet, anyway."

"Oh, so you're a fortune teller, too? You can read the future and so you know I'm going to start giving you orders?"

"I don't need to read the future," she told him, stiffening her spine and lifting her chin in defense against his tone. "All I have to do is look at the past."

"That makes no sense, either," he told her.

"It does to me," she said simply.

Lucas shook his head and tried to rein in the million and one thoughts churning through his mind. Then he gave it up. How could he find logic in what was unreasonable to begin with? Was his plan for revenge going to end right here, beneath a flickering, ready-to-burn-out parking light?

"I can't believe any of this," he muttered, more to himself than to her.

"I know. You probably don't hear it often."

His eyes narrowed. "Try never."

She winced. "I am sorry, but Lucas, I really need this job and I don't want us to work together under false pretenses."

A part of him relaxed a little. She wasn't walking away at least. She was just trying to put him on notice. "Uh-huh."

"That kiss notwithstanding, I really think we should just keep our relationship to teacher and student. Okay?"

Man, he thought, if Sean were here listening to this, his brother would be laughing his ass off. Hell, if it were happening to one of his brothers, Lucas would be doing the same thing. But it was damned hard to see the humor in the situation from his perspective.

On the other hand, Lucas mused as he watched her, Rose was the one to initiate that steam-inducing kiss—and she would have kept on kissing him if he hadn't called a halt and taken a step back. Say what she wanted now, he had tasted her desire, felt her need wrapping itself around him. Rose Clancy wanted him as much as he wanted her—which would only work in his favor as he went about seducing her. Good to know that beneath her cool, prim, good-girl demeanor, she was burning with the same fire that was licking at his insides.

So…fine. He'd play along. Let her think she was in charge. Eventually, the game would shift in his favor.

Things always did.

She was watching him warily, waiting for his response, and damned if he wasn't tempted to tell her to take her rules and get lost. He'd never before had a woman turn on him like this, especially after a kiss so hot—his lips still felt burned. And swallowing her "rules" was going to be hard to do, he knew. Yet, if he wanted his plan to work—and he really did—then he was going to have to go along with her…at least for now.

It grated, though, Lucas thought, as irritation spiked within him. He wasn't used to sublimating his own wants to anyone else's and if this is what it felt like, he had no interest in getting any better at it.

He looked at her and wanted her. He looked at her and wanted to turn and walk away. He looked at her and remembered her brother stabbing him and the rest of the Kings in the back and knew without a doubt that he wasn't willing to give up on his plan. Not yet.

So he'd go along. He'd let her think she had won this round, because winning a battle didn't mean winning the war. When this was over, it would be Lucas standing up and taking a bow. And it was that thought alone that had him nodding.

"Fine," he growled. "We'll do this your way."

She blew out a breath and flashed him a grin. "That's great. You'll see, Lucas. This will all work much better now that we both know the rules."

He watched her go to the passenger-side door and climb inside the already unlocked car. Alone in the flickering light of that lamp, Lucas clenched his jaw and promised himself that when this seduction ran its course and his payback had been achieved, *he* would be the one giving the not-my-type speech to Rose.

That realization had him smiling all the way home.

A week later, Rose was working on her home computer. This was her least favorite part of being self-employed. Well, there were also the quarterly tax reports. Frankly, anything to do with paperwork made her want to lie down on the couch until the resulting headache went away.

She loved cooking. Loved teaching others to do what she did best. But making what she loved a business demanded that she do a lot of what she hated, too.

Studying the spreadsheet across her computer screen, though, she had to smile. Thanks to Lucas King and the ridiculous amount of money he was willing to pay for cooking lessons, her bottom line was looking perceptibly better these days.

And her nerves were looking a lot worse, she acknowledged sadly. Picking up the mug in front of her, Rose took a long drink of her coffee and nearly gagged when she realized it had gone stone-cold. Grimacing at the taste, she carried the cup into the kitchen, saw the coffeepot was empty and automatically set it up to brew a fresh pot.

While the coffeemaker steamed and hissed and dripped, she leaned against her countertop and let her mind go to where, lately, it spent so much time.

Straight to Lucas.

In seconds, she was reliving that kiss again, as she had so many times over the last week. *What* had she been thinking? She should have edged away. Made an excuse. Laughed the tension off. But no, she'd had to grab his jacket lapels and drag him down for a kiss that was still reverberating through her seven days later.

"God, you're an idiot," she muttered, slapping one hand against the cool, gleaming surface of her cream-colored granite countertop.

She could still feel the hard thump of her heartbeat and the waves of desire that had crashed over her, nearly swamping her with a sense of need more desperate than she'd ever known before. Shaking her head, Rose absently reached for a dishtowel and dried and put away the few dishes sitting in the sink drainer while her mind taunted her by playing the memory of that kiss on a nonstop loop.

When she tired of torturing herself, she moved past that kiss and on to the strained conversation that had followed. She'd had to force herself to say what she had and heaven knew he hadn't taken it well.

"But then," she murmured, "why would he? No woman in her right mind would be pushing Lucas King away. No wonder he looked at me like I'd lost my mind."

Maybe she had, at that. She considered the suggestion objectively. She was single. Unattached. Clearly drawn to Lucas and his kiss had practically curled her toes and she had still turned him down. "Yep. Crazy."

When the phone rang, she jumped, then had to slap one hand to her chest to hold her heart in place. Shaking her head, she reached across the counter, and checked the caller ID. Smiling, she answered it.

"Dee, hi."

"I hate caller ID," her best friend said. "There are too few surprises in life anyway. Answering the phone should be like biting into a chocolate. A lottery, sort of. Will you get caramel or fruit and nuts?"

"Speaking of nuts," Rose said, still smiling, "what's going on?"

"Seriously?" Delilah James laughed and it was a deep, rumbling chuckle. "I'm calling for a passion update, of course."

"There is no update, and I'm sorry I ever told you about that kiss," Rose said, staring at the coffeemaker as if willing it to finish already. She'd need a lot more caffeine to deal with her best friend.

Delilah and Rose had met as roommates their freshman year of college and had bonded like sisters before the end of the first month of school. With similar backgrounds—each of them having been raised by wealthy, domineering fathers—they'd had a lot in common. The only difference being that at college, Dee had found the strength to stand up to her family's demands, while Rose hadn't.

"Of course, you're going to tell me about a kiss that fried all of your circuits," Dee said now. "I'm the best friend. Who else are you going to tell?"

"Nobody," she said and gratefully poured a fresh cup of coffee. "Honestly, it didn't mean anything."

"Right. That's why you were still babbling a day later. Why you said that you'd never experienced anything like that *and* it's why you said Lucas King kisses like a man who was just giving a woman a preview of the big event."

Rose closed her eyes on a sigh. "Did you take notes or something?"

"Are you kidding? I'm so jealous that description is seared into my mind." She gave a wistful, dramatic sigh. "So, what's the second chapter? Fondling in the kitchen? Playing touchy-feely while chopping parsley?"

"No to all of the above," Rose told her firmly, though her body did a quick hop and skip at the thought.

"You mean to tell me you're sticking to the rules you laid down? Strictly business?"

"I am," she said with a sharp nod that Dee couldn't even see. "I have to. I need the money he's paying me."

Dee snorted. "Oh, please."

Rose took the phone away from her ear, frowned at it, then slapped it back into place. "That's the reason I took the job in the first place, remember?"

"That's what you told yourself, anyway," Dee said. "Come on, Rose. We both know that Lucas King makes you shiver in all the right places."

True, she thought, rolling her eyes heavenward as she took a sip of hot coffee. Rose had been shivering for a solid week. And working in the man's house every night, in very close quarters, wasn't helping anything. Although, ever since that one, blistering kiss, Lucas had been absolutely, rigidly, polite. He hadn't made another move. Hadn't even so much as given her a look that would lead her to think that he'd spent nearly as much time daydreaming about that kiss as she had.

So *why* was she making herself crazy over this?

"Okay, yes, he does," she admitted, when Dee's silence began to scream at her. "But that doesn't mean I'm going to do anything about it."

"Pity."

"I'm sorry?"

"Rose, you know I love you…"

"I hear a *but* coming," Rose said.

"But," Dee continued, "you don't know a good thing when you trip over it."

"Oh, yes, I do," she countered, wandering across her small kitchen to stare out the window at the winterized backyard. The trees were looking a little sad, their browning leaves clinging to the branches, refusing to drop. The grass was brown, too. In fact, the only splotches of color out there were her chrysanthemums—yellow, purple, white—in the flowerbeds that needed weeding.

She'd lived in this house since her divorce, and she'd been happy here. Her own space, just a tiny bungalow in one of the older sections of Long Beach, the house was nothing like the palatial mansion where she'd grown up and, frankly, that was Rose's favorite part. Big houses felt cold. Empty.

Well, she amended silently, that wasn't entirely true. Lucas's house was gigantic, but there was an easy warmth to it, too. She had felt at home the moment she walked inside. Which probably wasn't a good thing.

"If you did," Dee was saying, "you'd kiss Lucas King senseless, tip him into bed and have your wicked way with him."

"You're writing your romance novel again, aren't you?"

Dee laughed. "Guilty. But my point is, why are you backing away? He's single. You're single. Finally."

"You know why," Rose said and opened the back door. It was cold outside, but right now, that sharp, ocean air felt good. As if it was going to blow right through her mind, chasing away thoughts she had no business indulging in.

Stepping out onto the back porch, Rose cradled the phone in one hand, her coffee cup in the other, and slowly sank down onto one of the weathered Adirondack chairs. Easing back, she stared into the yard, but wasn't really seeing it. Instead, she looked into her own past and didn't like the view.

"He's too much like Dave. And my father. And Henry," Rose said quietly.

"Rich men aren't all alike, sweetie," Dee said, her voice just as quiet, letting Rose know that she understood completely.

"No, but there are enough similarities between the Clancy men and the King men to make me wary."

"Okay, I get that," her friend said. "But you're not the same person you were in the past, Rose. There's not a man alive who could walk over you now. You're stronger than that. Not afraid to speak up for yourself."

She was, Rose thought with not a little pride. She'd worked hard to develop her own confidence. Her own strengths. For as long as she could remember, her father and her older brother had looked at her as if she were some plaster saint. She was always the good, compliant, pretty daughter and sister.

Part of that, of course, was her own fault. Her mother died when Rose was ten, and after that, she was in a constant state of fear that she would lose the rest of her family. That somehow, something would go wrong and she would be alone. She'd even convinced herself that if she wasn't perfect, they might not want her around at all.

So she had been better than perfect. She never made waves. Never questioned. Never argued. Never stood up for herself, not once. Even after college, she had maintained that air of perfection for her family and when her father had asked her to marry Henry Porter, she had agreed.

"Maybe Lucas King is just what you need," Dee was saying. "You've been celibate way too long. That creep of an ex-husband of yours really messed with your head and I'm thinking a little attention from the right person could just give you a whole new outlook."

Rose shook her head, took a sip of coffee and watched the neighbor's cat walk with balletic precision along the top of the block wall fence that separated the yards. She smiled to herself as the rotund calico paused long enough to bat one paw at a trembling leaf.

"What is whirling around in your devious mind?" Rose asked, though she knew she probably shouldn't.

"Seduction."

"What?"

"I'm just saying...if Lucas isn't a long-term guy, why can't he be a short-term one?"

"Because I work for him," Rose argued, shifting in her seat as a sudden surge of heat shot through her.

"Uh-huh, and one has nothing to do with the other," Dee insisted. "Live a little, sweetie. Have a fling. Enjoy. Don't you deserve some fun?"

Rose laughed. "Lucas? Fun? He's not an amusement park, Dee. He's...dangerous."

"Even better."

"You're hopeless."

"Thank you."

Rose heard the smile in her friend's voice and knew that Dee meant well, but... "I don't think so. I gave him the stay-away speech, remember?"

"Take it back."

"Hah! Just like that?"

"Why not? You said it was a great kiss."

"Practically a world record," Rose admitted, reliving that memory of his mouth locked with hers for what had to be the millionth time.

"One word from you, and I guarantee he'll forget all about your little hands-off speech."

"Then what?"

"Sweetie, if you have to ask that, it *has* been too long," Dee told her with a sigh. A second later, she said, "Oops, gotta run. My date's here."

"Right. Talk to you tomorrow."

"Okay, and Rose…live a little. Will you at least think about it?"

Once she hung up, Rose could acknowledge, at least to herself, that she would probably think of nothing else.

Five

"So we're agreed," Lucas said, glancing from Rafe to Sean. "We fire Warren."

"Hell yes," Sean muttered.

"Agreed," Rafe chimed in. "The man's used up his last chance with me. The mess he made out of the Johnson job is going to put us back at least two weeks. Not to mention we'll have to eat the cost of repairs to the water pipe and putting the yard back to rights."

"And there was water damage to the patio—redwood deck," Lucas reminded them.

"Perfect." Rafe sighed. "You know, we should fire him and send him over to work for Clancy's outfit. Serve 'em right."

Sean looked to Lucas, who shook his head firmly. He knew his youngest brother was about to tell Rafe all about Lucas's plan with Rose and, frankly, Lucas didn't want to hear it.

Naturally, that didn't stop Sean.

"Speaking of the Clancys," he said, shifting his gaze from Lucas to Rafe, "have you heard the latest? Big brother Lucas is taking cooking lessons from Rose Clancy, sainted sister of Devious Dave."

"Cooking lessons?" Rafe asked, confused. "Why the hell are you doing that? Hire somebody to cook for you if you can't figure it out yourself."

Lucas opened his mouth to speak, but Sean beat him to it. Really, now that he thought about it, he should have dropped Sean in the lake when they were kids.

"Oh, it's not just cooking Lucas is up to," Sean said quietly. "He's setting something up. Looking to use Rose as payback for what Dave did to us."

Rafe stared at him. "You're doing what?"

Lucas sighed and took a sip of his beer as Rafe went on a long-winded rant. He knew trying to interrupt would be pointless. Lucas didn't know how Katie, sweet woman that she was, could stand being married to the know-it-all. As the oldest of the three of them, Lucas was also the most patient of the three. He simply kept quiet and let Rafe go, knowing he'd eventually wind down and they could talk about this.

Once a week, the three King brothers who owned King Construction held a meeting to keep each other up-to-date on what was going on in the company. They rotated the meetings between each other's houses and this week, they were at Sean's place.

Great views, Lucas acknowledged, but then why wouldn't there be? Sean lived in a former water tower, which had been completely rehabbed and remodeled, of course. The water-tower home stood on a giant steel skeleton and the only way to the front door was a private elevator at street level. There was a wide, wraparound balcony surrounding the place, offering 360-degree views, and the living room where they sat boasted a wall of tinted windows that overlooked the ocean.

Out on the slate-gray waves beyond the glass, sailboats skimmed the surface and a few hardy surfers, outfitted in wetsuits, rode their boards into shore. From Lucas's perspective, the ocean scene looked peaceful and serene.

The direct opposite of the atmosphere here in Sean's coolly casual home. Everything had been going fine a few minutes ago. They'd wrapped up their business talk and after hearing yet another blissful take on the newlywed life from Rafe, Sean had mentioned what Lucas was up to with Rose.

That alone had been enough to throw a wrench into the conversation. Now, Rafe stared at Lucas from across the room and demanded again, "You're doing what with who?"

"Isn't that *whom?*" Sean said with a grin.

Rafe glared him into silence then turned his gaze back to Lucas. "Are you crazy?"

"Not the last time I checked, no." Lucas stood up, walked to the wet bar and poured a splash of single malt scotch into a crystal glass. He took a sip and turned to face his younger brother. "Dave Clancy cheated us. Used a spy in the company to steal contracts right out from under us. Why wouldn't I want to pay him back for that?"

"For God's sake, that was two years ago. Let it go already," Rafe said.

"Not a chance." Lucas bit the words out and felt the swell of indignation filling him.

Rafe was feeling magnanimous now, due to his happily married lifestyle. Two years ago, it had been a different story. Back then, all three of them had been furious and frustrated by the fact that they couldn't go after Dave legally because there was no evidence against him. Time passed and Rafe and Sean had both moved on, putting it behind them.

But for Lucas, the sting was still there. Maybe it was because *he* had been the one to introduce Dave to his brothers. *He* had been Dave's introduction to King Construction. Small wonder then that Lucas was taking this more personally than his brothers were.

"I tried to talk him out of it," Sean said. "But his head's as hard as Dad's."

"Nobody's head is that hard," Rafe said automatically, but kept his gaze fixed on Lucas. "If you're pissed at Dave, go after Dave. Using his sister is just sleazy."

"Exactly," Sean agreed.

A quick flicker of irritation spiked inside him because truthfully, it felt like that to Lucas sometimes, too. But the feeling wasn't strong enough to get him to back off.

"Rose is the way to make Dave pay. She's his baby sister. You remember how he was always bragging about her."

"Again," Rafe pointed out, "years ago."

"Family doesn't change."

"Amen to that," Sean muttered, then shrugged when Lucas stared at him. "Fine. Happy trails. Good luck on seducing then losing the lucky woman."

"Damn it, Sean…"

"Why be mad at him?" Rafe countered. "It's exactly what you're doing."

"Yeah?" Lucas met Rafe's stare and didn't give an inch. "And I seem to remember a guy whose plan was to topple the cookie queen into bed and then explain to her how all King men weren't jerks. Where were all your high standards then, Rafe?"

A flash of anger crossed Rafe's face at being reminded of how he'd tried to trick Katie when he first met her. But a second or two later, he said simply, "Yeah, you're right, and I almost lost her because of that stupid plan. You might want to think about that."

"Difference there is, I don't *want* to keep Rose," Lucas said. Not forever, anyway. But he wasn't in any hurry to send her on her way, either.

He scowled to himself at that thought. For a week now, Rose had been in his home every evening. They worked together in the kitchen. They talked, laughed and never once had either one of them brought up that staggering kiss they'd shared.

But it was there. Unsaid. Simmering in the air between them.

"Well, that makes it okay then," Rafe muttered.

"Yeah, were you planning on marrying Katie when you guys met? I don't think so." Lucas set his glass down and walked across the room to stand in front of Rafe. "I'm going to make sure Dave understands what stealing from a King means. And you're not going to talk me out of it."

"See?" Sean asked. "This is why I gave up trying to reason with either of you."

"Stay out of it, Sean," Lucas warned.

"Why the hell should I?" He stood up, too, and gave Lucas a hard stare. "You're not the only one Dave Clancy screwed. All three of us own the company. All three of us took a hit when he worked us over. But you *are* the only one acting like an ass about it."

Lucas bit down on his temper. Arguing with Rafe and Sean was pointless. They'd never understand why this was important to him. How could they? The three of them hadn't grown up together—none of Ben King's sons had—except for the summers all of them spent with Ben every year. And when those idyllic summers were over, Lucas went home to a woman who was constantly trusting the wrong men, only to have them break her heart.

Lucas had grown up with betrayal. He'd watched it happen to his mother over and over again and had finally realized that the only thing that really mattered in life was trust. Being able to trust those closest to you was priceless.

And no matter how angry he might be with his brothers, or them with him, he knew that they would be there for him, no matter what. For a man like Lucas, that was a gift beyond anything he could imagine.

The Kings stood together. No matter what.

It wasn't until two nights later that Rose appeared at Lucas's house. He saw her pull into the driveway and fought down a rush of expectation that he didn't want to either feel *or* acknowledge.

But it was damned hard to deny that he'd missed her. He hadn't seen her until now because she'd had standing cooking lessons to honor. She hadn't said with whom. It hadn't been with Kathy Robertson next door, though, and knowing that, Lucas had tortured himself, wondering if she was alone with some other guy. Cooking. Laughing. Talking.

Which was ridiculous, he knew. Why the hell should he care if she was at another man's house, spending time alone with him? She didn't belong to Lucas. They weren't a damn couple. She was, simply, a handy weapon he was preparing to wield.

And yet, he looked out the window and watched her lean into that silly van of hers with the skillet on the roof. His gaze locked on the curve of her behind and his groin tightened painfully. The ache of wanting her was stronger than ever.

Which should only help with the seduction plans, right?

When she straightened up and headed for the house, Lucas walked to the front door. He opened it and stood on the porch, waiting for her as she neared.

"Hi."

"Hi, yourself," he said, coming down the steps to take the heavy, cast-iron frying pan from her. "Why are you bringing your own pans? I've got plenty here."

"Ah, but you don't have a cast-iron skillet, and tonight, we need one."

They were stopped beneath the front porch light. Out on Pacific Coast Highway, cars streamed by, and on the sidewalk, a solitary woman walked a poodle so small it hardly qualified as a real dog.

But the rest of the world might as well have dropped away for all Lucas cared. His gaze was fixed only on Rose. Her eyes were bright, her lips curved into a smile and her long blond hair was loose around her shoulders. It was the first time he'd seen that thick mass free of the ponytail she usually wore and his hands itched to touch it. He wanted to wrap her hair around his hand and pull her in tight for a long, slow, deep kiss that would make the first one they'd shared look like a peck on the cheek.

He took a deep breath of the cold night air to try to dispel some of the heat charging through him. She got to him so fast and so completely, it kept catching him off guard, filling his mind with images that were designed to tempt and taunt him. Her scent drifted to him, and

Lucas's body hardened to the point of pain. In another minute, he'd be lucky to be able to walk to the kitchen.

If he wasn't careful, he might end up caught in his own trap. So to prove he was still in charge here, he pushed aside the urges rising within and forced himself to ask, "What are you planning for tonight, anyway?"

She looked a little startled at his gruff tone and he warned himself to dial it back. A second later, she edged past him into the house and headed for the kitchen without answering his question.

He knew what *his* plans would entail, but he didn't think she'd agree. At least, not yet. But soon, he promised himself as he turned and followed her into the house. His gaze locked on her retreating form, he repeated that vow silently.

Very soon.

"It's a surprise," she called back over her shoulder.

Lucas winced as he walked after her. He'd had enough surprises already, up to and including just how deeply he was being drawn into this little payback scheme. Many more surprises—without a little relief—and he'd be permanently in pain.

"Did you get my voice mail earlier?" Rose asked as he followed her down the long hallway, which was lined with framed family photos.

"If you mean did I take the steaks out of the freezer, yes," he answered. His gaze was locked on the fall of her hair, sliding down her back, swaying with her every step. On the curve of her hips, the lean length of her legs. He shook his head and swallowed a groan.

The flat heels of her shoes tapped against the wood floor and he liked the sound. Her steps were brisk, no-nonsense, and he had always liked a confident woman.

Funny, that wasn't how he remembered Rose, though.

When he'd first met her, she had seemed shy and a little standoffish. She'd hardly spoken to him the few times he'd seen her. But, he thought in retrospect, that had probably been due to Dave standing guard over her like a rabid pit bull.

He remembered being intrigued by her. He also remembered Dave shutting him down, fast. Back then, Rose's older brother had made it clear that she was off-limits. Now, Lucas had to wonder if she'd been off-limits only to *him,* since Dave was already planning on using Lucas to worm his way into a position of trust. Already planning on using the Kings and stealing from them.

And wondering that, Lucas had to also ask himself if Rose hadn't been in on it from the jump. Maybe, instead of being the carefully protected sister, she had been the bait in the trap. Beautiful. Seductive. Always kept out of reach, but dangled in front of a man until he stopped paying attention to whatever else was going on around him.

He watched her now through narrowed eyes, suspicion clawing at him. She moved around his kitchen, humming under her breath and even shuffling her feet into a little dance move to accompany whatever song was playing in her mind. She looked lovely. Innocent.

But how innocent could she really be? he wondered now. She was, after all, a Clancy.

Damn it, why had he never considered this before? Dave hadn't let Lucas get close to Rose, but he'd made damn sure that Lucas had had a good look at her. Can't catch anything if the victim never sees the bait.

Victim.

A rush of fury pushed through his veins. No. He wouldn't accept that. He wasn't a damn victim. He had been the target of an unscrupulous family. That didn't

make him a victim. It made him…what, exactly? A fool
for trusting? Well, he already knew that and accepted
it.

The tide was about to turn, though. He'd get even
with Dave for what he'd done to Lucas and the Kings.
The upside was, now that he'd considered Rose might
have been a part of the whole setup, he felt less…not
guilt, precisely, but regret, about using her.

Lucas set her iron pan onto the stove with a clatter
that got her attention. She whirled around and grinned
at him. "You're going to love dinner tonight. And it's
easy enough that you'll be able to make it again on your
own anytime."

"Good to know." He tucked his hands into his jeans'
pockets, leaned one hip against the edge of the black
granite counter and watched her.

Frowning a little, she slipped out of the bright yellow
windbreaker she wore over a cream-colored shirt and a
pair of black jeans. "Is there something wrong?"

"No," he said with a shrug he hoped was convincing.
"What could be wrong?"

"I don't know. You seem…" She paused, then shook
her head. "Never mind."

Lucas told himself to lighten up. He didn't want to
make her uneasy. Couldn't afford to scare her off before
he had a chance to make her brother pay. So he smiled
and offered, "Sorry. Bad day at work."

"What happened?"

"Why do you want to know?" he asked and wondered
if she was reporting in to her brother on everything
Lucas had to say. Then he scowled at himself and let
that one go. There was such a thing as going overboard.
Dave had already taken the Kings for all he was going

to get. No doubt he'd forgotten all about them and had moved on to steal from someone else.

"Just curious, jeez," she said. "Thought you might want to talk about it, that's all. But no big deal if you don't."

"Sorry again," he said, shoving one hand through his hair. "I'm in a crappy mood and taking it out on you."

"It's okay, everybody needs to unload once in a while."

"Understanding of you," he muttered.

"Well, growing up in our house, believe me, I heard my father and Dave complaining all the time. I'm sort of used to it."

He didn't stiffen this time when she mentioned her brother, though damned if he didn't want to question her. Find out exactly what Dave had had to say about *him* two years ago. But he wouldn't. Not yet, anyway.

Instead, he gave her a brief description of the minor crises at King Construction. "One of the crews had to shut down. A retaining wall crumpled and a man was hurt."

Worry sparked in her eyes. "Is he going to be okay?"

"Yeah." Lucas shoved away from the counter, walked to the opposite side of the cooking island and looked at her. "Broke his leg in two places, though, so he'll be out for a while. Meanwhile, the crew was pulled out so a different one can go in tomorrow to reinforce the retaining wall. And there's a customer complaining about her new block wall fence. Seems when she told us to build it five-and-a-half-feet tall, what she really meant was six feet and we should have known."

She grimaced, then smiled in sympathy. "According to Dave, women customers are the worst."

"I don't know. I usually like working directly with

the woman of the house. Most times, she knows what she wants and she can make a decision quicker than her husband." He slapped both hands onto the cool granite. "Men tend to look at a situation from every possible angle. A woman will look, see what something needs and just do it."

She tipped her head to one side and studied him. "You were right before."

"About what?"

"When you said you were nothing like my brother," she told him.

In the overhead lights, her eyes blazed a clear, summer-sky blue. Her cheeks were still a little pink from the cold wind outside and when she licked her lips, a knot of something hot and needy settled inside Lucas.

It seemed, he thought, that every minute with Rose Clancy, he was fighting to maintain control. Something about this woman sneaked past every defense he had ever had in place, and despite suspecting that she might have had a hand in what Dave had done to the Kings two years ago—or maybe because of it—he wanted her. Bad.

When she reached behind her head to gather her hair into a ponytail, he stopped her.

"Leave it loose," he said quietly. "It's beautiful."

She blinked up at him, surprised by either his words or his tone…or both. Pleasure shone in her eyes and battled with the spark of confusion he could read in her expression.

"Thanks, but when I'm cooking it just gets in the way."

"Right." Lucas nodded and told himself to get a grip.

Yes, he was trying to seduce her, but he was also trying to stay clear of the web he already felt her spinning.

Women like her were dangerous, and Sean's warnings came flying back into his mind suddenly. Things like... *no way does this end well.*

Damned if he'd back away now, though. He took an emotional step back and changed the subject entirely. "So, what's the menu?"

She frowned, probably wondering why his tone had shifted so abruptly. But a moment later, she seemed to push aside any misgivings and said, "We're making steak quesadillas, Mexican rice and roasted asparagus."

"Well, you had me up until the asparagus."

She laughed. The sound rippled from her and seemed to drift through the kitchen. Lucas smiled and realized that he'd really missed her over the last couple of days. He hated like hell to admit that even to himself. But when she wasn't here, the big old house he loved felt... empty, in a way it never had before.

Easily explained, he assured himself silently while she gathered her hair into a ponytail, then moved around the kitchen with a familiar air.

Normally, he didn't bring women to his home. When he had a woman in his life, they either met at her place or wound up at a luxury hotel for the night. He didn't bring them here, because an invitation to his house sent out the wrong signals. The minute a woman started getting comfortable, she'd begin to think of what she had with Lucas as something more than temporary.

And it never was.

It wasn't just that, though. His gaze swept the kitchen quickly, taking it all in. This house was his sanctuary. His man cave, he guessed. And sharing it with a parade of women would only make it less than what it was to him.

"Serious thoughts?"

Caught, he glanced at her and shook his head.

"No," he lied. "Just watching the teacher. Making mental notes."

"Ah," she said with a quick smile. "Then step right up, student, and let's get to work."

Six

"That was *great*," Lucas said, lifting his glass of red wine for a long sip. "Seriously good."

"Thanks." Rose smiled to herself at the compliment. The dinner really had turned out well. "I hoped you would like them. You'll have to get a good cast-iron pan and then season it before you use it."

"Season it?"

"I'll show you how. But the cast iron makes all the difference when you're frying the quesadillas—makes them crisp and keeps the cheese-and-steak filling nice and hot. And when you make them for yourself, remember you can add diced green chilies if you want to spice them up a little."

"Nothing wrong with spicy," he said softly.

Rose got a chill just from the look in his eyes and the timbre of his voice. Any spicier right now, she thought, and she just might burst into flames.

He set his glass down, leaned his forearms on the table they shared beneath the big bay window and said, "You're a terrific cook, Rose. Why're you doing this when you could be running your own restaurant?"

"Oh…" She sat back, looked at him and sighed a little. "I admit, the thought of owning a restaurant and creating amazing dishes is wonderful. I actually wanted to go to the CIA—"

"And be a spy?"

She laughed. "Culinary Institute of America."

"Ah. Entirely different sort of classes then," he said, smiling.

"Completely."

"Why didn't you go?"

"Lots of reasons," she admitted, though she wouldn't go into specifics. What would be the point of telling him that at first her father and then Dave had submarined her plans. And then she had married Henry for all the wrong reasons, trapping herself in a marriage that was way less than happy. No, she didn't want to talk about any of that, so she said only, "Mainly, money. It's expensive, and I just can't do it right now."

"I don't get it," he said softly.

She read the confusion on his face and knew what he was thinking. Why would money be a problem for one of the Clancys? She had grown up wealthy and could be still, if she was willing to give up being her own boss and slide back under the protective and suffocating cloak her big brother wanted to throw over her.

"Doesn't matter," she said.

"Sure it does. You're a Clancy, Rose."

She didn't want to get into this. It was no one's business, after all. But sitting here in the dimly lit kitchen across the table from a gorgeous man looking at her with sincere interest in his gaze was hard to ignore.

"The truth is, I could go to the CIA if I were willing to move back into the family home and have Dave dictate my life for me."

"What?"

"Wow." She blew out a breath and laid one hand against the fluttering nerves in the pit of her stomach. "I can't believe I said that out loud."

"Well, you did," Lucas said, "and you can't leave it like that. Explain."

"Now that I've started," she agreed, "I really should explain. Look, I know you and Dave don't speak anymore…"

His features iced over in a blink.

"And, I can tell by your expression you don't want to talk about that. But let me just say, I love my brother. He's always been good to me. He's just a little…"

"Overbearing?" Lucas supplied.

"Overprotective," she corrected. "And since Dad died, Dave's gotten worse."

"I was sorry to hear about your dad," Lucas murmured.

She looked up into his eyes and did read genuine regret there, and she was pleased. Whatever had gone wrong between Lucas and her brother, at least he wasn't taking it out on *her*. Staring at him across the table now, she felt at ease with him as she didn't with many people—men, especially.

Usually the men she met were after something. They wanted to use her to get to her brother. Coming from money wasn't always the happy thing that most people imagined it would be. For one thing, you never knew if someone liked you for yourself or for your bank account.

Which, she admitted with a rueful inner smile, wasn't a problem for her these days. Not since she'd cut herself off from the family coffers to go her own way.

"Anyway," she said, inhaling sharply to bring her mind back into line. "The bottom line is, after my divorce I told Dave what I wanted to do and he actually tried to tell me no. That I should do volunteer work— not that there's anything wrong with that at all," she added quickly. "But I wanted more. I wanted to build my own business. Be my own boss. And Dave thought it was too risky to invest in."

He snorted his disgust.

She appreciated the gesture even though she had the strangest urge to defend her brother. Shaking her head free of that notion, she said simply, "So I took the small trust fund my grandmother left me, opened my own business and am now alternately sinking and swimming all by myself."

"Good for you," he said, leaning back in his chair. "I can admire someone who knows what they want and goes after it."

"Thanks. Wish Dave felt the same," she admitted and felt a ball of tension in her stomach disappear.

"Yeah, well, Dave's a special case, isn't he?" Lucas muttered.

Studying him, she said softly, "I told you my deep dark secrets…why don't you tell me what happened between you and my brother to break up your friendship?"

"No."

"Just 'no'?"

"Get Dave to tell you," he said.

"Yeah, he won't talk about you, either," Rose told

him. She tossed her ponytail back over her shoulder and said, "Secrets usually come out though. Eventually."

"Not if you're careful," Lucas said, meeting her gaze until she was forced to look away from the heat she could see in those deep blue eyes.

"And you are?" she asked. "A careful man, I mean?"

"Always," he said, leaning toward her. "I'm a King. We might make mistakes, but we never make the same ones twice."

She looked up at him and tried to read what she saw in his eyes, but there was an emotional barrier there that she couldn't see past. There was more to his statement than she knew, Rose told herself. But getting any more out of him wouldn't be easy.

There was a warm, intimate feeling between them right now, she thought. Maybe it was the soft lighting, or the darkness beyond the windows. But it felt as though they were the only two people in the world. And that was a dangerous feeling, she realized.

Lucas King was temptation personified. Even his usually gruff manner wasn't enough to dispel the fantasies that seemed to arise with more and more frequency lately. Then Rose thought about everything Dee had said about maybe just "living a little." Why not enjoy Lucas in the short term?

Her stomach spun as she actually entertained the idea of seducing Lucas King. Could she do it? Hah! Of course she could do it. She'd seen the way he looked at her. She felt the heat pouring from his body into hers every time they so much as brushed against each other.

Oh, more and more dangerous, she thought, and said abruptly, "You know, I really should straighten up."

She bolted from her chair and with her back to Lucas, she grimaced tightly at her own cowardice. She had thought about this man for years and now that she had the opportunity to do something about it, what did she do? *The dishes.*

Flipping the water faucet on, she was grateful for the rush of water into the sink. At least the soft roar filled the silence. Then she heard Lucas walking up behind her and she braced herself. *Be strong,* she told herself silently.

"Don't," he said.

Startled, Rose wondered if she'd actually spoken aloud, but in the next moment, Lucas reached past her, turned the water off and said, "Don't hide from what's happening."

"Lucas..."

"You don't want to do the dishes, Rose," he murmured into the strained quiet. Then he laid his hands on her shoulders and turned her around to face him.

Stomach swirling, mouth dry, she lifted her gaze to his and inhaled sharply. Desire played out in those cool blue depths and he was making no effort to disguise his need for her.

"I've wanted to do this since that first night we kissed," he whispered and bent down slowly, lowering his mouth to hers.

Rose felt her heartbeat jump into overdrive as Lucas got even closer. Her hands were braced on the edge of the counter behind her, her chest heaving with each shallow breath she took. Heat zoomed through her until she felt like a sudden fever had slapped her.

His mouth was just a breath away from hers when her mind started racing.

Did she dare risk a very good-paying job for the momentary satisfaction of having the night she'd always dreamed of with Lucas King?

Did she dare *not* do it when she had the chance?

Did she want to live to be a hundred and go to bed every night, filled with regrets, asking herself, *Why didn't you sleep with that man?*

No. She really didn't.

"Rose?"

He had stopped, his lips a fraction of an inch from hers. Waiting. Waiting for her to be the one to decide. For her to put a stop to this or welcome him with open arms.

He lifted one hand, smoothed his fingertips across her cheek and instantly, wild heat skittered through her body. Want and need clawed at her.

Lucas King's touch was magnetic. Electric.

And just like that, her decision was made.

"No more hiding," she whispered and leaned into him, offering her mouth up to him. And as his lips closed over hers, she sighed.

She was ready for the electricity.

She was more than ready for Lucas King.

He cupped her face in his palms and kissed her so thoroughly, so completely, Rose was lost in the sensations whipping through her. If she hadn't already made up her mind to do this, the kiss would have convinced her. This kiss shook her completely, even more than the one they had shared only the week before, and, until that moment, she wouldn't have thought that possible.

A desperate sort of longing filled her. This was what she'd been looking for most of her life. This...magic that sent waves of pleasure crashing through her. Rose leaned into him, wanting more, wanting it all. Heat pooled in her center along with a throbbing ache that pulsed in time with the ragged beat of her heart.

Rose's skin hummed with anticipation as her tongue tangled with his. Lucas growled low in his throat and that rumble of sound awakened something vital inside her. His response to her was every bit as intense as her own. Knowing that, *feeling* that, gave her a heady sense of feminine power like she had never experienced before.

Always, she had been the good girl. The one that men treated like either a friend or a nun. Even her ex-husband had never really wanted her. But tonight, Lucas was changing all of that. Until him, no one had ever made her feel so sensual. So *desired*. Her dreams of Lucas from so long ago were now splintered beneath the reality. His hands slid down her neck, over her shoulders and around to stroke frantically up and down her back as if he couldn't touch her enough. She shivered with pleasure, yet wanted more. She wanted to feel his hands on her skin. Feel the hard brush of his palms against her naked flesh.

Crazy, her mind whispered.

Quiet, her body answered.

He tore his mouth from hers and lowered his head to nibble at the line of her throat. Rose arched her neck to one side to give him easier access. A second later, he groaned, lifted the hem of her shirt and pulled it up and over her head. She raised her arms to help, needing to feel his body against hers.

She didn't care that this was all happening too fast for her to think her way out of it. She didn't *want* to stop and be rational. For once in her life, Rose simply wanted to surrender to the thing she craved.

"I need you, Rose," he whispered, shifting his

hands to cup her lace-covered breasts. His thumbs and forefingers toyed with her sensitive nipples and even through her bra, the sensations were almost too much to bear.

He couldn't have said anything more perfect, she thought. Rose opened her eyes, looked up into his and said, "Yes, Lucas. I need you, too. Now."

"Good. That's good." He kissed her, hard, fast. A half smile curved his mouth briefly before intensity filled his gaze and he said, "Be sure, Rose. Once we start, neither one of us is going to want to stop."

"Nobody's stopping," she promised him, reaching out to stroke her hands over his chest.

He sucked in a gulp of air, gritted his teeth and said, "Thank God."

Reaching behind her, he unhooked her bra in a smooth, practiced move and then pushed it down and off her arms. He took a long look at her then and Rose felt his gaze as surely as she would have a touch.

"You, too," she said, tugging at his T-shirt. He nodded, yanked it off and tossed it to the floor behind him.

Rose sighed and enjoyed the view briefly before Lucas grabbed her and pulled her in close.

Skin to skin.

The friction was almost unbearable. He dropped his head to her shoulder and then pulled her head to one side so he could kiss and lick and nibble at her throat again. Rose couldn't breathe. With his hands on her, his mouth moving over her, she couldn't find any air and, oddly enough, she didn't care. Nothing mattered beyond the next kiss. The next caress. Time slipped away. The world disappeared.

All that existed was this moment.

This man.

Her mind went blessedly blank under the furious assault of too many sensations to keep track of.

"You feel so good," he murmured, splaying his hands against her back before letting them drop to the curve of her behind. He pulled her in close, aligning her body along his until she felt his hard length pressing against her abdomen and knew he was swamped by the same desperate need as she was.

"Not in the damn kitchen," he muttered.

Rose didn't care where they were. They could have been outside under the streetlights with neighbors sitting on their front porches watching and she wouldn't have cared. She just wanted his hands on her. His body moving inside hers. "Doesn't matter."

"Yeah, it does. Upstairs," he ordered, grabbing one of her hands and pulling her behind him as he headed for the hallway and the stairs.

Half-dressed, wild with desire, Rose kept up with him, but just barely. His long legs covered a lot more territory than she could. She stumbled, and wasn't surprised since her knees felt wobbly enough to collapse on her at any moment.

"Slow down," she finally said.

"Not an option," he groaned and whirled around to face her. "I already feel like I've been waiting years for this. No slowing down," he told her, jaw clenched. "No rethinking. No backing out."

His gaze was blue fire. Burning, glittering with more heat than she had ever seen before and everything in her roared to the surface to meet it.

She shook her head and said only, "You're walking too fast, I can't keep up."

He flashed her a quick smile that was born and gone again in an instant. "Why didn't you say so?"

He picked her up and swung her into the cradle of his arms, and Rose was absolutely romanced down to her soul.

He took the stairs two at a time, reaching the landing in a few long strides. Held close to his chest, Rose glanced briefly at his face as he stalked down the hall to the closed door at the far end. Even in her sexual haze, she noted her surroundings as they passed. Cream-colored walls, cherry-wood crown molding and a gleaming wood floor, covered by a deep red floor runner that muffled Lucas's steps as he relentlessly headed for their destination.

"Almost there," he murmured and Rose nodded, lifting one hand to smooth it over the sculpted muscles of his chest.

This wasn't a man born to wear a suit, she thought idly, while her fingertips moved across his skin, smoothing through the thatch of dark hair. His skin was bronzed as if he'd spent years in the sun and she could only imagine that the hard, chiseled planes of his chest had been born working on construction sites.

Her thumb moved over one flat nipple and he hissed in a breath as he kicked the bedroom door open, sending it slamming into the wall behind.

"Do that again and this is going to be over a lot sooner than either one of us wants it to be," he warned as his arms tightened around her like bands of iron.

That promise sent even more heat to her center, and she squirmed in his arms at the sudden discomfort of her jeans. She wanted. Needed. She took a breath and looked around. The huge room was darkened but for the moonlight pouring through the wide windows onto a gigantic bed. She didn't notice anything else.

Her gaze shifted to him and locked there as he stopped at the side of the bed, reached down and threw back the black duvet to reveal crisp white sheets. Mounds of pillows banked against the headboard and when he dropped her onto the mattress, Rose bounced a couple of times, still never taking her eyes from his.

Her entire body was sizzling. She swallowed hard at the look in his eyes. She felt like a banquet laid out before a starving man and heaven help her, she couldn't wait for him to take his first bite.

Desire pumped through her, making every nerve ending feel as though it was on fire.

"I've been thinking about this—you, here in my bed—for almost two weeks," he admitted, bending over her as she unsnapped her jeans then pulled the zipper down. He pulled the jeans and her panties off, pausing only long enough to tear her shoes off and toss them aside as well.

"I have, too," she admitted, though if she were going to be completely honest with him—which she wasn't—she'd have to say she had been thinking about this moment for three *years*. Since the moment her brother had introduced them and then metaphorically hung a No Trespassing sign over her head.

"Wait's over," he grumbled and peeled out of his own clothes in a heartbeat of time.

"Thank goodness," she whispered. Her gaze moved over him in a blink and everything hot and needy inside her stirred into frantic life. His body was amazing. She couldn't wait to feel it moving within her.

She lifted her arms in welcome and he bent over her, joining her on the wide bed, sliding his hands up and down her body, exploring every curve, learning every line. His breath came hot and fast against her neck, her breasts, as he took first one nipple then the other into his mouth, lavishing each of them with attention. His teeth scraped across the sensitive tips, and his tongue worked her until she was whimpering beneath the onslaught of feelings. He suckled her and it felt as though he were drawing her essence into his mouth. She clung to him, holding his head in place while her body arched and shifted on the cool sheets, looking blindly for release.

He fed off her response, ramping up his touch, his kisses. As if he felt everything she was experiencing, Lucas seemed to know just how to touch her. How to stroke and caress until she was babbling helplessly.

She writhed beneath him, hips rocking, back arching, moving into him, wanting, needing. Her mind shut down to everything but the incredible sensations he brought her. His hands seemed to be everywhere at once. Her breasts, her nipples, her abdomen, her… "Lucas—"

His big hand cupped her core and she gasped his name again, louder this time. Finally, her body seemed to shout. At last. What she needed. His thumb rubbed that small, sensitive bud at her center as he dipped first one finger and then two into her heated depths.

"Lucas, please," she whispered brokenly, hips moving into his hand, her head turning from side to side on the bed as she fought for breath, fought for completion.

Spirals of tension coiled inside her with every stroke of his fingers. He dipped his head to claim one of her nipples again and as he suckled her, he rubbed even harder at her center and the two sensations combined made Rose absolutely mindless with craving.

She moaned his name and fisted her hands in the sheet beneath her, trying to keep her grip on her unsteady world. Feet planted on the mattress, she rocked her hips ceaselessly, hungering for a release that remained tantalizingly out of reach. She worked for it, practically wept for it as each breath she drew grew shallower, more desperate.

He lifted his head, looked at her and in his eyes she saw the same frantic need she was feeling. "Fast and hard, that's how I want you, Rose."

"Yes. Be inside me. Now. Please," she whispered, twisting beneath him, parting her thighs even wider, her body issuing the invitation she couldn't find the breath to speak.

He reached over to the bedside table, yanked open the drawer and pulled out a condom. He tore the wrapping open, grabbed the latex and sheathed himself in one quick move.

"A careful man," she whispered, echoing the words he'd once said to her.

"You make me crazy, Rose," he muttered darkly, moving to cover her body with his.

She smiled, stupidly pleased by that remark. "I do?"

"Yeah. Hell, I almost forgot to grab a condom," he admitted, taking her mouth in a long kiss as his body slid into her heat.

"Oh, my…" She arched into him, lifting her hands to his shoulders, clinging to him as if she needed his strength to hold her onto the planet.

"Rose…" He groaned and held perfectly still for one heart-stopping moment. "Can't wait. Have to have you," he said on a sigh and, almost instantly, set a fast, hard rhythm that had Rose's heart racing. Again and again, he entered and withdrew. Their bodies moved together in the moonlight, each of them reaching for completion. Each of them clinging to the other.

And as the last, taut coil of tension inside her suddenly exploded, Rose called out his name and looked up into his eyes as the rest of the world fell away. A crashing wave of staggering pleasure washed through her, leaving her shaken and vulnerable.

She was still holding him, still meeting that passion-fueled gaze, when his body erupted into hers and, cradling him, Rose rode the wave of his release as fully as she had her own.

Seven

Lucas felt as though he'd just run a marathon.

His body still locked inside hers, his climax still rippling through his body, he hardened for her again. Rocking into her, he heard her sigh and felt her hook her legs at the small of his back.

"Mmm…" Her satisfied sigh rattled him, and at the same time fed the burgeoning hunger that was refueling itself inside him.

He groaned again and knew they weren't finished. A part of him wondered if they would *ever* be finished.

She flattened her palms against his chest and stroked his skin—her touch was like silk. He looked into her eyes and saw the passion-glazed stare of a woman completely undone and should have felt a jolt of satisfaction for a plan that was coming together all too well.

Instead, all he felt was more want. More need.

Her blue eyes were shining with every ounce of passion that was flaring inside him. She wanted him again every bit as much as he wanted her. The smoldering fire between them leaped into life like an inferno. Her short, neat fingernails scratched at his skin and every single touch was like the lick of flames. She thumbed one of his nipples and he felt the jolt of renewed passion zip through him like a lightning strike.

Heartbeat pounding, he took her mouth again. Their tongues tangled together, breath sliding from one to the other of them. Each of them fought their own need and offered it up to the other. Each of them hungered and Lucas did the only thing he could. He moved inside her again and heard her groan of satisfaction as his reward.

This wasn't seduction anymore.

This was *need*. Crashing, burning desperation—and it wouldn't be denied.

Easing up a bit, he unhooked her legs from his waist and draped them over his shoulders. She licked her lips and rocked her body on his, sliding him in even deeper than he had been.

Lucas hissed in a breath and fought for the legendary calm that seemed to have completely deserted him. When it came to this woman, he had no control. How could he have not noticed that before?

He was always in control. Always cool and composed. Distanced even, from the very women he slept with. There were barriers erected between him and the rest of the world.

But tonight was different.

She was different.

There was nothing he wouldn't do to have Rose, Lucas thought. For the first time *ever,* his mind was taking a backseat to his body's demands and he didn't care. Didn't want to think and could only be grateful for the complete shutdown of his coolly rational brain.

"Lucas…"

Her whispered plea slammed into him. He reached for their joining and stroked his thumb over the one nub of flesh he knew would make her the most crazed. She didn't disappoint him. Instantly, she rocked on him, swiveling her hips as best she could to take him deeper, higher.

And still it wasn't enough.

Shifting position, Lucas pulled free of her, drawing moans from both of them. Then he eased her legs off his shoulders, turned her over onto her stomach and lifted her hips.

Moving to accommodate what he was doing, Rose went up on all fours and in an instant, Lucas entered her body again, seating himself as deeply as he could. His hands on her behind, he squeezed and stroked while she moved into him, gasping for every breath.

He slid one hand down and around to cup one of her breasts, tugging at her nipple as he continued to move inside her. Faster, harder, deeper, he pushed them both beyond the edge of reason and into a world where the only hope either of them had was another crushing release.

Moonlight caressed her skin and silvered her hair. The cool sheets beneath them and the chill of the air in the room added even more sensation to what passed between them. And when he felt her climax stir, Lucas let himself go. This time when they made that leap, they made it together.

A few minutes later, Lucas was lying against the bank of pillows with Rose still spooned in front of him. He hadn't been able to separate himself from her yet. The heat of her drew him in and it was something he was in no hurry to give up. Breath churning from his lungs, he fought to get his brain back. He'd never experienced anything like this before. Rose was the first woman in his life that had emptied his mind and fired his body so that nothing else had mattered.

He could hardly believe what had happened. He hadn't been able to dredge up coherent thought beyond admitting to himself that she was so much more than he had originally thought. His natural restraint had dissolved. His rational self had taken a vacation, leaving his body in charge—and he hardly knew what to think about that. Hell, he'd never lost himself in a woman like that before. Sighing, he kissed her shoulder and reluctantly parted them. And—

A sudden, staggering realization punched him hard. How could he have not noticed? Been so careless?

Looking down at the woman cuddled into him he said, "Rose, tell me you're on the pill."

"What?" She sighed, rolled over and nestled her head more comfortably on his chest then licked her lips.

That brief sweep of her tongue sent another jolt of desire through him and he had to fight to ignore it.

"The pill, Rose," he repeated as she shifted lazily to turn her gaze up to his.

Her hair was a cloud of silvery blond, framing her face and lying across her pale, beautiful skin, making her look like some pagan goddess. And, despite the raging unease inside him, his body instantly went like stone again. If he wasn't careful, he was going to be repeating his stupendous lack of control.

"What did you say?" She stroked her palm up his

chest and around to his back and the brush of her fingertips against his skin felt like match flames.

He hissed in a breath, caught her wandering hand in his and growled, "Rose, the damn condom *broke*. Tell me you're on the pill."

That got her attention. She went absolutely still and her eyes widened. His stomach sank. He saw the flash of shock that became worry in her eyes, and he knew they were in trouble.

"Oh, God…" She pulled her hand free of his grip and covered her mouth with it.

Lucas sighed and briefly dropped one arm across his eyes as if he could shut out the whole image of what had just happened. He couldn't believe this.

"How did it…never mind."

"I don't know how the hell it broke, either," he muttered. "It's never happened to me before." He got out of bed, stalked to the bathroom to take care of the mess, then headed back to the bedroom. Sitting on the bed, he pulled her into his side and looked down at her. "Look, it's too late for this conversation, but you should know I'm healthy."

"Me, too," she assured him, though he hadn't for a second considered she might not be.

Not the sweet and pure Rose.

Irritation warred with the dregs of the passion he was still feeling. Even now, when he was reeling with the possibilities facing him, Lucas could admit to himself that his desire for her hadn't been quenched. Not even close. Which said exactly what about him?

She pushed her hair out of her face and reached for the edge of the duvet, dragging it up over her breasts as if somehow by draping herself in armor she could undo what they had already done.

"Is there a chance?" He actually winced at what had to be the dumbest question he'd ever uttered. Of course there was a chance she would get pregnant. He'd been stupid. Thoughtless. Allowed himself to be carried away by his body's demands at the expense of his damn brain.

"Forget it," he said quickly. "Stupid question. I know there's a chance."

"It's the wrong time of the month," she told him, "but that's no guarantee...." A moment later, she groaned and added, "I can't believe it broke."

His teeth clenched hard enough to snap his jaw, but he still managed to say, "My fault."

"Oh, please."

Not the reaction he'd expected. When he looked at her closely he was even more surprised by the irritated expression she was aiming at him.

"We're both grown-ups, Lucas. We were both here. We both wanted this and neither one of us handmade a faulty condom, so please don't treat me like a child and take all the blame for this."

"That's not how I meant it," he muttered. Women were damned confusing at times, he told himself. You don't take responsibility, they're pissed. You *do* take it and they're pissed anyway.

"Well, it's what you said," she told him, swinging her hair back from her face. "My God, you don't even see how insulting that is, do you? What? Am I some airhead who doesn't know how babies are made? Is that it?"

"No, damn it, what are you so mad about?"

"Oh, this is just typical," she muttered darkly, her hands fisting on the duvet until her knuckles went white. "I'm so tired of everyone around me acting as though I'm a porcelain doll or something. No mind of my own."

She scooted off the bed, still clutching the duvet tightly to her. "My father, my ex, Dave and now *you*."

He jumped off the bed, too, and stood there naked, watching her stomp barefooted around the edge of the mattress. "Don't lump me in with them."

"If it walks like a duck…"

"Great. Perfect." He threw his hands up and shook his head. Weirdest damn after-sex conversation he'd ever had. "You're an intelligent woman in charge of herself who might be pregnant because of a faulty condom. Happy?"

"Delirious," she snapped. "You just don't get it. I spent most of my life taking orders from the men in my life, who insisted they knew better than I did. I didn't argue, either, which is totally my fault," she added in a disgusted undertone. "I even married a man my father picked out because I didn't want to disappoint him."

Lucas shoved one hand through his hair. "Always wondered why you married that jerk."

"Now you know. Spineless Rose. That was me," she said with a shudder. "I look back and even I don't believe what a doormat I was." Flashing him a look that should have set him on fire, she added, "But you know what? Being married to Henry, living through the humiliation of him constantly cheating on me, was a valuable lesson."

"In what? Torture? Self-sacrifice?" He snorted a laugh. "Figures Saint Rose would find the silver lining in the middle of the storm."

She inhaled sharply and her expression was horrified. "*Saint Rose?* That's what you think of me?"

"That's what everyone thinks of you. The good. The perfect. The always proper and demure Rose Clancy," he said, despite the voice in his head warning him to step carefully.

She kicked the duvet away from her feet and, still clutching the top of it to her breasts, marched over to him, fury stamped on her features. When she was close enough, she poked him in the chest with her index finger.

Didn't look demure now, Lucas thought warily. Her eyes were flashing and her mouth was flattened into a thin, straight line that told him he was lucky she wasn't armed.

"I'm no saint," she snapped, defining each word with a sharp stab of her finger.

"I'm getting that."

"And I'm not the same Rose you used to know. I'm done taking orders from men—*any* man." She gave him a shove that didn't budge him an inch. "I'll make my own decisions, and I'll worry about my own mistakes, and I don't need you telling me what to do."

He crossed his arms over his chest and glared down at her. "Fine. Make your decision. Start with what do we do now."

"What do you mean?" she asked with a choked-off laugh that sounded just this side of hysterical. "There's nothing to do. It's done. A little late to be locking the old barn door, don't you think?"

"Yeah." He scrubbed one hand across the back of his neck and nodded to himself. "We'll just see what happens and if you are pregnant, then we'll get married and…"

"*Married?* What? You'll throw yourself on a funeral pyre? Gee, thanks. I feel so much better now." Shaking her head, she added in an undertone, "Ten seconds and he's back to treating me like an idiot again."

"How am I treating you like an idiot?"

"Hah! Just look at you. Acting like—" her voice dropped to a poor imitation of a man's "—poor, helpless Rose. I mistreated her badly. Better find a way to make it up to her." She slumped over dramatically. "I know! I'll just fall on my sword. That should take care of things."

"What the hell—"

She straightened up and flashed him another look that promised all sorts of retribution. "I don't need you sacrificing yourself for me, okay? It was sex. Great, earth-shaking and as it turns out, *unprotected* sex. I can deal. What I am not going to do is marry another man for all the wrong reasons. So come on out of the nineteenth century, Lucas."

He'd listened to her, dumbfounded, while she went on her rant. Well, now it was his turn. "Maybe this isn't about what *you* can deal with, Rose. Ever consider that?"

Turning his back on her, he scanned the floor for his jeans and grabbed them up. Shifting back to face her again as he pulled them on, he kept talking, irritated not just with himself, but also with the woman who only moments ago had had his engines roaring.

"Do you know who my father is?"

"What?" She scowled at him. "What does that have to do with—"

"Ben King, that's who," Lucas told her, shoving both hands through his hair with nearly enough heat to pull out every strand. "Ben King is to illegitimate sons what Johnny Appleseed was to trees. Do you get it now? Do you see why I'm taking responsibility for this?"

"No! What does your father have to do with anything that happens between us?"

He stomped to her side, noting that she held the duvet

higher and closer to her chest. The image of her as a pagan goddess slammed into him again. Moonlight sifting over her, outlining her in silver until she didn't even look real. She looked, actually, like every man's dream woman. Rumpled and sexy and ready to be tossed onto the nearest bed.

Which is just what he wanted to do.

Instead, he grabbed her bare shoulders and felt the heat of her blast into his hands. "My father spread his sperm in such a wide swath, we haven't even *met* all of our brothers yet," he told her flatly. "I promised myself years ago that I would never do that. I would never create a child that wasn't wanted. Planned for. *Loved.*"

Her features clouded up briefly, but her eyes had lost their fire when she said, "Okay, I can understand that, but Lucas, you did the right thing. You were thinking. I sure as heck wasn't. Protection never occurred to me, I'm ashamed to say. You thought of it."

"For all the good it did us. Doesn't change anything," he muttered and released her because if he held on to her any longer, he might not be able to let go at all. "If we made a child tonight, we're getting married. I'm not having any kid of mine grow up like I did. With a part-time father and a mother who spent all of her time trying to find a man to stay with her."

He'd never said that out loud before. Never let anyone catch a glimpse of the kind of childhood he'd had. Lucas had loved his parents, but he wasn't born blind. His mom was a nice woman who hadn't been strong enough to be a single mother. She had spent every waking moment looking for the love that Ben King hadn't been able to give her.

He wouldn't sentence any child of his to the kind of half life Lucas had known as a kid.

As if she sensed just how ragged he was feeling, Rose let her anger fade away. Her voice softened, too, as she said, "We're not going to settle anything tonight, Lucas. And we're probably going to war over nothing. I think I should just go."

Her skin looked milky against the dark fabric she held so tightly and her hair was as pale as the moonlight. Her eyes were shadowed, though, and he hated to see it.

His seduction plan had worked too well. Not only had he gotten Rose into his bed, but he'd also been seduced. Losing himself in the feel of her. The taste of her. Even now, knowing what they might be facing, his body ached for her again. His brain was racing, but his body only *needed*.

Nothing about Rose Clancy was turning out to be easy.

"Maybe we should talk this out more."

"I think we've already said plenty." She glanced around the room looking for her clothes. She grabbed her panties and jeans and tugged them on, then seemed to realize that they had left their shirts downstairs.

"Oh, for heaven's sake," she muttered, crossing her arms over her breasts. "I don't even have my shirt with me. What was I thinking?"

The problem was, Lucas thought, that neither of them had been thinking at all. This whole seduction thing had gotten way out of hand. He'd thought he was in charge. Totally on top of the situation. What a joke. Now he was caught in a web of his own making and he didn't have a clue as to whether there was a way out or not—or hell, whether or not he even *wanted* a way out.

Which was so far out of orbit for him, he dismissed the thought the minute it rose up in his mind. This was not about forever. Hell, this wasn't even temporary. This was just supposed to be a one-night seduction and then revenge. Plain and simple.

Only problem was, *simple* was off the table.

"You know what?" Rose was saying, shaking her head as if she couldn't believe she was standing there half-dressed. "I just have to go. Now."

Only minutes ago this woman had practically set his bed on fire. Now they were awkward with each other, neither of them sure of their next move. And for Lucas at least, that was a first.

"No point in hiding your breasts from me now, is there?" he asked, taking her elbow to escort her downstairs.

"In bed, it's different. Just standing here…" She closed her eyes and huffed out a breath that could have been anger but was probably embarrassment.

He snatched up a T-shirt off a chair in his room and handed it to her. "Here."

"Thanks," she muttered, turning her back on him to pull his shirt over her head. The hem of the dark green shirt fell to the middle of her thighs and made her look smaller, more vulnerable somehow—and he didn't think she'd like knowing that.

When she looked at him again, she refused to meet his gaze. Everything had changed now. They'd let each other in and exposed too many secrets and now they were both busily rebuilding personal barriers. Lucas steered her out of his room and down the hall, sensing the emotional distance between them as they walked in strained silence.

And all he could think was that Sean had been right. Revenge really did have a way of turning around to bite you in the ass.

* * *

Staring at the computer screen doing the books for her business wasn't taking Rose's mind off of Lucas King. She rubbed her gritty eyes, shook her head and tried to focus again, but even she could see it was useless.

Everything on the screen might as well have been in Greek. Numbers seemed to run together. Red and black. Clients and suppliers. Appointments and schedules. All of it was blurred into a distorted mess that seemed to taunt her feelings of ineptitude. That's what she got for trying to work when she was so tired she could hardly see straight.

"But to be fair," she said aloud in the stillness, "I suck at this end of the business even on a good day."

Frowning, she kicked back in her chair, lifting her sneaker-clad feet to the corner of her desk. Her small home office was brutally organized. Not a paper out of place. There were file cabinets, a three-in-one copier/ printer/fax machine and a top-of-the-line computer on a simple wood desk. She glanced at the framed poster of Ireland hanging on the wall and briefly wished she were there on that rocky coast, with the wind in her hair.

But that thought only lasted a moment as she sighed and glanced around the room. She had been so determined, when she started Home Cooking Taught at Home, to be the quintessential businesswoman. And for a while, she had made a good job of it. Until last night. Rose was pretty sure *quintessential* didn't mean sleeping with your clients—or rather *not* sleeping, but having amazing, soul-shaking, body-burning sex.

Her feet dropped to the floor as her stomach pitched. "Oh, God." She lowered her head to the desk until her forehead hit with a *thunk*. Rose sat up abruptly, reaching to rub her forehead.

She could be pregnant.

"No, don't think that, and for heaven's sake, don't say it out *loud*," she whispered, shaking her head. All she needed was to throw that challenge out to the universe.

Pregnancy was *not* in her business plan. Or in her life plan for that matter. Sure, someday, she'd love to have children. Had always wanted them, in fact…but not yet. She knew there were women out there who managed to be single moms and work and have a life and pull it off beautifully.

But that's not what she wanted.

Even with her miserable marriage in her background, Rose still wanted the fairy tale.

"Of course, they were called *Grimm* fairy tales for a reason," she told herself with a sigh. Oh, yeah, she was in great shape. Her mind wandering down long, twisting paths that went exactly nowhere and made her feel absolutely no better.

Trying to work was pointless, she finally admitted. No way was she going to be able to concentrate. Her gaze shifted to the noticeably silent phone on the corner of her desk. She had half expected Lucas to call and didn't know what she would say to him if he did. But the fact that he hadn't was beginning to really tick her off.

What had happened at his house after she left last night? Did he crawl right back into bed and sleep like a baby? No worries? No thoughts about her or them or what might be happening inside her body right at this minute? Was he really that cold? Was he so unemotional he couldn't even be bothered to call and say, "Hey, you okay? How's the baby?"

"He's right. Women aren't logical," she mused, pushing out of her chair to walk into the kitchen. "But how are we supposed to be logical when dealing with *men?*"

Her own kitchen was much smaller than the one at Lucas's house. But it was cozy and familiar and on this foggy, gray morning, it felt like sunshine with its white and yellow walls.

She filled the teakettle at the sink, set it on the stove and turned the fire on underneath it. While she waited for the water to boil, Rose leaned back against the counter, folded her arms over her chest and wondered what she was supposed to do now.

"Excellent timing," she murmured. "Why didn't you do some thinking last night when it might have helped? Because," she added ruefully, "you were too busy *feeling* to want to do anything rational."

Oh, terrific. Not only was her world sort of crumbling down around her, but now she was also talking to herself. That couldn't be a good sign.

Plus she was exhausted. She had been up all night. Every time she had closed her eyes, she saw Lucas. Heard his voice. Felt his hands on her body.

If she had managed to fall asleep, no doubt her dreams would have been in 3D with surround sound. So instead, she'd spent the last several hours cleaning her house until it was shining and then watching infomercials on television. Now her eyes felt like two marbles left out in the sun too long and fatigue dragged at every muscle.

Steam pushed out the spout of the teakettle, making an ear-piercing noise that shattered her thoughts and got her moving again. She took the kettle off the flame, poured the boiling water into her waiting teacup and idly stood there while the lone decaf tea bag brewed. She'd had so much coffee during the night her stomach needed a caffeine break. Besides, tea was soothing and damn it, she needed to be soothed.

Or, at the very least, she told herself silently, commiserated with. Gripping the mug, she walked to the phone on the counter, picked up the receiver and hit number three on the speed dial. She sipped at her tea while the phone rang, then winced when Delilah's slurred voice demanded, "Who is crazy enough to be calling me at this hideous hour?"

"Sorry," Rose said quickly. "Really, sorry, Dee. I didn't even look at the time."

She did now, though, and cringed. Five o'clock in the morning. "Look, I'll talk to you later, okay? Go back to sleep."

"Sure," Dee said with a groan. "That's gonna happen. What's going on?"

"Have you got an hour or two?" Rose asked on a sigh. Before Dee could answer, though, she shook her head and said, "It's nothing that won't wait. We'll talk later. I can't do this on the phone, anyway. I'm really sorry."

"Rose!"

But she hung up, feeling as though she was batting a thousand. Sex with a client, followed by a big fight and ooh, maybe pregnant. And then finally, she'd awoken her best friend. Maybe she could find a puppy to kick and make everything perfect.

"Okay, that's it. You need to get out of this house for a while." She grabbed her bright pink sweatshirt off the back of a chair, picked her keys off a hook by the door and, carrying her tea with her, headed for the front door.

She stepped out into the damp, cold mist of the fog and a few steps from the house, she was lost in it.

Eight

Lucas was grateful to have somewhere else to focus his mind. He'd been up for hours, thinking over what had happened with Rose, and he needed a damn break before his brain exploded.

"You sure you want to do this now?"

Lucas turned off the engine and glanced at Sean. "Why wouldn't I?"

"I don't know," his brother said, taking a sip of his extra-large latte. "You look like you want to punch somebody, is all. And since I don't want it to be me and since if you punch Warren we could get sued, I just thought you might want to wait a while. Cool down from whatever's got your jets firing so hot."

"Well, you thought wrong," Lucas muttered.

"Okay, then," Sean said with a shrug. "Let's start the show."

They were at Long Beach harbor, not far from Terminal Island. Mostly, this area was filled with naval vessels and the cargo ships that sailed in and out of the harbor every day. The air was cold and smelled like fish and diesel oil.

It was almost six in the morning and people were already moving at the King Construction yard. The security guard at the gate had opened it for them the minute he recognized Lucas's SUV. Now the car was parked beside the warehouse-size building that stored the company's tools and machinery. Men and women—King Construction didn't discriminate against women on a work crew—moved around the building and surrounding yard, talking, laughing, getting their gear for whatever projects they were on.

Every morning, the working crews would come here, to the warehouse, to get what they needed for the jobs that started precisely at eight. A lot of construction firms didn't store their equipment in one central location. But the Kings figured it was easier to protect their investment in the tools this way and it gave all of their workers a chance to get to know each other. Friendships on a job site made the work go better.

And, Lucas told himself, this way he had known exactly where he could find Warren. Sure, he could have fired the man over the phone but that was damned impersonal. The least he owed someone who worked for him was a face-to-face when that job was ending.

"Hey, Sean!" someone called out. "Come on over here and settle a bet for me!"

Sean glanced at Lucas. "You handle this on your own?"

Rolling his eyes, Lucas snapped, "Yes, Mom. I think I can handle it."

"Without hitting him?"

"Go away, Sean."

"Right." Still, he gave Lucas another worried glance before moving off to where three of their crew were holding a loud debate over football.

Lucas shook his head, amused as he heard Sean jump right into the argument with an easy camaraderie. As good as he was with the tech stuff, Sean also was the most easygoing guy Lucas had ever known.

He put thoughts of his brother aside as he walked into the cavernous warehouse. Heavy thuds and clanks sounded and seemed to echo as the different crews loaded up what they would need for the day. The steel walls reverberated with the roar of one of the diesel engines and men shouted to each other to be heard over the noise.

It was a good sound, though. Lucas had always enjoyed being on a job site. Most of the time now, he worked on the phone from the office, but every once in a while, it was good to get back to the basics. Check in with their crews. And just as Rafe had only a few months ago, actually work a job. Though Rafe had done it because he had lost a bet, Lucas enjoyed working a job occasionally just to keep his hand in.

The tension in his shoulders eased a little as he let his surroundings soak in. Whatever else was going on in his life, here at King Construction, he knew exactly what he was doing.

He nodded at the people he passed, stopped to answer a question, then asked one of his own, "Julio, have you seen Warren around this morning?"

"Yeah." Julio Vega, about thirty-five with a thick black mustache and sharp brown eyes, lifted one arm and pointed toward the back of the warehouse, where the loaders and cement mixers were housed. "He's back there."

"Thanks." Lucas found his quarry easily enough then, but by the look on Warren's face when he saw Lucas, he was guessing this wasn't going to go well.

"Boss," the man said, with a brisk nod and a clenching of his jaw.

"Warren, we need to talk."

"If this is about the WeDig problem—"

"It is," Lucas told him, slapping one hand to the cold, metal side of the cement mixer. "You know, you were lucky that the only thing the men hit was a water pipe. It could have been a gas line. The whole damn neighborhood could have gone up in an explosion and fire."

Warren was in his forties, balding, with a full red beard. His face flushed, but it wasn't embarrassment coloring his features, it was anger. "*Could have* doesn't count. It wasn't the gas line, Lucas. Yeah, there was a damn flood, but we got the pumps in, most of the water's gone and we'll have the damage to the redwood deck repaired by end of the week."

Defensive. Lucas couldn't blame him but he also noticed that the man wasn't exactly apologizing, either. He knew damn well what might have happened and *could have* always counted. On a job site, there were so many things that could go wrong at any given moment, it was up to the man in charge to stay one step ahead of all problems.

"Yeah," Lucas said, keeping his voice even and his tone calm. "But doing all of that means we're *not* doing the job we were hired to do. Plus, we have to eat the cost of the repairs to the deck."

Shaking his head, he noticed the other man's temper

spiking, in the way his jaw muscles twitched and his hands continued to fist and relax at his sides. Warren could be as mad as he liked, but it was the wrong damn attitude to take with the boss when it was your own blasted mistake that had caused the mess in the first place.

"Warren, you know as well as I do, we lose money every day we spend correcting what went wrong on your site. Now we're behind on the job, which puts us behind on the *next* job." He patted the cement mixer, then folded his arms across his chest. "You were in charge, and you should have made sure WeDig cleared you before any of the guys so much as lifted a shovel."

Warren's barrel chest expanded with the huge gulp of air he took in. "You can't lay all of this off on me."

"Who else?" Lucas demanded, his own temper beginning to build. Hell, he knew mistakes happened— briefly, he thought about last night with Rose and could admit that he made mistakes, too—but he didn't have a bit of sympathy for someone so stubborn they couldn't even own up to it. "*You* were the foreman on the job."

"Every one of those guys has worked for you long enough to know better than to start digging," the man argued hotly. "Am I the babysitter, too?"

Warren's voice was getting louder, and Lucas heard other sounds in the warehouse quiet down. He knew people were listening and couldn't seem to care. He'd have preferred that he and Warren could settle this quietly, but maybe it was just as well that everyone here was reminded of the rules. The Kings believed in second chances, sure.

But *keep* screwing up and you're out.

"You're not the babysitter, Warren. You're the man who gives the orders on the site." His anger suddenly fading away into a mass of just-plain-tired, Lucas added, "This isn't the first time you've made mistakes on a job, either. King Construction has a solid reputation, and we'll do what we have to, to protect it."

"Like *fire* me?" Warren demanded. "That's what this is about, right? You came down here to fire me?"

"That's right," Lucas said flatly. He was done here. He'd said what he had to say and now he just wanted it finished. "I did. You'll get two weeks' severance, plus your vacation pay, but I want you off King property in the next half hour. One of the guards will walk you out."

"A guard? Now I'm a thief you have to follow around until I leave?"

"It's standard procedure, Warren, and you know it," Lucas told him.

"Standard procedure. That's great." Warren was clearly furious, but he was also surprised. Lucas saw it in his eyes. Apparently, he had expected the Kings to give him another warning and that would be the end of it. He backed up a step, muttered under his breath and ran one hand across the top of his bald head. Finally, he glared at Lucas. "Five years I've worked for you and you toss me aside this easy?"

And just like that, Lucas thought, his own anger was back. "Like I said, this wasn't your first mistake. And hell, I could even accept the mistakes if you'd just *once* taken responsibility for them. But no. You always push it off on the guys. Their fault. They didn't listen." Lucas took a breath and blew it out. "Well, Warren, when you're in charge, you better make damn sure they're listening to you."

"You son of a bitch. What am I supposed to do now?"

"No longer my problem," Lucas told him simply and started past him. His task was over and he didn't feel any better. Now he had to head back to the office and try to concentrate on work, when the reality was, he knew damn well Rose would be front and center in his mind all day—just as she had been all night.

"Don't you turn your back on me—" Warren reached out, grabbed Lucas's arm and spun him around. Drawing his right arm back, the man took a swing at him, but Lucas blocked the punch easily enough and threw one of his own into Warren's stomach that had him bending over and wheezing for air.

Irritated beyond belief, Lucas just glared at the man. "What the hell were you thinking? Throwing a swing at me? On top of being fired you want to be arrested?"

"You hit me."

"Yeah," Lucas said. "I told Sean I wouldn't, but you just couldn't help yourself, could you? Had to ratchet this up into a fight. You really are an idiot, aren't you?"

"I'll sue!" Warren managed to say, raising his furious gaze to Lucas.

"No, you won't," Julio said from right behind Lucas. "I saw the whole thing. You took the first punch. Lucas was defending himself."

Grateful, Lucas nodded at the younger man. A lawsuit would have been expensive and time-consuming. With Julio stepping forward, they'd avoid the hassle, and he appreciated it. "Julio, get security back here to escort Warren to his car."

Julio sent the still wheezing man a disgusted look, but nodded and said, "Right, boss."

Lucas moved away, still feeling a nagging sense of something unfinished inside him. Even hitting that moron hadn't helped any.

He walked out of the warehouse, oblivious to the noise, the laughter and conversation. The fog was burning off and the sun was a hazy, rising ball of fire overhead. He shoved his hands into his pockets, took a deep breath of the sea air and told himself that the real problem wasn't Warren, and he knew it.

It was Rose. How they'd left things.

When she'd walked out of his house last night it had taken everything in him not to go after her, carry her back into the house and tie her to his damn bed. He could still see the look of wild fury in her eyes when he had called her *Saint Rose*. And he remembered, too, that arguing with her had been as damned intoxicating as making love to her.

The woman was getting to him on so many levels he couldn't count them all.

So it was best that she'd left last night. And good that he hadn't spoken to her since. After all, he reminded himself sternly, this had been the plan. He'd gotten her into his bed. Now all he had to do was tell Dave all about it and then stop seeing Rose altogether. Perfect.

Except for the niggling question of whether or not they'd created a child. Gritting his teeth, Lucas reined in his thoughts and tucked them at the back of his mind, where no doubt they would continue to torture him all the damn day.

"You hit him, didn't you?" Sean asked when he strolled up alongside him.

"What?" Lucas turned and frowned at his brother. "How'd you know?"

"The guys are talking about it. You came off really well in the telling, by the way."

"That's just great," Lucas muttered. "Warren took the first swing, but yeah. I punched him."

Sean handed over his latte. "Here. Have some."

Lucas took a few long swallows, welcoming the caffeine before handing it back.

"I knew you'd hit him," Sean said with a shrug. "That's why I wanted to go in with you."

"To stop me?"

"Hell no," Sean said. "*I* wanted to hit him."

Reluctantly, Lucas grinned. No matter how screwed up his life was, it was still good to have brothers.

The knock at the front door came only a few minutes after Rose had returned from her predawn walk through the fog. She was still exhausted, still struggling with her thoughts and in no mood for company. She pulled back the edge of the curtains to peer out and sighed.

"Ready or not," she muttered, "company's here, and it's not going anywhere."

Her own fault, she told herself as she walked to the front door and unlocked it. If Rose hadn't called an hour ago, Dee wouldn't be standing on her front porch right now, with two lattes and a bag that hopefully included doughnuts.

She opened the door and gave her friend a half smile. "You didn't have to come over, you know."

"Right," Dee said, walking past her into the living room. "My best friend calls me at the crack of dear-God-why-am-I-awake, and I should just roll over and drop back into dreamland."

Wincing, Rose closed the front door, locked it and followed her friend into the small, cozy living room. Dee was already on the couch, her sandal-clad feet propped on the coffee table and the serving tray of lattes on the cushion beside her.

Even at six-something in the morning, Delilah James looked gorgeous. She wore a body-hugging pale yellow shirt tucked into skintight dark-wash blue jeans. Her red hair was styled and fluffed, her makeup was flawless and her green eyes were practically glowing with curiosity.

All in all, Rose thought sadly, as she walked to the couch in her baggy sweats and battered sneakers, she felt like the ugly stepsister next to the shining Cinderella.

"I hope there are doughnuts in that bag," she said as she took a seat on the opposite end of the couch.

"Am I breathing? Yes, there are doughnuts in the bag. And a latte with your name on it."

"Thanks."

"Skip the thank-yous and tell me what's going on." Dee took a sip of her own latte and waited. One of her best skills as a girlfriend was that she was a terrific listener.

Rose knew all too well that Delilah would sit right there on the couch all morning and into the afternoon if she had to, waiting for Rose to spill her guts. Then she would listen without judging—mostly—and after that, she would support whatever it was Rose decided to do.

If only she *knew* what to do.

"It's a long story," Rose said, taking a sip of the latte and letting its heat slide through her system like a blessing.

"I brought a lot of doughnuts," Dee pointed out. "So start talking."

Surrendering to the inevitable, Rose dug in the bag for a doughnut, took a healthy bite and started talking.

An hour later, she was stuffed full, her eyes were grittier than ever and she was more exhausted than she'd ever been in her life.

"So," Rose said on a sigh as she rummaged in the

now empty bag for the few remaining crumbs, "that's the story of my incredibly screwed-up life."

"It's a beauty of a story, I'll give you that," Dee said, taking the bag away to crumple it, ignoring Rose's frown. She tossed it onto the coffee table beside their empty latte cups. "The question is, what are you going to do now?"

"Heck if I know." Rose laid one hand on her flat belly and tried to imagine the reality of carrying a child.

An instant later, she was wishing for more doughnuts.

"You're probably not pregnant," Dee said thoughtfully. "I mean, people try for *years* without conceiving. What're the odds you could do it in one try?"

"True," she agreed, not really believing it.

"And I know you probably don't want to hear this, but as the best friend, I have to at least suggest it…"

"What?" she asked warily.

Dee sighed. "There is a pill you can take the morning after, and you know it."

"I know," Rose said. "I actually thought of that around three this morning." Then she shook her head. "But I can't, Dee. It would be like wishing the baby away—if there is one—and I couldn't live with it. With Mom and Dad both gone now, if there *is* a baby, it would be my family, you know? So I can't, you know? I mean, it's good that it's out there, but it's not for me."

"Yeah. Wouldn't be for me, either." Dee leaned over and patted Rose's hand in support. "So, we'll just have to hope for the best, and wait and see on the baby front. On the Lucas front…"

"Oh," Rose told her with a quick shake of her head, "trust me when I say there is no Lucas front."

"Please. You can't even sleep for thinking about the man."

"That doesn't mean there's anything there, Dee. It just means that we had one wild, incredible night of sex followed by a humiliating argument." She took a breath and blew it out again. "Saint Rose."

Dee laughed, and Rose sent her a look.

"Sorry," her friend said, making an effort to stop the chuckles. "But if you could see the look on your face when you said that."

Rose grabbed one of the throw pillows, tugged it out from behind her back and held it in front of her, wrapping both arms around it. "The Saint-Rose thing notwithstanding, you should have seen the expression on *Lucas's* face when he told me that we'd be getting married if I turn up pregnant. He meant every word, Dee."

"So what?" Dee scooted closer, draped one arm around Rose's shoulder and said, "He can't force you to marry him, sweetie. All he can do is bluster and demand. You don't have to do a damn thing you don't want to—beyond sharing custody, of course."

Rose dropped her head to the back of the couch and stared up at the ceiling. "Custody battles. Doesn't that sound like a good time?"

"You play, you pay," Dee told her gently.

"Isn't this the part where you're supposed to comfort me?"

"Right. Well, here's the comfort." Dee gave her shoulders a squeeze. "You're probably not pregnant, so chances are, you'll never have to see Lucas King again."

Never see Lucas again. Four words that left a cold,

dark empty feeling inside her. Rose looked at her friend. "Sadly, that thought isn't much comfort, either."

Dee nodded. "Yeah, I know."

Nine

After Dee left, Rose had a brief cry and a long nap, then woke up feeling almost human again. She still didn't have a clue what she was going to do next, but whatever it turned out to be, she was sure she could handle it. If she never saw Lucas again, at least she'd had that one night with him that she used to dream of experiencing.

Of course now, she would be dreaming *about* that night for the rest of her life, but that was okay, she thought firmly. She could deal.

"Hear that, universe? I can take it." She stirred a big pot of beef-and-barley soup and took a deep breath of the amazing scents wafting into the air.

Outside, it was dark, and a storm had blown in off the ocean. Wind rattled tree limbs and rain tapped at the windows like nervous fingers. But inside, all was warm and cozy.

Cooking had always soothed her. As a child, she remembered standing on a chair at the counter while the family cook taught her to make cookies. And as Rose got older, the lessons became more complex. By the time she was a teenager, she spent most of her spare time in the kitchen.

She hadn't had boyfriends—not with her father and brother standing guard over her. So she spent most nights alone in the house, coming up with new recipes to ease the boredom.

Now, Rose set the spoon down on the ceramic-duck spoon rest in the center of her stove and realized that she'd come full circle. Years later and here she was standing in her kitchen daydreaming about guys. Well, *one* guy.

"And that's just pitiful."

She took a seat at the kitchen table and reached for the dark green shirt she had left hanging over the back of one of the chairs. The shirt Lucas had loaned her the night before, she'd meant to wash it today, but hadn't. Lifting it to her face, she inhaled the scent of him and let pangs of regret and disappointment rush through her.

"No," she whispered, "*this* is pitiful."

God, she didn't know what was wrong with her. It wasn't as if she'd never had sex before. And fine, yes, there was the pregnancy worry hanging over her head, but that wasn't what was bothering her, either. Why was she so torn up inside? Why couldn't she take a deep breath without feeling as if there were iron bands around her lungs?

"And why are you asking yourself so many questions when you already know the answers?"

Her fingers trailed across the gold crown and the King Construction logo on the shirt. An image of Lucas sprang up in her mind—dark hair tumbled across his forehead. Blue eyes going hot with passion as he covered her body with his own. And Rose finally admitted to herself what the problem here really was.

She was in love with Lucas King. A part of her had loved him for three years, she thought, fingers still tracing across the King logo on his shirt. From the moment Dave had brought him home and she looked up into those blue eyes. He had been polite, a little distant—no doubt having gotten the off-limits warning from Dave already—but he had smiled at her and something inside Rose had come to life.

She'd been lost even back then.

Maybe that was why she had never found another man that made her heart race and her knees go weak. Maybe that was the real reason she'd agreed to marry Henry Porter when her family asked her to. Somewhere inside her, she had realized that she'd never have the man she wanted, so what did it matter?

Which had been a really bad reason to get married. But looking back, Rose knew she wouldn't have changed anything even if she could have.

Oh, her marriage had been awful—but in a weird way, it had also been good for her. She had changed a lot, thanks to Henry's being such a miserable husband. By the time that very brief marriage fizzled out, she had found the kind of courage and confidence she had always lacked before.

Without that sharp learning curve, Rose didn't know if she ever would have had the nerve to open her own business, let alone take a stand against her older brother. When their father died, Dave had stepped into the patriarchal role as if he'd been born to it…which, he really had, actually. But Rose had already grown too much to give him the kind of power over her their father had once claimed.

She smiled wistfully to herself, remembering the expression on Dave's face the first time she had said no to one of his orders. It had been well worth the jittering anxiety and the hot ball of tension in her stomach. It hadn't been easy to take that first step, but when she did, the world hadn't ended. Dave hadn't stopped loving her.

In fact, to give Dave his due, once she had set down ground rules and let him know that she wouldn't be bossed around for the rest of her life, he had actually backed off. Oh, he was still authoritarian, but half the time she didn't listen and he didn't really expect her to anymore.

Which was a victory of sorts, wasn't it?

But Lucas…he was a different matter. She could still see him in his bedroom, glaring at her as he told her that if she were pregnant, they'd be getting married, like it or not.

Resentment jumped into life inside her. She straightened up in the chair and unconsciously squared her shoulders. Rose wouldn't trade one bossy man for another. She wouldn't stand her ground against her brother and then cave for Lucas.

Rose had already done marriage for the wrong reasons. The next time she said *I do,* it would be because she was madly in love—and loved just as fiercely in return. She wouldn't accept less and if she did turn out to be pregnant, she certainly wouldn't marry him just because of their child.

Her mind racing with arguments she couldn't use because Lucas wasn't there, Rose couldn't sit still another minute. Dropping the shirt on the chair back again, she got up and walked out to the living room.

Mindlessly, she straightened the already tidy room, fluffing pillows, stacking magazines on the corner of the coffee table. She could have turned on the stereo for company, but her thoughts were already so busy, she didn't need the extra distraction. A little silence, she told herself, was probably just what she needed. She should have known it wouldn't last.

When the doorbell rang, she jumped and whirled around. Her silly heart raced suddenly as her first thought was that Lucas was there. But in the next instant, that hope died.

"Rose!" her brother called out, hitting the doorbell again just for good measure. "Rose! I know you're home. I see your skillet car in the driveway."

Just what she needed, she thought, the other hard-headed man in her life. Hurrying to the door, she threw it open and instantly, wind-driven rain slapped at her with icy needles of wet. "Dave, what're you doing here?"

"Nice to see you, too, sis." He bent down and briefly kissed her forehead before walking past her into the house. He shook his head, swiped one hand through his wet hair and asked, "Wow, what smells so good?"

Rose sighed. Looked like she would be having company for dinner. "Beef-and-barley soup."

He looked at her and his eyebrows lifted. "Home-made?"

She had to smile at his hopeful expression. "Of course. You want some?"

"That'd be great." He shrugged out of his jacket and hung it on one of the hooks behind her front door. As he followed her to the kitchen, he kept up a running monologue. "This storm's got lousy timing. I've got a crew out on Pacific Coast Highway trying to shore up a retaining wall before the rain gets too bad. There's a mud hole where another family's new den was going to be and I've been out at a site helping the crew tack plastic up on a torn-off roof before the house flooded. The rain caught everybody by surprise."

Rain clattered at the windows, and the wind moaned as it swept under the eaves of Rose's old bungalow. The lights in the kitchen were bright against the dark, and the scent of the bubbling soup welcomed them into the room.

"Did you get the roof covered?"

"Yeah, but it was close," he said, scrubbing both hands over his face as if trying to rub away the memory. "We're putting in a second story, so we had the tarps ready to go—they just had to go up a lot faster than we thought. And did you notice? Not one damn weatherman predicted this storm?"

Rose was used to hearing construction stories. She'd grown up on them. And usually, Southern California weather cooperated nicely with builders. But every once in a while…

"Sounds like you've had a busy day," she said, going directly to a cabinet and taking down two soup bowls. She grabbed spoons from a drawer and carried them to the narrow table. Then taking the bowls to the stove, she filled each of them with the soup that had been simmering most of the afternoon.

"Busier than I'd like," Dave admitted, arms braced on her narrow table. "What about you?"

"Hmm?"

"Haven't talked to you in a couple of weeks, so thought I'd stop by and—"

"Get dinner?" Rose finished for him as she carried the steaming bowls of soup to the table.

He grinned, and she couldn't help returning his smile. She loved her brother. She really did. Rose just wished they had the kind of relationship that would allow her to tell him what was happening in her life. But not only could she not talk to Dave about a man, she also knew only too well how he would react to the mention of Lucas King. She just wished she knew why.

Dave pulled one of the four chairs out for her to sit down and that's when he spotted the green T-shirt.

Rose held her breath and then made a grab for the shirt before he could get a good look at it. But Dave was faster. He held it up and immediately saw it was a man's shirt.

"So who's the guy, Rose?" he asked, smiling at her in a way that made her think this might turn out all right after all. "Is he a secret? Because as the big brother, I should be able to check him out before you get too attached. Make sure he's good enough for my baby sister."

"Dave…"

Rose knew the moment Dave spotted the logo. Her stomach sank as her brother's eyes frosted over and all semblance of a teasing smile slipped away.

"King Construction?" He stood up, still staring at the gold crown on the green shirt crumpled in his fist. "Is this some kind of joke?"

"No," Rose said on a sigh as she tugged the shirt out of his grasp. So much for a touching brother-sister bonding moment. "It's my private life and it's none of your business, Dave."

He stalked the short distance to the kitchen sink, turned around and stomped right back again. Glaring at her, he argued, "The hell it's not. One of the Kings has been here. And left his *shirt*."

"He wasn't here," Rose said tightly. "I went to his house. I...spilled something and had to borrow one of his shirts."

"Uh-huh." He crossed his arms over his chest and braced his feet wide apart. "And why were you at his house?"

"Cooking lessons." Rose threw both hands high, realized she was waving the shirt around like a red flag in front of a bull and tossed it to the counter behind her. "It's what I do, remember? He hired me to teach him to cook."

"Sure he did." Dave shook his head fiercely, and his mouth worked as if there were dozens of words clogged up inside him that he wouldn't set free. He looked disgusted, worried and furious all at once. "Which one?" he said flatly. "Which King?"

Here it comes, she told herself. The argument of the century was about to get started.

Lifting her chin, she folded her arms over her chest, too, in a perfect imitation of his stance. Locking her gaze with his, she said simply, "Lucas."

Astonishment filled his eyes and had his mouth dropping open. "Are you serious? Lucas King? Damn it, Rose! Why him?"

"Why not him, Dave?" she demanded. "You and Lucas used to be friends. Then you weren't, and I never knew why."

"You didn't have to know," he muttered, turning away from her to walk to the closest window. He braced his hands on the wall at either side of the glass and stared out at the rain-splotched night beyond.

Rose could see her brother's reflection in the glass,

and she felt a twinge of sympathy at the taut misery etched into his features. But that didn't change the fact that it was past time for him to tell her the truth. What was the awful secret that had destroyed his friendship with Lucas? Why was the mere mention of the King name enough to shift Dave into defensive mode?

"I need to know now, Dave," she said quietly, her words dropping into the silence like stones into a well.

"Why?" he asked just as quietly. "Why can't you just take my word on it and stay away from the Kings? Especially Lucas?"

She took a breath and let it go on a sigh. "It's too late for that."

He turned around then and looked at her, hard and long. She held his gaze and when she saw the unmistakable question in his eyes, she nodded. "That bastard slept with you?"

"I slept with him, too. So if you're going to be mad…"

Defeated, Dave's shoulders slumped and he muttered, "Damn it, Rose, not Lucas."

"Talk to me. Tell me what went wrong," she said, laying one hand on her brother's arm.

Absently, he gave her hand a pat, then turned away again, apparently not able to meet her gaze while he talked. "You're right. You should know. Maybe if I'd been honest about this before, you would have kept your distance."

"Just tell me," she repeated.

"I paid one of the King assistants for insider information, and I used that information to undercut their bids on jobs." Finally, he turned back around to look at her. "Basically, I stole from the Kings."

Staggered, Rose could only stare at the man she had thought she knew. "I don't believe this. Why?"

Sighing, Dave dropped into his chair again. "I have excuses. Reasons. Dad was sick, jobs were in short supply, we needed the money. We invested in a few bad deals and took a beating." He braced his elbows on his thighs. "There were hospital bills, payrolls to be met and…like I said. I have excuses. But the bottom line is, I stole from Lucas. My friend."

"He knew?" Rose asked, slumping into the chair beside her brother's. Of course he knew, she told herself. Why else would Lucas's features freeze up at the mention of his old friend's name?

"He guessed," Dave told her, looking into her eyes. "He couldn't prove it. No evidence. But yeah, he knows."

Rose was so shaken she didn't know what to say. Or think. Her brother was a thief, and the man she loved was his victim. And to think that just a few hours ago, she had thought her life was as complicated as it could possibly get.

"Why didn't he say anything?" she whispered. "I mean, I get why you didn't, but why would Lucas keep quiet?"

"Like I said, no evidence. And without that, if he made accusations, he'd just look like a poor loser." Dave blew out a breath and reached over to take her hand. "Rose, has it occurred to you that Lucas hired you and then romanced you not because he wanted you, but for revenge on me?"

"No." She tugged her hand free of her brother's and jumped to her feet. Walking across the room, she slapped both hands palm down onto the counter and felt the cold of the granite seep into her skin. "He wouldn't."

"You're sure about that?"

She shot Dave a look as he stood up and came toward her. "Yes. Lucas wouldn't have—he never would have…" Her words trailed off as her mind and heart began a silent battle.

Her brain insisted that Dave was right. Why else would a man like Lucas King be interested in "Saint Rose," but for revenge? But her heart and body remembered every stroke of his hands, every kiss, every whispered word of passion and heat and would not believe that none of it had been real.

The storm pelted Long Beach for three days.

By the third day, Lucas was like a tiger in a too-small cage. He couldn't get out to a job site because of the rain, and if he had to sit in the damn office and calm down one more client, his head was going to explode.

That afternoon, he got in his car and started driving. As if on automatic pilot, his SUV took him directly to Rose's house. She hadn't been hard to find. All he'd had to do was look up the name of her business and there she was.

Now he sat outside the tiny, sky-blue bungalow, listening to the rain beat against the roof of his car. She was inside, he knew. The skillet car was in the driveway. A reluctant smile curved his mouth as he looked at the ridiculous thing. Only Rose would drive that car. And only Rose could have turned him inside out as she had.

For days, all he'd been able to do was think about her. He saw her in his sleep. Caught traces of her scent in his kitchen and every time he lay down on his bed, he wanted to reach out and find her there. He'd actually come to care about Rose.

Which told him it was time to end this.

His plan had worked fine, so it was done. He wasn't looking for a relationship. Wasn't the marrying kind and if he was, he sure as hell wouldn't be marrying into

Dave Clancy's family. So there was no point in leaving things between he and Rose up in the air. It was time to cut and run.

If it turned out she was pregnant, he'd worry about it then.

Getting out of the car, he walked slowly through the driving rain, his gaze fixed on the windows where lamplight played behind sheer curtains. Before he made it to the front porch, the door opened and Rose was standing on the threshold, watching him.

Everything in him eased as his gaze moved over her. Her blond hair was loose around her shoulders, and she wore faded blue jeans and a scoop-necked red blouse that displayed just the tops of her full breasts. Her eyes were guarded and she had such a tight grip on the door that her knuckles were white.

"Lucas."

"Hi."

"You're soaked."

"What?" He glanced up at the sky as if surprised to find himself getting wet. "Yeah. Guess I am."

She stepped back, farther into the house. "You want to come in?"

He nodded and took the steps in one long stride. Then he was brushing past her, his upper arm sliding across her breasts as he walked into her house. The jolt of heat from that minor touch of their bodies stayed with him as he peeled off his jacket and handed it to her. She hung it on a hook and then stood there, staring up at him.

Waiting.

Everything in him wanted to grab her. To forget about his plan. To forget about Dave and revenge and anything else that wasn't as real as she was. But that wasn't why he was here.

He followed after her, not much caring for the stiff formality that was suddenly between them. She led him down a short hall into the smallest living room he'd ever seen.

Stepping into that room, he felt like Gulliver. Everything was too small for him. The couch, the chairs, the tables. The walls were covered in framed posters and a few family photos and the scent of something amazing was coming from the kitchen.

It was warm and cozy and he felt like the intruder he was. There was no welcome for him here. Clearly, he didn't belong and judging from the chill of her reception, he wouldn't be staying long, either. The sting of that thought vanished when he told himself that was how he wanted it, anyway.

When Rose turned to look at him, her eyes were dry, but there were shadows in those blue depths that bothered him more than he wanted to admit.

"Why are you here, Lucas?"

Good question. He'd come to say goodbye, but now all he wanted to do was reach for her. He fisted his hands at his sides to keep from giving in to that urge.

Lucas looked at her, and, for the first time, noticed that she appeared to be nervous. Uneasy. Hell, maybe the last few days had been hard on her, too. They'd left too many things in the air that night. Too many things unsaid. And there was still a major question hanging over both of their heads. No wonder she looked as ragged as he felt.

She'd probably be as grateful as he would to have the unfinished business between them straightened up. To make a clean break. "Look, I only came to say that I won't be seeing you again."

"Is that right?"

Not a flicker of emotion showed on her features, and Rose, he had already learned, wasn't a woman to hide from what she was feeling. Her laughter was always genuine and her anger just as up-front and easily recognizable. But right now, she looked…empty. As if she'd been drained of all emotion and left to deal with a hollow sensation inside, like the one he'd been carrying around in his chest the last few days.

He frowned, not caring for that image, but he kept talking, wanting to make himself clear. He had to make her understand that whatever there had been between them was now over. And maybe then, they could both just put the past couple of weeks behind them. "I won't be needing any more cooking lessons, either."

"I see."

His scowl went deeper. Damn it, didn't she feel a thing? He was having a hard time saying this, the least she could do was look as though it mattered to her. "It's nothing against you, Rose. I just don't see how anything good can come from what's between us."

"Right. Of course not."

Again, her words were flat, her eyes cool and distant.

"What the hell is wrong with you?" he blurted out, wondering where the woman he knew had gone. This woman—detached, aloof—was someone he didn't even recognize. Reaching out to her, he went to grab her shoulders, but she took a hasty step to the side, avoiding his touch. "Rose, what's going on?"

"You tell me," she said quietly, her gaze locked with his. "The reason you won't be seeing me again…is it because my brother stole from you?"

Stunned, Lucas felt her words like a blow to the chest. How… He stared at her, hardly able to process this. The only way she could have found out that information was from her brother. "Dave told you?"

"So it's true," she whispered, shifting her gaze from his as if she just couldn't look at him any longer. Scraping her hands up and down her arms, she added, "Yes. Dave told me."

This he hadn't expected. Who knew that Dave would finally come clean? After two years of keeping his silence, what had pushed him into a confession? To Rose, of all people? And if her brother and she had been talking, did that mean that Dave knew about Lucas and Rose?

Grinding his teeth against the anger and frustration pumping through him, he asked, "Did you tell your brother about us?"

"Why?" she asked, now wrapping her arms around her middle as if needing something to hold on to, even if it was only herself. "Was that a secret, too?"

He tried not to hear the pain she was finally allowing to show in her voice. He still had to know, so he asked again. "Did you tell him?"

"He guessed," she said on a tired sigh. "He saw your shirt. The one you gave me the other night."

"Great. That's great." Shaking his head, he felt the last of his plan shatter out from under him. He'd thought he had it all figured out. The perfect revenge. Now it was all gone, and he was left standing alone with the woman he'd dragged into the rubble.

He pushed one hand through his hair and tried to figure out how this could have gone any worse, but he didn't come up with anything.

"Now I need to know something from you," Rose said.

His gaze snapped to hers. "What?"

"Was Dave right? He said you were only with me to get back at him. Was this all for revenge?"

He hadn't planned to tell Rose about the revenge plot. He wasn't interested in hurting *her,* after all. It was Dave he wanted to make pay. But looking into her eyes, he couldn't lie to her, either. There'd already been enough lies between them. "Yeah. That was the plan."

"The *plan.*" She huffed out a breath and shook her head again. "Wow. There was an actual plan."

Her cool blue eyes locked on him, and Lucas shifted uncomfortably under that steady regard. It had been a long time, years maybe, since he'd felt the stirrings of guilt and regret that were starting to burn through him right now. He couldn't even remember the last time he'd felt like this.

And he didn't like it. Damn it, he had done what needed doing. Dave had had to pay for his betrayal, and now he would. Collateral damage wasn't pretty, but sometimes it was unavoidable.

Going for a bravado he wasn't really feeling, Lucas said, "Rose, I didn't set out to hurt *you.*"

She nodded jerkily as if she were a puppet having her strings yanked. "So, just a bonus for you, then."

Another sharp stab of something hot and painful poked at his insides. He looked at her and felt completely torn. She was the sister of the man he considered his enemy. But she was also the woman he had spent the last couple of weeks with, laughing. Talking. *Loving.*

No. He pushed that last word out of his mind so fast, it was really nothing more than a blur on his consciousness. He didn't love Rose. He didn't love anyone. What he felt for her was…hell, he couldn't even name it, but he knew it wasn't love. How could it be?

That wasn't part of the plan.

He took a breath. "This wasn't how it was supposed to turn out."

"Really? Then what? You were just supposed to get me into bed and then you would disappear? Never to be heard from again? Was that it?"

"Pretty much," he admitted, though the words tasted bitter and had to be forced from his throat. When he'd first come up with this scenario, it had seemed pretty straightforward. Now, it was all tangled up in things he didn't want to identify. Now, he was looking into a pair of blue eyes glittering with pain and humiliation and he felt like kicking his own ass.

She was still staring at him as if he were a stranger that had somehow wandered into her home, so he tried to make her see this from his side. "Rose, I didn't know you when this started."

"You still don't, if you think I'm going to stand here and listen to you try to explain away what you did."

Frustration boiled through the regret. "Dave stole from me. Betrayed my friendship."

"And what have you done, Lucas? Is it really so different?" She glared at him for a long minute before looking away and adding, "At least Dave had a reason for what he did, all you had was your own petty need for payback."

"Petty?" He grabbed her shoulders and turned her to face him.

Fine, he deserved to feel like a jerk for using her. He could accept that. But damned if he'd stand there and have her tell him that his need for revenge was nothing more than petty. "I *trusted* him. My brothers trusted him. He turned on all of us. I don't think it's petty to want some satisfaction for that."

She pulled away from his touch, and instantly, his hands felt cold and empty.

"And I was a tool to be used."

"Not just a tool, Rose," he said, hating the words as they came out of his mouth, but somehow, he was unable to stop them. "You were—"

"Pitifully easy to trick?" she finished for him.

"Rose, try to understand," he said, even knowing that she wasn't listening to him anymore.

He reached out to her again, but she jerked back as if protecting herself from something foul.

Which, he thought, was just about right.

"Don't touch me," she said, shaking her head and swallowing hard. "God, you're just like all the rest of them. You used me. Like my father. And Dave. And Henry. My God, I didn't see it."

She laughed, and it was a harsh, brittle sound that tore at something inside Lucas that he refused to recognize.

"You weren't supposed to see it," he said.

"Well then, big congrats to you! Mission accomplished! Saint Rose taken down a peg, and big bad thief taught a very important lesson, I'm sure."

"Look, Rose—"

"No. *You* look," she interrupted, anger churning in her voice now and fury coloring her porcelain cheeks. "Whatever was between us? You're right. That's over. You got what you wanted, so we don't ever have to see each other again."

He didn't like the sound of that even though he'd gone to her house to pretty much say the same damn thing. And that didn't make a bit of sense. Lucas didn't like confusion. He liked order. He liked knowing where he was going, how he was going to get there and what he'd find when he arrived.

But ever since getting involved with Rose, he'd been wandering around in a daze. Why was he only noticing that now?

"Get out, Lucas. Get out of my house."

She was looking up at him as if he were the enemy. He guessed he'd earned that. He'd never been tossed out of a house before, but he supposed that he'd earned that, as well.

But he wasn't leaving until she understood one more thing.

"I'll go," he told her. "But we're not completely done until we know if you're pregnant or not. And if you are, Rose, I'll be back."

Ten

"He sent me a *check*."

Three days of silence, Rose told herself. No contact at all from Lucas and this is what she gets in the mail? In the *mail*?

"How big a check?" Dee asked from her usual perch on the couch. Like the true best friend she was, Delilah had shown up a few hours ago with more lattes and, even more importantly, a fresh supply of doughnuts.

They'd spent the afternoon on the couch with Rose alternately feeling sorry for herself and wanting to go kick Lucas. Now, evening was crouched outside the windows and the rain was beginning again. It was as if the weather matched her mood lately. Southern California was getting the rainiest winter in twenty years, and Rose felt right at home in the gloom.

"How much is the check?" Delilah asked again.

"Does it matter?" Rose turned to look at her friend.

"For three days, I've been moping around here, missing that big ape, torturing myself and what does he do? He mails me a check for..." She glanced down and her eyes bugged out. *"Ten thousand dollars!"*

"Seriously?" Delilah bolted off the couch and snatched the check from Rose's numb fingers.

Even though she and Delilah had both been born into wealthy families, they had each been on their own for the last few years. Rose by choice; Delilah because her father had lost everything to the IRS. So ten thousand dollars seemed like a vast amount of money to both of them.

Which to Rose's mind only made this more insulting.

While her friend cooed over all the zeroes on the check, Rose's brain went into overdrive. Since the night she had practically thrown Lucas out of her house, she'd been miserable. Every minute, she'd ached for him—despite knowing that he'd been using her all along to get back at her brother.

What kind of sense did that make? Shouldn't love be more like a faucet? Turn it on when it was right and shut it off when it wasn't? She hadn't slept, had cried so much her eyes were no doubt permanently red and puffy and *this* is the thanks she got?

The universe had to kick her while she was down?

Was he really that cold? Had she romanticized every feeling she had about him? Rose swallowed hard and tried to look away from the offending piece of paper, but her gaze refused to shift. It was all there, her mind whispered. All the proof she needed that he had never cared. That every word, every touch between them had been a lie.

And what had the last few days been like for him? Was he out partying? Moving on to some bimbo who wouldn't care what he thought or said or did? Had he even given her a moment's thought aside from the time it had taken for him to write that stupid, insulting *check?*

"Ten thousand dollars," Delilah said. "'For services rendered.' Uh-oh."

"What? Services?" Rose grabbed the check so she could scowl down at Lucas's scrawled signature. That's when she saw the memo line. Delilah was right. *For services rendered.*

Her jaw dropped and her eyes widened even further than they had before. *"Services?"*

"Rose," Delilah said cautiously, "you know he meant the cooking lessons."

"Do I?" she snapped in a voice so high it cracked as fury rushed through every inch of her body like an out-of-control wildfire. She was practically vibrating she was so angry. And insulted again. And hurt. And humiliated.

"That no-good, lying..." She ran out of invectives when Delilah interrupted her.

"You know he's not paying you for sex."

"We don't know that," Rose told her, still so angry she could hardly draw a breath. "This was probably part of his 'plan.' The big goodbye speech after using me to get back at Dave, followed by a nice check—not too big, not too small. Payoff has to be handled carefully, after all...."

"Oh, boy," Delilah muttered warily.

Rose hardly heard her. Her blood was rushing in her ears and her heartbeat was pounding as if she'd just completed a marathon. "Who does he think he is, anyway?"

"Rose..."

Her fingers curled into the check, and it was only

through a supreme act of control she didn't tear it into bits. Lucas King had given her a metaphorical slap for the last time. It was her turn now and she had a few things she wanted to say to him. In person.

She glared down at his signature again. "Think you can pay me off without even facing me over it? Well, I don't want your damn money."

"Let's not be hasty," Delilah urged.

"No," Rose said with a sharp nod. "You're right. I do want his money. But only what he owed me for those cooking lessons."

"He did say he was going to pay you three times your usual rate."

"That still wouldn't be ten thousand dollars, Dee," she said, tapping the edge of the check against her fingertips. "No, he did this on purpose. He sent a check that isn't so large I'd have to kill him, but still big enough for me to understand this was the big goodbye."

"There are worse ways to break up," Dee muttered.

"Hah! What? They were out of trinkets at the jewelry store?"

Delilah sighed. "You're going to go see him, aren't you?"

"You're damn right I am," Rose said, with a glint in her eye and a lift of her chin. Lucas King may have started all this with his ridiculous plan, but she was going to finish it. He wanted a big goodbye? Fine. She'd give him one. And when she was finished, he'd be sorry he had ever heard of Rose Clancy.

"Okay, as the best friend," Dee said cautiously, "I feel it's my duty to remind you that you actually *love* this guy, Rose. Remember the misery? The doughnuts? You're angry right now, but you still love him in spite of everything."

"I know," Rose said, pulling in one deep breath after another. "And *because* I love that big creep, there is just no way I'm letting him get away with this."

"Uh-huh," Dee said, "and then what?"

"Then," Rose told her firmly, "I will come home and do deep meditations or something until I'm *out* of love with him."

"Yeah, that'll work."

"Supportive. That's your job, remember?"

"Right, right." Delilah held up both hands. "I'm supporto girl. Need a getaway driver? Here I am. But Rose, there's still the question of whether or not you're pregnant to consider, too."

"I know." She nodded again, glanced at her flat belly and wondered for the thousandth time in the last few days if there was a baby already growing inside her. And if there was, that baby deserved better than a mother who was crazy and a father who didn't have the sense to know what was good for him.

Her shoulders slumped as her fingers moved over Lucas's handwriting. Shaking her head, she said, "If I am pregnant, I'll have to deal with Lucas. But if I let this go…him treating me like a bill to be paid…then how will we ever work together to take care of a baby? He may not love me, Dee. But he has to at least *respect* me."

Delilah nodded and gave her a smile. "You're absolutely right. I'm with you. Do you want me to go with you to see him?"

"No." Rose threw a look at the window and the cold, rainy day outside. "I have to do this alone."

"Okay, then." Delilah picked up her purse off the coffee table and shrugged into her windbreaker, pulling the hood up over her perfectly styled red hair. "But call me when it's over, okay?"

"I will." She stood there in the center of the living room and watched her friend leave. Then she told herself to get a firm grip on her sweeping emotions. There was no point in facing down Lucas if she couldn't calmly and clearly tell him exactly what she thought of him and his stupid check.

Minutes passed and she realized she wasn't going to calm down. The best she could hope for was that she wouldn't shriek at him or maybe kick him in the shins.

"Did he really think I could be bought off?" she asked herself, and then in the next instant, answered her own question. "Well, why wouldn't he? He knew Dave stole jobs out from under him, so in the world according to Lucas King, that makes all of the Clancys thieves."

Turning on her heel, she headed for her bedroom. She needed to change. And fix her hair. And makeup. *This* Clancy was going to teach Lucas King a lesson he wouldn't forget.

If it was the last thing she ever did for him.

"Lucas…"

He didn't even look up from his desk. "Evelyn, if you don't want Katie's cookies in the break room, tell Rafe."

"This isn't about the cookies," his secretary said and waited for him to look up at her. "Someone's here to see you."

Someone? Evelyn usually wasn't so vague. He frowned, then understood as a man walked up behind Evelyn, then slipped into Lucas's office. "Dave."

Almost the last person he'd expected to see here at King Construction. The only way he could have been more surprised was if Rose had shown up unannounced. Something inside him jolted to life at the thought, and he ruthlessly squashed it down.

He and Rose were over.

Even if he hadn't called an end to it himself, after the way things had gone between them at her house, he knew she was done with him.

He didn't like it and maybe he regretted the whole useless revenge plan in the first place—regretted it more than he would ever have thought possible—but hindsight was pretty much useless in most situations.

"It's okay, Evelyn," he said, standing up from behind his desk. He looked at the man opposite him and realized that he didn't even feel the old anger anymore.

Lucas couldn't help thinking about what Rafe and Sean had said, about letting it go. And somewhere over the last couple of days, he now realized, he *had*. Wasn't sure why. Wasn't even sure how. But that hard, cold ball he'd been carrying around in his gut for the past two years was finally gone.

When his secretary left and closed the door, Dave said simply, "You shouldn't have gone for Rose, Lucas."

There was that sting of shame again. But he didn't owe Dave anything, so he squashed that emotion flat. "And you shouldn't have betrayed our friendship, Dave."

"Damn it," Dave countered, "this was between you and me. You didn't have to drag my sister into it."

"Wrong." Lucas met his stare evenly. "This was between our *families*. You didn't just cheat me, Dave. You cheated my brothers. You cost us seven jobs that winter."

"Yeah," he said on a snort of self-derision. Scrubbing one hand across his face, Dave said, "I know. Still can't believe it myself, really. And you should know, I didn't want to do it."

"Small consolation. Whether you wanted to or not, you *did*."

"I needed the money," his old friend snapped, shooting Lucas a look that mixed both pride and embarrassment.

It was an admission he hadn't expected to hear. Hell, the Clancy family wasn't as wealthy as the Kings, but they came damn close. "For what? What was so damn important?"

Was he finally going to get the answers to the questions that had plagued him? And when he had them, would it make any difference?

Lucas had spent far too much time over the past two years thinking about the betrayal that had cut him so deeply. He'd even questioned his own ability as a judge of character and that bothered him more than anything. If he could be so wrong about Dave, what was to say he wasn't wrong about a lot of other people in his life?

"My father was dying, and the business was going down," Dave said, his words spilling from him as though a dam inside him had finally broken. He looked at Lucas. "Dad had made some bad investments in the years before I took over. He lost most of our capital. There were suppliers to be paid, contracts to honor and hospital bills piling up. I had to make good on it all or we would have lost everything we had left. I needed the jobs, Lucas." He scowled at the memories, but added, "I had to protect my family. I'm not sorry I was able to do that, but I am sorry I used you to do it."

Lucas could look at his old friend and see what that confession had cost him. He could even understand now, why Dave had done what he had. After all, there weren't many things Lucas wouldn't be willing to do to protect his brothers. So now that he knew the truth, how could he hold it against the man?

"You should've told me," he said finally. "We were friends. I could have helped you out, and you wouldn't have had to do what you did."

"Sounds good now." Dave laughed shortly and shook his head. "I couldn't tell you, Lucas. Pride's the one thing you and I always had in common. And that pride made me steal from a friend rather than admit that I was about to lose the company my grandfather built. Hell, I didn't even want to admit the truth to myself."

Rain slapped at the window behind him, the only sound in the room as the two men looked at each other and each tried to finally put the past behind them. Absently, Lucas wondered if fate hadn't taken a hand in the weather lately. If not for this new storm, Lucas would have been out inspecting the latest job site, talking to the crews. But with the weather delay, he had spent all afternoon in the office, catching up on paperwork. So he'd been here to hash this out with Dave.

Maybe this was fate's way of telling him just what his brothers had. Let it go.

"I was sorry to hear it when your dad died," he said quietly, offering the olive branch that they both needed.

"Thanks." Dave met his gaze and nodded. "I appreciate that. And I know that this doesn't mean we're friends again or anything."

"Not yet," Lucas admitted, though he was willing to scratch Dave off his active enemies list.

"What I came here to say isn't going to help that any, either," Dave told him. "You shouldn't have used my sister, Lucas. You had problems with me, I get that.

But you and I both know you went after her to stick it to me."

"Rose isn't up for discussion," Lucas said shortly. He was willing to forgive Dave for the stealing and the betrayal. But he wasn't going to stand here and talk about the woman he'd slept with to her brother.

Which struck him as odd, since telling Dave about sleeping with Rose had been the whole point of this exercise.

"The hell she's not," Dave countered, leaning both hands on Lucas's desk. "She's not like the women you usually hook up with."

"What do you know about that? I haven't even spoken to you in two years."

"Some things don't change."

Lucas gritted his teeth to keep from saying something he'd regret. Instead, he just stared into Dave's eyes, not giving an inch.

"Or do they?" Dave asked, a half smile on his face. "She got to you, didn't she? You thought you'd use Rose and walk away without a backward glance, but it wasn't as easy as you thought it would be, was it?"

He was right, damn it. About all of it. Lucas hadn't been able to slice Rose out of his mind or his soul. She was in there, deep, whether he wanted it or not. But he wasn't going to tell Dave that. "Stop now. I'm not talking about her with you."

"Fine, then just listen." Dave pushed off the desk. "Don't mess with her head, Lucas. If you're really finished then stay the hell away from her. Because if you hurt her again…you and I are going to go a few rounds."

With that, Dave walked out of his office. Alone, Lucas stared blindly at the closed door. He didn't like taking orders. Never had. But he couldn't blame Dave for this one.

Lucas didn't know what to feel anymore. For two years, he'd been carrying around what felt like a boulder, and now it was gone. A simple, five-minute conversation with Dave Clancy and he had a truce of sorts with his former friend.

All it had cost him was Rose.

Bull, his mind corrected instantly. Rose had never been his and so he couldn't have lost her. But even as he thought that, an image of her face as she stared him down that last night at her house loomed in his mind, taunting him. Even when her eyes had been spitting fire at him, he'd wanted her. Even now, he wanted her, he admitted.

Which meant exactly nothing, he assured himself.

Rose had been a temporary thing. Sure, she was still in his mind and his body was still fantasizing about her. But that was only because she was new. In a few weeks, he'd be over her. And as long as she wasn't pregnant, they'd never have to see each other.

She had been a means to an end and that end had now been completed. Story over.

Absently, he rubbed one hand over his chest, trying to soothe the heavy feeling centered there. But it didn't help.

Nothing helped.

"All right, enough," he muttered and stalked to the closet to grab the battered, brown leather jacket hanging inside. He shrugged it on, threw his office door open and walked out. "I'm leaving, Evelyn."

"Wow, and before seven, too," she said, but Lucas just kept walking.

There were far too many clever women in his life.

Eleven

It had finally stopped raining. Rose was cold. And wet. What she wanted to do was be home, curled up on her couch with a cup of hot tea in her hands and a mindless program on TV shattering the silence.

But she was determined to stay put until Lucas finally showed up at his house. For what had to be the tenth time, Rose checked her wristwatch again. A little after six. Why was he late?

When they had their cooking lessons together he was always here before now. Irritation gave way to worry.

Her gaze fixed on the rain-slicked surface of Ocean Boulevard and the cars flying past, fan-tails of water flying out behind them. Californians were notorious for forgetting how to drive on rainy streets from one year to the next. There were always more accidents during a storm.

Sitting in one of the Adirondack chairs on Lucas's

porch, she gripped her hands together in her lap and tried not to imagine his car as a twisted hunk of metal.

"Okay, don't be crazy," she murmured. "He's fine. He's just not home. Probably on a date or something. With some rich, gorgeous…"

Nope, don't go there, either, she told herself firmly.

She shouldn't care. Rose knew that. Lucas had lied to her, used her and then tossed her aside as soon as he was finished. She couldn't really blame him for seducing her, since she was pretty much in on that as well. But for the rest…she patted her shoulder bag, where his check was tucked away, and that alone stiffened her spine.

"Who're you?"

A deep voice splintered her thoughts and she looked up to see a bald, burly man with a full red beard standing in the middle of the lawn. He looked big, angry and, if she wasn't mistaken, very drunk. His eyes were narrowed on her. He was soaking wet and swaying on his feet.

A trickle of fear spilled down her spine.

Carefully, she reached into her purse and pulled her phone out.

"Where's Lucas?" the man demanded, taking a halting step toward her.

She couldn't tell him Lucas wasn't there. She didn't want the man to know she was alone. And she *was* alone. A quick glance next door to the Robertsons' didn't make her feel better. The big house was dark and there were no cars out front. And because the rain had only just stopped, no one was out walking their dog or enjoying the ocean view.

She really was alone in the dark with a man who didn't look very stable. If she called 911, she couldn't report a crime…he hadn't done anything. But if she didn't call and he did do something threatening, how stupid would she feel?

"Um, Lucas is in the backyard," she blurted.

"Fine," the man said and took another slow step, as if lifting each of his feet was taking every ounce of his strength. His words slurred as he vowed, "I'll jus' go she him."

Rose kept her gaze fixed on him but for a brief glance out to her car, parked at the curb. She decided she'd run out to it as soon as the man rounded the corner of the house. Once she was away, she'd call Lucas to tell him what was happening. She didn't want him to show up unaware of the man who clearly was looking for some kind of trouble.

Her stomach churned as she stood up, slowly. He didn't seem to notice her while he looked around as if trying to remember where he was and why. The heavy, cloying scent of too much beer hit her like a wave on the next breeze.

Suddenly, his bleary gaze shot to her and he demanded again, "Who're you?"

"A friend of Lucas's," she said, keeping her voice low as she moved carefully toward the steps.

The man snorted. "He don't have *friends*. No-good bastard..."

Instinctively, Rose wanted to defend Lucas, which would clearly be a mistake, since the man obviously was furious with him. She had to clamp her lips shut to keep from speaking, though.

So maybe she shouldn't wait to get to her car, Rose thought, and eased down the few steps to the paved walkway. He watched every move she made, and Rose almost wished it would start raining again. She would take every distraction she could get. "Well, I've got to leave now, so…"

She stepped off the walkway into the still-sodden grass, trying to keep distance between them. But for a swaying, unsteady drunk, the man moved quickly. He was suddenly at her side, holding on to her arm with an iron grip.

"Jus' wait a damn minute here, girly. You know Lucas."

"Yes," she said, holding her breath as much as possible. The stench of alcohol was much harsher now. And his breath was horrifying. As was his tight hold on her arm.

He was big and angry and drunk.

Not a good combination.

"You could talk to him. Tell him to not fire me." He leaned in closer, lost his balance and almost took them both down before somehow finding his footing again.

Rose's arm hurt where he held her, and her nerves jangled like sleigh bells. She tried to pull away, but the man was so much stronger than she was, she didn't have a hope. She still clutched her phone and as unobtrusively as she could, lifted it so she could see the dial pad.

"Hey! No phonin' him," the drunk told her and knocked the phone from her hand.

She glanced down at her phone, lying on the wet grass, and felt her heart slide down into the pit of her stomach.

"Let me call Lucas. He'll come talk to you," she urged, her voice as placating as she could make it, despite the fear. "Straighten all this out."

"Yeah?" He looked hopeful for a moment, but then his fingers tightened around her upper arm until she winced with a fresh wave of pain.

Then he shook his head. "No. He won't. Damn Kings. Once they make up their minds…"

"I can help." She tried again because really, what choice did she have? "Just let me try."

He thought about it for a long minute. Frowning, he staggered in place, caught himself, then finally nodded and released his grip on her arm. The pain of release was almost as sharp as it had been when he held her.

As soon as she was free, Rose bolted, leaving her phone on the grass. All she could think about was getting away. Getting help. Something. As she ran, she fumbled in her purse for her car keys.

Behind her, she heard the man shout *"Hey!"* and then the heavy pounding of his footsteps as he came after her. He was too drunk, too unsteady to move fast, though, she told herself. She had the advantage, if only she could—

Headlights flashed in her eyes and she threw one arm up in defense. A car screeched up to the curb behind hers and a moment later, Lucas was jumping out of his SUV.

"Rose? What's wrong?" His gaze shifted to the man coming after her. Instantly, Lucas pulled Rose to stand behind him, placing his body between her and any danger. "Warren, what are you doing here?"

"Came to talk," the man shouted. "Your lady there was helping me."

Even in the glare of the bright lights, Rose saw Lucas's features tighten into a mask of pure rage.

"Damn fool," he muttered, then looked over his shoulder at her. "Are you all right, Rose? Did he hurt you?"

"No. I'm fine."

He took a breath and released it as he nodded. "Good. That's good. Go to the house. Wait for me on the porch."

"No. I just want to go home, Lucas. I'm leaving."

He checked on Warren again, then took one moment to cup her cheek briefly. "Please. The porch."

Rose looked from him to Warren and then back again. She saw anger in Lucas's face, but she also saw worry, so she nodded. Heck, she was too shaken to drive anyway. Rose walked a wide circle around Warren and then hurried to the porch, pausing only long enough to snatch up her phone. From her safe vantage point, she watched Lucas with the other man.

Fisting his hands on his hips, Lucas said, "Warren, you shouldn't have come here."

The man scraped one hand across his face and to Rose's mind, he suddenly looked more miserable than scary. "Din't have choice. I can't lose my job," he said and dropped to the grass, cupping his head in his hands.

Lucas still looked furious, but there was also something of pity in his face as he looked down at the man. "If you were looking for a second chance, coming to my home, drunk, and threatening my woman aren't the ways to get it."

His woman?

Those two little words punched at her heart. Rose shivered, then before she could make too much of it, told herself it meant nothing. He was talking to a drunk. Making a point. And still those two words reverberated inside her like a shout into an echoing canyon.

"Din't hurt her," Warren muttered. "Wouldn't hurt a woman."

"That makes this your lucky night," Lucas told him and pulled out his phone. He glanced up at Rose as if satisfying himself that she was safe, then he made a brief call before tucking the phone back into his pocket.

"You stay right there, Warren," he ordered. "I swear, if you move from that spot…"

Warren didn't even flinch. Just sat on the wet grass cradling his head and murmuring to himself.

Clearly disgusted, Lucas walked to Rose, pulled her into his arms, then set her back from him and held her face between his palms. "Are you sure you're okay?"

"Yeah. He didn't really hurt me. Just seriously creeped me out." She gave a quick look to the now-moaning man on the lawn. "Who is he?"

Lucas glanced back at the man. "He worked for me. Until recently. I fired him. And by the smell of him, he's spent the past few days in a bar."

"Did you call the police?"

He looked back at her and sighed. "No. I called Sean. He'll drive Warren home. I don't want him arrested. He's got enough problems. But if he had hurt you…"

She shook her head. "He didn't."

Nodding, Lucas pulled out his keys, opened the front door and said, "Will you just wait for me inside? I've got to stay with Warren until Sean gets here."

She should go, Rose knew it. After all, she had only gone to his house to throw his check back in his face. But looking up at him how, she knew she wasn't leaving. At least, not yet. "I'll wait."

He gave her a smile, then turned back to the yard. He walked to Warren's side, then went down in a crouch beside the man. His words were too low for her to overhear, so Rose did as he asked and went into the house.

A half hour later, Sean had come and gone and Warren was on his way home. Lucas smiled grimly at the memory of Sean's disgust as they loaded Warren into his car. Lucas had no doubt that Warren was getting an earful on the drive home. Sean was as easygoing as they came, but tell him that a woman had been scared or hurt or in any way bothered, and Sean went coldly ballistic.

He wouldn't do anything to the man, but Lucas was willing to bet that after having Sean give him the shout-down of the century, Warren would accept being fired and disappear from their lives.

Walking into the house, Lucas could smell fresh coffee brewing, and he followed the scent straight back to the kitchen. He'd been avoiding that room, unable to even so much as enter it without Rose's memory rising up and nearly choking him.

So when he pushed the door open and saw her standing in the brilliantly lit room, she took his breath away. She'd draped her coat over a chair. She was wearing dark blue jeans, a red, wide-necked sweater and her long blond hair fell over her shoulders in a cascade of silk.

His fingers itched to touch her again. To feel the smooth slide of her skin. And because the urge was so strong, he jammed his hands into his pockets to keep from doing just that.

She turned when he entered and the edge of her sweater dipped low over one shoulder. That's when he saw the marks on her arm. Furious all over again, he was at her side in two long strides.

"Lucas?"

"You said he didn't hurt you," he muttered, pulling the sweater down far enough on her arm that he could see the prints of Warren's hard fingers on her pale skin. "He left marks, Rose. You'll be bruised by tomorrow."

"He didn't mean to," she said, wincing a little as Lucas's fingers moved over her arm.

"I should have had him arrested," Lucas muttered, lifting his gaze to hers.

"No, Lucas. He was just drunk and sad and scared..."

"He put his hands on you."

She reached up and touched his face, and Lucas felt the warmth of her slide down into that cold, empty pit he'd been carrying around in his stomach for days.

"I'm okay. Really."

He pulled in a breath, looked into her eyes and said, "When I saw you there. With him chasing you—"

"I was really glad you showed up when you did," she admitted.

"Me, too." His gaze moved over her face. Her scent filled him and Lucas gave into the need that had been plaguing him for days.

It was over. He knew that. Accepted it. But she was here and his body was hard and thirsting for her so badly he could hardly draw a breath.

"Rose..."

She shook her head even as she leaned into him. "Lucas, this isn't why I came here."

"I don't care," he admitted. "I just need to taste you again. To hold you again."

"We really shouldn't," she said and met him halfway as his mouth came down over hers.

Instant heat and hunger leaped up to snare both of them into a trap of their own design. He pulled her in tight, loving the feel of her body molding to his. She sighed into his mouth, and he took her breath and held it inside him, wanting to devour all of her.

His mind, his heart, his soul, begged to be heard, but

the only voice he listened to was that of his body. She was here. In his arms. Where he needed her.

Groaning, he shifted his hands to the waistband of her jeans, undid the snap and zipper and in seconds, was sliding one hand across her bare abdomen. She kissed him harder, deeper, her tongue twining with his in a desperate dance of desire.

He lowered his hand, beneath the elastic band of her panties and down to the heart of her that waited for him. She broke the kiss on a gasp and rocked her hips into him as he touched and stroked and explored her damp heat. Again and again, his fingers moved on her, taking her higher as he watched her eyes burn and then glaze over with what she was feeling. What she was giving him in this one stolen moment.

And when her body couldn't last another moment, when she was so taut with tension there was no higher for her to reach, Lucas felt the first shattering climax jolt through her.

"Lucas!" She clutched at his shoulders, fingers digging in as she moved on his hand, riding the waves of sensation that poured through her in a tidal wave of release.

Finally, only the slightest ripples remained, and she shivered as he held her close. Her face was flushed; her eyes unfocused; her breathing short and sharp. Finally, she licked her lips and let her head fall to his chest as if she were unable to hold it up on her own.

He kissed the top of her head and tried to calm his own racing heartbeat. It was a futile attempt. What he wanted was to bury himself inside her. To feel her heat holding him as closely and deeply as before. Pulling his hand free, he sighed and said, "Come with me, Rose. Upstairs."

A choked-off chuckle scraped from her throat, and she shook her head against his chest. "No."

"What?" He pulled back so he could look at her and waited until she lifted her gaze to his. "Why not?"

Biting her bottom lip, she moved away from him, zipped up her jeans and straightened her sweater. Then she pushed her hair back from her face. Looking up at him, she took a deep breath and blew it out again before trusting herself to speak.

"Because it wouldn't change anything." Another short laugh escaped her. "I shouldn't have let what just happened happen, either."

He grabbed her, then eased his hold when she winced as his hand came down on the bruises inflicted by Warren. Remembering that, knowing that she had been in danger and he hadn't been there until almost the last moment, terrified him and infused his words with a kind of desperation.

"But it did happen, Rose. You want me. I want you. Simple."

"No, it's not," she said sadly and it startled Lucas to see a sheen of tears fill her eyes. But she blinked them back so quickly, they were gone before he could even really ask himself why they had appeared in the first place. "It's not simple at all."

Frustration bubbled inside him. He was aching for want of her and was apparently going to keep on aching, he thought. So he blurted, "Then why the hell did you come here?"

She pulled away from him and a second later, steely determination was etched into her features. "Not for this," she told him.

Lucas drew a long, deep breath, fighting the hunger inside and the sense of annoyance he felt at her easy dismissal of what was clearly simmering between them. "Fine. *Why?*"

Lifting her chin, she walked past him to the table where she'd laid her purse. She opened it, pulled out an envelope and thrust it at him. "Because of this. I wanted to come over here and personally hand that back to you."

"What?" He glanced at it and recognized the envelope and check he'd sent her only the day before. He had deliberately sent her much more than he owed her, not because he was feeling guilty, either, but because he had simply wanted her to have it. Apparently, she hadn't appreciated it.

"Take it," she said, waving the damn envelope like a battle flag.

"I don't want it."

"Neither do I," she countered, and pushed it into one of his hands before folding her arms beneath her breasts.

His fingers tightened around the damn envelope, crushing it. "You earned the money."

"Hah! That's more than triple what you owe me for cooking lessons, and you know it. So the only other way I could possibly have *earned* that much was if—"

She left the rest of it unsaid but he didn't need to hear it. Insult slapped at him. "Are you serious? You think I'm *paying* you for sex?"

One shoulder lifted in a half-hearted shrug. But her eyes burned with an inner fire that singed Lucas with its strength.

"What else am I supposed to think?" she asked.

Offended down to his bones, Lucas felt his own anger rise to nearly choke him. Deliberately, he tore the check in two and threw both halves into the air, letting them fall to the gleaming wood floor at their feet. "There. Happy now?"

"Yes," she snapped, not even glancing at the torn check. "I'm happy. You can't *buy* me, Lucas. You can't pay me off. You can't assuage your conscience by writing a damn check as if I'm an overdue bill."

He just stared at her. What the hell was he supposed to say to something so outrageously *wrong?*

"That's not what I was doing, damn it!" His shout filled the room and seemed to bounce off the beamed ceiling.

She stepped up close, her gaze boring into his. "Then what? Why would you do it?"

Lucas shoved a hand through his hair. "I was trying to help."

She snorted.

"You're a damn good cook, Rose," he said, voice harsh as if every word was being scraped out of his throat. "You need money to build your business. I was… investing."

"Investing," she repeated, shaking her head at him in disbelief. "You wanted to invest in a woman you said you never wanted to see again? Where's the logic you're so fond of, Lucas? That doesn't make sense at all. But I'm supposed to just accept it?"

"Believe what you want," he muttered. *Try to do a nice thing and have it thrown back in your face,* he told himself. He never should have started any of this. It was all turning out to be far more trouble than it was worth. Now he was left trying to explain his motives to Rose when he didn't completely understand them himself.

Accepting the inevitable, he growled, "I'll mail you a check for what I owe you for the cooking lessons and leave it at that. All right?"

"Fine."

His gaze met hers.

Ice to fire.

"Then we're done here," he told her, grabbing hold of what was left of his pride and clinging to it.

"We're done, Lucas," she agreed, snatching up her jacket and slipping into it. She lifted her purse, slung it over her shoulder and walked out of the room, her heels clacking loudly on the wood floor.

From a distance, he heard the front door open, then close.

He was alone again.

Twelve

Two weeks later, Rose ran into the local coffee bar, her gaze scanning past the late-afternoon crowd, waiting in line, seated at tables. A wail of jazz piped down through overhead speakers and the scent of fresh coffee and doughnuts washed over her in welcome.

But today, nothing could soothe her. Not even doughnuts.

Quickly, she looked at the employees behind the counters, searching for the one person in the world she could really talk to. Just then, Delilah came out from the back room, laughing at one of her coworkers. She looked up, spotted Rose and called out, "Hi, sweetie! Having a latte emergency?"

A couple of people glanced at her, then turned away again and another barista, Eric, grinned a hello.

Rose hardly noticed. She hurried to the end of the

counter and waved Dee over. As she got closer, her friend's bright green eyes narrowed in concern.

Voice low, she asked, "Are you all right, Rose?"

"I'm *so* far away from all right," she muttered, glancing around to make sure no one else was close enough to listen in. "Can you take a break?"

"Sure," Dee told her, concern shifting to worry now as she half turned and said loudly, "Eric, I'm taking a break. Back in fifteen."

He nodded and Dee slipped around the counter, took Rose's arm and steered her out of the shop.

Outside, the sun was beginning to set and its rays seemed aimed at Rose's eyes. She squinted in response and took a long breath as she tried to ease the jumping nerves in the pit of her stomach. It didn't help.

"What is it, sweetie?"

"The end," Rose said dramatically.

"What?" Dee tugged her over to one of the tables gathered in front of Coffee Heaven.

After the storms they'd been having, the locals were out in force, enjoying the winter sun and the dry sidewalks. Kids rolled past on skateboards and women pushed babies in strollers. A golden retriever sat placidly beside its owner, who read the paper and pretended he had the whole world to himself.

Rose was only vaguely aware of all of it. There was too much running through her mind. Too many variables to consider, and one undeniable truth she had to face.

She swallowed hard and blurted out, "I'm pregnant."

"Oh, Rose…" Dee leaned forward and lowered her voice. "Are you sure?"

"Three test kits later," Rose said with a sigh, "I'm way sure."

A couple of minutes of silence passed before Dee sat back in her chair, keeping her gaze fixed on Rose. "So now what?"

"That's the problem. I know 'now what,' I just don't want to do it."

"Talk to Lucas, you mean."

"Yes."

"Honey, you've been making yourself sick missing him for the past two weeks," Dee said softly. "Is this really such bad news?"

"God, yes—I mean, no…I mean…" God, Rose thought, she wasn't even making sense to herself. But hardly surprising. Her brain had been in a spin since the last of the three tests had come back positive.

Seriously, what were the odds of getting pregnant on the *one time* a condom breaks? There were people all over the country—heck, the *world*—trying desperately to have children. She should feel blessed, she knew. And that feeling would eventually come. But right now, all she felt was worried.

Rose chewed at her fingernail, noticed what she was doing and stopped. "The baby isn't bad news, Dee. I mean, it's a surprise, but not a bad one, you know?"

Dee nodded, but kept quiet so Rose could talk and get her thoughts straight in her own mind. A truly *great* best friend, Rose thought.

"The bad news is, once I tell Lucas, he's going to want to marry me—"

"And that's bad because—"

"Because he doesn't love me," Rose muttered and glared at the newspaper-reading man when he flicked her a curious glance. Immediately, he hid behind the paper again. Rose lowered her voice. "He'll offer to marry me out of duty. Because me and the baby are his 'responsibility.' I don't want to be that to the man I love, you know? I want him to want me because he can't live without me. Not because a layer of latex failed at precisely the wrong moment." She paused, then started again before Dee could say a word. "If we get married for all the wrong reasons, it would turn out just like my marriage to Henry did."

"Henry was a horse's ass," Dee pointed out.

"True. But the bottom line is, I didn't love him. He didn't love me. And we created a gigantic ball of misery together. I don't want that with Lucas."

"But you *do* love him," Dee argued.

"Yes, I do. And how long before that feeling just withers and dies because I know he's thinking he was trapped into marrying me?" She shook her head as that thought settled in and turned her stomach. "This isn't the fifties. We have choices now, you know? And my choice is to *not* marry a man who doesn't love me just because he's the father of my child."

"Okay, I'm right there with you," Dee told her firmly. "Anything you decide is okay by me. So the next question is, what do you *want* to do?"

"Sadly," Rose said, slumping against the chair back, "*want* really doesn't come into it. If it did, then what I would want is Lucas and I together, celebrating a baby."

But that wasn't going to happen and Rose was just going to have to come to grips with the fact. Lucas had made his choice, and it hadn't been her. In the two weeks since she'd last seen him, she had heard nothing from him. Beyond a check she received for the exact amount owed her.

It was as if he'd shut her out so easily that he hadn't even missed her. Which was both sad and infuriating. Here she was, moping around, thinking about him, dreaming about him, carrying his *child,* and he was probably not even giving her a passing thought.

Instinctively, Rose squared her shoulders as if metaphorically accepting the weight that had just dropped onto her shoulders. No, Lucas wouldn't be back and if he did offer marriage, it wouldn't be the kind she wanted. He'd already made that very clear. So it would be best all the way around to put aside dreams and start getting ready for reality.

As that thought settled in, she knew one other person she had to tell before facing Lucas with the news.

"I have to go see Dave."

"Really?" Dee just stared at her, surprised. "You sure your brother is the one to help with this?"

Rose shrugged. "He's been better lately. Since we had that talk and finally came clean with each other, we've sort of found a new and richer relationship. He comes over a lot now, and he does know about me and Lucas, so this won't be a shock." She stopped and smiled sadly. "I have to tell him. He's my family."

"Okay," Dee said and stood up when Rose did. "But if he lets you down by being an idiot about this, just call me."

Far from being the Mayor of Idiotville, Dave was the perfect older brother. Once Rose told him what was going on, he said and did all the right things. He was supportive and understanding and Rose was so grateful she could have cried. Now that there were no more secrets between them, she knew she could depend on him. And Rose was going to need him in the next few months and then beyond even that.

"Don't worry," he told her, giving her a hug that

reassured and comforted all at the same time. "Everything's gonna be fine."

"I hope you're right."

"I'm always right," Dave teased, pulling back to look down into her eyes.

She laughed as he meant her to. "Oh, yeah. Now I remember."

"Atta girl," he said, a quick smile flashing across his features. "We're Clancys, you and me. We can handle anything. And your baby will be just fine, I swear it."

"Thanks, Dave," she said, leaning into him just to feel the solid strength of him. She was so tired, she could hardly stand up. It was as if all of her energy was going directly to worrying about the new life she carried inside. It was exhausting. "I'm so thankful I can count on you."

"Always," he promised, then asked, "Have you told Lucas?"

"No." She pulled away, wrapped her arms around herself and dropped into the corner of her couch. Drawing her legs up beneath her, she shook her head for emphasis. "Not yet. I know I have to, but I'm not ready to talk to him right now."

"Okay…"

Something in his tone alerted her, and she snapped him a look. "I don't want you talking to him, either. I'm going to be the one to tell him, Dave. And I'll do it my way, all right?"

"Sure. Absolutely."

Her gaze narrowed on him, looking for some sign that he didn't mean what he was saying, but he just looked… supportive. For which she was grateful. Even knowing that she would be sharing custody with Lucas, raising a baby on her own was a daunting prospect. She was going to need moral support for the journey, and she was so grateful to know that her brother was on her side.

"Thanks for understanding."

"You bet, Rose," he said softly. "I'm here for you. Whatever you need."

"Right now," she said, with a rueful smile, "I think I need a nap. It's been a full day."

"Yeah," he said, walking over to her. He bent down to kiss the top of her head. "You do that. I'll lock your door when I leave."

"Okay." She scooted down on the couch and rested her head on one of the throw pillows. "And Dave… thanks again."

"Don't worry about a thing."

She was practically asleep by the time he walked out the front door.

So there was no way she could have seen his expression shift from that of concerned older brother to one of icy determination. She wasn't ready to talk to Lucas? She didn't have to be. Dave was *more* than ready.

He had a lot to say to his old friend, and there was no time like the present.

"These are *great*," Sean said, reaching for another steak-and-cheese quesadilla. He burned his fingers and hissed in a breath as he dropped the food onto his plate. Grinning at Rafe and Lucas, he said, "You gotta give it up for Rose. If she can teach *you* to cook, she deserves some kind of medal."

"He's right," Rafe said, leaning back in his chair and reaching out to grab his beer. "Even though it wasn't your 'plan,' you managed to learn how to cook. Impressive."

"Yeah. Real impressive." He could cook, but he had no one to cook for. Which was why when it was his turn to host the weekly King meeting, he had volunteered to make his brothers dinner. Now, he couldn't remember why he had offered. Being in this room, even using that new cast-iron skillet he had bought on Rose's orders, left him feeling...incomplete, somehow. As if there was something important missing from his house. His *life*.

Lucas looked at his brothers, then let his gaze track around the kitchen he rarely set foot in these days.

Just being in the room was tearing at him. How the hell could he ever relax in here when Rose was stamped all over the place? Her scent, her laughter and, God help him, since that last night he'd been with her, even her passion was etched indelibly onto this room.

In fact, everywhere he went in his house, he heard her, saw her, tasted her. He wasn't even sleeping in his own bed anymore because he would wake up in the middle of the night stretching out his arms to her and finding only emptiness. How could his life have come so undone in a matter of weeks? How had the home he loved become foreign to him?

His sanctuary had become a prison of his own making.

"You're not eating much," Rafe mused.

"Not hungry, I guess," Lucas said with a shrug. In fact, he hadn't been hungry for two weeks. The knot in his guts made the thought of food impossible. Understandable, he told himself frequently. Of course, he'd have an adjustment period after cutting Rose out of his life. But he was sure it would right itself. Eventually.

"Right." Rafe took a sip of beer and said, "So, Warren stopped by my office this morning."

Lucas shot him a look. "And you're just mentioning

this now? Why the hell didn't you tell me he was there today?"

"Take it easy." Rafe ignored the heat in Lucas's voice and continued, "The man's feeling like a fool and only came to see me to apologize in person."

"Notice he didn't apologize to you," Sean said with a grin. "Probably afraid you'd drop him again."

"I should have had him arrested," Lucas countered, remembering again the bruises on Rose's arm, her slight shivers as he raced up to find her alone, facing a drunk in the dark. "He scared the crap out of Rose that night."

"I know," Rafe said quietly. "He knows it, too, and he's ashamed. Actually, I almost fell out of my chair when I heard that man say out loud for the first time ever, *it's my fault.*"

"About time," Lucas muttered.

Rafe nodded. "He also asked that I apologize for him to both you and Rose, Lucas. And to tell you that you won't have any more trouble from him. He's moving back to Phoenix to start over."

Lucas was glad to hear that Warren was leaving town. He didn't want that guy anywhere near Rose. Not that she would ever know Warren had left. How would she? Lucas wouldn't be seeing her again so he could tell her. Ever.

Absently, he rubbed the middle of his chest at a mystery ache that seemed to have lodged itself there.

"Another miracle chalked up to Rose," Sean said. "Because of her, Warren stepped up to the plate and took responsibility for the first time in his life. She really is an amazing woman."

"Yeah," Lucas agreed somberly. "She is."

"So what're you going to do about it?" Rafe asked.

"What?" Lucas looked back and forth between his

brothers and noted they both wore the same expression. Exhausted patience.

"Come on," Sean said, taking another bite of his third quesadilla. "We're not stupid. We can actually see the difference in you since you stopped seeing Rose."

"I don't know what you're talking about."

"Sure you don't," Rafe said with a smirk. "Hell, even your secretary's complaining about your tiger-with-a-toothache personality lately."

"Yeah," Sean added. "Evelyn says she's going to start force feeding you Katie's cookies to try to sweeten you up."

Lucas scowled at both of them, and if his secretary were there, he'd have one for her, too. He didn't appreciate being talked about or wondered over. His personal life was no one's business but his own. They could all damn well butt out.

"But cookies won't do it, will they?" Rafe asked quietly, gaze locked on Lucas. "It's Rose. It's been Rose all along."

Yes, it was Rose.

It was always Rose.

She never left his mind. The gaping hole in his heart reminded him with every beat that she was gone. That he'd let her go. Hell, that he'd actually *walked away* from her. And why? Because of his stupid plan.

You can't plan your life that way, and he knew it. What was that quote of John Lennon's? *Life is what happens when you're busy making other plans.* That about summed it up. Lucas had planned to live his life alone. To never get entangled in the silky webs of love and marriage. To avoid any relationship that even looked remotely long-term.

And that had worked out well for him.

Until Rose.

Lucas had spent the past two weeks fighting every instinct he had that demanded he go to her. Hold her. Kiss her. No other woman had ever made him want her so much—even out of bed. Rose challenged him, laughed with him, argued with him and stood up to him, willing to go toe-to-toe with him, even when he was *right,* damn it.

And he missed her more than he would have thought possible.

Suddenly irritated with not just himself, but also his interfering brothers, Lucas pushed up from his chair. "I don't need an intervention or whatever the hell this is."

"Oh, hell yes, you do," Sean said with a grin. "You're a pain in the ass to be around, Lucas. More so even than usual."

He gave him a snide smile. "Thanks."

"You're in love with her."

Lucas gaped at Rafe. "I am not."

Sean laughed, and Lucas shifted his glare to him.

"Yes, you are," Rafe said amiably. "Think I don't recognize the signs? Wasn't so long ago that I was doing with Katie exactly what you're doing now with Rose. And I'm here to tell you that hiding from it or ignoring it won't make those feelings disappear."

"It's worth a shot," Lucas mumbled.

"That's where you're wrong," Rafe told him. "You think you're miserable now? Wait another month or two. Or a year. You'll still be torn up in knots over Rose and torturing yourself uselessly. Face it," he added with a smile, "when a King falls for a woman, he stays fallen. There's no escape."

"Damn, that sounds terrifying," Sean said, to no one in particular.

Rafe ignored him and focused his gaze directly on Lucas. "A *smart* man wouldn't want to escape."

Was he smart? Lucas wondered. Or was Rafe reading too much into this? Seeing love where only need existed? What the hell did Lucas know about love? He had never felt it before. How could he be sure that was what he was feeling now? Need and desire were so twisted up inside him, he wasn't sure of anything anymore.

Which was damned lowering to admit, even to himself.

Meeting his brother's stoic stare took every ounce of willpower Lucas had in him. Rafe saw too much. Knew too much. And Lucas couldn't hide the truth any longer. Not from Rafe. Not from himself.

This aching, gaping hole inside him was what was left after he carved Rose out of his life. And if he didn't get her back, the emptiness would eventually swallow him. He'd be forced to live a half life, always wondering what might have been.

"If you want my advice," Rafe said a second later, "and even if you don't…go see Rose. Do some groveling. Get her back while you still have the chance."

Sean snorted. "Lucas? *Apologize?*"

"If he's got half a brain," Rafe said, still staring into Lucas's eyes, "then yeah."

Thankfully, he was spared having to reply when the doorbell rang. He left his brothers arguing over whether or not Lucas had half a brain and stomped through the house to the front door. He didn't bother to look outside first to see who it was. He was too damned grateful for the timely interruption.

If he had looked, he might have had time to duck.

As it was, Dave Clancy's punch caught him squarely on the jaw and staggered Lucas back several steps.

Seeing stars, Lucas cupped his jaw and shouted, "What the hell?"

"You son of a bitch." Dave stalked toward him, ready to deliver another blow when Rafe and Sean came running down the hall.

"What's going on?" Rafe demanded.

Sean was already moving to Lucas's side, presenting a united King front.

Dave's furious gaze never shifted from Lucas. "He knows what's going on. Ask him."

"I don't know what you're talking about!" Lucas glared at him. "I opened the door, you hit me. End of story."

"You didn't see that coming?" Sean muttered.

Lucas shot him a murderous look before turning back to Dave. "What are you doing here? And why the hell did you slug me?"

"Rose is pregnant."

Three little words, dropped into the room, and it was as if a bomb had gone off.

Sean gave a low whistle.

Rafe grumbled something under his breath.

Dave looked like he wanted to go another round.

And Lucas had never been so happy about anything in his life. Dave's news had hit Lucas harder than the man's fist had. His mind raced. Rose. Pregnant. He was going to be a father. And something else. He was going to be a *husband*.

That word settled into him and to his surprise didn't rattle him much at all. Finally, he had a *reason* to marry Rose. To make sure she married him. He would accept nothing less.

Despite the pain in his jaw, he grinned.

Dave saw it and frowned. "You think this is funny?"

"Hell, no," Lucas told him, rubbing the ache in his jaw again. "Nothing funny at all about this. But it's the best news I've ever had."

"I think he's got a concussion," Sean murmured.

"No," Rafe said, smiling, "I think he just figured out what he really wants."

"Damn straight," Lucas told him, then looked at Dave again. Rose's brother. They would all be family soon, he told himself, and made a point to ease the protective streak Dave was displaying. "Look. You and I, we straightened a few things out between us, right?"

"Yeah…"

"And I told you then that I started the affair with Rose as a way of getting some payback on you."

Dave nodded and didn't look real happy with that reminder.

"Things changed," Lucas said simply. "Rose is… everything to me." God, it felt good to admit it. To say out loud what his heart and soul had been trying to tell him for weeks. "I'm going to get her to marry me, Dave. As fast as I can."

The other man studied him for a long moment before finally nodding his head in acceptance. "She won't be easy to convince. She doesn't take orders from anyone anymore."

Lucas laughed. "Believe me, I know."

"But if it means anything to you," Dave added, holding out his right hand, "you've got my blessing."

Stunned to realize that it did indeed mean a lot, Lucas shook his old friend's hand, then turned to his brothers. "I've gotta go. Lock up when you leave."

As he ran out to his car, he heard Sean ask, "So, now that we're almost related, you want a beer?"

Lucas drove straight to Rose's house. He probably should have stopped at a jewelry store so he could hold a big, shiny diamond out to her when he announced that they'd be getting married...but he couldn't wait that long.

He felt better than he had in two weeks. The ache in his chest was gone. His eyes were clear and his heart, mind and body were finally in agreement on something.

Rose was the woman for him.

No one else would ever do.

Spotting the ridiculous skillet car in her driveway, Lucas grinned, parked out front and ran to the front door. The streetlights shone down on the narrow street filled with tiny houses and even tinier yards. People were so close together here, he thought they could probably shout "Bless you" when their neighbor sneezed.

He pounded on the door a few times, then hit the doorbell just for good measure.

Rocking on his heels, he looked around while he waited. Next door, an older woman was holding one end of a leash while an ancient-looking beagle wandered aimlessly around the yard looking for a place to go.

The woman frowned at him when he rang the bell again, and Lucas grinned. Her expression didn't change, and he shrugged, turning back to face the door, still closed and locked to him. What was taking her so long? The house was so small she wouldn't need more than a minute to get to the front door from anywhere in the place.

"Rose!"

Silence, but for the hiss from the older woman next door. Lucas ignored her.

"Rose, I know you're there, talk to me!"

"No!" The answering shout came from the other side of the door, and he smiled at the sound of her irritable, contrary voice.

His world suddenly straightened itself out. And he had to wonder how he had managed to be so clueless for so long. All he really needed was Rose. It was all so simple. So perfect.

Or, it would be, if he could get her to open the damn door.

Leaning his hands on either side of the door, he said, "Let me in, Rose. We have to talk."

"There's nothing to talk about," she told him.

"Not according to Dave," he called back.

"That traitor."

"Rose, let me in."

"Go away."

"Not gonna happen. Not again," he swore vehemently, his gaze raking over the door as if trying to see past it to the woman on the other side. "Not ever."

"Lucas, this changes nothing," she said after a long, tense moment of silence.

"Everything's changed and damn it," he said, "if you won't let me in, then I'll just shout it to you through this bloody door!"

"You watch your language, young man!"

This from the neighbor. Lucas turned a glance her way, then focused on Rose again. He didn't have time to worry about who else was listening. All that mattered was making sure that *Rose* heard every word.

Remembering Rafe's advice, Lucas figured she was owed some groveling. Strangely enough, it wasn't as hard as he might have imagined it would be. It was too important. Too necessary to be difficult.

"I know I hurt you, and I'm sorry." His voice dropped from a shout, but was still loud enough for her to hear him, he hoped. "I was stupid. Shortsighted. I thought I needed revenge when all I really needed was *you*."

"Lucas..."

She sounded tired. Defeated. A word he never would have associated with Rose Clancy before this. And it cut him deep that he had brought such a strong, wonderful woman such grief.

"Rose, give me the chance to show you what you mean to me. I won't blow it again," he shouted. "Damn it, Rose, I *love* you. Did you hear that, Rose? I love you."

He glared at the door that stood between him and the woman he needed to see. To hold.

"The least you could do is open the blasted door so I can tell you to your face what you mean to me!"

"That's it for you," the woman next door called out. "I'm calling the police!"

"Go ahead!" Lucas shouted. "Maybe *they* can make her open the door!"

Instantly, he heard locks turn and then the door was thrown open and Rose stepped out onto the porch. She was wearing the faded jeans he loved to see on her and a V-necked shirt that dipped low enough to display the tops of her breasts. Her hair was back in a ponytail again, and her beautiful blue eyes were red-rimmed from crying.

A stab of something sharp jabbed him in the chest and he swore silently that he would do whatever he could to see that she never cried again.

"It's okay, Mrs. Klein," Rose called to the neighbor,

who was dragging her old dog to the house. "We don't need the police, but thank you!"

The older woman glared at Lucas again and sniffed loudly, but allowed her dog to go back about his business.

Rose gave Lucas a long look before stepping into the house and saying, "Come in."

She was still reeling from his confession. She had never hoped to hear him say "I love you." Oh, all right, she had hoped. But hadn't thought it would ever really happen. Not Lucas King. Not the man who claimed not to believe in love or marriage or any of the things that were so inherently important to Rose.

Closing the door behind them, Rose looked up at him and saw something new in his eyes. Something that gave her chills. Something that told her maybe *hope* wasn't an impossible word after all.

"God, I've missed you," Lucas said, his voice deep and raw with emotion.

Rose wanted more than anything to go to him. To feel his arms come around her. To nestle her head on his chest and listen to the steady beat of his heart. But she couldn't. Not until she was sure he had meant what he said. She simply didn't think she could take another heartbreak.

"Dave shouldn't have told you about the baby," she finally said.

"You're right," Lucas agreed, reaching out to gently skim his fingertips along her jawline. "You should have."

"I was going to," she said. "I just wanted a few days to let the news settle in for me first."

He frowned suddenly. "Are you upset? About the baby, I mean?"

"No." She said it quickly. Firmly. Placing both hands on her flat abdomen, she shook her head and said again, "No, I'm not."

"I'm glad."

"But Lucas, this doesn't mean you have to marry me." God, those words cost her. All she really wanted was to be his wife. To raise their child together. To be loved by the man she loved with all of her heart.

"You're right." He closed the distance between them, laid both hands on her shoulders and said softly, "I don't *have* to marry you Rose. I *need* to marry you."

"Lucas—"

"Not because of the baby," he told her with a half smile that tugged at her heart. "But because without you, there's nothing. These past two weeks without you were the longest of my life. I fought every day to keep from coming here," he admitted. "I told myself I didn't need anyone. That what you and I had was just a temporary blip on the radar. I was wrong. I was an idiot to ever walk away from you."

"I want to believe you, Lucas. So much, I want to believe." Her heart felt as though it was being squeezed by a tight, cold fist. Her stomach was spinning and her mind raced with possibilities she couldn't quite bring herself to count on. Not yet.

"Then do," he insisted, pulling her into the circle of his arms, where she most wanted to be. "Rose, I told you a little of how I grew up."

She nodded, not wanting to speak, or interrupt him now, when every word spoken mattered.

"Well, I never believed love really existed. Never saw it, up close and personal. Then you walked into my life and suddenly, nothing was the same. You changed me. You changed everything. Forever."

She rested her forehead against the center of his chest and bit down hard on her bottom lip. This was all so good, she was afraid to take the chance. He was saying everything she had hoped he would and still, a part of her held back, worried and too cowardly to take the next step—trusting him to mean what he had said.

Tears welled in her eyes and choked her throat as she whispered, "I just don't want you to be saying all of this because of the baby."

"I'm not, Rose," he insisted, shifting so that he could cup her face between his palms and tip her face up to his. Gently, his thumbs rubbed away the tears that spilled from her eyes. "I'm saying all of this because of you. Who you are. What you've given me. What I want us to give each other. I love you, Rose Clancy. I always will."

A wave of love so rich and thick she could hardly breathe moved through her, and Rose could only stare up at him through her tears.

"I want this baby, Rose," he said, bending to press one brief, heartfelt kiss to her mouth. "And all the others that will come after it…"

"All?" she asked on a laugh.

He grinned and added, "But make no mistake, ever. You are the prize for me, Rose. You are the heart and soul of me. You are all I will ever need. Without you, I have nothing. With you, I have the world."

"I love you so much, Lucas," Rose whispered.

"Thank God," he said on a heavy sigh. "You had me worried, I can tell you."

She smiled up at him. "I never want to be apart from you again. These past two weeks were just so lonely."

"Then marry me, Rose." He kissed her again, harder, deeper, letting the passion between them sizzle and burn like a promise. "Come and live with me in that big, empty house. Help me make it a real home. For both of us."

"I will marry you," she said, finally giving in to the magic that was happening. Somehow, her world had righted itself again. She believed. In love. In Lucas. And in the life they would build together. "And I promise, that beautiful old house won't be empty for long."

* * * * *

COMING NEXT MONTH

Available November 8, 2011

#2119 WANTED BY HER LOST LOVE
Maya Banks
Pregnancy & Passion

#2120 TEMPTATION
Brenda Jackson
Texas Cattleman's Club: The Showdown

#2121 NOTHING SHORT OF PERFECT
Day Leclaire
Billionaires and Babies

#2122 RECLAIMING HIS PREGNANT WIDOW
Tessa Radley

#2123 IMPROPERLY WED
Anna DePalo

#2124 THE PRICE OF HONOR
Emilie Rose

REQUEST YOUR FREE BOOKS!

2 FREE NOVELS PLUS 2 FREE GIFTS!

ALWAYS POWERFUL, PASSIONATE AND PROVOCATIVE

YES! Please send me 2 FREE Harlequin Desire® novels and my 2 FREE gifts (gifts are worth about $10). After receiving them, if I don't wish to receive any more books, I can return the shipping statement marked "cancel." If I don't cancel, I will receive 6 brand-new novels every month and be billed just $4.30 per book in the U.S. or $4.99 per book in Canada. That's a saving of at least 14% off the cover price! It's quite a bargain! Shipping and handling is just 50¢ per book in the U.S. and 75¢ per book in Canada.* I understand that accepting the 2 free books and gifts places me under no obligation to buy anything. I can always return a shipment and cancel at any time. Even if I never buy another book, the two free books and gifts are mine to keep forever.

225/326 HDN FEF3

Name _____ (PLEASE PRINT) _____

Address _____ Apt. # _____

City _____ State/Prov. _____ Zip/Postal Code _____

Signature (if under 18, a parent or guardian must sign)

Mail to the **Reader Service:**

IN U.S.A.: P.O. Box 1867, Buffalo, NY 14240-1867
IN CANADA: P.O. Box 609, Fort Erie, Ontario L2A 5X3

Not valid for current subscribers to Harlequin Desire books.

Want to try two free books from another line?
Call 1-800-873-8635 or visit www.ReaderService.com.

* Terms and prices subject to change without notice. Prices do not include applicable taxes. Sales tax applicable in N.Y. Canadian residents will be charged applicable taxes. Offer not valid in Quebec. This offer is limited to one order per household. All orders subject to credit approval. Credit or debit balances in a customer's account(s) may be offset by any other outstanding balance owed by or to the customer. Please allow 4 to 6 weeks for delivery. Offer available while quantities last.

Your Privacy—The Reader Service is committed to protecting your privacy. Our Privacy Policy is available online at www.ReaderService.com or upon request from the Reader Service.

We make a portion of our mailing list available to reputable third parties that offer products we believe may interest you. If you prefer that we not exchange your name with third parties, or if you wish to clarify or modify your communication preferences, please visit us at www.ReaderService.com/consumerschoice or write to us at Reader Service Preference Service, P.O. Box 9062, Buffalo, NY 14269. Include your complete name and address.

HDES11B

Harlequin® Special Edition® is thrilled to present a new installment in USA TODAY *bestselling author RaeAnne Thayne's reader-favorite miniseries,* THE COWBOYS OF COLD CREEK.

Join the excitement as we meet the Bowmans—four siblings who lost their parents but keep family ties alive in Pine Gulch. First up is Trace. Only two things get under this rugged lawman's skin: beautiful women and secrets. And in Rebecca Parsons, he finds both!

Read on for a sneak peek of CHRISTMAS IN COLD CREEK. *Available November 2011 from Harlequin® Special Edition®.*

On impulse, he unfolded himself from the bar stool. "Need a hand?"

"Thank you! I…" She lifted her gaze from the floor to his jeans and then raised her eyes. When she identified him her hazel eyes turned from grateful to unfriendly and cold, as if he'd somehow thrown the broken glasses at her head.

He also thought he saw a glimmer of panic in those interesting depths, which instantly stirred his curiosity like cream swirling through coffee.

"I've got it, Officer. Thank you." Her voice was several degrees colder than the whirl of sleet outside the windows.

Despite her protests, he knelt down beside her and began to pick up shards of broken glass. "No problem. Those trays can be slippery."

This close, he picked up the scent of her, something fresh and flowery that made him think of a mountain meadow on a July afternoon. She had a soft, lush mouth and for one brief, insane moment, he wanted to push aside that stray lock of hair slipping from her ponytail and taste her. Apparently he needed to spend a lot less time working and a great deal *more* time recreating with the opposite sex if he could have sudden random fantasies about a woman he wasn't even inclined to like, pretty or not.

"I'm Trace Bowman. You must be new in town."

She didn't answer immediately and he could almost see the wheels turning in her head. Why the hesitancy? And why that little hint of unease he could see clouding the edge of her gaze? His presence was obviously making her uncomfortable and Trace couldn't help wondering why.

"Yes. We've been here a few weeks."

"Well, I'm just up the road about four lots, in the white house with the cedar shake roof, if you or your daughter need anything." He smiled at her as he picked up the last shard of glass and set it on her tray.

Definitely a story there, he thought as she hurried away. He just might need to dig a little into her background to find out why someone with fine clothes and nice jewelry, and who so obviously didn't have experience as a waitress, would be here slinging hash at The Gulch. Was she running away from someone? A bad marriage?

So…Rebecca Parsons. Not Becky. An intriguing woman. It had been a long time since one of those had crossed his path here in Pine Gulch.

Trace won't rest until he finds out Rebecca's secret, but will he still have that same attraction to her once he does? Find out in CHRISTMAS IN COLD CREEK. Available November 2011 from Harlequin® Special Edition®.

Dear Reader:

The book you a
Martin's True Cr
leader in true crime: Each month, MW00256398
of the latest, most sensational crime that has captured the national attention. St. Martin's is the publisher of bestselling true crime author and crime journalist Kieran Crowley, who explores the dark, deadly links between a prominent Manhattan surgeon and the disappearance of his wife fifteen years earlier in THE SURGEON'S WIFE. Suzy Spencer's BREAKING POINT guides readers through the tortuous twists and turns in the case of Andrea Yates, the Houston mother who drowned her five young children in the family's bathtub. In Edgar Award–nominated DARK DREAMS, legendary FBI profiler Roy Hazelwood and bestselling crime author Stephen G. Michaud shine light on the inner workings of America's most violent and depraved murderers. In the book you now hold, CHASING THE DEVIL, Sheriff David Reichert tell the inspiring true story of his relentless search for the Green River Killer, a quest that ultimately led to the killer's capture.

St. Martin's True Crime Library gives you the stories behind the headlines. Our authors take you right to the scene of the crime and into the minds of the most notorious murderers to show you what really makes them tick. St. Martin's True Crime Library paperbacks are better than the most terrifying thriller, because it's all true! The next time you want a crackling good read, make sure it's got the St. Martin's True Crime Library logo on the spine—you'll be up all night!

Charles E. Spicer, Jr.
Executive Editor, St. Martin's True Crime Library

CHASING
THE
DEVIL

My Twenty-Year Quest to
Capture the Green River Killer

SHERIFF DAVID
REICHERT

St. Martin's Paperbacks

This book is dedicated to the victims of the Green River Killer. It is my hope that the tragedy they suffered will inspire a greater effort to prevent young women from being caught up in a life of desperation and danger on the streets. May we all remember these young women and the lives they should have been able to lead.

Published by arrangement with Little, Brown, and Company.

CHASING THE DEVIL

Library of Congress Catalog Card Number: 2004011629

ISBN: 0-312-93819-5
EAN: 9780312-93819-2

Printed in the United States of America

Little, Brown and Company hardcover edition / July 2004
St. Martin's Paperbacks edition / January 2006

St. Martin's Paperbacks are published by St. Martin's Press, 175 Fifth Avenue, New York, NY 10010.

10 9 8 7 6 5 4 3

CONTENTS

PROLOGUE

THE RIVER

THE GREEN RIVER'S SOURCE is one mile high in the Snoqualmie National Forest and just south of a spot on the map called Stampede Pass. From one small spring it trickles westward, gathering strength from dozens of mountain creeks with names like Champion, Wolf, and Cougar. By the time it reaches flat land, it is a steady flowing stream that in the springtime, when the snow melts in the Cascades, can run twenty feet deep in some places.

The people who live in the mountain valley carved by the Green River have always had a close relationship with its waters. It was a source of fish and drinking water for Native Americans, who also used it as a highway to Puget Sound. Early settlers depended on the river in the same way, and in modern times it provides irrigation for farms and pleasure to sport fishermen, rafters, swimmers, and anyone else who loves the outdoors.

But even as it brings life to people on the shore, the river has long been a site for tragedy. In the middle of the nineteenth century, white settlers battled Indians along the river, and men, women, and children died on both sides. In more recent years, the river periodically claimed drowning victims or gave up bodies that had been dumped by those who hoped the evidence of their crimes might be swept out to sea.

My own connection to the Green River goes back to the early 1960s, when, as a boy growing up in the city of Kent, I earned money picking fruits and vegetables at farms that nestled up to its banks. Later, when I was in high school, the riverside became a haven from my long-running battles with my father. We had good times, but I was always aware of the pressures my parents felt raising seven kids on limited wages. On weekends my dad might drink a little too much and get into a fight with my mother. When I was young, I would hide. When I got older, I tried to intervene. After one especially bad fight, I left home and lived for two months in a 1956 Mercury, which I had recently bought with money from my after-school jobs. I parked in a deserted spot beside the river, went to school and work during the day, and slept in the car every night.

I knew all the isolated and hidden corners of Kent where a kid on the run might hide away. But I wasn't the type who got in a lot of trouble. In fact, I was the opposite. I was a kid who lived in the tough neighborhoods, dealt with bullies and bad guys on a daily basis, and felt it was my duty to defend myself and my fellow underdogs from them. Part of this attitude came from the tough example my father set. He never backed down and was always ready to fight for what he thought was right. But while he always seemed to try to impose his will and his judgment on others, I developed a near obsession with keeping myself and others safe.

Childhood had brought me plenty of experiences with danger. I was seven or eight on the day when, as I was shooting marbles with a friend, a man pulled up in a station wagon and tried to abduct me. An escapee from a state mental hospital, he had me halfway into the car when my mother ran up and grabbed me by the feet. She tore me out of his hands, saving me from God knows what he might have done. At around the same time, I was kidnapped by three older kids who blamed me for something I hadn't done and tied me to a tree out in the woods. I escaped, but the lesson of that experience and others was clear: We share this world with bad people, and you have to stand up to them.

With all the violence and drama I faced inside my family home and outside on the street, it's little wonder that I had an early fascination with cops and firefighters, who, after all, are officially charged with keeping us safe. As a boy, one of my favorite games was called Rescue 8, after a TV show by that name. I would get my brothers and sisters and cousins to stage emergencies — some kids would hang from tree limbs or pretend to be trapped somewhere — and then the rest of us would come racing to their rescue. Bikes served as police cars. We made our throats sore trying to scream like sirens.

When I was old enough, I stopped playing rescue and started jumping into bad situations whenever someone asked for help or I saw the need. When a Peeping Tom was bothering the women at my future wife Julie's college dorm, I raced after the guy and jumped on the running board of his VW. (He dislodged me by crashing into a telephone pole.) On the football field, where I played quarterback, I got into the middle of a fight that broke out after we had won a game. I didn't like it that one of our smaller players was taking a beating from a giant lineman. I broke up the fight, but the lineman cracked me between the eyes with his helmet and I wound up in the hospital.

For some reason, my early interest in keeping the peace didn't move me immediately into law enforcement. In college I considered teaching, coaching, social work, and the ministry. My grandfather, whom I loved and admired, was a Lutheran pastor, and faith was, and is, the center of my life. I thought about it a lot as I served seven months of active duty in the air force. All along my girlfriend, then fiancée, then wife, Julie, said I would make a good cop and encouraged me to consider that option. We discussed it often and decided the time was right when I left the air force and transferred into the reserves and returned to the Seattle area. In 1971 I took the test to join the King County Sheriff's Department and scored high enough — number 82 — to get one of 110 deputy positions. I started work in 1972 and would stay on the job for more than thirty-two years as Julie and I established a home and made a family that included our children, Angela, Tabitha, and Daniel.

On my very first evaluation my supervisor wrote: "Officer Reichert has the ability to be quite a good policeman. Although he seems very quiet, his actions indicate that he will do a good job."

I was a quiet young man, and action was far more interesting to me than any conversation. But I could empathize with those in need, and that made me a good fit in a profession that still harbored a certain Wild West mentality. Thirty years ago, before training was upgraded and the department established more specific procedures, individual officers were expected to be creative and assertive. You raced to every scene at high speed with the siren wailing, and you called for backup only as a last resort. (One reason for this was that your fellow cops were probably miles away.)

Sometimes the results of this macho approach were a little less than perfect. Take the time I answered a call to a domestic dispute where a man was holding a knife to his wife's throat. A more senior officer arrived and suggested I sneak in an open window. I took off my shoes and managed to get into the house. I distracted the man. He turned away from his wife, she ran to me, and I helped her escape through a window. I then went to the living room to see if I could prevent the man from killing himself. But as I entered the room, the man saw my reflection in a window. In the fight that ensued, he slashed my throat from my right ear to my esophagus, barely missing the jugular vein.

When I tell this story, some people are shocked. Today we have negotiating techniques and special teams that handle these kinds of situations. But people are often more surprised to hear that my wife, Julie, wasn't hysterical over that incident. She was alarmed when someone called the house and said, "Dave's on TV, he's been hurt." But once she knew I was going to be okay, her attitude was, "There's nothing you can say. That's Dave." And she was right. I would always see myself as a competitor and a protector, and I preferred to play offense whenever possible.

Fortunately, a cop can be assertive without risking his life every day. In those early patrol years, I learned some subtler strategies, like developing sources on the street and using my imagination on every call I answered. Sometimes the results were even amusing. I'll always remember the teenager who broke into a suburban home and stole from the liquor cabinet and the candy drawer. I went to the backyard and followed candy wrappers to a power line right-of-way.

Eventually I found a school absence note next to one of the wrappers. It must have fallen out of his pocket. That gave me the burglar's name, and soon I was speaking with his mother, who led me to his room and a cache of items he had taken from houses all over the neighborhood.

Then there was the night when I surprised a burglar who had broken into a gas station. He leaped out of a broken window and ran into the woods behind the station. I followed but quickly lost him in the darkness. (A rookie mistake: I forgot to bring a flashlight.) I could hear branches breaking, heavy breathing, and footsteps as I chased him. Finally there was a loud thunk and a cry of pain. Although we didn't catch him that night, we returned in the morning to follow the trail of blood from the tree the man had run into to the nearby trailer where he lived.

Besides the challenge of solving crimes and the rewards that come from helping people, one of the main benefits of police work is the camaraderie you feel with fellow officers. You might bicker and complain about some of them, but the bonds you form are unbreakable. I felt this was especially true when it came to the person who influenced me the most during my years of patrol — Sam Hicks.

Seven years my senior, Sam had been on the force for about three years when I arrived. A big man with curly red hair, he enjoyed the job and was part of a new generation bringing a smarter, more professional attitude to the work. Sam was gung ho, but he also had more common sense than anyone I had ever met. And he never lost his sense of humor, especially when it came to himself. One night we went to a robbery suspect's house and were attacked by a snarling dog that charged out of the darkness. Sam whipped out his mace but pointed it in the wrong direction. He sprayed himself in the face, and we went running for our police cars. With his eyes swollen and red from the spray, Sam laughed as hard as I did.

Although I never forgot what Sam showed me about keeping my cool and staying alert, the most important lessons he taught me were about persistence and thoroughness. Both were on display the night we responded to a call from some fishermen who had spotted a man's boot, complete with a foot and a piece of leg bone, on the bottom of an isolated mountain lake. Months earlier someone had reported a missing hiker in the same area. The man had had a few enemies, so we were looking at a possible murder.

Sam and I arrived at the edge of the forest before dawn. Detective Bob LaMoria joined us. We grabbed our flashlights, hoisted packs onto our shoulders, and began a nine-mile hike to the lake in pouring rain. Sam never slowed down, and when we got there, we quickly inflated a rubber raft and paddled out to recover the leg and foot with a grappling hook. While we were in the raft, I looked up to see a human rib cage resting on the side of a mountain five hundred feet above us. Under Sam's direction, I scaled the mountain, recovered what bones I could find, and then packed them out. In the end, the death was ruled a suicide, but at least the man's family could lay him to rest. For Sam, an eighteen-mile hike in the wilderness to solve the mystery of a foot found at the bottom of a lake was all in a day's work.

Sam became my closest friend, and his example of intelligent, dogged pursuit became my template for effective investigations when I joined him on the homicide and robbery detective unit. Sam always pushed his cases, and he didn't like to wait. On June 24, 1982, when he was ready to arrest a murder suspect, he called my house, looking for me. I was out, but rather than wait for me, Sam grabbed another detective, Leo Hursch, and went after his man.

Leo and Sam spotted their suspect, Bobby Hughes, riding in the passenger side of a truck driven by his brother. They followed him along the country roads of rural southwest King County until the brother turned down the long driveway of a big, isolated farm. The brother dropped Bobby near a line of trees and split. As Sam and Leo drove up, a shot fired from the trees smashed the windshield of their car. They got out and ran behind a barn.

On that fateful day, Sam and Leo were unable to determine where their suspect had gone. While Leo carefully scanned the area, Sam slowly crept around the corner of the barn. In the split second that his body was exposed to the tree line, a shot was fired. The bullet hit Sam in the chest, and he fell to the ground. Leo ran to Sam and radioed for help, and the shooter fled into nearby Flaming Geyser State Park, a large wooded area bisected by the waters of the Green River.

My friend and mentor Sam Hicks was airlifted to Harbor View Hospital, but he wouldn't survive. The shot from a high-powered rifle had caused too much damage. But before we knew he was dead, while the doctors still worked on him, the sheriff's office responded to the shooting with a massive manhunt. Every available cop raced to the scene. Dogs were put on Hughes's trail. Helicopters crisscrossed the sky. Patrol cars cruised every mile of road.

At first my supervisors held me out of the hunt. They said I was too close to Sam and that emotion would cloud my judgment. But when they needed someone to deliver photos of the suspect to the scene, I volunteered, roaring down there with the lights on and the siren screaming. The delivery was just an excuse for me to get involved. I think they knew that when they sent me on the errand.

When I arrived at the farm, deputies and detectives were streaming in from all over. One of the first I saw was Fabienne "Fae" Brooks. The first black woman detective in the sheriff's office, Fae was usually assigned to sex crimes. But like everyone else, she had turned out for the manhunt. Fae must have seen the shock and sadness on my face, because even before we talked, she gave me a strong hug.

The search for Bobby Hughes would go on for three days and nights, with hundreds of people scouring the countryside on both sides of the river. I was part of the effort, putting in long hours on the hunt and returning home just once to see my family, weep over my friend's death, and struggle for a few hours of sleep.

Finally, on that third day, a motorist reported seeing a haggard-looking man scrambling up from the riverbank and then crossing a road. Detective Bill Henne and I were among the officers who responded to the call. A police dog got the scent and began chasing Hughes. We raced to position our car along a gravel road that was right in Hughes's path. Bill and I both grabbed shotguns. I lay on the hood of the car, facing the woods with my finger on the trigger. Bill positioned himself on the trunk, facing in the same direction.

While we lay in wait, we could hear the dog in the woods and the cracking of branches. But neither Hughes nor the searchers ever broke through. He had stopped and tried to hide under a fallen tree. The dog caught him, and the officers trailing behind apprehended him. I was the only homicide detective on the scene, so I was enlisted to ride with Hughes to the Auburn station, advise him of his rights, and take his statement. I later took him to King County jail in downtown Seattle. Through it all, I forced myself to stay calm as he told some bullshit story about how he thought Sam and Leo were bad guys out to kill him. He had fired in self-defense, he claimed. All I could think of was how this guy had killed my best friend, a husband and a father and one of the best cops I ever knew, with the twitch of his index finger.

My daughter Angela's ninth birthday fell seven weeks after Sam's death. About forty members of our extended family were coming to our house to celebrate her birthday and all the others that occur in August. Because our family is so big, we had long ago agreed to have one giant party every month. For Angela's big day, Julie had made sure there would be cake and ice cream and plenty of other food. The presents had been bought and wrapped, and more would arrive with our guests. With a crowd of this size, the monthly birthday bash was almost as exciting as Christmas.

Angela was barely able to contain her excitement as she waited for the guests to arrive. She was sitting at our kitchen table, a big oak hand-me-down from my parents, when the phone rang. The call was for me, and if Angela was watching my face as I listened to the voice on the other end, she knew what was about to happen. It was an emergency call from the King County Sheriff's Office, and Dad, the homicide detective, would have to go, again.

So much would flow from that single phone call — decades of struggle, worry, danger, and obsession — that I almost forgot that it all started on Angela's birthday. But many years later, she reminded me of this and recalled how she had cried and then felt ashamed because she had thought of herself, not the murder victim I was summoned to examine. "I thought it was so unfair," she told me. "But we knew you had no choice."

Everyone understood that I had to respond without hesitation. And they knew that this was more than a job to me. I believed that I had been entrusted with the responsibility to resolve the worst kinds of tragedies and bring some sort of justice to the victims and their families. It was a serious business, and given how deep my Christian faith runs, I considered it to be a calling.

But even though I answered calls to murder scenes with almost automatic calm and efficiency, this one did strike a few emotional chords. First, it tore me away from Angela's party. I regretted that. Second, it involved multiple victims, and that always made things more challenging. And third, this call was bringing me back again to the Green River.

On June 24, the river had been the backdrop for events that had brought me to my knees with grief when Sam was killed. Now the Green River held even more tragedy. The bodies of two young women had been found submerged near the shore. It would fall to me to lead the investigation to discover who they were, how they got there, and who was to blame.

ONE

SOMEBODY'S DAUGHTERS

IT MAY BE HARD TO BELIEVE that every time I took an emergency call at my home, my mind shifted smoothly from family life to murder, but that's the way it works for most experienced detectives. We have the usual human desire for peace and comfort when the workday is done. And like most people, we try to move between home and work without much cross-contamination. The only difference is that homicide is one of the most disturbing acts that human beings commit, and homicide detectives have to deal with it every day.

On August 15, 1982, I received a call about a double homicide — two female victims. I knew that the site where the bodies had been found — a spot on the Green River in the Seattle suburb of Kent — was going to be difficult to search. Sinewy blackberry plants sprout on both sides of the river. Covered with thorns and almost impossible to snap, the vines are six feet and higher, and they grow amid reeds and grasses that are just as tall. Besides the thick brush, the river is banked by steep slopes of rocks, placed there by the Army Corps of Engineers to contain the river as it rises every spring with the runoff from melting snow in the mountains.

In Kent, access to the river is along a winding, two-lane country highway called Frager Road. For an area that's just twenty miles from downtown Seattle, it's a remarkably rural place, just farms, nurseries, and a few private homes. The only substantial business around there was a slaughterhouse called PD&J Meat Company, which overlooked the river just south of the Peck Bridge.

What bothered me most as I drove down Frager Road in my unmarked car was that I had been there just three days earlier — to PD&J Meats, in fact — to investigate the death of another young woman. In that case, a slaughterhouse worker had gone outside to smoke a cigar. He had looked down at the river, to a place where a spit of sand broke the surface of the water and a few logs had become stuck. Up against the logs he saw what he took to be a large animal carcass. Curious, he followed a path used by fishermen to the water's edge. As soon as he broke through the blackberry vines, he realized that the sandbar had captured not an animal, but a human being.

In that case, I had photographed the scene, called divers to collect the body, and helped bring it up the bank for the medical examiner. For me, dead bodies were a normal part of my work, and I was trained to regard them as evidence. I also treated them with deep respect. A body represents a person who was once loved, who once looked forward to the future, and who was robbed of the experiences and feelings that future promised. And sometimes the body can speak to us, offering clues and evidence that might bring justice to the person who once lived inside. For that reason, I take extreme care with the remains we find.

In this case, the sun had beaten down on the body's

exposed skin with such intensity that parts of it were charred. Other portions of the body had been submerged and were beginning to bloat. Worst of all, egg-laying insects had been especially active, and larvae were crawling all over it. I paused for a moment to steel myself and then, like the other officers on the scene, did what was necessary to gently rescue the corpse and carry it to shore.

Once we had the body on the riverbank, we could see that though the young woman was unclothed, she was offering us some clues to her identity. She wore a ring and an earring. She also had a few tattoos. The most notable was the word "Duby" inside a heart tattooed on her right shoulder.

The official cause of death would be determined by an autopsy, which I would attend the next day. But on the scene, the medical examiner was able to estimate that the body had been in the river for at least two weeks. He found no water in her lungs — which meant she was dead before she reached the river — and no significant wounds or trauma.

During the investigation, I contacted a local tattoo artist named Joe Yates, who had once helped identify another body via the victim's tattoos, but in this case he was stumped. However, checks with area police departments, which record key features whenever they arrest someone, eventually turned up the name Debra Lynn Bonner. Twenty-four years old, she was the same height and weight as the woman found in the river, and she had the same tattoos. She had been arrested for prostitution at least eight times while using several different names.

All the facts of the Bonner case raced through my mind as I approached PD&J Meats on Sunday, August 15, but my most troubling thoughts were not of the body, but of Debra's mother. Just twenty-four hours earlier I had gone to one of the roughest neighborhoods in Tacoma and knocked on the door of her tumbledown house. Inside, the house was a monument to poverty and dysfunction. The furniture, what little there was, was beat-up and stained. Mice ran across the floor. Everything about the place said, "Here are people who have struggled through life." When we sat down and Mrs. Shirley Bonner heard me say her daughter had been murdered, tears filled her eyes and trickled down her cheeks. You might say that this woman had never been equipped to raise a child, and you might be right. But her grief was real and her sorrow was deep, and she cried a mother's tears. "I will not give up," I had told her. "I promise you, I will not give up."

Now I was headed back to the river, where two more young women, two more daughters of mothers who would weep when they got the news, waited to be recovered and examined. As the lead detective on the scene, I would take on these cases, too. That meant that I would be responsible for the crime scene, for identifying the bodies, and for every other aspect of the investigation, including making contact with grieving families. It was going to be a very long day.

The parking lot at PD&J was jammed with official vehicles, so I parked on the roadside. I grabbed the big, bulky Mamiya camera I used for crime scene photos, along with its huge battery pack and a logbook to record each shot. As soon as I got out of the car, some of the officers who stood on the roadside began filling me in on the scene: Robert Ainsworth, a rafter who collected old bottles and other junk that had been tossed into the river, had been drifting through the shallow water, poking at the bottom with a homemade hook. Whenever Ainsworth found something he couldn't bring up with his tool, he'd slip into the water and muck around in the silt and sand.

On this Sunday afternoon, Ainsworth had seen a man on the riverbank as he rounded a bend near PD&J. The two spoke briefly about an outboard motor submerged at that spot. Ainsworth also saw a man in a pickup truck on Frager Road, above the river. Moments later, after the two men departed, the rafter saw what he believed was a mannequin of a woman submerged in the water. He poked it with his hook and noticed that it was pinned to the riverbed by a large rock. Then, as he maneuvered the raft, he saw another female form lying submerged about ten feet away. Her limbs, hair, and hands were so perfectly formed, so lifelike, that he realized these were not mannequins at all but, rather, the bodies of young women.

In order to avoid contaminating evidence that may have been dropped by whoever put these women in the water, the officers already on the scene had made a fresh path through the blackberry vines and tall grass. Before I plunged ahead, I looked for one of them to take my photo logbook and accompany me to record each picture that I would take, noting the time, location, and other details. The duty fell to a rookie who had hung back while other, older officers had briefed me.

Officer Sue Peters had the good or bad luck (depending on how you look at it) to have been assigned to patrol this corner of King County. Barely five feet tall with brown hair and a youthful appearance, Peters looked more like a grade school teacher than a cop. About to have her first encounter with dead bodies, she was quiet as we climbed down the bank and walked north along the rocks to the spot where the bodies looked to be shadows in the shallows.

The first body we reached was lying facedown, unclothed, in three feet of water. She was weighted down with rocks that had been laid on her foot, knee, buttocks, and shoulder. The silt that had begun to cover her up made it impossible to determine her race. I snapped pictures and called out the details to Sue, who managed to stay calm and composed by keeping her focus on the task at hand.

The second body, submerged ten feet farther upstream in water that was a little deeper, was lying faceup and was nude except for a front-closure bra that had been opened. This body had been secured with rocks on her right leg and hip, left ankle, and shoulder. But nothing held down her right arm, and as the water flowed around her, it raised her arm and made her hand flutter back and forth. Her mouth and eyes were open. She looked like she was waving to us and saying, "Here I am. Help me."

I was already wondering about the person — maybe "creature" is a better word — who was responsible for this little horror show. We all were trying to imagine how someone would have handled the chore of lugging the bodies to the water and then moving the rocks to keep them submerged. And naturally, we speculated about the connection to the girl with the Duby tattoo, Debra Bonner, who had been pulled from the river within sight of this spot.

Did these two young women have anything in common with Debra? Did they move in the same dangerous underworld of prostitutes, pimps, drugs, and johns? And what about the killer, or killers? Were all the people involved in this crime connected in some way?

Once I finished taking pictures, Sue and I joined the others scouring the water's edge for evidence. The area was littered with cigarette butts, bottles, cans, and other trash that people had thrown out of car windows or left while tromping alongside the river. This was a popular fishing spot, and a couple of makeshift shacks for winter sportsmen sat between the road and the water. No one discovered anything of apparent value, but we collected everything we found just in case.

While the others worked nearby, Sue and I picked our way carefully down the steep bank, looking for any sign — footsteps, broken plants, litter — of the person who had dumped the two bodies. The underbrush was very thick, and we moved slowly, parting grass that was five or six feet high, carefully pushing blackberry vines aside to avoid the thorns. We couldn't see more than a foot or so ahead of ourselves, so I was surprised when, halfway up the bank, we moved through the brush and almost stumbled upon a body.

"I've got another one!" I called out.

While I waited for other officers to come help mark the scene and check for evidence, I had time to examine the body. She was a young African American woman. She was lying facedown. Her legs were straight, her heels almost touching. Her right arm was raised, with the elbow bent at a ninety-degree angle. The only clothing she wore was a white bra, still clasped but pushed up. A pair of blue pants was twisted around her neck.

In my mind's eye, I saw the killer getting spooked by something — the man on the raft? a passing car? — and simply dropping this body before he could reach the river. He had obviously miscalculated, believing that this stretch of the Green River was more secluded than it was. I hoped that he had made other mistakes, missteps that would give us some clue to his identity.

The search for evidence would go on for hours. In the meantime, I would photograph the body and the scene, with Sue recording the details. Down below us, divers waded into the river to retrieve the first two bodies. I went down to help.

It was a gruesome task. The bodies were terribly bloated and starting to decompose. At one point I lost my grip on one of the bodies when the skin simply slipped off into my hands. When we were finally able to get both corpses to shore, we slipped them into body bags and then struggled up the bank, where the medical examiner, Donald Reay, MD, waited.

After we opened the first bag for him, Dr. Reay quickly determined that the first victim taken from the water was African American and that she had been in the water for three or four days. She had no obvious injuries, but there was a sizable bruise on her left arm. The second body from the river, also that of a young black woman, was more severely decomposed, and Reay thought it had been underwater for a week or so. She, too, showed no signs of trauma. In fact, of the three discovered that day, only the body in the grass bore any scrapes or cuts.

The third body still showed signs of rigor mortis — a stiffening that begins to ease about twenty-four hours after death — so it was obvious she had been dead for just a couple of days at most. Dr. Reay also noticed petechiae, tiny dots that appear on the face from broken blood vessels or hemorrhages. Petechiae form when the pressure in tiny capillaries is so high that the vessel walls burst. People can get them under their eyes or on their nose if they have a bout of severe coughing or vomiting. They are also a telltale indication of strangulation.

I looked down at the young woman and imagined her death at the hands of the beast who had wrapped those blue slacks around her neck and pulled hard, closing off her windpipe and draining the life from her. Her face looked both distorted and sweetly innocent, and I thought to myself, "Each of these women is somebody's daughter."

It would take several more hours for us to clear the scene. The rocks that had been placed on the bodies were evidence, so we gathered them up. But nothing in the trash that we found on the riverbank seemed to be important. We could only hope that as we discovered the identities of the three women and traced their relationships and activities, we would see something important.

Nothing at the river connected the bodies discovered on Sunday to Debra Bonner, who was pulled from the water three days before, except for the fact that they were all young females. This came up as I stood beside Frager Road and discussed the case with Major Richard Kraske and other investigators. Debbie Bonner's parents had admitted she was a prostitute and they had complained about a man she had called her boyfriend, who was really her pimp and drug supplier. His name was Carlton Marshall, and *he* had called *them* three weeks ago to say Debbie was missing.

Prostitution had been part of the picture in two other recent murders. In January, I had investigated the killing of Leanne Wilcox, who had been strangled and then dumped nearby on dry land. In July, the local Kent police had handled the death of Wendy Coffield, a prostitute who was a friend of Leanne's and who had been strangled and dumped in the Green River.

Wilcox, Coffield, and Bonner made three young prostitutes strangled and dumped within a ten-mile radius. What were the odds that these three additional strangulation victims — all young females — were *not* pieces of a single grotesque puzzle? Any reasonable person would bet that we weren't dealing with six isolated homicides — crimes of passion or impulse — but, rather, an ongoing campaign of death carried out by a single-minded killer.

Catching the killer would be our responsibility because the bodies lay in our jurisdiction, the unincorporated portion of King County (Seattle and the county's other cities had their own police departments). At twenty-one hundred square miles, it's the twelfth-largest county in the entire United States. Once a sparsely populated place of mountains, rivers, and coastline, the county had grown to a population of more than half a million people. Add in the cities, and the head count exceeded a million. But even with all these people, King County included plenty of wild and isolated spots. It was a perfect setting for serial killings: a big, diverse population surrounded by countless hiding places. To make matters worse, we had just five hundred police officers to cover the entire area. With fewer than one street cop for every thousand people, our manpower was not even half the national average.

The people of King County and the Pacific Northwest have had their share of experience with serial murder. In 1974 Ted Bundy began his killing in Seattle, abducting women from colleges and parks around Puget Sound and then killing them. Coeds were his favorite victims, and people grew ever more terrified as young women disappeared and bodies were discovered. Bundy eventually carried his killing to Colorado and then to Utah, where he was captured. Remarkably, he escaped *twice* and went on to kill more women in Florida before being arrested, tried, convicted, and sentenced to death in 1980.

Though the "Ted murders," as they were called, had ended, Bundy was still alive and still making headlines with offers to help officials locate bodies so long as he was kept alive. These stories served to remind people that every once in a while a vicious human predator may arise and start killing with ruthless, remorseless abandon. And we all knew that the fear and revulsion created by Bundy would be renewed as soon as the Green River deaths were publicized.

We caught a lucky break on that afternoon at the river when the media failed to appear. Like almost everyone else, most reporters take weekends off, and maybe the few on duty forgot to turn on their police radios. Whatever the reason, we had been able to do our work without having the press looking over our shoulders from the riverbank or peering down from helicopters over our heads. But as soon as Major Kraske issued a formal statement about the investigation, which we had to do given the seriousness of the crime, it became the biggest story in the region. The next morning the *Seattle Post-Intelligencer* would greet its coffee-sipping subscribers with a bold headline: 3 DEAD WOMEN FOUND IN, NEAR GREEN RIVER.

The front-page story wouldn't contain the name Ted Bundy, but it would leave the clear impression that someone had embarked on a very aggressive killing spree, which the police had been unable to stop. This early coverage would establish the media's tone for years to come: Another devil was on the loose, and once again the cops were unable to stop him.

As investigators, we could brace ourselves for the criticism that the media would inevitably stir up. But we didn't have the luxury of stopping to worry about it. There wasn't time. On the night after the bodies were discovered, we fanned out to tap informants and other sources. A sergeant and I paid a brief visit to a woman named Michele Marshall, who was married to Debra Bonner's pimp, Carl Marshall. She admitted that Debbie had worked with Carl but insisted she knew nothing about her death, or any of the others'.

It was after ten o'clock. The ME hadn't yet performed the autopsies, and most of the police offices that we could contact for reports on suspects and missing persons were closed. There was little more we could do, so I said good night to the sergeant and got into my car to drive home.

Before I started the car's engine, I knew that I wouldn't burden my wife, Julie, with all the details from my day. It was bad enough that she had had to make up for my absence at Angela's party. She didn't need to hear a gory tale of bloated corpses and body bags. I would slip into the house quietly, remove my clothes, and jump into the shower. Then I would tell her that it had been a difficult day, but that I was okay.

On the way home, I noticed that the night sky was clear and dotted with stars. I could make out the shapes of the mountains that loom over Puget Sound, sprinkled with the lights of the houses that climb up their sides. With its sparkling sound crisscrossed by ferries and the pristine mountains always in view, Seattle and King County are truly beautiful. People feel blessed to live here. I know I do.

But while the average citizen and countless tourists see an ideal place to live and work and play, the landscape I traveled that night included landmarks they wouldn't recognize. As a homicide detective, I could recall all of the murders I had investigated in dozens of neighborhoods across the region. Memories of those bodies, the families left behind, and the killers brought to justice came to mind. And now there was a terrible new place on the map, another intersection of longitude and latitude where violent death had cast its shadow.

TWO

STRANGER TO STRANGER

ON AUGUST 16, 1982, the King County medical examiner had three bodies in his cooler and no names to go with them. When I went to the lab to collect photos of the women's faces, I learned that all three had been asphyxiated — probably strangled — and that semen had been discovered in two of their bodies. That wasn't all. The two corpses that had been pinned to the riverbed with rocks had come ashore bearing additional evidence: fist-size, pyramid-shaped stones that had been inserted into their vaginas.

You didn't have to be a forensic psychologist to interpret this kind of discovery. Whoever was killing young women and dumping them in and around the Green River was blending a grotesque kind of sexuality with his violent attacks. If all the victims turned out to be prostitutes, then we were obviously looking for someone who was making a statement about the women, the trade they practiced, and himself.

We would stay silent about the rocks found inside the bodies. That kind of information might help us sift out our future suspects, since only the killer could know about them.

We also decided to keep a lid on an intriguing bit of evidence found on the body we discovered in the grass. It turned out she had scores of little glass beads, microscopic in size, on her body. Those were collected and set aside in hopes that they might one day bring us closer to the killer.

In the meantime, we faced a series of immediate obstacles. We had no witnesses, except for a rafter who offered vague descriptions of two men and a truck. Very little evidence was acquired at the river. And we didn't even know the names of the victims.

Although I had worked dozens and dozens of previous murders, I had rarely encountered so much mystery·in the early stages of a case. In most homicides, police can rely on an official piece of identification or a witness to quickly determine the victim's identity. And crime scenes, especially indoor crime scenes, often harbor very valuable physical evidence. Bullets can be traced to a specific gun. Fingerprints are left on doorjambs and tabletops. Many killers leave behind their own blood, a few strands of their hair, or a bit of thread from their clothing.

The typical murder investigation seems even easier when you realize that most killings involve people who know each other. Often there are friends and associates who can name likely suspects and testify to a fight, a disagreement, or a long-running feud that suggests a motive. A significant number of homicides involve family members and occur in homes where the police have answered many domestic disturbances. All you have to do is check the reports to get the right names.

You would be surprised by how many cases are cracked when we simply pick up the most likely suspect and take him in for a conversation. Having committed a murder and spent days wondering when the cops will show up, most people feel tremendous guilt, anxiety, and fear. They are so close to confessing that all you have to do is provide the right atmosphere. Then you say things like "I can understand if things got out of hand" or "You're basically a good guy. We know that. Just tell us what happened." Eventually one of these questions will be like a pinprick on a balloon. Suddenly the suspect explodes with information. All the facts rush out, and you've got your killer.

In every case, you pray for such a quick resolution and worry about running into dead ends. The cases you dread the most are homicides in outdoor settings where there are no witnesses, little physical evidence, and no indication of a relationship between the killer and the victim. They are stranger-to-stranger crimes. This was the situation in the cases of Leanne Wilcox, Debra Bonner, and Wendy Coffield. With all three of these women, we had only the fact that they were engaged in a dangerous profession — prostitution. We could speculate about pimps and johns, but we had little real evidence. And with the additional bodies lying in the ME's lab, we had a total of six especially tough cases, and a killer who had been very careful to leave almost nothing to pursue.

While I was in the autopsy room, King County sheriff Bernard Winckoski had been meeting with Major Kraske and other senior officers. Fearing that we had another Bundy on our hands, they decided to put together a twenty-five-person task force. Detectives and patrol officers would be drawn from other duties, and we would work under the direction of the major crimes command staff. This move would put much-needed manpower into play, and assure the press and the public that we were serious. But it also signaled to me that I was dealing with a case that would be much bigger, more complicated, and far more demanding than any I had seen before.

I felt this burden quite keenly because I was, officially, the lead detective in all the murders, starting with Debbie Bonner and Leanne Wilcox. This was the way most police departments worked back then. When you had a case, and a related crime occurred, it became your responsibility, too. There was a certain logic to this practice. In those days, long before the computer became a ubiquitous tool, we had to rely on the facts in our heads and use our own intellect to make connections. So there had to be one lead detective who was present at the beginning and responsible for assimilating all the facts. For better or worse, I was that man for the task force.

Although I would direct the activity at every crime scene, read every report, and conduct a great many of the key interviews, I didn't have to organize the entire project all by myself. My superior officers, Major Kraske and various others, would handle long-range planning and daily management. But it would still be up to me to make sure that all avenues of investigation were followed and that all of the information that was gathered was processed and correlated. We were going to generate an enormous volume of data, and I would have to keep up with it all.

The first thing we needed to do was identify the three bodies recovered on Sunday. We checked our own records on runaways, missing persons, and previously arrested young women. Outside law enforcement agencies tried to help, and we received suggestions from police all over the Northwest. Every local department maintained a list of unsolved missing persons cases. If a match could be made with one of the bodies, then the task force and the local cops would make progress on two cases.

At the same time, we also heard from a steady stream of citizens who had ideas about the killings. Our phones rang nonstop as we struggled to move callers through their stories to determine if anything of value was being offered. Some of the callers gave us serious information. One had overheard a man discussing dumping a body. Another told us that his friend had recently raped a woman and threatened to throw her in the Green River. A third saw a suspicious-looking man in a baseball cap cruising Frager Road in a green station wagon. He made an abrupt U-turn when he saw police vehicles parked along the highway.

It was vital that we hear about the suspicious driver on Frager Road, but, as you might imagine, we also fielded a great many calls from people who were either misinformed or just trying to inject themselves into the drama of the case. One anonymous tipster recommended we look into a man who frequented taverns around Kent and might be into drugs. No other reasons were given. A couple of prostitutes pointed at their johns. One caller suggested that a lonely, old disabled man — he had a debilitating hunchback — should be our prime suspect. Obviously he was her idea of what a killer looks like, but she had no other reason for her suspicion. Several women told us to check out ex-husbands who hated women, collected pornography, and often disappeared without explanation.

We all took these kinds of calls, and in between, we met with every source — snitches, prostitutes, johns, and pimps — who might have seen or heard something important. Knowing that our earlier victims had plied the sex trade, we paid special attention to the nearest active area for prostitution, a section of Pacific Highway that everyone called The Strip.

*   *   *

In the late 1970s and early 1980s, The Strip had become an open-air market for those who would pay for sex. Lined with chain hotels, cheaper off-brand motels, bars, and twenty-four hour markets and cafés, this stretch of road was convenient for businessmen traveling through Sea-Tac airport, which served almost thirty thousand people a day. It was also handy for men who worked in the many industrial parks that could be found within a half hour's drive. At around four o'clock every afternoon, young women who had dressed to be noticed would start walking up and down the street as traffic built to around five to six thousand cars per hour. The activity grew as the night wore on. On peak weekend nights, you might see up to a hundred strolling women. Their customers made their "dates" by pulling to the curb for a chat with the vendor of their choice.

Every police officer who worked the area knew the dance performed by the prostitutes and johns. Once a woman got into a customer's car, he might take her to his hotel, or she might direct him to a room she had rented for the night. More times than not, however, the deed would be done in some secluded spot off the highway. Few places offered a better selection of these hideaways. That's because the airport authority had condemned entire neighborhoods around the airport and torn down the houses, leaving behind a warren of empty, unlit side streets and cul-de-sacs. Couples who wanted a quick sex act found a place to park and either stayed in the car or walked into the wild underbrush that grew everywhere. In a matter of minutes the date would be over and the woman would be returned to The Strip, where she could attract another customer.

As I write this in 2004, you would be hard-pressed to

imagine what was happening on The Strip in 1982. The sex trade has disappeared, going behind closed doors in suburban houses, and the stretch of highway that prostitutes once prowled has been renamed International Boulevard. Most of the dumpy motels are gone, and commuters who carry briefcases now occupy the bus shelters that once served as pickup points for johns.

But in 1982, The Strip was a bustling sex bazaar of a type that could be found in most major American cities. The phenomenon had several causes. New laws had made it difficult for police to enforce curfews or push teenagers off the streets. (When I started on the force, I could pick up underage kids for violating curfew and just take them home.) At the same time, huge numbers of teens and young adults were running away from their families, making it impossible for police to follow up on all the missing persons reports. Unless there were indications of a crime, missing persons reports involving adults were not assigned for serious investigation. Reports of missing teenagers were cleared off the books after thirty days, to make room for fresh cases.

Other ugly trends contributed to the picture. A crack cocaine epidemic had created a huge reservoir of desperate young female addicts. And finally, the threat of HIV and AIDS was not yet understood. A great many men and women thought it was safe to engage in prostitution. They didn't understand the odds when it came to violence and disease.

If you are wondering why this kind of activity was allowed to go on in metropolitan Seattle, the answer is the same as it was in every other major city. We never had enough manpower to shut down the trade. Those prostitutes and johns we did arrest got a slap on the wrist and were back on the streets in a day. And the community didn't press us to make cleaning up The Strip a priority. It was not a place that many considered to be very dangerous, and a great many voters viewed prostitution as a victimless crime.

But just as prostitution is never a victimless crime, the trade at Sea-Tac was never safe for the women or their customers. Pimps who promised to take care of women instead controlled them with drugs and violence. At the same time, every john who made a date was entering an unpredictable and potentially violent underworld. Sure, most of the time the exchange — sex for money — went off without any trouble. But there were enough instances when truly heinous crimes occurred that I had trouble understanding why any sane person would ever pay for sex.

Consider, for example, one of the murder cases I handled early in my career as a detective. It began when a cop on patrol got out to check a little Pinto parked in a tavern parking lot near King County International Airport, which is also called Boeing Field. The Pinto hatchback had a big rear window, and the officer couldn't help but notice a body lying behind the backseat. Sam Hicks and I were called to investigate. We eventually proved that the dead man was a john who had been killed by a pimp who robbed him at the Ben Carol Motel on The Strip. Superficially, the case simply illustrates the dangers in prostitution. But our investigation and its resolution gave me some hope that we would quickly find the Green River killer.

At the start of the Ben Carol murder case, we had nothing but an unidentified body in a car. We had no witnesses, no murder weapon, no fingerprints. We got a break when the manager of the Ben Carol Motel reported blood in one of his rooms. The registration information given by the man who had rented the room was fake, including his car's license plate number. But then we checked all the traffic stops made in the area that night. Bingo. There was a plate with the same numbers and letters as the one on the motel register, but in a different order.

To make a long story short, the plate led to a pimp and his stable of prostitutes. We found one of the women in Portland, Oregon, and after six or seven hours of talking, she told me the story. Twenty-three years later, the pimp is still in state prison. The lesson of the tale is not that Sam and I were superslick detectives. The lesson is that killers almost always leave a trail that can be followed. They rent rooms, use credit cards to buy gas, get stopped for speeding. And even in the netherworld of prostitution, where everyone is devoted to being invisible, it is possible to trace identities, unravel mysteries, and solve crimes.

These insights are not unique. Every patrol officer, detective, and sergeant who took to the streets in the days after those bodies were discovered at the Green River had had similar experiences. We believed that someone had seen the killer. Someone could identify the vehicle he drove. Someone could give us an accurate description. Someone knew something that would solve the case.

"Don't you worry about me. I'll *know* that fucker when I see him. Shit, he's going to regret it if he tries anything with *me*. I won't let him get away with it."

Like every one of us, Fae Brooks heard one woman after another blow off her warnings about the Green River killer. A longtime veteran of the sex crimes unit, Fae knew many of the women on The Strip, and they trusted her. In the early days of the task force, she met with dozens of them. None of them knew who the killer might be, but they didn't seem very concerned about themselves. Young and hardened, they mistakenly believed that their "street sense" would protect them.

Fae and I talked about this problem on a regular basis throughout the Green River investigation. No matter what we said to these women, they wouldn't get off the street and they wouldn't believe they were vulnerable. The danger in this attitude became very clear as we gradually established the identities of the three women whose bodies were recovered on August 15. The first "hit" was made on a set of fingerprints taken from one of the bodies and matched to prints that belonged to a prostitute who had been arrested by us in the past. (No doubt she thought she had perfect street sense, too.) The prints came attached to a long list of prostitute aliases: Marcie Woods, Belinda Bradford, Belinda Woodies, and so on. Ultimately, we got to the name Marcia Faye Chapman.

Marcia Faye Chapman, called Tiny by her friends, was so small and youthful that it was hard to believe she was thirty-one and the mother of three children. Unlike so many others out on The Strip, she used her money to support a family. She also maintained a relationship with her mother. Her mother was the one who identified Marcia Faye's body. She also told me that her daughter had recently had a run-in with a man who hit her with the butt of a pistol as he accused her of stealing from him. She told me that Marcia Faye had been missing since mid-July. Grandma had been taking care of the kids ever since. She had filed a missing persons report on August 2.

Much more work would be required to trace the identities of the remaining bodies. We sent photos to the FBI and police agencies throughout the Northwest. Drawings of the victims were published in the newspapers. We began tracking missing persons reports. At the same time, families of missing young women came in to look at pictures. I met with one couple, Namon and Marilyn Marshall. Their daughter — Namon was actually her stepfather — had been gone for about three weeks. They reviewed the pictures of the unidentified women and suffered a terrible shock. Yes, they said, one of them was their daughter. Her name was Cynthia Hinds.

I cannot imagine what it was like for the Marshalls as they struggled to absorb the fact that their daughter was dead, the victim of a sadistic killer. It must have been nearly as difficult for them to return the next day and tell me what they knew about her. Mrs. Marshall admitted that her daughter, all of seventeen years old, was a prostitute. Cindy had been spending a lot of time in a prostitution district in downtown Seattle, around Pike Street, and on The Strip.

As detectives interviewed more than 150 subjects and followed up on tips, we developed a list of names for the third and last body. Dental records led us to believe she was probably a sixteen-year-old from Kent named Opal Mills. I was the one who notified the Millses that we thought their daughter was dead, and I brought them in to make the identification. There is no more heartbreaking scene than the moment a parent recognizes that a child has been murdered. Like the Marshalls, Opal's parents were devastated. But when we talked about the circumstances of their daughter's death, they became defensive and even angry with me.

Although Opal had been arrested for soliciting, Kathy Mills kept insisting that her daughter had never been a prostitute. In quiet but firm tones she said her child was still an innocent, a girl who could not have been selling herself. Kathy Mills had warned her daughter about the dangers lurking on the highways. She knew about Debra Bonner's murder and had feared that her daughter would get into trouble while hitchhiking.

Robert Mills was much louder in his protests. He didn't want to hear anyone mention that Opal had traded sex for money, preferring to say that she was just a random victim. (We would learn, much later, that Mr. Mills appeared grief-stricken only when people were around. In private moments with his wife, she said, he admitted to feeling relief that a troublesome child was gone.)

There was something about the way Mr. Mills talked about Opal, the way his face looked and his posture changed, that made me think there was more than a father-daughter relationship here. His attachment to her seemed almost romantic, and he sometimes sounded like he had lost a girlfriend instead of a child. In my gut, I suspected that he had been involved in an incestuous relationship with Opal.

A gut feeling is not evidence, but the idea that a very young prostitute was once sexually abused is not so far-fetched. A high percentage of prostitutes were molested as girls, many by family members. How else does a child of fifteen or sixteen feel so comfortable ignoring every taboo and choosing to use sex to get what she wants?

I'm not saying every prostitute in the land was once molested by her father. And that certainly wasn't the case with the Green River victims. But many of the investigators in the Green River case took note of these kinds of relationships and made sure to check on these men as possible suspects. Neither Mr. Mills nor any of the others would turn out to be a murderer. But the very fact that we had to consider so much dysfunctional, even criminal, behavior in the families of the victims made our work that much harder.

Eventually our investigation would reveal that Opal was a smart but very angry and streetwise kid with a bad temper.

Her schoolmates didn't believe her when she bragged about making money through prostitution, but in fact it was true. We also found out that she had been in school with Wendy Coffield, the sixteen-year-old who was found in the Green River on July 15.

All of the Green River victims seemed to be connected by more than the fact that they were involved in the sex trade. Coffield, Bonner, Chapman, and Hinds had all worked The Strip, sometimes in the exact same locations. In fact, the heavy legwork done by the task force placed each one of them on that part of Pacific Highway in the moments before they disappeared. Finally, through our work with the telephone company, we were also able to confirm that the last call Opal Mills ever made was from a pay phone on The Strip. Three days after she made that last call, I had stumbled upon her body in the grass alongside the river.

In less than a week we had gone a long way toward solving one half of the stranger-to-stranger equation. We knew all of the victims' names. We understood that each one of them had worked on The Strip, disguising their true identities and occupying a world of darkness and mystery. Three were still of high school age. The other two were small in size, and could easily have been mistaken for women far younger. In short, they were perhaps the most vulnerable and least powerful victims a killer might select.

They were also among the hardest people for investigators to check out. By design, their connections to friends and family were weak and their movements were shrouded in secrecy. They rarely told the truth, which made reconstructing their last days difficult. And most of the men and women who knew them would deny it to protect themselves. This made sense. They were all engaged in one kind of crime or another. No matter how much we told them that we didn't care about other activities they might be involved with and that we only wanted to stop the killing, most were reluctant to trust us.

Even with all the difficulties, we were making much more progress on the victims than we were when it came to naming any suspects. Hundreds of men cruised The Strip on weekends. Very few of them bore the appearance of a killer. In fact, no one out there could say that he or she had seen someone forcing women into his vehicle or menacing them with a gun or other weapon. As far as most of the prostitutes were concerned, it had been business as usual for months on end. Johns came, johns went, and if anyone gave them any trouble, it was most likely a pimp.

In my first day of investigating Debbie Bonner's death, I had talked to a bail bondsman who knew her. He said that Debbie had complained of being threatened by a man named Mathews. The same name had turned up in a note written by Debbie that her parents had given me. In that note, Debbie had said that Mathews planned to kill her if her pimp, Carlton Marshall, didn't pay off some sort of debt.

It would be logical to think that Debbie had predicted her own murder and left behind the evidence. Interviews conducted by other officers seemed to point to the possibility that the pimps who hovered around the prostitutes on The Strip might be engaged in some kind of war. Maybe the Green River victims were casualties of this conflict, killed by a man who was determined to ruin his enemy's business.

Unfortunately, this theory ignored a lot of what we knew about the sex business. Pimps might beat up a prostitute, and they might try to poach someone from a competitor's roster. But the women are too valuable to be killed. And if one pimp was going around murdering prostitutes, he would quickly turn up dead himself.

Despite these flaws, we followed up the pimp-war idea. But when we found Carlton Marshall, it turned out that he was no more certain about who killed Debbie than we were. After trying to get us to go away — "Fuck you, I ain't sayin' shit" — he finally started to talk. Carlton insisted that he cared about Debbie. He liked her, and when she disappeared, he had been worried. The note about Mathews was genuine, he said, but the information in it was not. He had only told Debbie that Mathews was nursing a murderous rage. Marshall had lied in order to motivate her to stay out on the street and make as much money as she could, as fast as she could.

This was the way it was going to go. Leads would arise. Tantalizing bits of evidence — Debbie's letter, for example — would come into our hands. And then, just as quickly, the promise of progress would evaporate. Deceit was a way of life for the people who made their living on the sidewalks and in the motels of The Strip. Very few of the stories they told would turn out to be accurate, and we would have to pour a huge amount of time and energy into barreling down dead-end streets because some unreliable person gave us information that was only half correct.

Unreliable witnesses gave us one huge set of problems. The phenomenon of serial killing provided another. A proficient serial killer, and it seemed we were dealing with a very skilled one in this case, considers murder to be a kind of art form that he will perfect over time. (I say "he" because in almost all cases they are men.) Serial killers typically leave no evidence, speak to no one about what they are doing, and get more clever with practice.

In the early 1980s, experts were just beginning to use science, psychology, case studies, and other tools to construct so-called profiles of serial killers. One of the most experienced experts happened to be a former King County detective — and my old partner — Robert "Bob" Keppel. After chasing Ted Bundy unsuccessfully, Keppel had put plenty of time and effort into the study of serial killers. He had pioneered many of the methods used to hunt for these killers. And in 1981 he had been recruited to help solve the Atlanta child murders.

In Atlanta, Bob got to meet and confer with other detectives who had pursued serial killers in other jurisdictions. Together they helped steer authorities away from the notion that a white racist was killing black kids. They suggested police look for a black man who worked with children and may have been hanging around crime scenes. After spotting him during the stakeout of a river dumping site, police arrested the killer, a man named Wayne Williams. He was, as the profile suggested, a black man whose work as a school photographer brought him into contact with kids. He had also tried to enlist as a volunteer in the hunt for the Atlanta child killer.

By the time the Green River Task Force was created, Bob Keppel had built a reputation as a brilliant if sometimes overly confident man. (I liked his assertiveness, but some people resented his fame and considered him a self-promoter.) Bob had left the sheriff's office to become the chief investigator for the attorney general of Washington State. Middle-aged and seasoned, he was a good choice for the job, and my guess is that he got a big bump in pay and was able to work a much more reasonable schedule. No more emergency calls to view dead bodies. No more crawling around on his hands and knees to find bits of bone and other evidence. But he was still available as a consultant for our case, and Major Kraske brought him in for a meeting I attended with a host of other task force detectives.

I briefed the group about the Green River cases, reviewing the identities and activities of the victims as well as our meager leads. Detectives from other jurisdictions talked about unsolved murders involving young women, especially prostitutes. And we heard about a large number of missing persons. We went back and forth over possible links between the Green River murders and other homicides. Some people thought they were all the work of a single killer. Others thought that none of them were connected.

When it was his turn to talk, Keppel separated what I called the Green River victims — Coffield, Bonner, Mills, Hinds, and Chapman — from the other cases of missing and murdered women. (Wilcox was temporarily ruled out.) In those five he saw the possible "signature" of a single serial killer. Each one of the victims had been asphyxiated, some with ligatures discovered on the scene. Each one had been left in a sexually degrading condition, naked and dirty. The rocks placed inside two of the victims represented an exaggerated statement of the same sexual hostility.

There was no doubt in Bob Keppel's mind that the Northwest was once again the hunting ground for a predator who tracked and killed young women. The victims were a little different — prostitutes instead of coeds — but the pathology was similar. We were facing a brutal and obsessed man who was engaged in a rampage that wasn't about to end. In fact, he was likely to expand his range, traveling farther to catch his victims. And he wasn't going to stop until we caught him or he died.

Among those of us who listened to Bob talk, there may have been a few who just didn't want to accept that we were dealing with another serial killer. Nothing we face in law enforcement is more urgent, demanding, gruesome, or difficult than a serial murder case. The public fear that serial killers generate, and the fact that they keep on finding new victims, put tremendous pressure on those who are supposed to stop them. At the same time, there are few crimes more difficult to solve than a string of stranger-to-stranger homicides.

While some detectives may have wanted to deny the existence of a serial killer, others simply disagreed with Keppel's ideas. The men and women in that room had plenty of experience with homicide and had developed reasonable theories of their own. Some looked at the way the bodies were dumped and the estimated timeline for the killings and wondered if a copycat was at work. Others thought that no self-respecting serial killer (they're supposed to be smart) would have used the river for a dumping spot after Coffield and Bonner were discovered.

I could imagine that the killer might go back to the river. After all, a truly bold serial killer might indeed return to a spot known by the police in order to taunt us with more bodies. On this point, I agreed with Keppel.

But unlike Keppel, I didn't yet see a "signature" in the appearance of all the bodies. Rocks had been found in just two of the victims. The same was true for the ligatures. Only two had cloth around their necks. No, if there was any signature at all, it was in the size, age, and occupation of the women who had been killed. They were all on the small side. They were all young or looked young. And they were all prostitutes who worked The Strip. The key similarity was the victims, not the killer's signature.

As the meeting broke up, there was near-unanimous agreement that our monster was going to kill again and that he might have already claimed more lives. He would need a place to dispose of the bodies. He obviously liked the river. Maybe it was symbolic — a baptism for the dead prostitutes — or maybe it was because the waters could wash away any evidence, such as hair or fibers, that he might leave on the body. Whatever the reason, he obviously liked the Green River, so we decided to quietly stake out the section of Frager Road that offered access to the dumping site to see if he returned.

We got a lucky break when we went out to establish the surveillance at the Green River. A top-floor apartment in a small complex set back from the west bank of the river happened to be empty. We were able to post officers in there with binoculars and night-vision equipment. They had a good view of both sides of the waterway as well as a stretch of Frager Road.

The road provided the sole access to the site where the bodies had been dumped, and there were only two ways to access it — on one end, the Peck Bridge; on the other, the West Valley Highway. We hid unmarked cars, which would be manned twenty-four hours a day. The officers would record the make, model, year, and tag number of every vehicle that passed.

What were the odds that we would catch our target with this setup? They were very slim, indeed. But everyone makes mistakes. It was possible that the killer would be overconfident. He might even think that we were assuming that the river was "too hot" for him to use again, and therefore we weren't watching. No matter what, we had to keep an eye on the place and avoid being noticed.

It worked for about a day. Then, as the local TV stations prepared to broadcast the evening news, a reporter flying over the river saw our unmarked cars, which, though hidden on the ground, were visible from above. Our surveillance must have been an irresistible new angle on the story. Whatever the reason, when the anchors turned to their reporter in the sky for an update on Green River, our cover was blown. If the killer wasn't watching, he would likely hear about our surveillance from one of the many thousands who were.

We all understood that Seattle is a highly competitive news market. Reporters for our two major papers and many TV stations fall all over one another trying to get a scoop. And of course it's not a journalist's job to help our investigations. But they were human beings, too; you would think that they would want the killing stopped. Instead, they were interfering, and perhaps giving a serial killer advance warning so he could avoid arrest.

It is impossible to assess the damage done by that airborne reporter. We can never prove what might have happened if we had been able to maintain our surveillance. But I can say that the report on the unmarked cars signaled the start of a long, difficult relationship between the press and our task force. Sometimes they would help by alerting the public and encouraging people to contact us with information. But often they would get in the way, contaminating the thoughts and memories of potential witnesses and making it almost impossible for some of us to get into the field and do our work.

THREE

SAVIORS AND SINNERS

IN A TYPICAL MURDER CASE (I know there's no such thing for victims and their families), you focus your energy on catching the person who stole a life. You do it for the victims, their families, the community, and the not-so-abstract ideal of justice. With the start of the Green River case, we faced that challenge, multiplied by at least five victims. But we had another, even more urgent purpose. Because we were dealing with a predator who was out there committing homicides for sport, we understood that we had to prevent future killings. This was not just an investigation. It was a war against an enemy who used classic guerilla tactics, carefully choosing the time and place for his stealth attacks. And we believed he would attack again.

We could only speculate about the killer, basing our guesses on the circumstances of the murders and the advice we got from experts. Bob Keppel was the first to give us this kind of advice, but soon afterward, we got an analysis of our case from the FBI's behavioral science unit in Quantico, Virginia. The author was John Douglas, a man who would one day be world famous as a profiler of criminals. At the time, the whole profiling field was still in the early stages of development. But there was general agreement that killers like the one we were chasing were acting out long-standing violent fantasies of sexual control. Once they began acting out those fantasies, they didn't stop.

What profilers had to say about the motivations of serial killers was often very interesting. We could expect that our guy had been abused, humiliated, maybe even tortured as a child. As an adult he would be driven to fulfill his grisly fantasies, which were all about overcoming his lack of control as a child. The urge to control and kill was too powerful for him to resist, even if he tried. But most killers would be so lost in their need to degrade and kill women that they not only didn't *want* to resist their compulsion but actually *needed* to fulfill it.

We understood this analysis of the generic serial killer's psyche, but we had to have more specific guidance. Here Douglas was a little hard to follow. He saw the killer as both meticulous, because of the way he weighted down two of the bodies, and impulsive, because he neglected to bring killing tools and sometimes had to improvise ligatures. Meticulous and impulsive. Aren't we all a little bit of both?

After considering the isolated, watery dump site, Douglas said the killer was probably an avid outdoorsman, maybe even a fisherman who was familiar with the place. He also saw clues in the killer's choice of victims. This guy had serious sexual problems. He hated prostitutes and maybe all women, and was making some kind of statement with his crimes. And of course anyone so damaged and also dominated by the urge to kill would have trouble making a normal life. He probably had trouble holding a job or getting close to other people. I appreciated Douglas's observations. They were sensible. But most of them had already been raised in our own meetings. They didn't point us in any new direction.

Finally, Douglas told us that our target might be drawn to the investigation. Like a fire starter who hangs around to watch the blaze, he might even stand in the background when we recovered a body, or call in with tips. This was a good point, but again just a reminder of something we already knew. For generations cops have understood that people who commit a string of high-profile crimes are proud of their work. They like seeing us sweat over an investigation, and they like feeling as if they have had a big impact on lots of people. Some are even police buffs, the guys with scanners in their cars and kitchens, who get so excited by being around law enforcement that they stage crimes to bring us close.

If the experts and the profilers weren't going to identify the Green River killer, we had to hope that people who worked the sex trade, including his potential future victims, would. By "future victims" I mean the women who continued to work The Strip and other street-prostitution areas — Pike Street and Rainier Avenue — despite the danger. It was possible that some of them had met the killer, "dated" him, or even escaped an attack. If we asked the right question of the right woman, we might just get a breakthrough.

As the lead detective, I would have to help plot the strategy for our sweep, read every report, and make suggestions for follow-ups. I suspect that it was about this time that I began to develop the intense debriefing style that would eventually drive some detectives to distraction. After reading their reports, I would pepper them with questions: Does she have a boyfriend or husband? Does she drink or take drugs? What about her friends, sisters, or brothers? My mind churned endlessly, and I'm sure my obsession bred a little resentment among my colleagues. But we were all obsessed with stopping this killer, and scared that we might miss the clue that would help us catch him.

At the start of our initial canvasing of the streets of Seattle, we turned to recent missing persons reports involving women who were probably prostitutes. We had dozens on file from friends, parents, even pimps. In many instances, the person wasn't missing at all. She had run away to escape a bad situation, or she had returned and the case was closed. But among the unresolved reports were several where a woman had been seen on The Strip, or leaving home for a night turning tricks, and then simply disappeared, abandoning everyone and everything she cared about.

Retracing anyone's movements long after they have disappeared is a daunting task. But we did this with all the key missing persons files, interviewing friends, family, pimps — anyone who might know something. Since these women lived and worked in the shadows, trying hard to escape notice, we hit a lot of brick walls. For all the evidence they left behind, some of these women might as well have been lifted to heaven.

As we looked for the missing and worried about their fates, we also tracked down working prostitutes who might have seen or heard something on the street. Some of these women were worried about the killer and eager to help. They would let down their guard and reveal that they were weary, vulnerable, and scared. They talked about the lives they had left behind when they became prostitutes — their brothers and sisters and old friends. Many admitted they had taken to the street to get away from abusive fathers and stepfathers and mothers who had failed to protect them.

Although a number of the women were very cooperative

and let us get close, others couldn't stop playing the same kind of games they used to fend off vice cops under more ordinary circumstances. I'll never forget one hard-core prostitute who just wouldn't believe that I didn't care about her criminal activities and only wanted her help to stop the killings. We spent fifteen minutes haggling over the ground rules for our interview before she threw out a proposal she hoped would give her protection: "Okay darlin,' how 'bout we do it this way? I'll put a little coke on your dick and then give you a blowjob. You'll like it. I'll like it. Then we'll talk."

It was ridiculous for her to think I would do any such thing. I kept repeating that she didn't need to bribe anyone. I wasn't going to arrest her. I just wanted to talk about what she saw on the street. Eventually she believed me and told me what she knew about dangerous pimps and so-called sick tricks — johns who behaved in strange ways.

With so many detectives collecting so much information about them, it was a very bad time to be a john in greater Seattle. We questioned a lot of bullies and sadists and a few men who thought it was fun to talk about killing prostitutes. Some were brought in for polygraph tests. Not one turned out to be a serious suspect.

Part of the trouble was that our witnesses were giving us vague and unreliable statements. For example, at the county jail, I spoke with a prostitute named Sharlyn, who was concerned about an encounter she had had prior to her arrest. She told me about a man in a station wagon who had given her a ride when she was hitchhiking. She described a big guy with blue eyes and reddish blond hair who kept carpenter's tools in the car. He talked about Debbie Bonner as if he had known her. Sharlyn thought we should check him out. As an afterthought, she noted that he had demanded oral sex as payment for the ride in his car. Accustomed to the rules of the street, Sharlyn had obliged.

Sharlyn, who offered a sketchy description of a man who was nasty but not necessarily murderous, was typical of our sources. Some also blended bits of information they had learned from the case — thanks to the heavy media coverage — with their own experiences. We could never be sure whether a witness was relaying an actual experience or a tale blended with facts from TV broadcasts and newspaper articles.

But at least Sharlyn was available to talk. As often as not, the tips we received led to phantoms. On one afternoon, a task force sergeant gave me a note about a woman named Wanda Mercury who was in the King County jail. According to her probation counselor, Wanda had valuable information. But when I got to the jail, they said that she had been released. Finding her again would be tough. Wanda was probably one of a dozen street aliases she used. The next day, a missing persons report was filed by a pimp named Anthony "Pretty Tony" Lee. One of his prostitutes, who happened to be his wife, had gone out to get food and never came back. One of the aliases Pretty Tony reported to the cop who took the report was Wanda Mercury.

Although Pretty Tony and his pimp colleagues were bad characters who exploited vulnerable, desperate women, they were essential to our investigation. Many pimps made it their business to observe their prostitutes at work. They would sit in cars parked nearby, or hole up in a $20 motel room and peer out the window at the street where one of the women walked. They took note of when a woman left with a man, when she returned, and how many tricks she turned in a night. This kept them abreast of the most important matter in this business — how much money was changing hands. It also made them some of the best-informed sources we could find.

Besides pimps, young prostitutes were in regular contact with taxi drivers and other tough characters who worked on the street. In the early days of our investigation, I went looking for one of these men — James M. Tindal — to ask him about a seventeen-year-old named Gisele Lovvorn.

Tindal was the kind of oddball we often found behind the wheel of the beat-up cabs that prowl the airport district late at night. With his ponytail and leather vest, he tried to come off as a tough biker type. But he also claimed to be sensitive and caring. He said he was so sensitive that he had taken in Gisele when she was just fourteen and had cared for her ever since. Yes, he had had sex with this underage girl — they were lovers — but that wasn't important at the moment. What was important was that Gisele was missing.

In July, before the bodies in and around the Green River had horrified the public, Tindal filed a missing persons report on Gisele. He had also supplied a photograph that showed that she was a very young-looking teen with blond hair and blue eyes. She was small — under five foot five and 120 pounds. He said that she had turned to prostitution to pay for his bail after he had been arrested for credit-card fraud. Gisele was going to stop working the street as soon as she developed a string of regular customers who would "date" her by appointment, said the cabbie. Then, on July 17, she took off, leaving behind all her clothes and jewelry — even a notebook where she had written her johns' names.

Earl Tripp, the detective who took Tindal's initial report, couldn't offer him much help. Patrol officers would keep an eye out for Gisele, but in those pre–serial killer days, they had to assume that she had simply run away, perhaps because she had gotten tired of her taxi driver friend. But when the task force swung into operation, we gathered up every recent report of activity on The Strip. I went out with Tripp to follow up on Tindal.

When we caught up to him, Tindal said he had spent the better part of a month playing amateur detective. He had shown Gisele's picture around, reminding people that she had a tattoo of a bird on her breast and wore a ring shaped like a snake. He told a wild story about a stranger he described only as "a black man" who had threatened to harm him if he continued to look into Gisele's disappearance. Other than that alleged encounter, he had met nothing but dead ends. Pretty Tony wasn't involved with Gisele, and neither were any of the other pimps on The Strip.

By the time we left him, I had shifted James Tindal from the category of "source" to "possible suspect." This didn't mean we had real evidence that he had killed anyone. Further work would have to be done to rule him in or out. However, he fit part of the killer profile we were working from — underemployed, familiar with the area, highly interested in the Green River investigation. He also seemed a bit inconsistent in his concern for Gisele. Maybe he truly cared for her as a runaway teenager, but he had also exploited her for sex and money.

How could a fourteen-year-old girl — pretty, bright, and energetic — fall in with a much older man who used her for sex and couldn't even earn enough money to keep her out of prostitution? Consider the girl's situation. When she met him she was probably frightened, traumatized, and desperate for food, a place to stay, and a little human comfort. Out on the street, he may have been the nicest man she had met in a long time. He must have looked good to her. This is what one of our witnesses, another girl who had fallen in with Tindal, told us after we tracked her down. This street kid really got to me as she described some of the sexual acts that her "savior" had persuaded her to perform in exchange for his attention. After the interview, we were able to get her back into her foster home, but I worried that she had already acquired some fairly twisted ideas about what passes for normal in the adult world.

Tindal's type can be found wherever runaway kids go. Men like him imagine themselves to be heroes, providing safety and shelter for kids adrift in a world of evil sinners. Many of them "like" kids a little too much and wind up having sex with them — with both boys and girls. They might also get them hooked on drugs and alcohol and then steer them into prostitution to support the habit.

In 1982, downtown Seattle was home to a significant population of down-and-out kids who would be vulnerable to the Tindal types. Hundreds hung out in parks and slept in secret places like highway overpasses and sheltered loading docks. Many fell into the clutches of the self-appointed saviors who cruised the center city area, from the Space Needle to Pioneer Square.

On September 6, a couple of street kids named Pinkie and Shannon came into our downtown Seattle office and spoke with Detective Bob LaMoria. Bob, who had gone with Sam Hicks and me on that long hike to recover a body in the mountains, was easy to talk to. Pinkie and Shannon opened up to him, sharing their concern about two men they knew from the streets. One, a taxi driver they called Melvyn, lived down near Olympia but was always in Seattle, hanging around with runaways and street kids. He had warned them to stay away from another cab driver named Dan Smith, who drove for a company in the community of Federal Way. According to Melvyn, Smith was a bad guy who had talked about killing the women found in the Green River.

It was after 7:00 p.m. by the time the kids left. Bob was way past the end of his shift. He handed the tip to me. As he left, I called our surveillance team and asked them to look for Dan Smith's cab. I then read some more reports and, when I couldn't concentrate any longer, straightened up my desk and headed for my car. I would be back in the office in about nine hours. I rode home, thinking about all the material we had gathered, all the leads we were following, and the mountains of information I had to assimilate.

Every member of the task force was working double shifts, following up every tip that came in and every lead that flowed from the interviews we conducted. We contacted the family, friends, and schoolmates of every victim. We talked to people who owned businesses on The Strip. We consulted probation officers, school principals, landlords, hotel desk clerks, waitresses, and bartenders. At the same time, patrol officers were part of the effort, picking up prostitutes and pimps, taking names, writing reports, and making arrests.

Some of the stuff we chased was just plain bizarre. Female construction workers on a crew working near the Green River reported that two men had driven by in an old brown Nova, throwing women's purses at them. Five were recovered. One contained used sanitary napkins and human waste. Of course we had to follow up.

We also had to investigate three anonymous notes telling us that a former police officer nicknamed Tonto was the Green River killer. The man named in the letters had been caught having sex with a sixteen-year-old in a city vehicle. Of course we had to spend manpower checking him out. We even sent the notes to the state crime lab. We were told the former police officer had been one of Debbie Bonner's johns, but we found nothing connecting him to any of the killings.

All of these details filled my mind, alongside the names that echoed in my ears. Wilcox, Bonner, Tindal, Melvyn. That last one, Melvyn, rang some sort of bell. Yes, he was the guy those two kids had discussed with Bob LaMoria, but there was something more, I felt. I had come across that unusual name someplace else. And it had been recent. As I pulled into the driveway, I made a mental note to check it in the morning.

I don't have any real vices, unless you count certain sweets — chocolate gets me every time — and that's probably a very good thing. Some people turn to drink or drugs to get through the strain of something like Green River. I relied on my wife, Julie, who was very supportive, and a stress-reducing exercise regimen.

I have always enjoyed working out, and when I became a cop, I made it my job to stay in shape. It was part of staying safe and maintaining my ability to protect others. On many mornings these workouts also offered moments to reconnect with my children. I would wake up, put on some motivational music — the Pointer Sisters or Oak Ridge Boys — and one or more of them would toddle in to talk or sing along. Often we'd break into some crazy dancing, which would lead to a lot of giggles and laughter. I always got my exercise in, but the kids made sure my sense of humor got a workout, too.

On the morning of September 7, I was up so early that I had finished my exercise routine and showered before anyone else in the family was even stirring. I then drove to the Lucky Spot Tavern — a place that catered to the least lucky people you can imagine — in Tacoma. Debbie Bonner used to hang out there, and I wanted to talk to the bartender, Shorty. Although the tavern had opened for the morning trade, Shorty wasn't around, so I went to the task force office with the name Melvyn on my mind.

After an hour of sifting through records, I found it — a tip sheet with the name Melvyn Foster. He had called us to say we should investigate — you guessed it — Dan Smith. I asked our intelligence unit to get me a report on Foster, and they came back saying he lived near Olympia, just like the Melvyn the two street kids had described.

To be sure, we tracked down Smith and brought him in for questioning. We showed him photos of the victims, and he insisted he didn't know any of them. He went on to say that he had nothing to do with the Green River killings and he would be happy to take a polygraph. As he predicted, the test showed he was telling the truth about everything. That left one big unanswered question: Why was Melvyn Foster saying that Smith was a likely suspect?

It took a couple of days, but eventually Bob LaMoria and I pieced together the truth about Foster and Smith. It turned out that Foster had never seen or heard anything that could connect Smith to Green River. Smith was just one of many denizens of Pike Street who was probably up to no good. Yet Foster was obviously intent on spreading the word that Dan Smith was a possible serial killer. And he was equally determined that we hear the same charge and investigate it. He even volunteered to go out and collect people who would come to us and second his opinions. With his talk on the street and adamant statements about Dan Smith, Melvyn Foster was a little too interested in the Green River case and a little too eager to help us pin the murders on Smith.

Police departments in other jurisdictions had sent us reports on Foster that made him a more serious concern. Just as the forensic profiles predicted, he had been in trouble with the law — two terms in prison for auto theft. His employment record was spotty, and he had a terrible track record with women, marrying and divorcing four different women he had met when they were teenagers. He was also fascinated by life on the street and frequented areas where prostitution flourished.

Detective LaMoria and I both saw the red flags with Foster. We grew even more suspicious when Pinkie rushed in to report that Shannon was missing. Fortunately, we soon discovered that this was a false alarm. Shannon had been arrested by the Seattle Police Department vice squad and was in juvenile detention.

None of us could be blamed for worrying about Shannon. The whole Pacific Northwest was terrified of the serial killer, and we all feared that additional murders were taking place. As frustrated as we felt about not catching the killer, we were also grateful that no more bodies were turning up. We could hope that this particular madman had defied the experts and simply stopped. Or maybe the killer was someone already in our sights, someone who knew our investigation was running at full power and was trying to throw us off his trail.

Melvyn Foster acted like he had nothing to hide. He agreed to come in for a lie detector test, and even arrived twenty minutes early for the appointment. He was an old-looking forty-four. He had slicked-back black hair and was dressed in a leather jacket and boots, and he was very talkative. He liked flowery language and would always use a three-dollar word when a fifty-cent one would do. He talked about himself as if he were a kind of superhero, a big strong guy who jumped into fights to protect the innocent and used his physical presence to intimidate bad guys. In this, he seemed a little deluded. He couldn't have weighed much more than 150 pounds, and whatever muscle he may have once possessed had obviously withered while he spent long days and nights driving a cab.

I had told him that the lie detector test was routine, and that he shouldn't be concerned. It was also routine to conduct an interview beforehand in order to establish a suspect's story and help us devise the questions the polygrapher would pose.

In our previous conversation, Melvyn had said he knew Debra Bonner. But when we handed him photos of other Green River victims — Coffield, Mills, Chapman, and Hinds — he said he didn't recognize them. Then we showed him pictures of other known prostitutes, and he seemed to know a lot of them. He said that night-shift cab drivers know all the women on the street. They jump in to get warm, offer services to drivers on a slow night, and use the cabs to take their tricks to motels.

As the interview continued, we focused more on Foster's lifestyle. We asked him about the two teenage girls he had brought to live in his house. Where had he been in the month of August?

Suddenly Foster asked why the polygraph was being delayed. "Why all the questions?" he inquired. "Just let me show you that you're wrong." After we agreed to stop the interrogation and let him take the polygraph, we gave Foster some coffee and left him alone. I called the FBI behavioral science unit in Quantico, Virginia, where a consultant told me to pressure Foster a little by making him think we had a lot of evidence pinning him to the killings. We used this advice as we worked up the questions for the polygraph operator. Half an hour later, Foster got wired up and began answering the questions. It didn't take long for the machine to tell us that he was lying when he said he didn't know the identity of the Green River killer and that he had had nothing to do with the murders.

When we got back to the interview room, we first talked a little about the test and the story he had told. When I felt the time was right, I let him know that he had failed. He said it was impossible. The machine is 90 percent accurate, we answered. Then he said he must be part of the 10 percent. If that was true, Bob LaMoria shot back, let us search your house and your car.

"Go ahead," said Melvyn.

It was already late afternoon. An appointment that Melvyn thought would last an hour was entering its sixth. But he wanted this over with, so he signed releases permitting us to go to Lacey and search his home and his car. He was daring us to find something, and demanding we do it right away or let him go.

You might think that when a subject takes this kind of stand — "I didn't do it, so go ahead and search" — it's a sign of innocence. Not necessarily. I've been involved with some criminals who take this position as a roll of the dice. They're betting that you won't do a thorough search. Others are bold about giving police access to certain places because they know those places are clean. They have another location where they have hidden the evidence.

We enlisted Detective Rick Gies for added security and put Foster in a car for the hour drive south on Interstate 5. Soon after we got on the road, Foster warned us that we would find two pairs of panties in his car, under the front seat. He didn't want us to get the wrong idea. One pair belonged to an underage girl who had had sex with him in the car. The other pair belonged to a young girl who had changed her clothes in the backseat of the car. He talked about these incidents in a very casual way, as if every middle-aged man in America used his car for casual sex with teenagers and kept their underwear under the front seat.

Detective Gies, who sat in the back of the car with Foster, had brought along the photos of the victims. He took them out and began handing them to Foster, one by one. Rick suggested that Melvyn think harder about whether he recognized them.

After repeating that he knew Debra Bonner well, Foster surprised us by saying that perhaps he had been mistaken about Marcia Chapman. Now he recalled that he had met her at a restaurant in Seattle in January or February and may have given her a ride to the airport. We were all a little surprised by this admission. It was almost as if he wanted to solidify his position as a suspect.

There was more. As we drove along and Foster kept studying the photos, he admitted that he recognized Cynthia Hinds and Opal Mills. A pimp named DJ had introduced him to them, said Melvyn. Later he had seen them on the streets.

As we approached the exit from I-5, Melvyn pointed to a picture of young, blond Wendy Coffield. Now he remembered. He had seen her on Pike Street near Second and also on The Strip. A prostitute nicknamed Pretty Eyes had introduced him to Wendy, who later flagged him down for "short shots," quick trips around The Strip.

Now that he was talking, Melvyn couldn't seem to stop. He said he had never had sex with any of the victims, but he had fantasized about approaching Wendy and Debbie Bonner. When Bob LaMoria reminded him that Wendy was just a teenager, Foster was quick to tell us where he drew the line for underage sex. It was somewhere around age fifteen.

"Anyone who would have sex with a fourteen-year-old female," he said, "would have to be a pervert."

That was one of the most unusual car rides I have even taken, and that's saying a lot when you're a cop. Here was a guy who knew he was a target of a massive investigation of a serial killer, admitting that he knew almost all the victims and had thought about having sex with them. This was on top of his statements about sexual relations with other teenagers and the failed polygraph test.

Still, Melvyn Foster directed us through the town of Lacey and to the street where he lived. He brought us inside, introduced us to his father, who was watching football on TV, and the two of them signed consent forms allowing us to search the entire premises, including the yard and any outbuildings. Melvyn's dad accepted his son's explanation that we were there "to clear something up," and the two of them sat down to watch the game while we went through every room, every closet, every drawer, and every cabinet. The scene was made just a little bit stranger by the appearance of one of Melvyn's children, a small boy who followed us around with a tape recorder, narrating the search like he was announcing a ballgame. He even followed us outside, where we searched two cars and a shed.

I had hoped that we might find incriminating photos or a collection of items taken from the victims. Many serial killers have accumulated such "souvenirs" as trophies or reminders of their crimes. We found none of these items but confiscated a few magazines that contained advertisements for mail-order brides. In the car, we found Polaroid photos of nude women and some pubic hairs, which Melvyn said must be linked to a friend who had borrowed the car and may have used it to have intercourse with his girlfriend.

"I did not kill anyone," he repeated.

The search ended at 10:15 p.m. We informed Melvyn that we were taking him into custody, not as a murder suspect but because he had warrants out for a long list of traffic violations. He didn't protest as he got back in the car for the ride to Seattle. He was booked at the jail a little after midnight. I went home at 1:30 a.m., tired but more optimistic than I had been in weeks. After hundreds of tips and thousands of investigative man-hours, we had a real suspect.

In the morning, twenty-four hours after he appeared for his lie detector test, Melvyn Foster was cranky but still cooperative. He voluntarily gave us hair and blood samples and agreed to answer more questions. We decided to try something different, sending Fae Brooks into the interview room. We figured that as a woman, and an African American, Fae might shake Foster out of his comfort zone. But we also wanted to tap her experience as a detective who dealt with men who commit sex crimes. Compassionate by nature, she was able to convince these men that she understood them and that she knew they were only showing "love" to their victims. This made them feel safe, and it made many of them talk.

It didn't take long for Fae to get under Foster's skin. In a matter of minutes he was shouting at her, and cursing a blue streak. He called her a nigger and worse, and told her to get her "ass out of here before I stick a shoe in it."

I watched all of this through a two-way mirror and went to see Fae as she left the room. She wasn't much bothered by what had happened. She knew it was just part of the job. Her mere presence had rattled Foster, though he would later misrepresent what happened and say she goaded him to the point where he became furious.

When I went back into the interview room, I chastised

Melvyn and he backed right down. Even though he claimed to be furious and fed up, he didn't ask for a lawyer, and he didn't ask to leave. To be safe, I repeatedly told him that he could call for an attorney, but he kept insisting that he didn't need one. He knew he was innocent. He wanted to clear things up. "Let's keep talking," he said.

For the next few hours, we interviewed him about his background — where he had lived, his education, work history, relationships — and he responded like someone appearing on that old TV show *This Is Your Life*. He enjoyed talking about himself, and he considered us his audience. The mood was so relaxed that he even told us that he suffered from sexual impotence and that he had been heartbroken ever since his last girlfriend left him in March.

It was important for us to get Melvyn to tell us about his activities in a way that would account for his time and also lock him into a story that we might dissect to test his honesty. I left the interview room and grabbed a couple of the blank calendars that we keep around for this purpose, and the photos of the Green River victims. When I came back, he agreed to go through the calendars and write his whereabouts on specific dates. I put them down on the table. As he began writing, I laid out the photos so that he would see them out of the corner of his eye. After a minute or two, he stopped writing and reached out to pick up Debbie Bonner's picture.

"It's too bad they're gone," he said. Then he put the photo down and covered it with a blank piece of paper, like he was drawing a white sheet over a corpse.

While we had talked through the afternoon, going over Melvyn's contacts with the Green River victims, his father had come to Seattle and posted bail for his release on the traffic warrants. At 6:30 p.m., we told Foster he was free to go but said that we had more questions and would prefer him to stay. He volunteered to continue, still insisting that he was able to explain away all his connections to the murders as innocent coincidences.

We did want to give Melvyn a chance to clear himself, but that's not the only reason we had for continuing our session with him. Marathon interviews, like the one we were having with Foster, sometimes lower a suspect's defenses and lead to a confession. At the very least, they offer police one good shot at extracting new details or even pulling apart a suspect's story as he repeats and even contradicts himself.

As the hours passed and he went over and over the same territory, Melvyn did offer bits of new information He described brief encounters with Marcia Chapman and Wendy Coffield in February. In March he saw Wendy again on Pike Street. She was with a young woman who called herself Pretty Eyes. In the same month, he ran into Cynthia Hinds, Debbie Bonner, and Opal Mills.

In this time period, Melvyn told us, he had spent many nights in cheap motels around Seattle instead of going home at the end of his shifts. In May he went on a trip to California with some of the street kids he had befriended. In Stockton the parents of one young woman called the police. They checked out-of-state reports, found that the kids were all runaways from Washington State, and arrested Melvyn for contributing to the delinquency of minors. He was released from jail in mid-May and returned to Washington State.

As Melvyn finished this little anecdote, Major Kraske came into the interrogation room, holding a pair of handcuffs. They had been found in a search of Melvyn's car, which was parked outside. They were "a conversation piece," claimed Melvyn. He sometimes told people to get in the car and put them on, but he had never actually used them.

By 8:00 p.m., after ten hours of conversation, writing, and explaining himself, Melvyn had had enough. He asked to leave and was taken back to the jail for processing and release. While he was doing that paperwork, we arranged for detectives to wait outside and discreetly follow Melvyn home. Out of hundreds of contacts, no one had given us more information about so many victims. No one else had admitted to being so close to the five women. And no one else fit the serial killer profile more closely. For the indefinite future, Melvyn Foster would be the subject of around-the-clock surveillance.

FOUR

A Prime Suspect

FOR THREE OR FOUR DAYS in September of 1982, the members of the task force had good reason to hope that the Green River nightmare would be brief. Although we had several troubling missing persons reports, the number of women unaccounted for at the time wasn't extraordinary. And there had been no bodies found, no Green River–style murders in more than a month. We also had identified a very likely suspect and put him under constant watch.

However, we didn't talk openly about our hopes that we had stopped the Green River devil. It was much too early for that. We continued to operate as if the case were unsolved. For me, that meant following up on Melvyn's story. One of my first contacts in this chore was a woman named Karen who came into the major crimes unit to volunteer information about him. She said she knew many of the people Foster considered his friends, and she provided us with a long list of streetwise citizens who could complete our picture of Melvyn Foster. The lineup of new witnesses provided by just this one woman can give you a good sense of the strange and complicated world that Melvyn lived in. Among those whom Karen suggested we contact were Bambi and Breezy, two teenage girls who were friends of DJ the pimp; Bud, who also went by the name Space Case and saw everything that happened on Pike Street; Buzz, a "very ugly" guy who wore a cowboy hat and walked around downtown with a cat on his shoulder; and Wheels, a friend of Buzz.

As I looked for these characters and many others, I continued to test our theories about Melvyn. When I called John Douglas, he repeated that Foster was a valid suspect, and he offered some ideas about pinning him down. First he suggested we look for young women who may have flagged down Foster's cab. We should ask them whether he had tried to take them to secluded areas against their wishes. Families should be contacted to determine whether Melvyn had attended the funerals of the Green River victims. (People who kill for the thrill get pleasure out of seeing the grief they inflict on friends and family.) Douglas also thought we might try to take Foster to a motel room where we could stage a scene with pieces of evidence, like the pyramid rocks found in the two river victims, and see if he got upset.

The stage-set idea was classic FBI. They favor this kind of psychological warfare, believing that bad guys will crack if they see that a pile of evidence has been collected against them. It wasn't a terrible idea, but I worried that Melvyn might be too smart to fall for it. He had already figured out that we were watching him and had called to complain of harassment.

At that point in our surveillance operation, we were hardly engaged in harassment. All we did was post one or two detectives in an unmarked car near Foster's home. (The Thurston County sheriff, who had jurisdiction, was aware of this operation.) When Melvyn left the house, we followed him at a distance until he came home. We didn't pull him over or crowd him. If we restricted his ability to cruise areas of prostitution or pick up street kids, we couldn't help that.

My first few shifts watching Melvyn were unremarkable, except for some of the heart-to-heart conversations I had with fellow detective Fae Brooks when we spent a couple of cold dark nights in the car together. Like people always do, we wound up sharing our life stories. I told her about growing up in a house where fighting was considered normal. She told me about being born in Harlem and growing up as a navy brat in places as distant as Connecticut, Kansas, and Japan. Fae had graduated high school in rural Alaska, where she was the only black kid most people had ever seen.

At first I thought that the challenges that Fae had dealt with while moving from town to town and culture to culture were the key to understanding why she was so good at her job. She was an excellent sex crimes investigator. She showed so much empathy to victims that they found it very easy to talk to her, to go over the most humiliating and disturbing aspects of their experiences. That same empathy helped Fae manipulate perpetrators into making incriminating statements. She knew that they all considered themselves good guys who were merely showing "love" in a way that society would never understand. Fae let them think that she understood them and that it was safe to share their secrets with her.

I was right that Fae's youth had played a role in the development of her people skills, but there was more to it than I could ever have guessed. On a 10:00 p.m. to 6:00 a.m. stakeout shift, as the steam rose from our cups of hot chocolate, Fae explained the real reason why she was so skilled at her work. Facing new kids every few years and dealing with racism and sexism were all part of it. But the key was that she had been a victim of sexual abuse herself. When she was just a child, her stepfather had trapped her in an incestuous relationship, violating her body and her trust. Ever since, she had spent a whole lot of time trying to understand what had happened. She also put that experience, and all that she learned, to work for others.

More than most people, Fae understood that the women who were killed by the Green River monster were innocent victims who deserved everything we could pour into the investigation. They were not second-class citizens, and they were not to blame for what had happened to them. In fact, some had been all but programmed for a life on the street. Family patterns of shame, violence, and dysfunction are learned and repeated by many children of abusers. It's a miracle anyone can break the pattern. "There but for the grace of God," said Fae, admitting that she had much more in common with the women we found in the Green River than anyone might guess.

During our surveillance, Melvyn acted as if he were locked into some sort of contest with the sheriff's office. When he drove his car, he did his best to shake us. If he succeeded, he would call our office and taunt us. He bragged about eluding us on the highway and asked why we weren't confronting him with evidence linked to his hair and blood samples. The answer, he repeated, was that we had no evidence because he was innocent.

On some level, Melvyn was enjoying being a suspect. He may have thought that this was a sort of sport, and it was appropriate to try to goad us. We didn't need any more motivation, and we certainly didn't take his statements personally. But we all received a little extra jolt of incentive when, after our few days of hope, Port of Seattle police called for our aid. A dirt bike rider had smelled something sickeningly pungent as he had roared through an undeveloped area south of Sea-Tac Airport. He had looked around in the underbrush — wild blackberry bushes — and found the decomposing body of a young woman who was nude except for a pair of men's socks, which had been knotted together and wrapped around her neck.

The recovery of a body, and the search of an outdoor site where it has been left, are never easy tasks. You always have to steel yourself for the appearance of the body and the grisly jobs of inspecting it, moving it, and searching for every bit of flesh, hair, and bone. You must control your own reaction to the smell of decaying human tissue. Nothing on earth is more nauseating than the sickening odor of a rotting corpse. You can wear a surgical mask or smear your nostrils with Vicks VapoRub, but nothing will block it. Otherwise strong and able people retch and turn away when confronted by this odor. Those of us who are able to get past it and still work are blessed with an unusual ability to focus or a profound facility for denial, or both.

This search and recovery would be especially difficult because the body was only partially decomposed. In cases involving skeletal remains — like the time Sam Hicks, Bob LaMoria, and I trekked in the mountains — the pieces are easy to handle. The same is true when a comparatively fresh body is found and it retains its integrity. But bodies that are halfway to the skeletal stage tend to be quite fragile. Extreme care must be taken to preserve them and move them without causing damage.

This body was discovered on a Saturday night, so I left

home again on a Sunday morning, when I should have been going to church with my family, to direct the recovery of another body. As I drove to the site, I reviewed the procedure in my mind. We would establish a perimeter and slowly search the ground and brush for evidence until we reached the spot where the body lay. Everything we might find would be preserved as evidence, and then we would carefully collect the remains.

The light rain that fell on the morning of September 27 made the scene gloomier, but it didn't slow us down. The search for evidence didn't turn up anything significant. When we directed our attention to the body, it was bagged, lifted to a stretcher, and then removed. It was left to me and some of the other cops to get on our knees and search for smaller particles of flesh, bits of bone, and hair. To make sure we didn't miss anything, we even dug up the soil that had been under the body, and scoop by scoop poured it through a screen. It was a long, tedious process, and in the end, nothing was found.

This time, identifying the body would be fairly easy. Although dirt and decomposition had made it hard to make out when I saw the body, the ME at the lab immediately noted a tattoo of a bird on the victim's breast. On her hand was a gold ring shaped like a snake. Dental records would make it definitive, but there was already no doubt. This was seventeen-year-old Gisele Lovvorn, the young woman who had left James Tindal's apartment on July 17 never to be seen again. On a Saturday afternoon when others her age were flipping burgers, playing soccer, or cruising the mall to meet boys, she had gone out to turn a few tricks. She had become the sixth victim in the Green River murders.

Although Tindal had made a big show of his concern for Gisele, we had to consider him a suspect. When I went to see him, he immediately assumed we had found her body and demanded to view it. That wasn't going to happen. Instead, we took him downtown for a long interview, where we asked him to go over his story about Gisele's disappearance and also tried to find out what he knew about the other six dead women. Nothing he said went beyond the facts reported in the newspapers and on TV. And unlike Melvyn Foster, when Tindal took *his* lie detector test, he passed.

The polygraph didn't end our business with Tindal. In the course of our investigation, Fae Brooks had met one of the runaways to whom he had given shelter from time to time. As she did so often, Fae sat down with this young woman — a girl really — and listened as she described how the older men she met on the street gave her comfort in exchange for sex acts ranging from the ordinary to the downright bizarre. Usually these kids flatly refused our help. But this time Fae got through. We were able to get her back into her foster home, and we followed up several times when she slipped out at night. We always brought her back.

During the long grind that would become the Green River investigation, Fae and I would look back on the rescue of that one lonely girl and consider it a high point. We would also have to acknowledge that those early weeks had been eye-opening. Although we were both accustomed to dealing with the rough sides of society, and Fae had worked exclusively on sex crimes, the level of depravity and danger we saw on the street was truly alarming. Most of the young women we encountered had taken to the street as girls. So many predators prowled the city, looking for them, it was inevitable some would be snared. And once they fell in with one of those guys, there seemed to be no limit to the disgusting and degrading things these girls would do under the guise of love.

*   *   *

After a few weeks of relative calm, the press reports on Gisele Lovvorn revived the public's concern about the Northwest's new serial killer. But unlike during the Bundy era, when daughters of the comfortable middle class were killed and everyone felt the terror, most of the people who were truly frightened about the Green River murders were Seattle's untouchables, the women who worked the streets and their families.

In the six weeks since the three bodies were recovered at the river, several families had asked us to look for young women who had disappeared. Four of these women, Mary Meehan, Kase Ann Lee, Terry Milligan, and Debbie Estes, fit the victim profile to a disturbing degree. They were teenagers. They were runaways or known prostitutes. And each of them had last been seen around The Strip.

The youngest of the four, Debbie Estes, was only fifteen years old, but like a lot of kids her age, she felt she was wise beyond her years and quite capable of taking care of herself. She had been arrested and told the cops her name was Betty Jones. She was small and had been born with blond hair, which she dyed black in the summer of 1982. On The Strip she told people to call her Star.

Weeks before anyone had thought up the phrase "Green River killer," Debbie's parents had reported her missing. Tom and Carol Estes operated a trucking company from their home on The Strip, so they knew how many young women tried to make money flagging down cars and taking big risks. They passed them while driving to and from work. When some of them started turning up dead, Debbie's parents came back to remind us about their missing child and to press us to do more.

In fact, we had been doing everything possible to locate Debbie Estes and all the others. But we didn't know that she and Betty Jones were one and the same. At the end of August, Betty Jones had filed a complaint about a man in a blue pickup truck who had stopped in the area of The Strip, offered her a ride, and then brandished a pistol to force her to give him oral sex. This incident had become a significant lead, and we had officers looking for the man and the truck. But we would never hear from Debbie Estes, aka Betty Jones, again.

We were hearing a great deal from Melvyn Foster — our surveillance annoyed him — and all of greater Seattle was about to hear from him, too. On October 1, Melvyn left his house in Lacey, and a detective who was parked in a hidden driveway on the same street pulled out to follow him. What ensued was not so much a chase as a little game of cat and mouse as Melvyn weaved in and out of the lanes of traffic on I-5 and then jerked his car off the highway at a downtown exit.

Our man glided to a stop behind Foster when he got out to use a pay phone. The slow-motion pursuit continued when Melvyn got back in his car and drove around the city until he pulled into the parking lot of KIRO, a local TV station. Reporter Hilda Bryant was standing outside with a camera crew. Bryant and the crew ran down the block to our unmarked car, put the microphone and camera in the detective's face, and asked him what he was doing to Melvyn Foster.

That evening the television audience got to see our cop's flustered response and listen to Foster laugh. Those who didn't watch KIRO got Melvyn's take on the situation from interviews he gave to the newspapers. The *Post-Intelligencer* story noted that Melvyn knew five of the six Green River victims and reported the fact that he had failed a polygraph. The paper allowed Melvyn to claim he was a guardian of Seattle's street kids, but then added that he had accepted "sexual favors" from prostitutes in exchange for cab rides. Our official statement said that he was "under suspicion." Melvyn declared, "I haven't done anything."

It was hard to understand what he was up to. In all my experience with murder suspects — including many who were innocent — not one had gone to the press to announce that he was under investigation. Most were so worried about what it would do to their reputations and relationships that they tried to keep their contact with detectives secret. They wouldn't even tell their friends and family.

Why did Melvyn do what he did? It's possible he thought that by taking a very public stand early in the process he could get his complaint about unfair treatment on the record. Later, if things got tight for him, he could say, "I told you way back when that they were after me for no good reason. I'm being railroaded."

I think it's more likely that Melvyn loved the attention and had trouble controlling his impulses. In more than four decades on this planet, Melvyn Foster had never been at the center of anything big. He was a former car thief who scraped by driving a cab and got his kicks with teenage girls. Then he injected himself into the Green River investigation and got caught up in the excitement. Never a man of good judgment, he had gotten the idea of driving to KIRO and failed to think through the consequences.

One consequence was that we decided to continue the surveillance, even if that meant he would get more upset.

One morning when he came out of his house, he saw Fae and me parked on the street near his house. He went back inside to retrieve a baseball bat and then stormed toward us. I started the engine and looked in the rearview mirror. When he got close enough to raise the bat over his head, I jerked the car forward. He kept coming. I waited again and then pulled away as he swung. We did this three or more times, and couldn't help but chuckle, until he stormed off in a rage.

Though he was easy to unnerve, Melvyn was a quick study. The next time he decided to confront us, he slipped out the back of his house, loped through the neighborhood, and came up behind Detective Pat Ferguson, who was parked on a side street. Pat heard the footsteps, saw Melvyn behind him, started the car, and drove away. Melvyn ran to his own car, got in, cranked the engine, and took off.

On this particular night, we happened to have blanket coverage on Melvyn's neighborhood. Fae and I were in another car, and a detective named Larry Gross had been hanging around on a motorcycle. We all saw Ferguson leave and were surprised to see Foster take off after him.

"I'm being chased by Melvyn," said Pat over the radio. I looked at Fae, and she smiled as I pulled out to join them.

Ferguson, who was in a clunker that belched blue smoke, drove straight to the interstate and headed north like a bat out of hell. Melvyn, who was also driving an old, beat-up car, somehow managed to keep up with him. We traveled for several miles — Ferguson followed by Melvyn, followed by Fae and me, then by Detective Ben Caldwell and Major Kraske in another car, and then by Larry on the motorcycle.

Pat was able to shake Melvyn and pull off the highway. Melvyn went flying past the exit, got off at the next one, and turned back toward his home. After we saw that Foster was done, we joined Ferguson in a parking lot. We all had to get out and laugh before we could go back to work.

Always willing to play every hand to the last card, Melvyn later called the Thurston County sheriff to report that he had been involved in a dramatic and dangerous high-speed chase. According to his version of events, there were bullets flying and near-collisions with regular traffic. None of this was true, of course, but their dispatch center called us to make sure.

It may seem strange that we laughed about some of what happened with Melvyn. But it's impossible to work so long and so hard on such a difficult case without moments of humor. This doesn't mean we were lighthearted about the investigation. I took it very seriously when a threatening note was taped to the door of my house by someone who knew all about our involvement with Foster. In very flowery language, it warned that something bad was going to happen to my family.

For the next few months, my children went back and forth to school in a school bus followed by a police car, and officers were posted at my home whenever Julie and the kids were there. On the surface, the kids took this in stride. Sometimes they were excited by it. But they were also worried. Tabitha, age seven at the time, made private plans for what she might do if a bad guy broke into the house. After testing different places, she decided she would run and hide in the cabinet under the bathroom sink. She tried it out a few times and found that she could get inside and close the double doors completely. Other kids might hide under the bed, she thought, but that was too obvious. Who would think that a person could hide in a bathroom vanity?

At the time, the kids didn't tell me much about these worries. The practical steps we took minimized the danger posed by these letters. In fact, we all took the threats in stride and tried to go about our lives as if nothing were wrong. I certainly believed that I was as strong as a rock and handling the stress well. It was only many years later that Julie told me that about this time, I began to have a lot of trouble sleeping. I was so exhausted that I didn't have any trouble falling asleep. But I tossed and turned all night long. Even in my sleep, I was trying to catch a killer.

FIVE

A CIRCLE OF EVIDENCE

EXCEPT FOR GISELE LOVVORN, who had disappeared weeks before we put Melvyn Foster under surveillance, we had discovered no new victims since that awful day on the river. This meant that one of three things had happened: Foster was our man, and we had stopped him; Foster wasn't the killer, but the fact that we had twenty-five detectives on the hunt had forced the real monster into hiding; or more murders were taking place, but we weren't aware of them because the killer had gotten better at hiding the bodies.

What we knew about serial killers and their compulsions told us that option two was the least likely choice. It's almost impossible for these guys to stop once they overcome the inhibitions that once restrained their desire to kill. So we had to believe that if we were wrong about Melvyn Foster, we would eventually have more bodies on our hands, and among them would be some of the women who for the moment were runaways and missing persons.

In the meantime, we could use the period of calm to pursue other suspects and dig a little deeper into Melvyn's background and what he had told us about his recent activities.

On TV shows and in movies, key bits of physical evidence and critical statements from witnesses fall into detectives' laps and they soon solve the case. In real life, physical evidence is hard to come by, most people don't want to talk to you, and snitches can push you in the wrong direction. As a result, investigators spend an awful lot of time chasing down the witnesses, associates, friends, and acquaintances who might fill in the details of a crime suspect's story. Although we often discover contradictions and startling revelations that blow a story apart, our goal is to get at the truth. If a second, third, or fourth party confirms what we have been told and that helps us rule out a suspect, that's a good thing. It means we can move on to another lead.

When it came to Melvyn Foster's many tales, we faced a big challenge just finding all the young women who had been in and out of his taxi, and his life, in recent months. Runaways, prostitutes, and street kids don't have reliable phone numbers and addresses. You have to contact them through other people on the street, and *they* will pass along the word only after you've convinced them that you're not interested in arresting their friend.

A good example of how this works involved the girl name Tracy Woods, who came in to see me after she was certain that I was only interested in Melvyn and didn't want to hassle her. In May, Tracy had gone on Melvyn's California road trip, the one where he was charged with contributing to the delinquency of minors. Other than Melvyn's run-in with the cops down there, the trip had been uneventful, said Tracy. But in mid-August, he had said some things on the phone about the Green River murders — how he had known the victims — that had made her think twice.

A lot of people like to connect themselves to big events. They recognize a name in the newspaper and start acting like they are in the know so they can impress their friends. For this reason, it was important to know whether Melvyn's big talk came after the killings hit the press or before. At first Tracy said the conversation occurred on August 17, which meant that Melvyn could have plucked the names out of the newspaper. Then, as I carefully avoided making any leading remarks, she began to reconsider. August 17, the Tuesday after the bodies had been found, might not be right, she concluded. Her conversation with Melvyn had probably taken place on the fourteenth, the day before anyone knew there were two bodies in the river and one on the bank.

Tracy wasn't the only source who connected Melvyn with the Green River victims. A cab driver nicknamed Punkie said Melvyn had ridden with Wendy Coffield in her cab many times during the month of March. And we were also beginning to get some physical evidence that pointed to Melvyn. The state lab had reported that Foster's hair was similar to hair found at the Green River site. The tests that could be done in 1982 were not definitive, but they did not rule Melvyn Foster out either.

With so much at stake, it was important for us to move slowly and weigh the value of everything we had against the quality of our sources. When I added it all up at the end of October, I had a list of what you might call "Foster factors" that included the following, in descending order of importance:

- Foster had failed his polygraph.
- He flip-flopped on knowing the victims. First he said he recognized only Debbie Bonner. Later he admitted to knowing all the Green River victims.
- Hair similar to Foster's was found at the Green River dump site.

- The FBI serial killer profile matched Foster in some ways.
- Tracy's and Punkie's statements linked him to the victims.
- A woman who had lived with Foster in the late 1970s told me he kept a large collection of newspaper articles about murders.
- Women's underwear and photos of nude women had been found in his car.

These elements, all produced through time-consuming investigation, formed a circle around Melvin Foster that was almost complete. If we wanted to fill in the gaps, we would need the full force of a court order to get telephone records, bank records, and credit-card receipts and to perform a second and more thorough search of Foster's home and vehicles.

The petition that we began developing to get the orders we needed would make a little bit of history. For the first time in Washington State, and perhaps the first time anywhere, a criminal profile would be submitted as evidence, along with an affidavit suggesting that a specific suspect matched it. The court would soon agree and give us the authority we needed.

But while we hoped that the additional investigative powers those court orders supplied would lead us to a quick arrest and indictment, we never rested when it came to other leads. In fact, while we were making every effort to pursue the Foster end of the case, I also screened leads that came in from as far away as Saskatoon, Canada. When police there arrested a man who tried to bring a gun onto an airplane, he talked on and on about Green River. While the Saskatoon tip went nowhere, another one was so ripe that I had to travel to California to make sure that the

Green River killer wasn't sitting in a prison there on unrelated charges.

The initial tip came from the Seattle Police Department. They told us about a suspect named John Hanks who was connected to a couple of assaults that had the earmarks of the Green River killings. They could have been failed murder attempts. When we asked our patrol officers and detectives to start looking for him, they turned up a few signs that he had been in the area, including a bunch of receipts for porn rentals at a local video store, but no one had seen him in weeks. Finally we discovered he had recently been taken into custody on warrants in Solano County, about two hours north by car from the Bay Area.

Bob LaMoria and I went together to the prison at Vacaville, California. We were both impressed by the man we met in a tiny interview room. At five foot nine and two hundred pounds, John Hanks was big enough to intimidate and overpower women the size of our Green River victims. When we started talking, he showed he was bright enough to manipulate them into a false sense of security.

Although we had said we were there to talk about assaults back in Seattle, he knew we wouldn't have come all this way for that. He wouldn't relax until I told him that we also wanted to talk about "some murders around the Green River."

"Well, I don't know *nothing* about that," he said, and he offered to take a polygraph to prove it.

Clearly a man with experience in the criminal justice system, Hanks immediately began to talk about how the test would clear him. But he was still worried. He said that if he heard too much about the Green River case, it might affect him when he was taking the lie detector test. He stopped the interview, insisting that he would continue only after a poly-graph session cleared him of suspicion.

We had heard one other suspect make noise about his in-nocence, demand a polygraph, and fail, so we made no as-sumptions about Hanks. He could be telling the truth, or he could be betting that he could beat the machine. We had no choice but to go along with his demands.

While we waited for a test to be arranged, we visited Hanks's family and looked for evidence in the belongings he had left at a former residence. We found none. We also arranged for a court order to take blood and hair samples from Hanks. Getting him to comply was a difficult matter. He protested to prison officials, and we had to get the judge who signed the court order to back us up.

Finally, three days after we first visited at the prison, Hanks's lawyer informed us that the polygraph test was off. It would take several more weeks to establish the ground rules for the polygraph. When it was finally conducted, I had to wonder what all the fuss had been about. Hanks passed it with no problem.

During the time I spent in California, the Foster investiga-tion continued. I returned to find that his phone records had been obtained by other task force detectives, and they seemed to clear up the confusion over when he had talked to Tracy Woods. They showed that he had made one call to her on the thirteenth of August and another on the fifteenth. The next calls were placed to her a week later. If Melvyn had been talking about the murders at a time near their discov-eries at the river, it was *before* the news broke and the public learned about them.

Soon we could add more circumstantial evidence to our case against Melvyn. We found a neighbor who said she had taken care of Foster's two children from August 13 through the fifteenth, leaving Melvyn free to roam around the region. Another source told us that Foster had been overheard talking to Gisele Lovvorn about joining him in a hot bath just prior to her disappearance.

The weight of all our discoveries, from the failed polygraph to Foster's apparent involvement with every one of the victims, led to two important decisions. At ranks high above mine in the sheriff's office, commanding officers had concluded that the task force had achieved its purpose and could be disbanded. We had ceased to find new bodies. We had our man, or so the thinking went. And the detectives and patrol officers were needed for other duties. (Unbeknownst to me, Sheriff Winckoski was on his way out, and county officials had been complaining to him about the cost of the task force. Whether this had anything to do with the shutdown, I may never know.)

The second major development came from the courts. In mid-November a judge considered all the information and evidence we had compiled and authorized another search of Foster's house in Lacey. A few days before Thanksgiving, about a dozen men and women from the sheriff's office went to conduct the search. We closed off the street and set a troop of Explorer Scouts to the task of searching the two and one-half acres of land around the house. Detectives went into and searched a large shed, even pulling up the floorboards to look underneath.

Inside the house, we inspected every square foot of carpet and every closet, cabinet, shelf, and drawer. We turned over mattresses, shook out the bedding, and lifted up sofas and chairs. We collected hair and textile fibers and vacuumed carpets to collect microscopic evidence. Everything we found would go to the crime lab.

While we were searching, we could hear helicopters circling overhead, so we knew that Melvyn Foster had notified the press that we were there. When we finally left the house, we saw that the street just past the barricades had been jammed with vans from TV stations and cars belonging to reporters and photographers. Some of the TV crews were preparing to transmit live reports back to stations in Seattle. We followed policy, keeping quiet about the purpose of the search and what we may have found. But Melvyn had a field day, standing for one interview after another.

As we left Lacey, I knew that it would be the last major operation of the task force. The following day, I would be the only detective assigned to the case full-time. All the records — thousands of pieces of paper — would be moved out of the major crimes office, where the task force had worked, and into a lonely little space wedged between two floors of the courthouse.

The space, on what was called floor 1-A, was a windowless alley roughly eight feet wide and twenty-five feet long. It had once been called the Bundy Room, and during that investigation its walls had been covered with maps, photos, and charts relating to that case. When I got up there, it was empty except for half a dozen very old wooden desks and some old gym lockers. I took the last desk in the back and buried myself in the piles of paperwork that still needed to be processed.

Along with all the paperwork, I was still expected to monitor missing persons cases, maintain intermittent surveillance on Melvyn (I would tap other cops to help with this duty), and field reports that came from our sources and other jurisdictions.

The tidal wave of information that came to us after we put out bulletins on the Green River case brought with it glimpses into an underworld of suffering, perversion, and death. Up and down the West Coast, predators were killing prostitutes, runaways, and young women who had simply met up with the wrong men. In San Francisco, for example, two bodies had been found with objects inserted in their vaginas in the same way the Green River killer left rocks in two of his victims. In British Columbia, three women had been found strangled, and one, in the city of Richmond, had been hidden in a river, like those we discovered on August 15.

If these kinds of reports weren't enough to make you feel like the world was a dangerous place for the innocent, all you had to do was leaf through the transcripts of the dozens of interviews we had done with suspects and witnesses. There you would find rapes, child pornography, attacks on crying infants, kidnappings, and sadism. In the aftermath of the publicity about Green River, more than one rapist had mentioned the murders during an attack on his victim.

Given the torture inflicted on women and children, it was easy to conclude that there was a hell on earth, and it was ruled by psychopaths who disguised themselves as mild-mannered, middle-aged men. Certainly it occurred to me, as I waded through all the reports, that young women needed to be protected and warned away from dangerous situations. My own daughters were still grade-schoolers, and I was already a pretty firm parent. But there was no doubt, once the Green River case began, that I would be an extra-vigilant dad for the rest of their lives.

SIX

STALLED

As autumn turned into the winter of 1982–83, I continued to process the mountains of information the task force
had collected and built a file on Melvyn Foster for the prosecutor. After months with the task force, with all its manpower and activity, I felt strange to be working alone in the
isolation of floor 1-A. But I wasn't the only member of the
sheriff's office who felt a little adrift. In December, Sheriff
Winckoski quit, leaving a vacuum at the top. The new sheriff, Vern Thomas, wouldn't take the helm for another four
months.

Staying true to form, Melvyn continued to involve himself in the case in a way that would have seemed strange if
we were dealing with any other suspect. He contacted the
attorney general to ask that I be taken off the case and called
the sheriff's office repeatedly to say he was impatient with
the slow pace of the work being done by the state crime lab.
He often stopped to talk to officers conducting surveillance.
Once he turned up at a rural murder scene where Thurston
County sheriff's deputies and detectives were dealing with
the body of an elderly man. We never found out how he

knew a body had been found at that very isolated site and that police were at work there.

Not content with his law enforcement contacts, in February 1983, Melvyn appeared on a local television show called *Town Meeting* to complain about how difficult his life had become once the public knew he was a suspect. He didn't mention that he was the one who had gone to the press in the first place; nor did he say anything about how he had injected himself into the investigation over and over again. After the broadcast, we heard that he contacted F. Lee Bailey to see if he could get on the celebrity lawyer's TV program, where he could take a polygraph test in front of a national audience.

Strange behavior and odd occurrences are to be expected in serial killer cases, and I was dealing with plenty of both. One citizen who wanted to be helpful called to say that she knew a man who hated the color green so much that he had killed one of our victims because she was dressed in green and dumped her in the Green River as some sort of statement about its name. I reassured her that none of our victims were found wearing that color and thanked her for her concern.

While I never heard again from the lady who was focused on the color green, I had repeated contact with a middle-aged woman named Barbara Kubic-Patten, who was fixated on the Green River killings and claimed to be both a private investigator and a psychic. In fact, she was the kind of person we often find hanging around crime scenes and interfering with investigations out of curiosity and a misplaced sense of his or her own importance.

In one conversation after another, Kubic-Patten warned me that I was in grave danger. She said she had experienced a psychic vision in which I was killed while I was seated in a green — there's that color again — automobile. She said that the Green River killings had nothing to do with prostitution and that her psychic abilities had given her advance notice of Opal Mills's murder.

Nothing that Barbara Kubic-Patten said led me to believe that she had supernatural abilities. However, she had struck up a relationship with Melvyn Foster, and every time she saw him, she then reported to me whatever he had told her. In one of their meetings, she claimed, he told her that the victims of the Green River killer would have been easy to control if their attacker had come at them from behind and twisted their arms. This causes so much pain that anyone would become submissive. This story caught my attention because one of the clues in the Coffield case, which we had purposely withheld from the public, was the fact that she had suffered a broken arm at the time of her death.

Unfortunately, Barbara wasn't always helpful. She gave people the impression that she was working for the sheriff's office, which wasn't true, and she didn't always exercise good judgment. This became clear when she said something that made me think that she had helped Melvyn discover where I lived. From that moment on, I was even more cautious in my dealings with her.

The trouble with so much of the information collected on Foster was that it was not very firm stuff. As I discussed the case with the assistant prosecutor Al Mathews, we both recognized that we didn't have enough solid evidence to bring charges. Mathews and I had worked well together on other cases. He had won the conviction of a pimp in the murder of that john at the Ben Carol Motel. And when it came to

Foster, I knew what was lacking even before Al talked about it, so I wasn't surprised when we concluded that we weren't ready.

But understanding why the case was stalled didn't make it any easier to accept. I'm a very competitive person, and it was hard to keep telling people that the circle around Melvyn Foster still wasn't closed. I was also getting a little tired of the sympathetic looks I got from colleagues in the sheriff's office. Every once in a while, a detective, patrol officer, or supervisor would go out of his or her way to look in on me on floor 1-A, where I occupied a desk at the back of the room. These exchanges all went something like this:

"How's it goin', Dave?"

"Okay. We're makin' progress."

"Well, just hang in there."

"I will. We're gonna solve this."

"I know. But I'm glad it's you up here alone and not me, buddy."

If there was a little bit of sympathy in the voices of my occasional visitors, it grew stronger when we received some bad news from the FBI crime lab about one of the few physical items that we hoped would connect Melvyn to the bodies.

Remember the tiny beads recovered at the Green River site? It turned out that some were also recovered when we vacuumed Melvyn Foster's home near Olympia. We were excited by the possibility that the beads connected him to the bodies. Unfortunately, the lab reported, those sparkly little granules come in the paint that highway departments use to mark the lines on roads. The beads make the paint reflective, and they are so much a part of the environment that we've all had them on our shoes or trousers at one time or another.

I was further discouraged by the fact that many of the women reported missing in the summer and fall had yet to turn up. Included on this worrisome list were the following names:

Kase Ann Lee, 16
Terry Rene Milligan, 16
Mary Meehan, 18 and pregnant
Debra Estes, 15
Denise Bush, 23
Shawanda Summers, 17
Shirley Sherrill, 18
Rebecca Marrero, 20
Colleen Brockman, 15
Alma Smith, 18
Delores Williams, 17

These missing young women were known or suspected to be prostitutes and were last seen in areas where the trade is rampant. In one of these cases, we had managed to collect some useful information. Denise Bush had been hanging out in a motel on The Strip when she lost a coin toss with a pimp and ventured out on a rainy afternoon to get some cigarettes. She wore a hooded sweatshirt — no coat — and left all of her belongings in the room. We found a witness who claimed to have seen her get into an old pickup truck with wide side mirrors driven by a white man with a medium build who was about thirty years old.

We had been watching Foster so closely that I had to doubt he was responsible for these disappearances. This highlighted the chilling possibility that the Green River killer was quietly continuing his depraved activities safely out of our view. I refused to believe that we would not solve the case. The intense investigation of Melvyn Foster would have to be set aside, but we were never going to give up.

I had been arguing for help all along, and after some delay, I finally got one more detective, Fae Brooks, to come back on the case. I wanted someone with experience on the street, knowledge of sex crimes, and good people skills. She had all three. Fae and I went back to The Strip to meet with more young women and, as usual, warn them about the dangers they faced. We both were dismayed to discover that everyone out there seemed to think that Melvyn Foster was the killer, that the murder spree was over, and that all they had to do was stay away from this prime suspect. Very few of the women we met were aware of how many young prostitutes had recently disappeared. Maybe they, too, had believed the danger had passed.

Although we worked day and night, often pulling sixteen-hour shifts, there was no way that Fae and I could keep up with the work that had once occupied a twenty-five-member task force. Our progress was slow, and our worries continued to grow. Fortunately, the incoming sheriff was worried, too.

Vern Thomas was my idea of a dedicated, modern cop. He had been a reformer on the city of Seattle police force, where jobs were once routinely handed out to ex-athletes and tough guys who had political connections. Thomas had fought against the corruption he found in the police department. He had been punished for it by his superiors, but he maintained his integrity. As time passed, and power shifted, Vern's standing improved. County Executive Randy Revelle, who named Thomas sheriff, had been one of his few allies on the city council. He naturally turned to him when it came time to appoint a new sheriff. Revelle expected Thomas to bring the same toughness and integrity to his new job, where his immediate priorities would include a review of the Green River case.

Smart enough to know that he didn't have the time to review Green River top to bottom, Vern gave the job to Bob Keppel. Because of the Bundy case and his work as a consultant, Bob had experience in serial murders. Thomas asked him to use what he knew to assess everything we had done and make recommendations.

Initially, my supervisor, Major Kraske, and I were opposed to this review. We worried that it was being done in response to political pressure and criticism in the press. Besides, I had been in regular contact with Keppel all through the investigation. I knew we had problems, the most significant being the lack of manpower and the widely held notion that the case was about to be solved. If Keppel was going to give Vern Thomas the kind of report that would renew the office's focus and add more people to the investigation, I was all for it.

But as much as I welcomed anything that would beef up the Green River investigation, I was wary of what any reviewer might do. It's all too easy to jump into the middle of someone else's investigation and find fault. No two detectives do the job the same way, and it's only natural to believe that your own methods are best. As much as I respected Bob, he possessed a strong ego and it was possible that his analysis would be affected by a desire to demonstrate superiority. Finally, I was well aware of my own emotional investment in the work I had been doing. For more than eight months, I had worked very long hours on a nearly impossible task. During half that time, I was the only full-time detective on the case. If anyone was going to examine it, I sure hoped they would acknowledge both the effort and the value of the work done so far.

From the start, Bob seemed to have trouble seeing anything good about what we had done. His first big complaint was about the organization of our materials. This was before we had computers, so the information was all on paper, and indexing it was difficult. Still, we had a system in place, and if you were patient, you could consult the names and subjects on three-by-five cards to find reports that might relate to each other.

After a cursory look, Bob declared that our system was cumbersome and confusing — it could be, especially to someone coming to it cold — and asked us to revamp it. Eager to get the review going, Fae and I did what he asked.

For two months we guided Bob through the investigation, including all the materials generated by the task force. Whenever he asked for a change, we did it. This included building an Evidence Master List and Chart, to make it easier to weigh what we had collected and identify similarities from victim to victim.

When Bob finally submitted his review to Vern Thomas, on May 18, 1983, it was thirty-three pages long and included ten pages of general comments, fifty-six direct criticisms of the task force's work as it related to five victims, and no fewer than fourteen recommendations for improving the investigation.

Much of what Keppel wrote was hard for me to accept. It was clear, from the very first page, that he wouldn't recognize the progress that had been made and that he was going to interpret much of what he saw in the most negative way. Although I felt my blood pressure rise as I read on, I tried hard to look past my own pride and to assess his findings as coolly as I could.

Many of Bob's specific points about witnesses we never located and tips that fell through the cracks were valid. He was also correct to criticize us for failing to seek out certain people mentioned during interviews or ask certain questions that might resolve discrepancies in the stories told by witnesses.

However, among Bob's direct criticisms were many that were simply wrong because he had overlooked reports that would have helped him understand our work better. Time and again he wrote that we had failed to contact a certain witness, or follow a particular line of questioning, when in fact we had done so. In other instances, he wanted us to go back over well-trod ground with people who had very poor memories and had already shown themselves to be unreliable. There is always a danger, when you press people too hard, that they will start making things up just to satisfy you.

Aside from these specific problems, two so-called major deficiencies in our work were highlighted. One had to do with the Evidence Master List. By the way that Bob addressed this issue in his report, you would never know that we had only just finished developing it. The other big problem related to Melvyn Foster. He wrote that in our interviews, we had failed to ask certain friends and family members of the Green River victims about Foster. He was right about this, but the problem was not as significant as he suggested, and it was being addressed.

On a more general level, Bob believed he had found a problem of attitude with some task force members. He said they had suffered from "indifference, impatience, or a negative attitude toward some of the witnesses (prostitutes and pimps)." He went on to say that this problem "reflects more on the interviewer than upon the cultural background of the person interviewed. One has to work harder at interviewing these types of witnesses."

If there were people on the task force who harbored the kind of prejudice that Bob described, I didn't know who they were. Having been at the center of the investigation from the first day, I knew the level of dedication and seriousness my colleagues had brought to the job. If anyone had ever shown a loss of focus or concentration, it was no doubt the product of fatigue, not insensitivity. We all knew that the lives that had been lost were as precious as our own, and no one ever said anything to suggest they thought that crimes against prostitutes were somehow acceptable.

With the front end of his report so heavily loaded with negatives, I had to believe some of the rumors I had heard about Bob's ambitions to take over the Green River project. Several people in the office had spoken to me about this possibility, and it certainly seemed that he was making a case for his own expertise. It wasn't until the twenty-seventh page out of thirty-three that he finally acknowledged the handicap that Fae and I had operated under: "No serial murder case has been solved utilizing the abilities and time of one or two investigators. An immediate formation of a full-time Green River TEAM of detectives is necessary."

These were the two sentences I needed to see in the report, and I was happy to come upon them, even if they were buried at the end. I was also pleased to see that Bob agreed that the Green River killer was probably still at work, and that he had changed his method of disposing of bodies to escape notice. Gisele Lovvorn, who was found quite by accident, had been dead for many weeks before the discovery. There was no reason to expect that we would find other bodies any more quickly. And the pattern set by previous serial killers — Bundy, John Wayne Gacy, Wayne Williams, David Berkowitz — showed that these men don't stop killing until they are captured.

Other recommendations at the end of the report matched my own priorities. Since serial killers tend to widen their area of operation in order to confuse police, any new task force should include representatives from all of the region's police agencies. The activities of detectives needed to be coordinated to avoid covering the same ground twice. We should begin surveillance, especially at night, of subjects other than Foster. And every prostitute booked through the King County jail should be interviewed before her release

Taken altogether, Bob Keppel's call for a new task force and his major recommendations for the organization and direction of the team were encouraging, and I hoped that Sheriff Thomas would act on them quickly. Sure, some of the criticisms bruised my ego, but I could live with them as long as I got the reinforcements. Besides, there was no time to dwell on differences of opinion. Fae and I had too much work to do, and the load was about to get much heavier.

SEVEN

A One-Sided War

In the spring of 1983 I worked to get Bob Keppel all the information he requested, and as I began the reorganization that he had advised, the tips and new missing persons cases continued to accumulate. Five young women who fit the general profile of the Green River victims, including four teenagers, were among those who disappeared in April alone. Three of them were last seen on The Strip, but a more intriguing element was noted in two of these cases — a beat-up old pickup truck.

The best description of this truck came from a pimp named Bobby Woods, who reported that his girlfriend, Marie Malvar, a five foot two, 105-pound eighteen-year-old, had disappeared while working The Strip on the night of April 30, 1983. Bobby had been sitting in his car, keeping an eye on Marie, when the truck slowed and pulled over near the bus stop where she was standing. The truck was dark-colored, with primer spots where repairs had been made to the body.

Marie got into the truck, and the driver pulled out of the lot and turned north. Bobby decided to follow and was able to pull up next to the truck and get a quick look at the man behind the wheel. The guy was white, in his thirties, and he seemed to be arguing with Marie. After traveling about five blocks, he pulled into a motel parking lot. Bobby followed but kept his distance.

There's no telling what might happen when a john picks up a prostitute, and the man in the truck wouldn't have been the first to get into a heated discussion over what was going to happen and how much it would cost. But with the Green River killings, and his strong attachment to Marie, Woods was being extravigilant. When the truck started moving again, leaving the parking lot and heading back south, so did Woods.

What ensued was not exactly a high-speed chase, but the truck did accelerate as it traveled down Pacific Highway, and Woods did the same. At the intersection of 216th Street, the truck made a sudden left turn as the signal turned red. Woods had no choice but to stop as cross traffic started to flow. He sat and watched the truck disappear. He went after it when the light changed, but in the darkness he was unable to find it again. His anxiety and fear began to rise as hours passed and Marie did not return. He thought about contacting the cops, to get their help finding her, but he was reluctant to get them involved.

Woods had good reason to delay contacting the police. First of all, at age eighteen Marie was legally an adult and had the right to drive off with anyone she chose. In fact, in the first twenty-four hours, she wasn't even missing as far as the law was concerned. Second, both he and Marie were engaged in criminal activity, and it was natural for him to be shy about pointing that out to authorities. When he finally did go to the suburban Des Moines police to file a missing persons report, he left out the part about prostitution, but it was easy enough for them to figure it out.

The Malvar case took a strange turn early on. Marie's family actually joined with Bobby Woods to go looking for her. (Even though they hated the life that Marie shared with Woods, their love for her was so strong that they decided to work with her pimp.) Woods, Marie's father, Joe, and her brother James went looking for the old pickup truck with the primer spots. They started at 216th Street and drove up and down every side street.

The search took them through a typical suburban neighborhood of crisscrossing streets and cul-de-sacs. They looked in every driveway but found no truck matching the one Bobby had seen. Before giving up, they went farther east on 216th Street, passed under Interstate 5, and turned right onto Military Road, a north-south route that cut through an area that was less densely populated, almost rural.

A thousand yards south of 216th Street, they came upon an isolated little side road called Thirty-second Place. They took a right there, and followed it as it curved back to the north. Just a block long and isolated between I-5 and Military Road, Thirty-second Place was quiet and secluded. Traffic was light, so the Malvars and Bobby Woods could take their time scanning every property. Halfway to the end, Bobby had them stop. There was the truck, parked in the driveway of a rundown little house. When Marie disappeared, it had been too dark for him to be sure of the color. In the light of day, he saw it was dark maroon. The color and the spots painted with primer were consistent with his memory. This was the truck. He was almost sure of it.

The Des Moines Police Department cops who responded when Joe Malvar called were skeptical. Bobby Woods wasn't exactly an upstanding citizen, and the idea that Marie Malvar's disappearance might be solved by a pimp and Marie's family was far-fetched to say the least. It was more likely that Bobby was engaged in some elaborate ruse, they thought, in order to deflect attention that should have been focused on him.

Nevertheless, the cops knocked on the door of the house. The man who answered said his name was Gary Ridgway. Like thousands of men in the area, he fit Woods's description of the man who picked up Marie — white, medium build, midthirties. He confirmed that the truck was his but added that he had no idea what Woods and the Malvars were talking about. There was no woman in his house, and he hadn't picked one up on The Strip the night of April 30.

Although it was hardly a routine call, the Des Moines police didn't recognize their stop at Gary Ridgway's house as something vital to the Green River case. It was just another lead, among hundreds that were sent to floor 1-A. At the time, Fae Brooks and I were still working overtime to keep the investigation going and respond to the criticisms and recommendations in the Keppel report. One task that she and I both regarded as a high priority was our work on Gisele Lovvorn's murder.

To get the fullest picture of Gisele's life, we went back to her friends and the other prostitutes who had seen her on The Strip. One of them volunteered to get in our car and show us the spots she would use for "dates" who wanted brief sexual services. The second place she showed us was in a desolate former subdivision that had been taken over by the airport authority. South of the main runways at Sea-Tac, it was very near where her body had been discovered months before.

The exact spot was along a dirt road that came off Twenty-second Avenue South. As we drove in, I saw something very strange: a rectangle of dirt outlined with rocks and a wooden cross stuck into the ground. If it wasn't a burial site, then someone had gone to an awful lot of trouble to make it look like one.

With a couple of radio calls, we arranged for someone to bring a shovel to the site and set up a meeting place where we could retrieve a camera from another officer. When all the equipment was ready, Fae and I walked carefully to the grave, and I began gently pushing at the sandy soil. My heart pounded in my chest, and Fae looked on with both dread and curiosity. A little more than a foot down, I ran into some very small bones and a skull. Someone had buried a family pet. We both sighed with relief, and I quickly covered it back up.

While other women gave us information on Gisele's whereabouts in the weeks prior to her death, we turned to James Tindal's new live-in girlfriend to find out about his behavior. She gave us enough information on potential sex crimes to get a search warrant for his apartment. On a Sunday morning, Fae and I took some uniformed officers over there and woke him up. We searched his place and found some photographs of nude young women, along with some credit cards and identification cards belonging to a number of different women. We also found a collection of newspaper clippings about the Green River killings, and a scrapbook filled with pictures of Gisele.

The conversation I had with Tindal was oddly candid. He admitted that he had engaged in sex with underage girls and apologized up and down, as if I could give him some sort of absolution. But he was very firm when it came to Gisele's death and the other Green River murders. He insisted that he had nothing to do with them and was willing to undergo further questioning, and a polygraph, in order to clear himself.

With all I knew about Tindal, I was not going to be swayed by the fact that he had been honest when it came to having sex with minors. Lots of liars try to cover their deceit by being carefully truthful about other matters. Tindal obviously saw teenage girls as objects, not human beings, and he had prowled the streets to obtain a steady supply of them. I wasn't going to take him at his word when he said that this predatory behavior was limited to using them for sex and then pimping them on The Strip for money.

Having failed to find anything that directly linked Tindal to the murders, we didn't arrest him. Instead, we went back two days later, to bring him in for another chat and a polygraph. At the same time, we collected the girl who was living with him. She refused to file a statutory rape complaint, but she did allow us to arrange for her to return to her foster parents.

Freed from the threat of a rape prosecution, Tindal performed almost flawlessly for the polygrapher. He answered most of the questions without hesitation and left us with only one possible conclusion: he didn't kill Gisele, or any of the others. When he learned this, Tindal tried to show an even greater willingness to help us. He sat with us for another hour, answering every question we could ask him about Gisele and their life together. I considered the test a useful tool. Although he wasn't eliminated, given the lack of evidence, Tindal would not be regarded as a high-level suspect.

Which brought us back to Melvyn Foster. Even if we didn't want to make him a priority, Melvyn continued to call attention to himself. Melvyn's favorite reporter, Hilda Bryant of KIRO, arranged for him to take a lie detector test. (We were told the test was inconclusive. Melvyn told everyone that he had passed.) Foster also began saying some inflammatory and even threatening things to self-proclaimed psychic private eye Barbara Kubic-Patten, who told us that Melvyn was bragging about firing a pistol at surveillance officers and locating my father, just in case he wanted to use him to apply pressure on me.

In her many calls to me, Kubic-Patten talked about Foster's familiarity with the Green River. He had supposedly picked beans on nearby farms — just as I did as a boy — and fished there with his father. He also quoted Bible verses, which he said related to the serial killer's victims, and then offered a bizarre analysis of the crimes that only a psychic might accept. According to Kubic-Patten, Foster said that the number three was the key to the murders. Three white women and three black women had been killed. This was somehow related to the Holy Trinity. And before the murders stopped, there would be twelve deaths — four times three — one for each of the ancient tribes of Israel.

Most of what Barbara reported could be set aside as the product of two poorly organized minds conspiring to produce a lot of nonsense. However, I didn't like hearing Barbara say that Melvyn felt like going to my house, kicking down the door, and beating me with a baseball bat. She also told me that Melvyn had mentioned getting a crossbow and shooting me. After these threats, the office went back to keeping an eye on my home and my family.

As the summer of 1983 passed, Melvyn decided to be more assertive. He sent a long and rambling letter to the county executive, Randy Revelle, complaining that Fae and I had harassed him and violated his civil rights "132 separate times" with activities that included tapping his telephone and stealing his mail. None of this was true. At some points in his letter, he sounded as if we were coworkers and he was appealing to the boss for a transfer. "We have a serious personality conflict," he wrote, and then he pleaded for the executive to have me taken off the case because I was causing him so much stress.

Revelle was obviously not going to take this kind of complaint seriously. He passed the letter to Sheriff Thomas, who responded with wise counsel. After explaining that the charges against Fae and me were baseless, Thomas warned that in replying to Foster, Revelle would give him "another forum to appeal to the media and thus complicate our investigation."

Sheriff Thomas, who checked in on me every once in a while, knew that the Green River investigation had been getting more complicated with every passing day. In the second week of May, some people who were looking for wild mushrooms came upon a woman's body. They were in a rural area about ten miles east of the airport and perhaps a thousand yards north of another popular fishing stream, the Cedar River.

The discovery must have shocked the mushroom pickers. The woman, fully dressed, had been left with a paper bag over her head. A wine bottle was placed on her body, and dead fish had been laid on her throat and breast. Ground sausage was piled on her left hand. A driver's license identified her as Carol Ann Christensen, age twenty-one. Her address was near The Strip.

Although she was the right age, and she came from the right neighborhood, at first it was hard to say for sure that this was another victim of the Green River killer. The body was dressed, after all, and the macabre decoration was nothing we had seen before. However, the more we investigated, the more these differences receded. The medical examiner found that Christensen had been strangled with some sort of ligature. And she had been undressed and then redressed. There were signs that the body had been in water for a time before it was left on dry land. Doctors also recovered semen from inside the body. This was the third sample we had been able to obtain from Green River victims. The other two came from Marcia Chapman, who had been found in the Green River on August 15, 1982, and Opal Mills, who had been discovered in the grass near the river that same day.

What about the fish, the wine bottle, and the meat? When I spoke to FBI profiler John Douglas, he said there was no reason to believe that this "staging" excluded the Green River killer as a suspect in this case. No doubt the killer was aware of our investigation and proud of his ability to elude us. The gruesome additions to the site where the body was found may have been a statement of defiance. The fact that it deviated from the established pattern — either no staging or rocks placed inside victims — might just mean that the killer was able to express his sickness in a variety of ways. Or he was trying to persuade us that we had two killers on the loose instead of one.

In addition to the new body, we had to respond to more missing persons reports. Connie Naon, age twenty, was last seen at a hotel on The Strip. Eighteen-year-old Keli McGinness went out to look for johns outside an airport area motel and was never seen again. Carrie Rios, who was just fifteen years old, was missing for two weeks before a report was filed.

By the fifteenth of July, exactly one year after Wendy Coffield's body was found in the Green River, we had eight bodies and knew of at least eight other young women who had gone missing under very suspicious circumstances. The sheriff's office announced that three more detectives and one support officer would be added to the case. The task force was being restored. I welcomed the additions, especially since I would help pick the people who were assigned, but I knew they weren't enough.

Three weeks after the task force was reconstituted, a ninth victim was discovered and added to the Green River tally. This body was found by a man picking apples in an abandoned orchard on the north side of Sea-Tac. The corpse had been there long enough to decompose, so that all that was left were bones, teeth, and a gold chain. Some of the bones had been broken.

Once again we had to cordon off an area around the body and make sure we recovered everything that might have meaning. Rodents had dug burrows around and under the bones, so we used hand tools to open up these tunnels to make sure we weren't leaving behind small bones that might have been gnawed off the corpse and carried under ground.

Despite all this effort, we found little that might suggest the victim's identity. The medical examiner was able to say it was a female, aged fifteen to twenty. But the woman's race and the cause of her death were impossible to determine. And even though we had recovered teeth, none of them matched the records supplied by the dentists of the women who had been reported missing. If this was a Green River killing — and I suspected it was — then the victim was someone we hadn't heard about before.

All the signs pointed to one obvious conclusion: Women were still being snatched off the streets and killed, and it was likely the work of a single evil individual. But while some in the local press, notably KIRO's Hilda Bryant, were sounding alarms about the case, in general it seemed like the public didn't much care. We heard nothing from citizens groups, and no one was organizing rallies or petitions to demand we put more resources into the investigation. (I would have been glad if this had happened.) Whereas once the murder of coeds and young women of the upper middle class had sparked a hue and cry for the capture of the serial killer known as Ted, the deaths of prostitutes and street kids were met with indifference.

I was not indifferent. Each time Fae and I followed up another missing persons report or recovered a body, my sense of outrage and frustration grew. I had become a police officer in order to catch this kind of bad guy and protect the very people who were being killed. But this devil had chosen to attack the most isolated and vulnerable women — they were practically invisible — in a place that was all darkness and shadows. I could drive up and down The Strip all night — and many nights I did just that — and he could still get away with it. There were just too many women in too many secluded hiding spots for me to stand a chance.

I took the murders so personally that I struggled to tear myself away from work, and even when I did, I had trouble getting them out of my mind. On most nights, I was able to set the investigation aside well enough to connect with Julie and the kids. But they were aware of the stress I was feeling. They could see it in my face and no doubt hear it in my voice. And no matter how hard I tried to make it up to them, they noticed that I just wasn't around as much as I used to be. This became painfully clear to me one night when I managed to get home to be with the kids. I scooped up my daughter Tabitha and we read one of her favorite books. When the story was finished, she turned to me with a serious look on her face.

"Daddy, where do you *go?*" she asked.

"What do you mean?" I replied.

"Where do you *go* all the time, when you're not here?"

"I'm still trying to catch that bad guy, the Green River killer," I told her.

"Well, do you know his name?"

"No."

"Do you know what he looks like?"

"No."

"Do you know where he lives?"

"No."

"Do you know who he is?"

"No."

"Then how can you catch him?"

Without a name, a face, or an address, it was going to be very hard to catch the Green River killer, especially since he appeared to be getting smarter. Though we found signs of sexual trauma in some of the victims, he had apparently begun to use condoms to avoid leaving evidence behind. He had also learned to use better hiding places for the bodies. The Green River was a very active recreation area, not the ideal place to hide a corpse. But the body in the orchard had gone unnoticed for so long that it had become a skeleton. And it was sheer luck that led to the discovery of Carol Ann Christensen. If not for those mushroom pickers, her body could have lain there unnoticed for years.

But I refused to believe that this killer was infallible. He had already messed up a little, depositing semen for us to discover, and that gave me hope that he would make more mistakes in the future. The need to discover those mistakes, and then exploit them, put me in a bizarre position. While I dreaded the next call about a body or a skeleton found in some isolated spot in our sprawling county, I knew that the victims we had yet to find could tell us what we needed to know.

I was getting impatient. How long would we have to wait, I wondered, until someone just happened upon another body? Wouldn't it be a good idea to go out looking for bodies? Given the way the bodies had been dispersed so far, it seemed clear to me that the killer was picking up women on the Sea-Tac strip, killing them, and then hiding their bodies in secluded spots not far from the airport. He may even have been killing them near the dumping sites. After all, these women were accustomed to wandering around in cars or trucks to find an out-of-the-way place to do their business without the police or anyone else taking notice. The perfect hidden spot for a "date" was also the perfect spot for a murder.

With this much information about the killer's territory, it made sense to me that we should start searching for bodies ourselves. We could identify vacant lots, wooded areas, and abandoned acreage — including all the property that was seized around the airport — and comb them one by one. If we didn't have enough of our own personnel, we could enlist Explorer Scouts or search-and-rescue teams.

When I proposed this idea to my supervisors, they listened and saw some merit in it. We all hated the waiting and liked the idea of taking positive, aggressive action. But it would take a large number of people and a substantial amount of time. At higher ranks it was decided to hold back on this idea. I believed there were bodies waiting in those areas and disagreed with the decision. Unfortunately, it wouldn't be long before I was proven correct.

On September 18, more than a year after the first bodies were found at the Green River, we were called to recover a skeleton found lying facedown in a boggy area off Star Lake Road, a winding two-lane highway where developers were just starting to build big new homes. The body was on the north side of the road. Beyond was a steep ravine. We marked off a wide area and brought in both sheriff's deputies and Explorer Scouts to search for any evidence that might have tumbled down there, but once again we found little that might assist us. We found no clothing or jewelry that might help identify her. The teeth we recovered didn't match any of the records we had on file.

Five weeks later, another anonymous body was found. This skeleton was located on the side of Auburn-Black Diamond Road, on an embankment that led down to a trickling little stream called Soos Creek. We found no clues to her identity, and no physical evidence related to a killer. Teeth found with the body didn't match any X-rays on file.

This last site was even farther from The Strip, at least twenty-five highway miles away. It was not the kind of place you would choose at random. But this didn't mean that the killer had abandoned his preference for dumping his victims close to where he found them. On October 27, a young couple looking for apples had stumbled on a skull in the area south of Sea-Tac. This would be our eleventh recovery of remains left by the Green River killer.

I got to the apple orchard a little after dawn the next morning. For the first time in the Green River investigation, I saw a body that had been buried in a grave that had been covered with rocks, twigs, and dirt. We removed the debris and carefully scraped at the earth. The body was in an advanced state of decay. A mass of brown hair was visible near the skull, but most of the flesh had disappeared. What little remained was chalky and fragile. If it wasn't moved very carefully, it would fall apart when it was handled.

As we scraped away the soil to expose the remains, we made a startling and disturbing discovery. Inside the pelvis, at a spot where the victim's vaginal canal once existed, was a rock shaped like a pyramid. It was possible that the rock had come from the pile placed on top of the grave. It may even have been in the earth below the body and only appeared to have been inserted because the remains had settled. But none of us who were there as the earth was brushed away and the stone emerged thought that it just happened to be there. No, it was too much like the rocks found in the victims at the river and too perfectly located beneath the pubic bone to be anything other than a sign from the Green River monster.

While we were considering the implications of this piece of evidence, we heard someone shout. Not a hundred yards from where we stood, one of the Scouts was waving excitedly. By the look on his face I didn't have to guess what he was standing over. I knew it was another set of remains.

In this case, we found no carefully dug grave, no pile of stones, and no pyramid-shaped rock. Instead, we saw a female body, almost fully decomposed, covered in trash and leaves and broken branches. It had been there long enough that weeds and saplings had grown up from between some of the bones, making the recovery just a little bit more difficult.

These new discoveries made me feel even more motivated to find the killer, and even more frustrated by the lack of evidence. At about this time, we got a little good news. Two of the mystery bodies had been identified. One, the first apple orchard find, was Shawanda Summers, who was last seen on The Strip in October 1982. The other, the body we had found near Soos Creek, was Yvonne Antosh, a twenty-year-old from Canada who had been reported missing from The Strip in May. Soon we would have names for the last two women found in the orchard. One was Constance "Connie" Naon, twenty, missing since June. The other was Kelly Marie Ware, twenty-two, who disappeared on July 18.

Connie, Kelly, Yvonne — these could have been the names of my own kids' classmates. It was certainly easy for me to imagine them as kids in school, since we had photos for all of them and they looked a lot like class pictures. Yvonne, whose hair was parted in the middle, looked shy, even a little scared. In her picture Connie had her hand on her chin, like she was thinking about something. Kelly looked out from her picture wearing a big smile and gold hoop earrings.

It wasn't so much the discoveries of bones and flesh that tortured me but, rather, the lost lives, the shattered dreams, and the devastated families. And as the death toll continued to mount, I felt almost haunted by these faces. I owed them justice, but even with the task force help that arrived in the summer, I knew we still faced enormous challenges. As of November 1, 1983, we had a dozen bodies, and I was arguing that they all were connected to the Green River killer. We also had at least twenty missing persons reports that bore all the earmarks of a Green River murder.

More bodies. More missing women. Few clues. It was as if we were in a one-sided war with an unseen enemy. He was knocking off the soldiers on our side, but we never got to fire an answering shot. We experienced all of the tragedy, collecting bodies and noting who was missing in action, but none of the satisfaction that might come with fighting back.

I was finding it harder to set aside the investigation and

rest, even when I went home. Julie and the children noticed that little things bothered me a lot more than they should. For example, if I got home after the family had eaten dinner (this happened a lot), I was more likely to complain about the leftovers I got. The plate was cold. The meat dried out.

Julie was patient with me. She even started making soups, stews, and pasta dishes that were easy to warm up when I came home late. Daniel, Tabitha, and Angela were also understanding. But I know they were affected by how stressed out I was. Tabitha would take it upon herself to distract me. She would tell me a joke, sing a song she had just learned, or launch into a long funny story about what had happened at school that day. It was her eight-year-old's strategy for making a tense moment lighter, and it worked as often as not.

I felt blessed to have a family that was able to recognize that I wasn't just a crabby guy but that I was under tremendous pressure and there was very little I could do about it. I was grateful for the help they gave me. It made our home a refuge from the Green River killer, and the time I spent with them did relieve the stress. But if the murderous devil was going to be stopped, I needed much more help during the long days and nights when I was on the job. Fortunately, help was on the way.

EIGHT

PLAYING CATCH-UP

SHERIFF VERN THOMAS sent in the reinforcements in January 1984. More than two dozen detectives and officers were added to the Green River case, giving us more than thirty-five full-time personnel. I remained the lead investigator, but there would be more managers above me, and so much more activity — interviews, follow-ups, and surveillance — that I would have to invest a lot of my time in just keeping up with new discoveries and angles on the case.

The expanded force was moved into space at the King County Sheriff's Office precinct 4 in the suburb of Burien, putting us within a few minutes' drive of The Strip. Eventually some resentment would arise over the resources we received. Any time you create a team within a team, there are bound to be misunderstandings and jealousies. But there was no way around this. You don't stop a serial killer until you arrest him, and it was obvious that this guy wasn't going to be taken down with anything less than an all-out effort.

Unfortunately, the sheriff's move to expand the task force got lots of press attention, and this sometimes made our job tougher. For a while, it seemed as if every time we left the office, reporters were waiting to ask us questions or follow us to interviews. The competition among the reporters was intense. It also led to some behavior that I thought was out of bounds. In mid-January, for example, Carlton Smith of the *Seattle Times* contacted me to say he had some information about Melvyn Foster. But before he gave it to me, Smith wanted to be assured that I would provide him with some sort of scoop in exchange. I refused to play that game.

Frank Adamson, the captain assigned to the task force, tried to deal with the media onslaught by restricting press contacts. He and Fae Brooks, newly designated public information officer, announced that they would answer all requests for information. In those contacts with the media, Adamson was generally upbeat. Others in the office were optimistic in a way that I thought might be unrealistic. They thought we could wrap things up in a matter of months. Not realizing that I had lacked proper support, they assumed that I had mishandled things and missed important evidence.

Certainly anyone who looked at the enormous volume of information that had been collected could have imagined that clues to the killer's identity were somewhere in there. And additional important information came in every day. In February, the *Seattle Post-Intelligencer* turned over to us a strange letter about the "greenriverman." The envelope was marked VERY IMPORTANT, and the message was typed, without any spaces between the words. Each line contained a question or a statement intended to illuminate the mystery.

"whysomeinriversomeabovegroundsomeunderground?"

"thinkchangedhismo"

"outofstatecop"

Included in the letter were references to facts that were not widely known. The author mentioned a stone in a vagina, the wine bottle found with Carol Christensen, and the possibility of necrophilia, which is something we had suspected. These statements were almost taunting. So, too, were lines about how "fearofdeath" was forcing women off the street. Was this the killer describing his motive? Were all the murders part of some campaign against prostitution? Or was the Green River killer a woman hater who sought out prostitutes because they were easy prey?

We sent the letter to the FBI for analysis. The only fingerprints they found came from staffers at the newspaper (four different people had handled it), and the contents practically defied a rational assessment. Could the letter have come from the killer? Perhaps. Was there anything in the letter providing a clue to his identity? No. Least helpful of all was the signature — "callmefred." In the end, the FBI said the letter was probably not from the killer.

With all the new personnel, we were able to follow up more leads like the Fred letter as soon as they came in. For example, I responded immediately to a call from a frightened young woman who requested a private meeting because she was afraid of people finding out what she had gotten herself into. When we got together, she told me that she may have had a brush with the Green River killer, and he was a prominent Seattle sportscaster.

The young woman's story began with a chance meeting at a fashionable restaurant in South Seattle. She was flattered that a locally famous man was interested in her, and she felt a close connection to him. (This may have been because she thought she knew him from hearing him on the radio over the years.) One thing led to another and soon she was in a hotel room with him. She became a bit concerned as he produced a bag full of sex toys — dildos, vibrators, handcuffs, lubricant — and then got alarmed when he started to choke her during sex. He tried to explain that cutting off a person's air supply could enhance orgasm, but she would have none of it. The incident scared her so much that she came to us.

The sportscaster didn't quite fit our profile, and if you spend enough time investigating sex crimes, you learn that this kind of behavior is not as unusual as you might have thought. Nevertheless, we quietly checked out the man's background and his whereabouts on the days when the Green River killer committed his murders and dumped the bodies. The sportscaster's work records, provided by his employer, cleared him.

Ruling out a suspect was nearly as important as ruling one in. I was glad, in the sportscaster's case, to be able to wrap up an investigation quickly, and without having to leave King County. Other avenues of investigation stretched across the state and across the country. For example, in March of 1984 I had to travel to Buffalo, New York, with Bob LaMoria to look for a car and three witnesses connected with the death of Leanne Wilcox, the young woman whose body was discovered months prior to the Sunday afternoon when we found three victims at the Green River.

Two of the witnesses were prostitutes; the other was a pimp who had worked with Wilcox. Buffalo authorities had responded to a national Teletype with a report that he was probably in their jurisdiction. They also believed they had found the car. Preliminary identification had been made based on tire types we discovered using plaster casts of tracks left at one site where a body had been recovered.

It happened that snowplow drivers were on strike when we arrived in Buffalo, and if you have ever been to that city in the winter, you know what that means. Major thoroughfares were passable, but every side street in the city was blocked. The local cops got us to within a few blocks of the house where the car was parked, but we couldn't make a positive identification because everything was under snow.

Back at police headquarters we met with the homicide night-shift detectives. If they thought we were a couple of Dudley Do-Rights, and I believe they did, then these guys were characters straight out of *Barney Miller*. They all sat at a single long table with just two phones, which they slid from detective to detective. When one of the phones rang, a cop would bang on the end of the receiver so that it flew up in the air. He would grab it and then bark, "Yeah, Buffalo PD" and demand to know the caller's business.

During the night shift in this high-crime city, what many of the callers wanted was to report a body. The detectives would go into the field, take names, collect evidence, and recover the corpse. If they could make an immediate arrest, they did. Otherwise, the case was turned over to day shift detectives who were charged with longer-term investigations.

Although they had a strange way of working, at least to my eye, the Buffalo cops were happy to help Bob and me. They had given us enough information for us to discover that our two witnesses had left town for Reading, Pennsylvania. Bob and I made plans to go look for them. The Buffalo cops said the snowplow strike would be over when we returned, so we could go see that car then.

In Reading, Bob LaMoria and I met with a city detective who knew the prostitute we were hoping to find. We went to stake out her building. A few hours into the surveillance, the battery on the local cop's radio went dead. Certain he wouldn't miss anything, he said he would cut through some backyards to reach a police precinct and retrieve a fresh one.

Of course, not long after the Reading detective was out of sight, the woman we were after came out of the apartment building. She got in her car and began to drive. I had no choice but to follow. She snaked around the neighborhood and finally stopped at a light. I looked in the rearview mirror and saw the missing detective running for me. He jumped in, and we took off after our target. On the way, he explained that he would have come back sooner, but he had been reported to the cops as a prowler and detained by patrol officers who didn't recognize him as one of their own, working undercover.

When we finally stopped and interviewed our witness, she had little to offer on the Wilcox case, but she did say the two other witnesses had returned to the Buffalo area. Another plane ride took us back there, where, thankfully, the snowplows were again operating.

With a warrant we were able to recover the car, but then we ran into a snag. I asked the Buffalo cops to use a new technique involving superglue to help us get fingerprints from the car's interior. This method involves placing a hot plate and a pan smeared with superglue in the car. The fumes from the glue float around and stick to prints, which can then be lifted. The Buffalo cops had never heard of this and couldn't do it for us. But they volunteered to pack the whole car onto a freight train for Seattle. Though I explained that we didn't have a court order to take the car, this didn't seem to matter much to them. They hated bureaucracy and just wanted to get the job done. It took quite a bit of talking to keep them from just going ahead and doing it. (I also had to talk them out of a "special" hotel deal they cooked up for us. We would pay $50 per night but get receipts for $75. They couldn't understand why we didn't want this "travel bonus pay.")

Ultimately, we got the FBI to test the car with superglue, and they found nothing of value. The car, we would discover later, was not the right one anyway. As for the witnesses, a Buffalo detective took me to every seedy neighborhood in town to look for them. At every address I'd get out and lock the car door. After three or four stops, he looked at me and said, "Would you quit fucking locking the door? I want someone to steal this piece of shit."

Our witnesses were finally located in Niagara Falls but proved to be disappointing. They had known Leanne Wilcox, but they could tell us nothing new about her death. After more than a week on the road, Bob LaMoria and I went back to Seattle with nothing much to show for it. But we did have a few morale-boosting stories to tell in the task force office.

A week after we returned from the East Coast, four hundred people marched in downtown Seattle as part of a "Take Back the Night" demonstration. A few of the marchers were relatives and friends of victims of the Green River killer, but most were either women who spent a great deal of time on the street or members of local activist organizations.

The placards carried by these women made their views plain. Some were specific to the serial murder crisis. Others addressed broader concerns about the rights of women and the status of women who worked in the so-called sex industry:

STOP THE GREEN RIVER MURDERS
NO BAD WOMEN, ONLY BAD LAWS
END VIOLENCE IN OUR LIVES

I would quarrel with the idea that laws against prostitution were bad. If you knew as many prostitutes as I did and had seen how they were violated and degraded every day, you would want the law to stop it, too. But I couldn't blame anyone who wanted the killings to stop. We should all hope to take back the night and make it safe for everyone.

However, there was one big sign, carried by Opal Mills's mother, that provoked anger and resentment in me. It said:

MY DAUGHTER MURDERED, ATTITUDE = TOO BAD
POLICEMAN'S DAUGHTER MURDERED, ATTITUDE = KILLER
FOUND NEXT DAY

I knew that some people thought we were less than aggressive about the Green River investigation because the victims were not middle-class women. But I knew that we were giving the case everything we had. We couldn't have been more dedicated, and Mrs. Mills should have understood this. We were open to every question she could have asked about our work and had made no secret of our own frustration.

I understood that any parent whose child is killed goes through a natural psychological process that includes anger and grief. Anyone in that position wants to assign blame, and who better to blame than the police? Because I understood their sadness, I could tolerate criticism from parents. But I had more trouble listening to people who wanted to make political points at our expense. We were not part of some judgmental and antiwomen establishment. We were men and women who felt the loss of the Green River victims, and sometimes cried with those left behind. We worked thousands of hours of overtime. We sacrificed time with our own children. And here they were, saying we didn't care.

Ultimately, I came to understand that many people have

an unrealistic view of police work. They believe that we can solve any crime if we only try hard enough. We do have good investigators and a few tools at our disposal, like fingerprinting and lie detector tests. But the miracle discoveries you see in the movies and on TV rarely happen in real life. Nothing is harder than finding a bad guy who attacks strangers and knows how to hide his tracks. I know this isn't much solace to those who have lost loved ones. But it's a fact that when we're dealing with the most skilled type of killer, we often need more time, and more luck, than anyone can imagine.

Although the protesters didn't know it, at the time that they were rallying downtown, the task force had been making real progress. We were combing lists of men arrested for harassing, assaulting, and soliciting prostitutes, as well as lists of men who had fishing licenses and drove pickup trucks. All of this was done by hand, in that precomputer era, and we'd found names that appeared on several different lists and had narrowed down the number of potential suspects.

Some of us began to hope that we could get ahead to the point where we might identify a number one suspect. But unfortunately, the Green River killer wasn't going to let us catch up in this way. He had continued to murder women, and bodies were out there, waiting to be discovered. Every time this happened, investigations into suspects and our searches for the missing had to be delayed while the new site was analyzed and searched and the body was recovered.

Between Valentine's Day 1984 and April 20, fewer than ten weeks, eleven new bodies would be recovered by our team. Two were found near exit 38 of Interstate 90, the east-west superhighway that starts in Seattle and ends in Boston. Both were skeletons, and it would take time to confirm their identities — one was Lisa Yates, nineteen, and the other was Delise Plager, age twenty-two. Both fit the victim profile. Their location, far from the Green River, made it clear that the killer was making a greater effort to hide his crimes.

Unfortunately, the same blessings of nature and geography that make the region a wonderful place to live also made it an ideal place to get rid of murder victims. If you've ever flown into Sea-Tac, you know what I mean. Within fifteen miles of downtown, development gives way to vast stretches of wilderness bisected by two-lane highways and logging roads. From an airplane you can see how easy it would be to hide something as small as a woman's body.

In March, the remains of four more bodies turned up. Three were near the airport; the fourth was found near a logging road a good thirty miles from The Strip in an area near Enumclaw. It was Debbie Abernathy, who was reported missing back in September. A few months before the body was found, a man changing a tire found her driver's license on the side of Route 18. We had publicized the fact that a lot of women were missing, and this man had the presence of mind to call about his discovery. I met him at the scene and organized a search. We eventually found a birth certificate for Abernathy's son. Obviously this stuff had been thrown out the window of a passing vehicle. It was potentially a big break because the killer had had these materials in his possession. But when we checked them for fingerprints, none were found.

We didn't have time to dwell on our disappointment, because within a few days, we made a number of discoveries well south of the airport district, along Star Lake Road. On that day, a man looking for mushrooms in the woods found a human skull. We didn't get the report until the sun had set, so a patrol deputy guarded the site overnight. But by

8:00 a.m. on April 1, we had dozens of people assembled to start a search.

The area was overgrown and littered with fallen trees. Waist-high plants disguised dips in the terrain, making it hard to keep our footing. To make matters worse, it had rained overnight, and the dense shade meant that everything would stay wet and slippery all day.

A skeleton that apparently belonged to the skull was found in short order. Then we came upon a second set of bones, and then a third. All were located within sight of a little gravel turnout, a spot where someone would have been able to park a car or truck and have a pretty good view of the roadway to see if anyone approached from either direction. Obviously the killer had scouted the spot and found it so safe, and convenient, that he used it again and again.

Sad experience had made us pretty good at recovering remains. We marked grids around the bodies and systematically searched the ground. Much of the brush was hacked away, but not before each leaf was inspected for fibers and other trace evidence. In the areas adjacent to the bodies, we were even more meticulous, sifting through all the natural debris and collecting every bone and fragment of bone.

We made an odd discovery near the third body, which lay beside a fallen tree. Once leaves and sticks and twigs were moved away, we were startled to find a second skeleton. But this wasn't a person; rather, it was a fairly large dog, which had been placed head to head with the human remains.

At this site we got a little help, and education, from a professional tracker supplied by the U.S. Border Patrol. At first it was hard to accept that this man, Joel Hardin, could see things that we were missing. But I became a believer when he managed to spot footprints that everyone else had passed over. He studied them carefully and came up with the following information:

- The regrowth of various plants crushed by footsteps suggested the prints were made about a year ago.
- Sure footsteps indicated the man came in daylight and knew the terrain.
- The size ten or eleven prints were made by the type of walking shoe worn by people who work on their feet.
- The man appeared to walk in a purposeful, unhurried way.

These observations weren't going to send us running to the killer's door. But they could be added to the pile of clues and contribute to our overall sense of who we were chasing. He was comfortable in the woods and very careful about his activities. Since he was depositing bodies in daylight, it was obvious that the killer was willing to hold on to his victims — dead or alive we didn't know — for some period of time after he met them on the street. This boldness made me think he was going to keep right on killing.

Two more bodies were found later in April. One was discovered by a Weyerhaeuser Company cedar scout, who was working just off a logging road near I-90 when he stumbled upon a human bone. I went searching in the area with Bill Haglund of the medical examiner's office. After spending hours in the woods of the adjoining area, I noticed a shaft of light coming through the trees. The bright warmth of this light drew me out of the shadows and into a quiet glade. But where the sunbeam reached the ground, it fell not on ferns or flowers but on a bleached-out human skull, complete with teeth and jawbone, that had been perched on a stump.

No matter how many bodies and skeletons you see, the sight of a perfect human skull, with its empty eye sockets and lifeless smile, is always frightening and stomach-turning. In other cases where heads were separated from bodies, we might have assumed that a wild animal had been at work. Here, I knew a depraved human being was responsible and that he was playing with us. The skull on the stump was a message. It said, "I know you're here, but I'm one step ahead of you, and I always will be."

An odd thing happened the next day, while we were conducting a broader search. Barbara Kubic-Patten, self-named psychic and confidante of Melvyn Foster, arrived with her two kids. This in itself was not unusual. Barbara had continued to inject herself into the case, even though we were no longer focused so intently on Melvyn. On this day, we chased her away. She drove a couple of miles down the road, pulled over, and walked into the woods. There she spotted a sheet of plastic, lifted it, and found a mostly decomposed body. Long hair still attached to the skull showed it probably was a female. We would identify her as Tina Marie Thompson, age twenty-two. She had last been seen at a motel on The Strip in July of 1983.

Because it was only partially decomposed, this second body was more difficult to recover than a skeleton that was bone and nothing more. I felt frustrated, angry, and disgusted with the monster who was responsible for so much death. The body count was now twenty-three, and we had dozens of missing persons reports involving young women who worked the streets.

As much as I tried to prevent it, the case was getting to me in ways that I would not be able to recognize for many years. Although I believed I was putting on a convincing display of professional detachment, my family, friends, and coworkers noticed a change in me.

My wife experienced the change in the most direct and difficult way. It was around this time, when the bodies were piling up and there seemed no limit to the depravity of the killing machine we were trying to stop, that something in me snapped. I began to question the whole idea of human compassion. I asked Julie to stop saying "I love you" as much as she did. I couldn't bear to hear it, not when I knew there was so much evil in the world and there were so many victims who would never hear those words again.

Julie quietly agreed to my request. She restrained her normal loving impulses. Many years would pass, and I would almost forget that I had asked her to do such a painful thing. But one day she would recall it and explain how much it had hurt. And I would understand more clearly how the Green River killer had forced her to pay a price, too.

So much was happening in the investigation that communication was a key issue. We tried to share information freely and also began meeting weekly for a breakfast conference in a room reserved at a local restaurant. These briefings were critical if we were going to maintain an overall picture of the case.

As the summer of 1984 approached, I could see that we were making progress on many fronts. We had applied for a big grant to computerize all of our data and had received preliminary approval. Eventually staff and volunteers would begin entering all kinds of information — tips, motor vehicle registrations, fishing licenses, arrest records, and so on — so that we could locate men who fit the killer's profile.

At the same time, a handful of primary suspects had emerged from our street-level investigation. Melvyn Foster was on this list, but in my mind he had dropped down a few pegs. His failed lie detector test was a red flag, but I was starting to think that he was being evasive about something other than the Green River murders. After all, we had him under fairly tight surveillance during the time when the later murders took place. It was hard to imagine he was responsible. He had also become quite eager to cooperate. He had volunteered to take truth serum in order to clear himself (a request we turned down for legal reasons) and had begun to talk to me like I was his good buddy.

In the meantime, task force detectives were identifying possible new suspects at a pretty fast rate. Typical was a man named Gary Ridgway, whom Detective Randy Mullinax brought in for questioning in May of 1984. A prostitute named Rebecca Guay had identified Ridgway. She had come to us with a story about an assault that took place in the fall of 1982. While working The Strip, she got into a maroon pickup truck with a john who said he would pay $20 for oral sex. She told him to drive to a secluded spot off the main road, and they both got out.

Things went bad when the john was unable to get an erection. He suddenly accused her of biting his penis, and he hit her and shoved her down onto the ground. He then grabbed her around her neck in a choke hold. Terrified that she was in the presence of the Green River killer, Rebecca fought for her life, screaming that she had a family and didn't want to die. She managed to escape, and after following her for a few steps, her assailant got back in the truck and drove off.

For two years, fear had kept Rebecca from coming forward, but the more she heard about the Green River case, the more pressure she felt to speak up. When she came to us, she was still able to recall every detail of that assault, including the fact that she had seen the man's employee identification card. It was from the Kenworth truck manufacturing company. Randy showed her a series of pictures, including one taken when Ridgway had been arrested in a prostitution sting operation. She picked him out.

When Detective Mullinax met with Ridgway, he admitted to the run-in with Rebecca Guay. But he insisted that he had just overreacted to the bite and that once he realized what he had done, he had turned Rebecca loose. He would have had trouble denying that something had occurred. We knew he frequented The Strip, and she had identified him and his truck. Randy Mullinax didn't know, however, that the Des Moines police had gone to Ridgway's house on the Malvar case in May of 1983. That information had not been transmitted to us.

In the crazy world of pimps, johns, and prostitutes, there was nothing extraordinary about the story of Rebecca Guay and Gary Ridgway. But to be sure, Randy asked if the man would take a lie detector test. He agreed immediately and came back on the day it was scheduled. A very skilled polygrapher administered the test and found no sign of deception. Ridgway would remain a person of interest for us, but with no additional evidence and many similar suspects, he was moved well down on the list.

NINE

SOMEBODY KNOWS SOMETHING

ONE OF THE most troubling paradoxes in our investigation revolved around the discovery of human remains. We dreaded getting called to a scene and were truly relieved whenever it was a false alarm. But whenever a body turned out to be a victim of the Green River killer, it gave us an opportunity to look for new evidence. There was always a chance that the killer had been noticed by a witness at the site or had left something behind.

So, as much as we hated being confronted with new deaths, we became a little concerned when the pace of discoveries slowed. In the second half of 1984, only two bodies were found. In the same time period, we received no new reports of missing women. But this didn't mean that the Green River killer had stopped when our tally passed two dozen victims. We still had that number of missing women and more. He might just have gotten better at hiding the bodies.

No one was more upset by the mystery of the Green River killings than those parents who had reported their daughters missing months and even years ago. We heard from some of these mothers and fathers almost every week.

Others, like Mertie Winston, tried hard to restrain themselves. Mertie didn't want to bother me, so she saved up her questions until she couldn't bear it anymore and then called me to go down the list.

"Why haven't you caught him?"

"Do you have any evidence at all?"

"Why is this so hard for you to do?"

Sometimes I could share information with Mertie, and sometimes what I knew had to be kept secret. Many parents, Mertie included, had theories about the killer. She would focus on someone and push us to investigate. When the lead didn't pan out, she would get frustrated and then angry. Later, though, she'd bring cookies to the task force office.

It was often hard to tell whether these parents believed their daughters were alive or had concluded they were dead. Either way, they needed some sort of physical evidence before they could even think about trying to return to their normal lives. Like us, they both dreaded and welcomed the news that a body had been discovered. I would visit or call them as soon as I could share anything about the identity of new remains. It was our policy to have the lead detective on a case make personal contact with a victim's family whenever important information had emerged.

For many years I was also close to Carol and Tom Estes, whose fifteen-year-old daughter Debbie had disappeared in 1982. Debbie had been running away from home for years before she went missing. Her parents spent many long days and nights looking for her up and down The Strip and in downtown Seattle. As years passed, whenever a body was found, they wanted to know if it was their daughter. There were dozens of times when I had to tell them no.

The strain of not knowing took a toll on these mothers and fathers. Occasionally Tom, a long-haul trucker, would call from the road and just roar into the phone: "You guys are idiots! What the fuck are you doing?" I would ask him to calm down and assure him that we were doing everything we could. Then, when he was back in town, he and Carol would call, looking for information. After these talks, things would get better for a while. I understood the pressure they were under. If I had been in their position, I would have yelled and screamed myself.

The decline of new discoveries did allow us to pursue some more creative investigative ideas. For example, in November of 1984, we helped one of the local TV stations do a monthlong series of public service announcements and pleas for information. Captain Adamson, Fae, and I appeared in these spots. The theme was "Somebody Out There Knows Something."

The station also put up a $100,000 reward for information that might lead to an arrest. The news pieces did generate a flurry of new tips, but none was valuable enough to earn the $100,000.

A month later, Bob Keppel and I went to Florida on one of the more unusual investigative fishing trips of my career. Ted Bundy — once the Northwest's most famous serial killer — had written from his death row cell to offer his services as a consultant on our case. He had followed the Green River investigation in the news and become so interested that he took out a subscription to one of our local papers.

Bundy was an egotist, and there could be no doubt that he was jealous of the attention that had been focused on the killer he called "the Riverman." He may also have felt competitive. This new serial killer was working the same area where Bundy started his career in murder. And he was killing at such a rapid pace that he was likely to surpass Bundy's record. Finally, Bundy may have harbored some admiration and curiosity about this new killer. He wanted to get inside information, to satisfy his own perverse obsessions. He was also out of the limelight, trapped in his eight-by-eight prison cell, waiting for his execution and craving attention.

After exchanging a few brief letters with Keppel, Bundy sent him a long letter filled with questions. He wanted to know about the sites where the bodies had been found and the profiles of our victims. (They might not all be prostitutes, he said.) He speculated about the killer's way of operating, suggesting that he might have posed as a police officer to win the trust of his victims. Bundy had done this himself.

Most of what Bundy wrote matched our own ideas about the case. We already suspected that the killer was an ordinary-looking guy who would seem nonthreatening to his victims. We also understood that he was picking up women in specific and limited areas frequented by prostitutes and their clients. This meant that people who worked the street were accustomed to seeing him around, and not afraid of him. Finally, we suspected that, like Bundy, the Green River killer watched the news and very much enjoyed seeing reports on bodies that were discovered and the frustration of the police and family and friends of the victims.

But even though we could anticipate some of what Bundy might say, there was still a chance that he could help us. He was an intelligent person who understood serial killers in a way we could not. There was even the possibility — admittedly remote — that he would receive some kind of communication from the Riverman. These guys are like members of a very unusual club. Who could appreciate their experiences better than a fellow practitioner? If they were in contact, maybe we'd find a clue to the Green River killer's identity. We also hoped that Bundy might talk about his own killings in Washington State, to fill in some missing details.

We were willing to let Bundy use us as a source of information and entertainment and to bolster his own self-esteem. Unfortunately, I had to agitate a little to make sure a King County detective was in on the interview, because initially Bob Keppel was assigned to go alone. I reminded our captain that we always used two detectives to conduct important interviews: one to watch for body language, take notes, and devise new questions while the other spoke directly to a subject. Besides, this was a King County sheriff's case. In fact, the Bundy killings were King County's, too. The captain saw my point. I would guess this irritated Keppel a bit, but we had no trouble working together once we left Seattle.

We flew to Jacksonville and then drove about an hour southwest to Starke, home of the Florida State Prison. But when we arrived, we were informed that Bundy wasn't available. (How often is someone on death row so busy he can't meet?) It turned out that he had a previously scheduled visit. We agreed to come back.

The next day, Florida prison authorities cleared us through their security, reminded us that Bundy was a master manipulator, and then walked us through the belly of the prison to the death row area. We were deposited in an interview room that was bare except for three plastic chairs and a table bolted to the floor. When the guards brought Bundy in, I shook his limp hand to establish some rapport, but as I did, I recalled all the lives he had taken.

People had talked to me about how charismatic and good-looking Bundy was, but the man I met was unimpressive.

He was dressed in prison coveralls, and his hands were chained to his waist. He hadn't shaved in a day or two. He tried to smile and be gregarious, but it didn't feel right. He seemed lost, even a little humiliated to be the guy who was so desperate for attention that he would reach out to a couple of cops.

In our first hours with him, Bundy asked us about the victims and tried to analyze what the Riverman was up to. A few of the women he had killed had not been arrested for prostitution, though they frequented places where prostitutes worked. Bundy said that killing these women might have been a mistake, a deviation from the Riverman's real goal. He also suggested that those women could be the victims of a different man, one who was not so intent on killing women who took money for sex. Ted looked down on the Green River killer's choice of victim, because it didn't take much effort to capture and isolate a prostitute. In contrast, Ted had had to use all his charm and charisma to persuade his victims — bright and attractive college girls — that it was all right to get in his car.

Like others, Bundy thought that the killer we were chasing was an avid outdoorsman. After studying the dispersal of the bodies, he concluded that more must lie in the forest outside Enumclaw, where we had found Debbie Abernathy's skeleton. It was a remote and yet accessible place, so perfect for the killer's purposes that he must have continued to use it.

After a couple of hours, I could see that Bundy was getting excited. A little more color appeared in his face, and his eyes brightened. When a prison guard brought him a lunch tray, he was too distracted to eat. Instead, he just picked up his spoon and pushed the beans and potatoes around until they were all mixed together.

As he talked about the dump sites, Ted repeated his belief that they were preselected. Certain bodies were destined for certain locations even before the killer moved in on a victim. He also had no doubt that the Riverman was going back to visit those bodies after they were dumped. "He's going back probably a number of times," he said, "to bring bodies into the area or to check on a body, or check out an area."

Bundy had noticed, as we did, that the missing persons reports and body recoveries had slowed considerably. I asked him if it was possible that the Riverman had simply stopped killing. He almost laughed at me. "Not unless he was born again and got filled with the Holy Spirit in a very real way. He's either moved, he's dead, or he's doing something very different."

I agreed with him on this point. In the history of serial killers, not one of them had been able to simply walk away from the killing compulsion once the murder spree had begun. Bundy understood this. When he spoke about how the Riverman may have "straightened up," he meant that the killer had become more proficient, "more careful in the way that he disposed of their bodies. And there's no question that this explains the apparent drop-off in discoveries."

As we questioned him, it became clear that Bundy had made a very deliberate study of the Green River case. He knew all the victims' names. He knew where and when bodies had been found, and he had plotted out the relationship between the pickup spots and dump sites. But his analysis of these facts was unimpressive. He saw patterns where none existed.

At a moment when the conversation lagged, I decided to ask if the Riverman might have shown any mercy, releasing women whom he had intended to kill. I knew that Bundy would base his answer on his own sick experiences, but I was eager to know if it was possible, if a serial killer was capable of changing his mind and letting someone go.

"I think there's an excellent chance that he has picked up a number of prostitutes who he's later released for any number of reasons," said Bundy. "Perhaps he just felt an unusual wave of compassion. Maybe he was surprised at some point and felt it was too risky to kill that particular individual. Maybe somebody saw him at some point in time after he had made contact with her, or maybe it's just entirely too risky to go through with it. But I think he's doing it fairly quickly — he's probably killing them fairly quickly."

In fact, we had spoken with a number of prostitutes who reported run-ins with violent johns. Some described what sounded like attempted strangulations. But there was no apparent pattern to these stories.

Although Ted was eager to discuss the Riverman's stalking and killing — no doubt he got vicarious pleasure from this — he was more evasive when it came to events that might transpire after a victim's death. We knew that Bundy was a true necrophiliac who had gone back to the places where he left bodies to rape the rotting corpses. In fact, you could argue that he had killed women for the sole purpose of having an object to exploit sexually. This is common behavior for serial killers. They want total control and are excited by the hunt but often have trouble performing sexually with a live woman.

One of Bundy's few apparently normal psychological responses was his shame about raping dead bodies. He carefully avoided saying anything directly about this. But we eventually got him to admit there was a "fatal link between sex and violence" in the Green River case. Added to his earlier observations about how the killer would invariably go back to visit the bodies he had hidden, this statement suggested that we might actually catch the killer at one of the dump sites.

This was what Bundy had in mind when he suggested that we might want to hold off any public announcement about the next body we discovered, especially if it was not yet decomposed. If, instead, we established very unobtrusive surveillance, the killer might actually come to us. As he explained this, Bundy seemed to get some pleasure out of criticizing the way police departments generally respond to the discovery of a body.

"I know the instincts . . . [of] the police," he said. "Everybody is called in and scours the site. The Explorer Scouts crawl on their hands and knees and this has always fascinated me, and appalled me, because I said, 'If they'd only waited, they'd have found somebody. The guy would have come right up to them.'"

Bundy was saying that the sexual lure of the body was too much for him to resist. His other suggestions also depended on exploiting the killer's sexual interests. Ted was certain that the Riverman enjoyed violent pornography, especially slasher movies. He actually advised us to put on a film festival that featured so-called snuff films, in which it appears that someone is killed on camera. Some of these movies feature characters who are prostitutes. He advised us to show the movies in a theater near The Strip, where we could videotape the customers and record their license plate numbers.

"Hey, there's no better indicator of whether a man is capable of this kind of act, of killing all these women, than if he has that interest [in snuff films] and goes out of his way to indulge that interest."

Of course this kind of film festival would have drawn Ted Bundy's attention when he was a free man. And as he talked about it, he got quite excited. But it was an impractical idea.

For one thing, the cost of renting a theater for weeks and keeping surveillance teams on duty would have been enormous. But, more important, there was no way that a judge would have given us a warrant to pursue a suspect more aggressively — arresting him and searching his property — simply because he went to a movie.

The one thing you could say about the film festival idea was that it was inventive and original. It stands out in my memory because almost everything else Bundy said was self-serving and a rehash of ideas that were already established. He talked about the possibility that the Riverman was collecting items — clothing, jewelry, pictures — as souvenirs of his murders. He also insisted that he would appear completely "normal" to his friends and family, showing no hint of his criminal activity. And he said the killer was smart enough to learn from what he read in the papers and saw on TV to refine his methods.

Ultimately we would spend two full days interviewing Bundy. This exercise required a great deal of patience, because Bundy frequently repeated himself and often acted as if he were far more insightful and intelligent than any detective. Bob Keppel, who was building a reputation as a serial killer expert, seemed to appreciate the chance to learn more about how Bundy thought and how that might be applied to serial killers in general. I could understand this, since Bob had put a good deal of time into chasing the phantom "Ted" only to have detectives in other jurisdictions slap the cuffs on him.

But for me, the Bundy interviews turned out to be less about information and more about inspiration. Ted Bundy certainly knew everything about his own exploits as a serial killer, and he had studied other monsters the way an athlete studies his competitors. But in the end, he had used us to get some relief from the prison routine and to make himself feel important. He was also trying to delay his own execution by demonstrating that he had some value to society that would be lost upon his death. I didn't buy any of that. But I did appreciate getting so close to such an arrogant, self-important, and disgusting character. It renewed my sense of anger and my determination to get the Bundy-like devil who was still at large back home.

The eerie calm that had settled on the case in the fall of 1984 continued into early 1985. But while the street scene was quiet in Seattle, we were hearing about missing prostitutes and murders in many other places, including North Carolina, Florida, Texas, and British Columbia. Authorities in those jurisdictions contacted us for advice on handling crime scenes and to compare cases. None of them involved murders quite like the Green River killings, so it was hard to conclude that our murderer had moved away. But we were able to help solve some of the crimes — including murders — that took place outside King County.

In the Seattle area no new bodies were found until March, when a teenager walking in the woods found bones in the area off Star Lake Road where we had previously recovered bodies. The condition of the bones led me to think the body had been lying there during our previous searches. But I didn't beat myself up over the fact that we hadn't seen it before. The vegetation in this spot was so thick and overgrown that we almost had to step on an object to find it. The mud was so thick and sticky that it practically pulled our boots off with every step.

Although we would never know exactly why we missed this body before, forensic analysis determined that the murder took place in 1983 or earlier. When we stepped back and analyzed the pattern of our discoveries and the estimated dates for the murders, we could see that all of the people we had found were killed prior to the spring of 1984. Captain Adamson was so sure that the killings had stopped, at least in our region, that he began saying so publicly.

When I heard this, I began to worry that the politicians who controlled our budget would begin to lose interest. They could decide that the crisis was over and that the killer had either ceased his attacks or moved to another jurisdiction. Either way, they might have an excuse for cutting back the Green River Task Force.

If anything, we needed more resources, not fewer, especially when it came to processing all the evidence we had gathered. The Washington State crime lab had been overwhelmed by all the items we were submitting for analysis. They were literally years behind schedule on ordinary requests, and even if we identified a certain piece of evidence as a very high priority, months might pass before we received a report. This wasn't the fault of the lab staff members. There were just too few of them.

Although we understood the problems all law enforcement agencies faced, we didn't always cope well with the frustration. At one point, the detectives on the task force decided to have a closed-door meeting. During the session, we aired our complaints about how our time was managed, the command staff's priorities, and important tips that had been set aside in favor of various pet projects. Most of all, we felt that our input wasn't valued.

After compiling a long list of concerns, the group elected me to present it to Captain Frank Adamson.

Frank and I got together in his office. I handed him the list, told him about our frustrations, and then waited for him to read it over. I expected him to say, "Okay, Dave. You guys have some good ideas. I'll get back to you on this."

Instead, I could see his face turn red and his eyes start to water.

"You know, Dave," he began, "you don't understand the influence you have on these people you work with. You have tremendous impact on what they believe, what they say, and what they will do. Whether you like it or not, or believe it or not, you are *the* informal leader of this group."

He paused for a moment. I said, "Okay."

"And right now you are leading these guys in a mutiny," he said, his voice growing more serious. "You better get on board. I need you to be part of this team."

Until that moment, I hadn't realized that I could have usurped the command staff and that they needed my support just to keep the task force operating smoothly. I didn't get any assurance from Adamson that he would take action on the list of suggestions, but he did say he would consider it seriously.

The one certain thing I did take away from that encounter was a better sense of my own responsibility. Adamson made it clear that I was the leader that the other detectives were watching. If I showed some confidence, faith, and determination, they would, too.

In the weeks to come, I would redouble my efforts. I followed leads on the Leanne Wilcox case all the way to Alaska, where Detective Randy Mullinax and I interviewed witnesses who had met Wilcox when she worked in Anchorage. I also reopened certain avenues of investigation regarding Opal Mills.

On my way to and from work, I would detour to drive The Strip and talk to prostitutes, warning them of the danger.

And whenever I passed a site where one or more bodies had been recovered, I made sure to drive slowly when I reached the spot where the killer had unloaded his cargo.

One afternoon I drove down Frager Road and came upon a car parked near PD&J Meats. When I saw a man standing by the trunk, I stopped to talk to him. He was about thirty-five years old. Inside the trunk he had waders and a fishing pole. I believed him when he said he was a fisherman, but I took his name and the license plate number on his car so I could search for matches in tip sheets, arrest reports, and other key databases. I didn't get any hits.

TEN

BAD BEHAVIOR

IMAGINE THAT YOU are the chief of police in Portland, Oregon. One hundred and seventy-five miles to the north, the Green River Task Force is wrestling with what may be the worst serial killer case in American history. After a streak of horrible discoveries, the body count tapers off. It looks like the serial killer has stopped, or moved on. Then you notice that a couple of prostitutes have been murdered in your jurisdiction.

In the fall of 1984, the Portland police responded to the murders of two prostitutes in their city by limiting their cooperation with us. They said that their cases were different. I knew that a different modus operandi didn't prove that the murders in Portland hadn't been committed by our guy. Some serial killers will stab a woman who refuses to be strangled and then shoot her if the knife doesn't work.

We were frustrated when Portland rejected our offer to help, but the macho world of law enforcement is notorious for turf battles. Maybe it was a matter of pride for them. Or maybe they didn't want to do anything to suggest that the Green River killer had moved into their community. Every cop in the Northwest understood that the Green River Task Force was under enormous public and political pressure. At the same time, we were trying to do something that was extremely difficult — find a nondescript man who was killing women who lived in the shadows. Who wanted to take on those kinds of problems?

In the interests of maintaining a working relationship with them, I didn't press the Portland cops hard. After all, we had plenty of our own tips to follow — the task force had logged twenty thousand pieces of information by early 1985 — and it was reasonable to trust that authorities in Oregon would pursue their cases vigorously.

We knew that it was important for us to stay on good terms with other police departments, because the big breakthrough in our case was likely to be made by a street cop who had Green River in mind while he or she was performing routine duties. This is exactly what happened in the 1970s and early '80s with the case of England's Yorkshire Ripper. There, investigators thought they knew who the killer was, but they didn't have enough evidence to make an arrest. One night, an alert patrol officer who was driving through a lovers' lane pulled in behind a car. When he asked the driver to get out of the car, the man did, but first he asked and was given permission to go off behind a storage tank in the bushes to relieve himself. Then he came back to the patrol car.

Once the officer heard the man's story, he recognized him as a key suspect and called homicide detectives. While the detectives had the guy at the station, the police officer remembered that the man had briefly gone behind the storage tank. He went back to the lovers' lane, searched in the bushes, and discovered a ball-peen hammer, which was found to have blood on it that tied him to some of the murders. The case was solved.

The Yorkshire case became part of a presentation I made to our patrol officers, which we then put on videotape for wider distribution. Along with the tape, which was shown at roll calls and other meetings, we provided ten key suspect names and information about a pickup truck described by witnesses in four cases. Three witnesses said it was a Ford, and two of them described it as having a canopy over the bed and primer spots on the body.

In those precincts where bodies had been found, we reminded deputies and officers that the killer could be revisiting those sites. In general, this was something serial killers did. They went back to commit sex acts, relive the excitement of the murder, and check on how well police had conducted their search. In the Green River case, we knew, at the very least, that the killer had used the Star Lake Road spot over the course of fourteen months. This fact had to make every car that pulled to the side of the road in a deserted area the object of suspicion.

For nearly two years, we had been issuing regional and national bulletins about our case and requesting information on murders and suspects that might possibly be linked to ours. I thought these bulletins had produced an important break when I got a call from a detective in the Multnomah County Sheriff's Office. He asked if I had heard that the Portland police had arrested two Brazilians for the murder of a prostitute.

When I called the Portland police, I hit a brick wall. They would neither confirm nor deny the arrest. This was ridiculous. I knew that they had two guys in custody. Finally the detective on the phone admitted it, but he refused to give me their names.

"What do you mean?" I said. "Just give me the names. I'm not going to the news media with this. I just want to see if they're in the Green River files."

The answer was no, and the discussion was over, at least for the moment.

After I put down the phone, I went straight to my captain, and he agreed that if Portland had someone in custody, someone who may have been killing young prostitutes and dumping them in secluded spots, we needed to know more about it. We didn't have time to play games. Together we went to see Sheriff Thomas. I wouldn't have thought it was possible, but after I explained what was going on, Thomas seemed even more upset than I was. This is what I liked about him. He was a cop's cop who believed that catching the bad guy was the only important thing. Before I left his office, Thomas called the Portland chief, Penny Harrington, and made an appointment to meet the next day.

In the morning, on the drive south to Portland, Thomas asked me about the task force's work, and reiterated his support for what we were doing. It was clear to me that he wanted to maintain the effort, despite the manpower and money it cost, and I appreciated hearing that. We also talked about why the Portland cops were hiding the Brazilians. It boiled down to one of three possibilities: one, they feared that we would compromise their investigation; two, they didn't want to get dragged into the big Green River mess; or three, they thought they had nailed our serial killer and wanted the glory for themselves.

The meeting was held in Harrington's office with the two top executives in charge. We got to the heart of the matter immediately.

"Dave, tell the chief what happened," said Vern Thomas.

I explained that the detective who was sitting there had said he could give me no information on the arrests.

Harrington questioned the detective and quickly ordered him to take me to his desk to review all the files. It was as simple as that, but not exactly easy. The detective was still difficult to work with. And when I checked the time frame for the Brazilians' arrival in the United States and was able to rule them out as suspects for our murders, he gave me an "I told you so" attitude. All I could think was that we could have all saved a lot of time and energy if the guy had just gone over the files with me when I first asked.

For her part, Chief Harrington made sure to tell the people of Portland that there was no serial killer loose in their midst. "We're not going to close our eyes if we see a pattern," she said. "But we don't see anything."

It was a good thing that we cleared the air with authorities in Portland, because weeks after that showdown at police headquarters, a worker at a tree farm in the suburbs uncovered something that would take us back to Oregon: a human skull. Eerily enough, the skull was found near a river in Washington County and close to the Starlight Motel on Pacific Highway South and a municipality called King City. At Sea-Tac, which was in King County, the street where so many of our victims were last seen was also called Pacific Highway South, and it was also the site of a Starlight Motel. Were these similarities all just coincidences?

The Washington County Sheriff's Office helped us in the investigation. We recovered some additional bones, including pieces of a second skull. They then supplied the Green River Task Force with X-rays and dental charts. Within forty-eight hours, our medical examiner was able to determine that the first body was one of our missing persons, twenty-three-year-old Denise Bush, the prostitute last seen in 1982 when she went out for cigarettes. It would take a few weeks for the second set of remains found at the Oregon tree farm to be identified. She was Shirley Sherrill, age eighteen, who had disappeared roughly two weeks after Denise.

If Denise and Shirley had been reported as missing persons in Portland, they would have been assumed to be victims of a local crime. But they had disappeared from King County, and that made their murders an interstate matter. And that meant that the FBI might have reason to jump into the Green River investigation with both feet. This would satisfy many in the media who had been calling for the FBI to take over the investigation because we were supposedly incompetent. Like many people outside law enforcement, some members of the media seem to believe the bureau has special powers.

We had already turned to the FBI for technical expertise — including profiling from John Douglas and lab work on various pieces of evidence — and we had kept the local field office updated on our progress. Some local activists, politicians, and Washington governor John Spellman had also called for the FBI to come into the case in a big way. But as long as the crimes stayed inside the state, the bureau lacked jurisdiction.

Now that two of our victims had turned up in Oregon, the feds decided they had a clear role to play. Alan Whitaker, special agent in charge of the Seattle FBI office, announced only that a review was under way. But in fact, it was obvious to all of us that the bureau was gearing up to make a large-scale effort. In a public announcement, the bureau promised to coordinate its activities with the Green

River Task Force. But it was clear that the FBI was going to work beside us, rather than impose itself over us.

Civilians might be surprised to read that federal officials don't just come in and take over a case. The truth is that once you set aside their advanced technology and certain experts, the FBI's capabilities are no better than what you'd find in a large police department. Their agents were not very different from our detectives. In fact, many of our people had far more experience with violent crime and street-level investigation than most of the people the FBI sent to Seattle did.

I fully respected the FBI agents we met, but their duties rarely included chasing killers. And while some investigative techniques can be used to solve different kinds of crimes, homicides are a specialty. This became clear to me when I did a briefing for one of these agents. He stopped me during the discussion of a medical examiner's report to ask what the term "rigor mortis" meant. Anyone who has even the slightest training in homicide investigation knows that this is the physical stiffening of the body that occurs some hours after the heart stops beating, and it helps establish the time of death.

Add that we had been up and running since the summer of 1982 and that we had an extensive local network of informants and contacts, and you can see why we were glad to have the FBI's help but confident in our own abilities. We wouldn't expect to jump into one of their terrorism cases, but when it came to murders, we knew what we were doing.

Of course, the feds were just as certain about their expertise, and from the moment they established their presence, they were very aggressive in their pursuit of their own leads. As early as August, just a few weeks after they began, the FBI agents said they had a couple of good new suspects.

This was a bit of a surprise to those of us who had investigated the killings for so long, but if they had somehow pinpointed the right man in a matter of weeks, we would be happy about it.

In the meantime, September brought a dramatic development that had nothing to do with anyone's special investigative abilities or dramatic insights into the case. A man driving a blue taxi picked up a prostitute in Portland. He took her to a deserted spot about thirty-five miles east of the city near a 176-foot waterfall called Horsetail Falls. Once there, he raped her, choked her, and tried to strangle her with a ligature, and then stabbed her. It was just like a Green River murder, except for one thing — the victim survived.

Born in Seattle, this young woman I'll call Helen — her name was never made public — was already a tough street kid when she heard about the Green River killer and went south to Portland to get out of harm's way. On the night she was attacked, she knew within a few minutes after she got into the cab that she was headed for trouble. The driver pulled out a knife and ordered her to crawl onto the floor of the car. He gagged her and tied her up, and then headed east on Interstate 84. He got off at the Historic Columbia River Highway and then went east a few more miles to the falls.

When he finally stopped the car, he jerked Helen out of the passenger side, beat her, choked her, and then raped her. Then he wrapped a bandana around her neck and tried to strangle her. When the bandana broke, he took out a knife and stabbed her in the back. When this failed to kill Helen, he pulled, kicked, and pushed her down an embankment. He followed and stabbed her again, this time in the chest, leaving the knife in. Desperate to live, she yanked it out but then fainted, and her body went limp.

Believing he had killed her, the cab driver found an old fifty-gallon steel drum, which he laid on top of her, along with some branches and leaves. Helen started to come to but wisely decided to play dead. She watched him climb up the embankment, where he stopped to catch his breath. He lit a cigarette and gazed down to see if she was moving. Obviously worried that he hadn't finished the job, he went back down and checked her pulse. Helen played at death so well that he was convinced. In the distance, she heard a train and the sounds of the waterfall. She passed out again before he scrambled back up the hillside and left.

At dawn, Helen woke up again. She somehow managed to struggle up the steep slope. As she reached the roadside, an older couple was approaching in their motor home. These good Samaritans stopped, wrapped her in a blanket, and took her to a nearby hospital.

Detective Jim Doyon was my partner in this investigation. At first we ran into the same old Portland police attitude, only now they had allies — the Oregon State Police and some FBI agents. We knew, for example, that they were withholding from us the name of a pimp who may have had important information. When we pushed them on this, a state police lieutenant stopped everything and hauled his detectives into the hallway. When he returned, he suddenly announced that they were prepared to be completely open with us. He gave us the pimp's name, and it turned out we had already interviewed the guy.

With so many agencies involved, we were able to pursue many different angles at once. Cab companies throughout the Northwest were contacted in an attempt to locate the blue car. Surveillance was set up on Union Avenue, where prostitutes worked, and a police artist worked up a sketch of the subject based on Helen's description. Helen remembered that her assailant wore coveralls, tried to strangle her with a bandana, and hurt his hands during the struggle.

Jim and I spent two months on the Portland assignment. We had to work carefully because we didn't want the killer to know that the task force was moving into Oregon. This wouldn't be easy, because the press was monitoring every move we made, using police scanners to track us. For the time we were in Portland, Jim went by the code name "Columbo," and I used the name "Callahan," from the Dirty Harry movies. This tactic worked, and we were able to pursue our investigation without interference. But this didn't mean we were spared frustration.

At one meeting of the Green River Task Force, we gave a report describing what had happened to Helen and the efforts under way to catch the guy who had attacked her. When I described the suspect — coveralls, bandana, injured hands — I noticed one of the detectives in the back of the room suddenly turn pale. After the meeting, he pulled me aside so we could speak in private.

"I've got some bad news, Dave," he said. "I've got something to tell you and it's making me sick."

He stopped and looked at me. I told him to just get it out, and we would deal with it, whatever it was.

"While you were in Portland, I got a phone call from a guy who wanted to know if we had his brother as a suspect."

"Okay," I said.

"He gave me a first name and said, 'Can you tell me if you have a guy who's wearing coveralls and a red bandana? Somebody with cut knuckles?'"

At the time, no one at the Green River Task Force office knew about the cut hands, coveralls, and bandana. They hadn't been briefed.

This wasn't bad news to my ears. It was very good. I

August 12, 1982. Detective Reichert standing by with a camera as marine patrol officers recover the second known Green River victim, Debra Lynn Bonner. (PHOTO BY CATHY STONE, © *KING COUNTY JOURNAL*.)

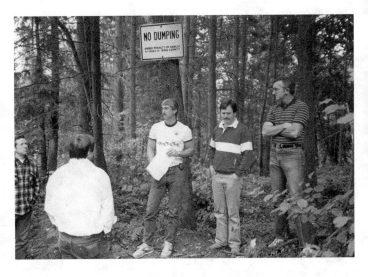

Detective Reichert leading new detectives assigned to the task force on a tour of the sites where bodies were found. *Left to right:* Detective Bob Seager, unidentified detective, Reichert, Detective Bob Stockham, and Detective Cecil Ray. This is the Star Lake Road site, c. 1986. (COURTESY OF THE KING COUNTY SHERIFF'S OFFICE.)

Photos of victims posted at task force headquarters in the mid-1980s — a constant reminder of the horror and tragedy of the case. (COURTESY OF THE KING COUNTY SHERIFF'S OFFICE.)

Detective Cheri Luxa (*left*) and Detective Fae Brooks discussing the case in front of the victim photos board, c. 1985. (COURTESY OF THE KING COUNTY SHERIFF'S OFFICE.)

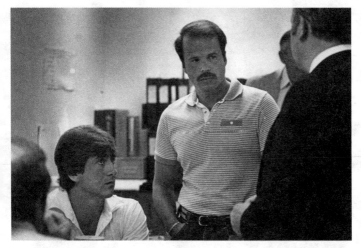

Left to right: Detective Reichert, Detective Randy Mullinax, and Sergeant Frank Atchley discussing the case, c. 1984–85. (COURTESY OF THE KING COUNTY SHERIFF'S OFFICE.)

The May 12, 1982, booking photo of Gary Ridgway, when he was arrested in a police sting after he propositioned a King County detective posing as a prostitute. Ridgway's next arrest would come in November of 2001. He was again arrested in a sheriff's office sting operation.

Sarah Christensen with a photo of herself and her mother, Carol Ann Christensen, killed by Gary Ridgway in 1983. Sarah was five years old when her mother was murdered. (© *KING COUNTY JOURNAL*.)

Debra Lorraine Estes, whose parents asked Detective Reichert to serve as a pallbearer at her funeral. (COURTESY OF THE KING COUNTY SHERIFF'S OFFICE AND THE *KING COUNTY JOURNAL*.)

Gary Ridgway being escorted into the King County Courthouse on April 15, 2002, where prosecutors announced that they would seek the death penalty in his trial. (PHOTO BY MATT BRASHEARS, © *KING COUNTY JOURNAL*.)

Ridgway's home for most of the 1980s and the site of many of the murders. (PHOTO BY DEAN FORBES, © *KING COUNTY JOURNAL*.)

Left to right: Detective Reichert, Detective Carolyn Griffin, Detective Bob Stockham, and an unidentified detective sifting evidence at a decomposition site in the mid-1980s. (COURTESY OF THE KING COUNTY SHERIFF'S OFFICE.)

Green River Task Force, 1987. (COURTESY OF THE KING COUNTY SHERIFF'S OFFICE.)

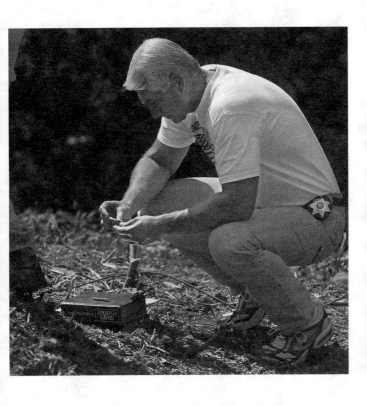

Sheriff Reichert examining bones. (PHOTO BY PATRICK HAGERTY, © *KING COUNTY JOURNAL*.)

Sheriff Reichert in the courtroom on November 5, 2003, the day Ridgway pled guilty to forty-eight counts of murder. (PHOTO BY ELAINE THOMPSON, ASSOCIATED PRESS.)

Gary Ridgway in the King County Courthouse, November 5, 2003. (PHOTO BY ELAINE THOMPSON, ASSOCIATED PRESS.)

asked the detective if he had taken a name and number from the caller.

"Yeah," he said. "I saved it for a few days and then I threw it away. I thought it wasn't anything."

It was a mistake. Everyone makes them. And the detective was already so distraught over it that I couldn't see any purpose in getting angry. So we focused on trying to recover any information that would help. We checked his notepad to see if we could raise the numbers from the impression he had made while writing the caller's number down. When this failed, we hypnotized him a couple of times to try to get the number. He recalled an Idaho area code and a prefix, but that was all.

With this information, we were able to zero in on Boise. But that was as far as we got. Boise's not a big city, but it's large enough that we couldn't ever find the man who called about his brother. After this, I don't think anyone at the task force ever threw away another sheet of paper.

We would never find the man who had attacked Helen. But we were able to help her recover from the attack and maintain her privacy. We accomplished this by moving her to a kind of safe house in Spokane, where she could rest and recover without being hounded by the press.

Not that some reporters didn't try. Soon after Helen was settled in Spokane, a husband-and-wife team of journalists posed as relatives to get in to visit her. They got through the first screener, but the second one called the task force, and we told them that the visitors were lying.

We felt a little satisfaction when we thwarted those reporters who wanted to exploit her, but otherwise the outcome of our investigation into Helen's near-murder was disappointing. We had been excited by the prospect of a so-called live victim, but in the end, we couldn't find the man or the car she described. We also came to realize that the man who attacked her was probably not the Green River killer. He was probably a different monster, one who may or may not have gone on to attack other women.

The letdown we felt when the Horsetail Falls attack became a dead end was made even worse by the changing political mood in King County. While we had been working with Helen and the authorities in Oregon, the county budget office was asking questions about the cost and effectiveness of the Green River Task Force. Tim Hill also happened to be running for county executive against Randy Revelle, the man who had appointed Sheriff Vern Thomas and backed the task force.

By questioning our effectiveness, Hill could make a play for two types of voters who occupied opposite ends of the political spectrum. The first group included the men and women who attended the "Take Back the Night" rally and believed we were both ineffective and callous toward the Green River killer's victims. The second group were conservative, anti-tax voters who resented that we had spent about $2 million per year chasing a serial killer who was still on the loose. This group may have also believed that the killer had stopped, and may even have moved away, so there was no longer a crisis.

Fortunately, the politicians who might exploit the Green River case were limited by basic common sense. No one could come right out and say we shouldn't seek justice for the dead and missing. At the same time, it was impossible to argue that we deserved a blank check. Responding to these two imperatives, Revelle did what a lot of politicians do when they need to address an issue but want political cover.

He appointed an outside expert to review the case and make recommendations.

The consultant Revelle chose was a pioneer of serial killer investigations named Pierce Brooks. Once a detective with the Los Angeles Police Department, Brooks had begun investigating serial killers in the 1950s. He was the first to realize that many of these killers left behind "signature" clues at crime scenes. He had been the first to advocate a national crime data system to help cops catch killers who moved from place to place, and he had been the leading figure in Joseph Wambaugh's book *The Onion Field*.

Not the type to sit down and write a report, Pierce eventually delivered his findings to us in a meeting that was tape-recorded. He said that county leaders should set aside any thoughts of cutting back the task force. He believed that the answer to the case was in all the data we were collecting, but it would not be found if we didn't have the personnel to continue gathering facts and analyzing them. The only other possibility for a big break — such as a patrol officer stopping the killer with a body in his vehicle — would require a whole lot of luck.

When he talked about the challenge of finding the Green River killer, Pierce kept returning to the way the man had selected the disposal sites for the bodies. (He and I had visited many of them and talked about the killer's activities.) The ones he used the most, like the riverside itself, involved steep terrain and heavy underbrush. Though they were good hiding spots, they were also so difficult to negotiate that the killer would have to expend a great deal of energy, and risk injuring himself, in order to dump a body. He would do this only if he felt some connection from a "prior relationship" with these places.

Who would have a prior relationship with the Green River, isolated logging roads, and hidden wild places close to suburban settlements? Most likely he was an avid outdoorsman, someone who liked to camp, hunt, fish, and hike. He may also have grown up near one or two of these places and explored them as a boy. As an adult, he might live near one of the sites and work close to another. It was also possible that his job brought him to various undeveloped tracts. Maybe he worked construction or for a local or state highway department.

Brooks's profile of the killer was not so different from the one we were working from. He thought the killer was probably a white male, approaching middle age, with a background in the military. (The killings were efficient and did not involve mutilation, noted Brooks.) To catch him, he suggested we do everything we could to generate more tips, more leads, and more data. We should trace back for many years the titles to property near the dump sites, collect names of retired servicemen, and gather up employee rosters for companies located near The Strip. Once all these many pieces were entered into computers, programs that found names in several different categories might spit out a list of good suspects.

In the end, Pierce Brooks gave the county executive his support for the task force, and he may even have quieted the critics, for a while. But Revelle lost the election, and Tim Hill would soon reveal himself as no friend of the sheriff's office. During one of his early visits to the task force office, he made not-so-subtle references to budget problems and the possibility of cutting our manpower, even though we had just received a $1 million federal grant, which eased the financial burden we were putting on the county.

As fate would have it, we got a reminder about our mission in the last week of 1985. A stolen car had wound up in a ravine near Mountain View Cemetery, which was in Auburn not far from Star Lake Road. Cemetery workers who went to check it out discovered that as the car had scraped through the underbrush, it uncovered a human skull. Our search team eventually found a second skull, and we concluded that we had found another Green River dump site.

The recovery near Mountain View Cemetery was difficult because the ravine was deep and the weather was cold and wet. My mood wasn't helped by the fact that I had been sleeping poorly for several weeks. A terrible image from one of our recovery spots had been popping into my mind whenever I was at rest. It was a picture of the bones of a sixteen-year-old who had been dumped near the bottom of a gully off Star Lake Road. The body had obviously been posed, naked, with the legs so far apart that both hips appeared to be dislocated. I understood what this meant. The killer had returned, maybe more than once, to rape the corpse. How could anyone sleep with those kinds of images in his mind?

No doubt this new search for skeletons would plant the seeds for fresh nightmares. Things were made worse when Lieutenant Dan Nolan agreed to let the media stand on the side of the road right above us and train their cameras down into the ravine. The detectives who were gathering evidence objected to this. We didn't want our faces on TV. We didn't want the public to see any evidence we might discover in our search. And most of all, we felt that the Green River victims' families should be protected from the sight of bones being pulled out of the ground.

I was elected to take these concerns up the hill to Lieutenant Nolan. He told me to get back to work. It was too late to move the press. They had already set up their cameras. I made sure Nolan understood how unhappy we were about this and then grabbed a couple of ropes and a few paper tarps to take back down to the search site.

At the bottom of the ravine, I told the detectives that Nolan had ruled against us but the issue wasn't settled. We tied the ropes to some trees and then draped the tarps over them. In a matter of minutes, the gravesite was hidden from the prying eyes of the TV cameras. The reporters complained, and eventually Nolan came down and forced us to remove our screen. But by then we were almost finished, and we used our own bodies to block the view for the remainder of the search.

When this little battle was over and I had time to reflect, I wondered why it was so hard for the press to respect what we were doing and understand the effort we were making. I had, literally, begun to turn gray in three and a half years of hunting for the Green River killer. I had sacrificed vacations, family events, and my own peace of mind. And I had put up with enough of the bad attitudes of reporters, other law enforcement agencies, and political know-it-alls.

ELEVEN

ONE OF TEN THOUSAND

THE FAMILIES OF THE WOMEN who had been killed or were missing were a high priority for every member of the Green River Task Force. It was important, I found, to let them control the level of contact. Some family members asked that we call whenever there was a big break in the case, but otherwise they kept their distance. Others sought us out on a regular basis because we represented some symbolic link to their dead or missing loved one. I recall in particular the parents of Marie Malvar, who invited some of us to parties celebrating the anniversary of their daughter's birth. There were balloons and a cake. They showed me Marie's bedroom, which hadn't changed since her disappearance.

I felt very sorry for the Malvars. They were suspended in a terrible place between life and death. They wanted to believe their daughter was alive, but everything they knew suggested she was dead. I had almost concluded that this was the case, but I would never have said that. They were very gracious and were recognizing our efforts on their behalf. I wanted them to know we cared.

In early 1986, the Malvars and many other parents started

to telephone me on a more frequent basis. They had good reason. Some of the people on the task force had begun hinting that we were close to making a big arrest. Captain Frank Adamson even told the press that he believed 1986 would bring the investigation to a close. In a story headlined SERIAL KILLER HUNTER PREDICTS CAPTURE IN 1986, Adamson said, "I'm fairly optimistic we will have him in jail."

I was shocked. I was still the lead detective, and as far as I knew, we did not have a strong enough suspect to make that kind of statement in private, let alone broadcast it to the world. But Adamson was quite impressed with the FBI and had spent extra time with them in recent weeks. All I could imagine was that he was being fed some information that the task force detectives were not getting. The likely source was the FBI.

Adamson was determined to solve this case, but he was also very frustrated by our lack of progress. Several of us thought that he had more faith in the FBI than he had in his own people. For these reasons, he may have succumbed to the FBI mystique.

As it turned out, the captain's bold prediction did come from information developed by the bureau, which had begun to send more agents to Seattle. We were all brought into the loop in late January at a series of briefings. Agents told us that a chief from another jurisdiction had tipped them off to a suspect that they had been working for months. (Why the chief didn't call the task force, I'll never know.) They were now ready to move on him, and they needed the task force's manpower to implement a complicated plan to take him into custody.

The target was a fifty-two-year-old construction worker who lived south of the city in Riverton. When agents briefed us about Ernest W. "Bill" McLean's background, they said he was an avid outdoorsman — he trapped animals for their fur — who knew the region's rivers and woods. Third parties had said he made some comments about picking up a prostitute and possibly killing her. The FBI had conducted an aggressive background check on McLean. They had used both a top secret team and a spy plane to conduct surveillance.

When the briefing was over, many of us had big doubts. My negative reaction had something to do with the fact that I had not been informed about McLean until the investigation was well on its way. But beyond this issue lay other problems. We didn't believe that the information gathered by the bureau qualified Bill McLean as a high-level suspect. Most of it was based on the fact that he fit a certain profile. After the meeting, a few detectives expressed frustration that McLean would receive such intense focus when their best suspects had been rejected. It had to have something to do with the aura of the FBI. They said this was the guy, and our command staff had fallen into line.

Once the die was cast, I was assigned to the intensive investigation of McLean. When the FBI learned that McLean had once belonged to a meat cutter's union, I was instructed to find out if he had ever worked at PD&J, along the Green River. It took days, but I eventually learned that he hadn't been a butcher for twenty years, and he had never worked at PD&J. He had committed a burglary there in the 1960s, and he was caught and prosecuted, and he served time.

Surveillance of McLean entailed other time-consuming assignments. When he was seen approaching a barn in rural King County, a whole team was assembled to search the place. Investigators were especially excited by what appeared at first to be a pile of women's clothing. After surrounding the place and working carefully through the entire building, we discovered that the "clothing" was actually nylon attached to steel ribbing and cables. From what I could see, it was the remains of either a hang glider or a hot-air balloon.

None of these dead ends discouraged our commanders from pursuing McLean. As they devised their plan for his capture, the FBI agents explained that they intended to "shock and surprise" McLean by taking him and his wife simultaneously, deploying teams to search his house and then delivering him to a specially built interrogation room. That room would be decorated with maps, charts, and three-ring binders all bearing McLean's name. After McLean saw all this, they would offer him a chance to help himself by confessing.

Our commanders looked past the warnings coming from their own detectives and bought into the suspect and the plan. The trigger would be pulled on the first Wednesday in February, just after McLean returned home from his job. Of course, the captain and FBI were not going to let me be in on the arrest, even though I remained the lead detective on the task force and had vastly greater knowledge of the murders than anyone in the bureau. They told me that McLean would not respond to me because I was too young and I had some doubts about the case against him. I didn't fight them too hard, even though we all knew that a good detective could play any role. I was so skeptical of their case that I wasn't terribly concerned that I was missing out on something big.

When the fateful afternoon arrived, we were to assemble at the Burien precinct, where the task force was housed. As I walked in, I noticed that someone had brought in a cake and some bottles of champagne for a celebration. I had never seen anything like this in a police office, and it gave me a sinking feeling.

I was teamed with FBI agent Bob Agnew to take McLean's wife, Fay, into custody at her workplace in the suburb of Des Moines. I respected Agnew. He was more like one of us, and he, too, had doubts about McLean's culpability. When we approached Fay outside her office, she said she would be happy to talk to us, but we needed to make an appointment. We followed her as she went back inside the building, where we made it clear that we weren't going to make an appointment, we were going to take her to the FBI office. She agreed to go with us but asked for a favor. She was supposed to drop a disabled acquaintance at his home. Would it be all right if we followed her there and then took her into custody?

It wasn't like she was armed and dangerous, so we agreed and followed her to the man's house. We arranged to have her Toyota pickup truck towed and then searched. She got into our car for the drive to the FBI office in downtown Seattle. On the way there, she didn't seem intimidated or frightened. She seemed angry.

Our interview of Fay McLean ran from about 4:30 in the afternoon to 10:30 at night. We learned a little about her background, such as where she had lived and gone to school. She spoke about her husband in general terms but was also fairly evasive. She wanted to know more about the case we were investigating. When we finally told her that her husband was a suspect in the Green River murders, she said, "That's impossible."

Few people have ever seemed more certain about anything than Fay McLean did on that night. She said that she and her husband shared the same hobbies and were together most of the time. When we said he might have called in sick from work to commit the crimes, she said that she had never seen any unexplained absences from work on his pay stubs. And he had given her every one.

When we asked Fay whether she felt that she and Bill had a normal sex life, she came back with an almost amusing response. "You define for me what's normal," she said, "and I'll tell you if that's what we have."

In the end, Fay McLean told us nothing that would implicate her husband in the killings. And though we told her that Bill was being questioned, too, she didn't seem worried about what might be happening to him. She was more concerned about practical issues. She wanted to know when she would get her truck back, how she could get clothes out of her house, and where she might be sleeping that night. We were able to arrange for solutions to all those problems, and as she left, both Agnew and I were convinced that Bill McLean was not the Green River killer.

While Agnew and I had been working with Fay McLean, another team had swooped down on her home in Riverton. At least half a dozen police vehicles were involved, and some of the personnel wore windbreakers with GREEN RIVER TASK FORCE printed on the back. If we wanted to do something discreetly, this was not the way. Local reporters, who had been primed for a big break in the case by Adamson's statements about an imminent breakthrough, jumped when neighbors called to tell them what was going on. Reporters raced to the house, to the task force center in Burien, and to the FBI office downtown. It was a full-court press, and soon anyone who was watching TV would see a special bulletin announcing that a major development was imminent in the Green River case.

The reporters who wanted to see the cops march a suspect out of the house were disappointed. Bill McLean had been under surveillance at a construction site where he worked. At quitting time he was followed and then pulled over. The agents who took him into custody and brought him north to the downtown federal building were a little surprised when he asked, "What took you so long?"

The command staff had selected King County detective Jim Doyon to be part of the team that would question McLean. Doyon was there when he was brought into the room that had been decorated for this purpose. One of the most impressive setups in the room was a poster-size picture of McLean surrounded by smaller photos of the women who had been killed. Red cords had been strung between the picture of McLean and the ones of the dead women. Also on display were the pyramid-shaped rocks taken out of some victims' bodies.

The idea behind all this stagecraft was not to induce feelings of guilt. Serial killers don't feel bad about their crimes. In fact, they are proud of their accomplishments. If the profiles were anywhere near accurate, the Green River killer was likely to believe that he was performing some sort of public service — by killing prostitutes — that benefited the rest of society even though we wouldn't see it that way.

So if guilt wasn't the way to get to him, what was? Fear. The sole purpose of the sudden confrontation, the simultaneous interview of his wife, and the search at his house was to make McLean believe we had enough evidence to put him on a fast track to execution. Even serial killers want to preserve their own lives. If he thought that a conviction was unavoidable, maybe he would talk in order to win some points toward a different sentence, like life without a chance of parole.

The problem was, McLean did not seem scared. He was impressed by the work that seemed to be reflected in all the props, but he didn't react at all to the rocks. And he was quite cooperative when it came to answering questions about the Green River killings. He did say he wouldn't talk about burglaries and possible violations of state game laws. This made sense, since McLean had been convicted of a burglary, and he was an avid game trapper who may have committed a few violations over the years.

Trapping animals for their fur was a big part of McLean's life. He explained that this was why he knew the woods, fields, and streams that were frequented by the Green River killer. The same factors that made them ideal dump spots — isolation, heavy brush, and inaccessibility — made them good places to catch game.

McLean's five-word statement at the time he was taken into custody ("What took you so long?") had jolted the agents who made the arrest. Maybe this guy was ready to confess to the murders. But early in the interview, McLean explained that he had been aware that he was under surveillance in recent weeks, and this was why he had expected to be picked up. But when it came to the Green River murders, McLean kept insisting, "I'm not the guy."

This firm statement, repeated several times, combined with McLean's willingness to answer questions and his apparent lack of fear, was enough for Jim Doyon to reach a quick conclusion: McLean was not the killer. And within an hour he was communicating this belief to profiler John Douglas, who had flown in to observe the questioning. Douglas agreed with Doyon. McLean was probably not the guy. But these expert opinions were not going to stop the process. Agents would continue the interview and up the ante by challenging McLean to take a lie detector test.

*   *   *

The Green River serial murders were the biggest story in the Pacific Northwest, and once the press got hold of the news that a man was in custody, they weren't going to let go. On the night of his arrest, the street in front of McLean's house was jammed with TV vans and cars belonging to people who just wanted to look at what might be history in the making. The crowd got so big that one enterprising man came by with a supply of snacks and hot coffee (it was a cold February night), and the gawkers quickly snapped up everything he had to sell.

Fae Brooks, as the public information officer for the task force, was stuck with the duty of answering but not answering the media's questions. She couldn't name Bill McLean as a prime suspect because the investigation had not yet established such a firm connection. She would say only that a "person of interest" had been brought in for questioning. The press knew we had gone into McLean's home, so it was easy for them to deduce the person's identity. But Fae was still careful to avoid using McLean's name, and she refused to offer up any details about the day's events. She even warned reporters about moving too fast on the story because they might get it wrong.

But with TV and radio stations already broadcasting and rebroadcasting reports about the search at McLean's home and the "person of interest" statements, the reporters seemed determined to push the story hard. Before the night was out, at least one TV station would reveal McLean's name and offer details about his activities as a game trapper. (Years later, detectives would still argue over who leaked this information.) And in the morning, the *Seattle Post-Intelligencer* would have McLean's name on its front page along with a picture of his house and another one of an officer bringing "evidence" out.

Anyone who read that story would have gotten the impression that we had a lot of evidence against Bill McLean. One quote, attributed to an unnamed task force member, said, "There is an awful lot that looks good. There is an awful lot of good probable cause."

The same source was also quoted as saying that there was a chance that the evidence could be explained away. And the *Post-Intelligencer* included in its story testimony from McLean's neighbors, who expressed the shock and surprise that always comes when people learn that someone they know has been arrested for a heinous crime. These statements are usually presented in the name of fairness toward the accused. But how many people really take them seriously? Statements like "he was a quiet neighbor" or a "nice guy" are so commonly made about the worst criminals that they are widely viewed as a joke and almost a sign that the guy must be guilty.

To make things worse, from Bill McLean's point of view, the newspaper went far beyond its front-page news story. Inside the paper, readers got a map that showed some of the sites where bodies had been found, as well as the location of McLean's nearby home. They could read thirty-four capsule descriptions of the victims. And a feature article portrayed McLean's neighbors as both baffled and suspicious. As one woman explained, "We don't know what goes on in other people's homes."

When I read that statement on Friday morning, I found myself wishing that the *Post-Intelligencer* subscribers knew what had gone on inside the FBI office overnight. McLean had insisted that he never picked up prostitutes and had never been arrested as a john. Police records confirmed this. He also challenged those sources who had told investigators he had made statements about killing prostitutes. This was "bullshit," he said, and anyone who said such a thing was lying.

McLean went a long way toward establishing his own truthfulness when he agreed to take a lie detector test. When he passed, the bureau asked him to do it again. McLean complied and then kept on complying until he had spent several hours hooked up to the polygraph wires. Five different analyses were made. All five said he was being truthful.

It could not have been easy for the investigators and commanders to accept the obvious. When the day began, they were so sure that they were going to catch the Green River killer that they had prepared a celebration. But at 2:00 a.m. on Friday, February 7, the cake and the champagne bottles stood as symbols of their overconfidence. Frank Adamson would have to go before the press and explain why McLean had been released. McLean, he said, was just one of "ten thousand people we're interested in."

It was, on its face, an almost ridiculous statement. If Bill McLean was no different from ten thousand other "persons of interest," why had we swarmed all over his house, taken him and his wife into custody, and impounded their vehicles? The answer was obvious. On Thursday, McLean was number one among the ten thousand, the man whom the FBI was going to nail with the Green River murders. On Friday, he was on his way off the list entirely. In fact, he would soon be officially ruled out as a suspect.

In the aftermath of the McLean fiasco, I felt more discouraged than at any time in the investigation. I believed that our commanders had been misled and that the FBI had looked for reasons to go after McLean while failing to check for facts that would eliminate him as a suspect. Good investigations follow both of these tracks. I don't know if the agents followed their standard procedure, but the bureau did have a different way of doing things. For example, we recorded all of our interviews. They would just take notes and paraphrase a witness's statement.

I was so upset about the time lost to the McLean detour that I angrily announced to Julie that I was going to quit. I seemed so serious that she actually called Sheriff Thomas, who quickly invited me to meet him.

It would have been unusual for a rank-and-file detective to meet with the sheriff, but Thomas had made the task force a personal priority and we had gotten to know each other pretty well. When I got to his office, he asked me to tell him what was bothering me. I didn't hold back, and when I finished lambasting my commanders and their decisions, he took a deep breath.

"You're frustrated with your supervision?" he asked, smiling. (All good, aggressive cops are frustrated with their supervisors.)

"Well, yeah," I answered.

"Dave, you have to hang in there," he said. "Someday you will be their supervisor. You'll get your chance. I'm sure of that. But right now we need you on the task force. I don't have to explain why. You know why. And that's why I don't believe you really want to get off."

He was right. I had just reached the point where I couldn't stay quiet, and our meeting gave me the opportunity I needed to vent my frustration. I went back to work at the task force office and did my best to avoid voicing my complaints. There was nothing to be gained by assigning blame. But I would have been a little happier if the FBI had stepped forward to acknowledge its role in identifying McLean and leading the investigation into his activities. Instead, on the day after McLean was cleared, more than a dozen FBI agents, including John Douglas, left town.

So, most of the feds were long gone when the media backlash began. Typical of the criticism we received was an editorial cartoon by Brian Basset of the *Seattle Times*. The drawing showed police approaching a tree house while saying, "He's white, male, harbors a deep resentment toward the opposite sex." The cops are shown moving in on a little boy as they shout, "Freeze, dog breath! Green River task farce!"

As someone who had lived with the stench of death and chased the Green River killer as if he were my own personal demon, I had trouble seeing the humor in that cartoon. But I was angrier still about the events that had opened us up to such criticism. I was also concerned about the loss of political and public support that was bound to follow the McLean failure.

Tim Hill didn't waste any time. He offered the sheriff some lukewarm support but then announced that he would require another review of the task force's work to see if we were anywhere close to finding the killer. If we weren't, he would consider cutting back our budget and our manpower.

If Hill had asked me for my analysis, I would have reminded him that the body count had slowed, but it hadn't stopped. In 1985 remains had been recovered in Oregon, at Star Lake Road and near Mountain View Cemetery. In May and June of 1986, we recovered the bones of two more women near Interstate 90 in Bend. Some of the remains had not been identified. But since they were found close to the skeletons of women whom we had confirmed as Green River victims, there was little doubt about who had killed them.

With thirty-six victims and more than two dozen reports of young prostitutes missing from the streets where the Green River dead had been picked up, the case remained a monstrous and compelling challenge. I was not ready to recommend that we reduce our efforts even slightly. I believed that this killer was still in our community and that he was determined to take more lives.

TWELVE

REFOCUSING

THERE WAS NO GREAT public uproar following the arrest and release of Bill McLean. No one held a rally at his house. And there was no mass protest outside the county courthouse in downtown Seattle. Why was the outrage confined to the newspapers' editorial pages? I came to believe that this was because the average citizen of King County didn't care very much about people like Bill McLean, didn't fear the Green River killer, and didn't relate to the women who were being murdered.

It is a sad but true fact of life in our society that certain victims merit a public outcry and others are considered expendable. The exceptions to this rule, at least in the Green River case, were the few dozen people who refused to forget those who had been murdered. Some of these were family members. Others were people who knew life on the street firsthand. And a few were activists who were outraged by the victimization of women and frustrated by our inability to catch the killer.

Because I understood their motivation, I wasn't bothered when I found a small group of demonstrators in front of our office on July 15, 1986, the fourth anniversary of the day when the first body was found in the Green River. When it started to rain, the protesters came inside the building and sat down in a circle in the lobby. There were only fifteen or twenty of them. They didn't bother us, and they were no threat to the facility. Their chants were somewhat familiar, including the charge that we didn't care about the victims because they were not middle class. We were used to hearing this, and we went on working. At quitting time they insisted on staying. The standard procedure in such situations calls for cooperation, not confrontation. We posted an officer to keep an eye on things and said good night.

I arrived the next morning with a couple of dozen doughnuts and some hot chocolate. Some of the protesters were still sleeping. A few were stirring. They all perked up when they smelled the cocoa and I started handing out the doughnuts. Hoping that I might be able to get through to them and convince them that we did care, I sat down and squeezed into their circle. As I was doing this, Lieutenant Nolan arrived for work. He shot me a look, shook his head, and walked by.

After I listened to the group complain about our failures and express their doubts about our efforts, I tried to convince them that we really cared and were doing everything we could. I wanted them to know me as a person, to trust me. But as we talked, I could see I wasn't getting through. Most of these women lived in a world where cops were the enemy. While a few were surprised and pleased that I would sit down with them, others viewed what I was doing as a sham. But they did thank me for my time and the doughnuts. And in a few hours, they decided that they were tired and in need of fresh clothes, and they left.

* * *

One of the fears expressed by the women who had occupied the task force office was that we would soon lose resources and be forced to cut back the investigation. This was one thing they got right. County Executive Tim Hill had continued to criticize the task force and was eager to reduce its budget. The McLean incident forced Sheriff Thomas to accommodate Hill by ordering a review of the investigation, which was done by a few veterans of the command staff. In late summer they finished their work and recommended a 40 percent cut. The main reason they cited for the cut was their belief that the Green River killer was no longer operating in King County. None of us who were actually investigating the murders were sure this was true. We still had missing persons, and plenty of leads to follow. And everything we knew about serial killers said they never stopped on their own.

Once the recommendation was made, County Executive Hill said he would come to the task force office and hear us out before making a decision. We still believed he had an open mind, and we put more than a few hours into developing a presentation, complete with a slide show and documentation. Most of the presentation was focused on the leads we were still pursuing and the progress we had made in using computerized data to highlight suspects. But we also pointed to a long list of cases that we had worked on even as we chased the Green River killer. We had helped solve unrelated murders, assault cases, sex crimes, and many hundreds of missing persons reports. We had also taught hundreds of police officers and detectives the most modern techniques for analyzing outdoor crime scenes and recovering bodies.

Hill seemed to pay attention to what we told him, but I noticed that Sheriff Thomas, who had accompanied him to the task force headquarters, looked tired and irritated. When we finished, the county executive didn't pose a single question. Nor did he offer a word of thanks or encouragement. Only later did we learn that the decision had already been made: We were going to have to accept reductions in manpower and budget.

Among the first to leave the task force were those who couldn't stand any more of the frustration that comes from not catching the bad guy and a lack of support from above. I understood their perspective. Most men and women become police officers in order to make arrests and put away criminals. The task force was concerned with arresting just one murderer, and we had been thwarted for four long years. I couldn't blame those who said, with great reluctance, that they wanted to go back to the kind of duty that would feel more productive and rewarding.

Some others on the task force hung in because they didn't want to seem like quitters. I understood this attitude. Good cops are, by nature, stubborn and resilient. It's a matter of honor to stay on a case to the very end. But when it came time for people to be reassigned, I'm sure some of these detectives were relieved to be chosen.

Finally, there were a few who were forced off the task force, even though they wanted to stay. One of these was John Blake, a detective whose main job had been analyzing information as it came in. Blake had developed a favorite suspect, a man who owned a lot of land near some of the sites where bodies had been left. He got frustrated when the command staff rejected his suggestion that the man be examined more closely. Instead of moving on, he went over the data again and again, trying to find tips that might be linked to his target. He couldn't let go of his theory and eventually started talking about how his suspect had some inside pull with the sheriff's office. What else could explain the commanders' decision to ignore such a viable suspect?

Blake eventually focused much of his anger on me. I had sided with those who didn't see a valid suspect in Blake's theory. But while we exchanged some pretty tense words, I had no idea that he was truly disturbed by what had transpired. It all came out when he was told he was being cut from the team. He blew up in a meeting with Captain Adamson, and, instead of following the captain's suggestion that he take some time off, Blake went out on temporary stress disability.

We all understood the pressure John felt and the enormous frustration that came with the Green River case. On one occasion, the sheriff's office sent over a psychologist to talk with us. We agreed as a team to participate, in part because we knew the command staff were sincerely concerned about us. The psychologist tried to get us to discuss our feelings and let down our defenses. It didn't work very well, in part because our defenses were what kept us functioning. There would be time enough for talking about our feelings once the killer was caught.

Those of us who were going to stay in the game after Tim Hill's budget reduction needed a little time to regroup. I remember a lot of lunches — with Detectives Brooks, Doyon, Mullinax, and Matt Haney — spent going over the work we had done and trying to plan for the future. Sometimes our conversations took place over sandwiches we purchased at a local deli. We'd park somewhere on The Strip, eat and talk, and watch the johns and prostitutes, hoping to see something significant.

The sting was starting to fade, but we all were still annoyed about the way the FBI and our command staff had pushed the McLean affair, which ended up damaging our credibility. Randy Mullinax had been especially skeptical before McLean was taken into custody, warning people, "You can talk yourself into believing in any suspect if you try hard enough." On the day of the operation, he even told certain relatives of the Green River victims to put their hopes on hold. He didn't think McLean was the guy.

Besides the damage done to the task force and the dashed hopes of the victims' families, consider what happened to McLean himself. More than once Randy paused in the middle of a conversation and wondered aloud what the future held for the trapper now that his name had been in the press.

I tried not to dwell on the past but focused instead on building morale. Sometimes a group of us would go for lunch to places like The Barn Door Tavern, famous for great burgers, just to get a break from the routine. But cops never really get away from the job. We were probably the only customers who knew that the tavern had been the site of a triple homicide a few years back. And some of us had seen the bodies and could picture the scene in our minds. But we had no trouble eating there. It was just another landmark of depravity to us, and we knew so many that it seemed like we were always spending time in places where mayhem and destruction had occurred at one time. You just had to put it out of your mind.

In a matter of weeks, we got over the county's decision to cut back the task force. The team was smaller, but it was still strong. Gradually we developed a healthy "we'll show them" attitude that renewed our energy. We also decided to refocus our efforts on a suspect who had been of great interest to King County detectives long before the bodies were found in Oregon and the FBI came in like a five-hundred-pound gorilla.

Some of the leads that we decided to revisit emerged from the computer runs we made to find names associated with the Green River data. One that popped out was Gary Ridgway, the Des Moines truck painter who had attacked a young prostitute who he claimed bit him. When Randy Mullinax interviewed him in 1984, Ridgway admitted to contact with one of our missing persons, Kim Nelson, a twenty-year-old last seen at a bus stop on The Strip in November 1983. But he had passed a polygraph and was moved onto the list of lower-priority suspects.

When Detective Matt Haney went back over the data we had collected, he noticed something interesting. Ridgway had been on strike for a three-week period in 1983. According to the best estimates of the medical examiner and detectives, three of our victims had been killed during that period. At no other time had the Green River killer been so active.

The data on Ridgway also included a 1982 report from the Seattle Port Authority police, who had stopped to talk to Ridgway while he was parked in a pickup truck at a baseball field near the airport. They noted in their paperwork that Ridgway was with a woman named Jennifer Kaufmann. With a little extra checking, Matt discovered that Jennifer Kaufmann was an alias used by Keli McGinness, who was a missing person last seen in November 1983.

The final connection that Haney made by working the computer was one that Randy would have wanted to know about when he met with Ridgway in May of 1984. It was the Des Moines police report on their visit to Ridgway's house at the request of Marie Malvar's family and pimp a year earlier.

There was the pickup truck — again — and a third woman on the Green River missing persons list.

We didn't need any more encouragement to swing into action against Ridgway, but we got it anyway. When Matt Haney went over the polygraph test with a couple of analysts, they pointed out a rather obvious concern. No one had asked Ridgway about Malvar and McGinness, so the test didn't clear him in those cases. Matt also gathered up all of the witness statements that made any reference to a vehicle. Quite a few of them described a truck that could have been Ridgway's.

Compared with the case the FBI had developed to justify its move against Bill McLean, we had more than enough connections to justify bringing Ridgway in. But we were extremely wary of repeating that experience. We began surveillance, using a camera posted near Ridgway's house, which was a few blocks off The Strip, as well as sending detectives and patrol officers in unmarked vehicles. The last thing we wanted was for him to strike again just as we were closing in.

In the scramble for additional evidence, Matt went looking for a witness who had given a statement when we first investigated Kim Nelson's disappearance. Paige Miley had been working alongside Nelson — staying in the same motel, standing on the same street corner — at the time she disappeared. A few days afterward, a man in a pickup truck stopped to speak to Miley as she was standing outside a 7-Eleven store on Pacific Highway South. He asked about her friend "the big blonde." Kim Nelson was a tall, striking woman with blond hair. The man Miley had described was in his thirties and had brown hair and a mustache, just like Ridgway.

When Matt went looking for Paige Miley in late summer

1986, the denizens of The Strip told him they hadn't seen
her in months. He put out a bulletin and got lucky when the
Las Vegas police called to say that their vice squad knew
Paige well. Matt met with her once, with mixed results
Then, in the fall, when more information was in hand
Randy Mullinax went to Las Vegas to try again. (Matt was
unavailable.)

As Randy reported when he got back, Paige Miley didn't
make it easy on him. First of all, she failed to show up at the
place and time set for their meeting. Randy had to ask the
Vegas vice squad's help. When they found her at work on
the street, Paige agreed to go with Randy under one condition — that he buy her anything she wanted at a good
restaurant. Randy agreed, and Paige, who was dolled up in
a sparkly spandex tube top, miniskirt, stiletto heels, and
huge amounts of makeup, directed him to a quiet place frequented by middle-class families and couples.

If patrons at the restaurant failed to notice Paige as she
waltzed into the restaurant, they surely caught her loud
laughter and dramatic way of speaking. She ordered expensive appetizers and a huge rack of ribs, slathered in sauce,
which she got all over the place as she ate. Randy, who sort
of liked Paige, had to remind her to curb her outbursts of
profanity. He also had to reassure her that she was speaking
under the immunity of a "King's X." In the language of the
street, when cops give prostitutes a King's X, they can answer questions without being charged with minor offenses.

Eventually Paige repeated for Randy the details of her encounter with the man who had spoken to her about Kim
Nelson. She recalled that he was wearing a checked shirt
and jeans, and that he was drinking a can of beer. Finally
Randy reached into a file he had brought and took out six
photographs. He asked Paige to study each one carefully

to see if she saw the man who had talked to her at the 7-Eleven. Without hesitation she zeroed in on a photo of Ridgway and said, "That's him."

Randy and Matt would take the lead in the pursuit of Ridgway. They put together the information prosecutors needed to get warrants to search his home and his vehicles and to authorize us to take samples of his hair and saliva. (This was before DNA testing was available. Saliva was used to determine blood type.) In the meantime, they would manage surveillance — leading much of it themselves — and conduct even more investigation into the suspect's current and past activities.

Every detective who tailed Ridgway through the winter of 1986–87 noticed he enjoyed driving up and down The Strip and that he often hopped on Interstate 5 North to go to one of the county's other major prostitution districts along Rainier Avenue. These were the two areas where most of the Green River victims had been seen in their last hours.

It wasn't just *where* Ridgway went that interested us but *how* he operated when he got there. He spent hours driving slowly up and down the streets, often turning into parking lots where he could stop and observe the women who were on the curb, trying to attract johns. Sometimes he would get out and throw open the hood of his truck as a ploy to attract their attention. He seemed almost too casual in his approach, as if he wanted the women to make the first move. It was the perfect style of behavior for a man who wanted to appear harmless and easygoing.

What we saw in Ridgway led most of us to think we might have our man. But we had other viable suspects, too. And after so much disappointment, we fought against reaching a definitive conclusion prematurely. I had felt very strongly about Melvyn Foster, only to see the case against him dissolve. The FBI and the command staff of the task force were so certain about Bill McLean that they were literally ready to pop champagne corks. This time we were determined to contain our enthusiasm.

Background checks and interviews with people who knew Ridgway gave us even more reason to suspect him. As the various profiles had predicted, he was an ex-military man (navy) who had lived and worked in the area around Sea-Tac for decades. He also had a penchant for unusual and rough kinds of sexual encounters. One of his ex-wives told us he had taken her to secluded spots around King County to have sex in the woods, beside rivers, and down in ravines. Several of these places were near sites where we had recovered bodies. But this was not as remarkable as you might think. Ridgway lived in the area. A surprising number of people like to have semipublic sex, and prostitutes used these same areas routinely.

Even as we gathered all the information that connected Ridgway to the Green River killings, we also tried to find any information that would prove he couldn't have committed these crimes. Was it possible that he was at work when the victims were seized and killed? His employment records suggested the opposite. In the few cases where we knew the approximate date and time of a woman's death, Ridgway had been away from his job. Worse, for him, were credit-card receipts that showed him gassing up at stations near crime scenes at times when the killer would have been prowling around.

Since we couldn't rule Ridgway out, and everything we checked only added to our suspicions, we soon arrived at the point where we had to conduct a thorough search of his home, truck, and body for evidence. A superior court judge had no trouble finding probable cause and gave us the warrants we needed. Our team agreed to keep quiet about the plan to take Ridgway into custody on April 8. We wanted to avoid, if at all possible, the kind of press coverage that had turned previous suspects into household names. On April 7 I went home, fully believing that we would be able to pull it off. And though I fought against believing it, there were moments that night when it occurred to me that the Green River nightmare might finally be over.

The warrant did not allow us to arrest and charge Ridgway, and we were determined to avoid having our moves against him reported in the press as a big breakthrough in the case, as had happened with Melvyn Foster and Bill McLean. For this reason, we described him only as a "person of interest."

On April 8 we took possession of his truck, and brought him downtown for a conversation. He calmly insisted he had done nothing illegal. And he readily agreed to give us hair samples and to chew on a piece of gauze so that we might discover his blood type.

The saliva sample was taken as a matter of routine. We had recovered semen from some victims' bodies, but the crime lab hadn't been able to obtain much information from the samples. We could only hope that one day science would advance enough to change this outcome, and they were preserved for just this reason.

While Ridgway was being processed, I led a team to his home to begin a search. In order to maintain a low profile, we limited the team to six people, traveled in unmarked vehicles, and wore civilian clothes.

I was in for a shock when I arrived at Ridgway's house. Waiting for me out front was Mike Barber, a reporter for the *Post-Intelligencer*. We had all pledged to keep our mouths shut about this search in order to protect Ridgway and ourselves from the media, but obviously someone had leaked information about our planned search. Fortunately, Barber agreed to keep Ridgway's name out of the paper. And upon our request, Ridgway's neighbors promised to refrain from calling other reporters. When they finally did catch on, the other members of the media also decided to avoid a repeat of the McLean problem by refraining from using Ridgway's name.

Inside, we crawled over every square foot of the house, looking inside closets and drawers and moving every piece of furniture. The attic and crawl spaces were searched with bright lights. We cut samples from his carpets and ran vacuum cleaners to collect bags full of dust, dirt, and hair for the lab to analyze. Outside, we explored the grounds for bones, clothing, or any other items that may have been hidden or buried.

All the profilers and professors and ace detectives who have worked on serial killer cases say that most serial killers collect souvenirs of their victims. It might be jewelry or pieces of hair. Some have taken photos of their victims. The point is that they want to remember and relive the killings, and these totems help bring them back to the place and time when they exerted the ultimate control over another person.

In my wildest fantasy, I hoped that we would find a box full of macabre mementos that would put Gary Ridgway on a fast track to death row. But after the most thorough search imaginable, we found nothing of the sort. The only vaguely interesting items we took away included some rope and plastic sheeting. We also found some maps of King County.

While we held his truck for further inspection, Gary Ridgway was given a ride home on the evening of April 8. He had said nothing incriminating in the time we spent with him. And over the weeks to come, the state lab would find nothing significant in the stuff we collected from his house and truck. None of the hair and fiber matched what was found on the victims. (This may have been because, as Ridgway's brother later told us, he had replaced all his carpet in the past year.)

None of the hair we took from Ridgway's body matched hair found on the victims. And though carpet fibers and the contents of many vacuum cleaner bags were examined closely, there was no breakthrough. More time and more effort would have to be invested before we could pin anything on Ridgway.

Fortunately, patience is like a muscle. It grows stronger the more you exercise it. As the fifth anniversary of the Green River murders approached, I didn't feel terribly let down by the results of our search. If Ridgway was the killer, and we certainly had no better suspect, then he had enjoyed certain advantages. He knew that we had been conducting a vigorous investigation and that we would eventually discover some shred of physical evidence he had left behind. With this warning, he likely cleaned his home and truck many times over. He would have carefully disposed of or hidden his cache of souvenirs, if he had one.

But there is no perfect crime and there are no perfect criminals. I was convinced that the Green River killer had eluded us mainly through luck, and I knew that kind of luck doesn't last forever. We were going to do our best to make sure it ran out soon.

Anyone who wasn't inside the investigation or experienced in serial murder investigations might have judged all of our efforts up to and including the Ridgway search a failure. After all, we hadn't actually caught the Green River killer.

But people who knew our work could see that we had made remarkable progress. The most obvious and important development was the dramatic decline in the number of new missing persons reports and Green River–type killings. If we hadn't caught the killer, we certainly had slowed him down. No doubt this was due to our increased presence in prostitution districts and our aggressive pursuit of witnesses, evidence, and suspects.

Beyond what was obvious, we had made many other important advances. Bob Keppel and Pierce Brooks, two prominent experts on serial killer investigations, had urged us to make a big investment in organizing our data into a form that could be analyzed by a computer for key matches and trends. This had never before been done in a serial murder case. We did it. And the results, when you acknowledge the value of the Ridgway lead, were obvious.

We had also advanced law enforcement's standard for handling outdoor crime scenes. Through careful study, we had learned how to recognize the pathways our killer used to enter and leave sites. We had set rigid, almost mathematical protocols for isolating and searching a location without contaminating it. And we had established very scientific methods for recovering every shred of evidence, down to individual hairs that would otherwise have been lost.

Finally, some of the task force members believed we had managed to build the right kind of relationship with the press, allowing reporters to inform the public without affecting our work. The evidence for this belief could be seen in the way the newspapers and broadcasters responded to the Ridgway search. They withheld his name and reported our activities in an accurate way. The public were informed that we were investigating a "person of interest" but learned little else. As a result, no one made a huge deal out of the fact that our search didn't yield an arrest. At last, the media understood what we were doing.

Or so it seemed.

In the summer following the Ridgway search, while the state lab was still processing evidence and we were continuing to monitor his activities, we heard that the *Seattle Times* had begun research for a series of articles on the Green River case. Our commanders, who had been pleased with the reporters' behavior around Ridgway, ordered us to cooperate with the *Times* writers Carlton Smith and Tomas Guillen.

For months, Smith and Guillen submitted requests for information, conducted interviews, and pored over records. I heard from some of the victims' relatives that they were constructing reports on them, too. The families hoped that the newspaper's attention would raise the profile of our investigation. If the stories presented the victims as real human beings rather than as caricatures of street prostitutes, then maybe the public and the politicians who controlled the sheriff's budget would support what we were doing.

We didn't lose a lot of sleep worrying about what the *Times* was going to say. There was too much work to do. In June, a skeleton had been found near Green River Community College. It was Cindy Smith, a seventeen-year-old missing since early 1984. Then in early September we were called to an embankment of Interstate 5 near The Strip, where the body of a recently killed woman was found wrapped in plastic sheeting similar to material we had found at Ridgway's house. The most chilling element of this find was that the victim, Rose Marie Kurran, had been missing for only a few weeks. (In fact, I had warned her to get off the streets prior to her disappearance.) If her murder was the work of the Green River killer, then his long period of apparent inactivity was over.

* * *

Days after we identified Rose Marie Kurran's body and notified her family, the *Seattle Times* finally began to publish its report on the Green River investigation. I was glad to see that some families were presented in a sympathetic light. And the paper did point out the challenges created by the huge number of runaways and missing persons we had to follow and the commitment Sheriff Thomas had made once he took office. But the overall tone of the series was very negative. Each installment was presented under the headline GREEN RIVER, WHAT WENT WRONG?, and almost every article included criticisms that were based on facts that we couldn't have known as we were doing our work. These were presented under headings such as "Valuable Time Lost," "Ignored Possibility," and "Investigation Gaps."

Anyone with common sense could see that we were being subjected to unrealistic expectations, and hindsight made it seem as if we had operated like a bunch of bumbling idiots. I could almost accept this from the reporters because I understood that they were ignorant about the early days of the investigation. However, I could see that they were motivated, at least in part, by ambition and hunger for fame. Why else would they devote an entire article to a description of their own methods and adventures in what they called the "shadows" of The Strip? Why else would every installment of the series include a prominently displayed item called "Credits" that listed the writers, editors, and even the "paste-up" man, like the credits that roll after a movie? Obviously these people were going after more than the whole truth and nothing but the truth. They were gunning for a Pulitzer Prize.

But while the behavior of the *Seattle Times* was consistent with what I expected, the statements from Tom and Carol

Estes that they published hurt us and disappointed us: "'Police really don't care,' Carol Estes says of efforts to find her daughter. 'They feel the kids are out there because their family doesn't care. They are not doing their job.'"

Of all people, Tom and Carol Estes knew that the detectives who were assigned to the Green River investigation had poured their hearts and their souls into the case. I had made myself available to them every time they called, and other detectives had done the same. No tip had been ignored, and no angle had been left unexplored.

Eventually we would all be able to see that grief and frustration were behind the kinds of criticisms voiced by Carol Estes. And her statements certainly didn't affect our efforts to find the man who killed her daughter. But if I said it didn't hurt us, even more than the judgments of the reporters, I'd be lying.

If a temporary loss of public support had been the only fallout from the *Times* series, we would have taken it in stride and forgotten about it quickly. But in the months before, we had heard constant rumblings of trouble between Sheriff Thomas and County Executive Hill. The sheriff was behind the task force 100 percent, and that included paying whatever overtime was necessary. Hill had become obsessed with the cost of the investigation, and he belittled the sheriff in front of other officials. Eventually the county council came to Vern Thomas's defense over several issues, and that only increased Hill's irritation.

The newspaper series that attacked the task force provided cover for some anonymous letter writer to send a list of complaints about Thomas to the county executive. Written on sheriff's office stationery, the letter delivered a few outright fabrications and a lot of low blows. Hill chose to discuss it in a press conference. The sheriff resigned the next week. He said it was because he could no longer stand as a loyal department head for the county executive.

An interim sheriff — Jim Nickle — filled Vern's position while a national search was conducted to find a permanent replacement. Nickle would oversee cuts that included closing the large task force office and moving the remaining detectives to the old county jail and placing them under the command of Major Terry Allman of the criminal investigations division. (Prior to this, we had reported directly to the sheriff.)

Although Nickle wanted the job on a permanent basis, it went to James Montgomery of the Boise sheriff's office, who came to King County despite his reservations about the Green River case. As an appointee, not someone elected by the voters, Montgomery was clearly Tim Hill's man. And as a loyal member of Hill's team, he was obviously prepared to cut the task force further if necessary to satisfy some budgetary concerns.

THIRTEEN

MEDIA BLITZ

As DIFFICULT AS the Green River case could be — in the winter of 1987–88 we knew we were nowhere near the end — there were always moments of grace that brought relief from the frustration and allowed us to be regular cops, if only for the moment.

Sometimes it was a little thing. Just after Christmas, Fae Brooks and I went to interview a woman who may have known one of the missing prostitutes. She told us what we needed to know, and while we were with her, we noticed that her eight-year-old son was especially interested in us. Before we left he got up the courage to tell us that he had gotten a new bike from Santa, but it had been stolen from in front of his house.

By the time we got back in our car, I was already thinking about an old bike in my garage. It was just the right size, and with some shiny new rims and a coat of red paint, I made it look almost brand-new. The boy who had lost his Christmas bike was happy to get a new ride, but I did what I did as much for myself as for him. It felt good to be able to solve a problem so quickly and to win that kid's smile.

Many other members of the task force also offered help to the people we met during the investigation. I can only guess how many thousands of dollars our detectives and deputies pulled out of their own wallets to help a family that needed food or a runaway kid who asked for a bus ticket. I don't mention this because I think we were saints. I mention it to show that we never became so detached from the people involved that we stopped being human ourselves.

I was most committed to the families of the Green River victims, and that's why it was easy for me to forgive Carol Estes's critical remarks about the task force that were published in the *Seattle Times*. It was soon water under the bridge, and I was glad we were still friends in May of 1988, when Debbie Estes's remains were finally discovered in Federal Way by a crew constructing a playground.

The recovery scene was a little different this time, because the skeleton was found a few feet below the surface of the ground. (It is possible that the killer buried her, but it is more likely that the body was buried by earthmovers that graded the area prior to construction.) Many hours of painstaking effort would be required to find anything that might be useful. We were rewarded with some pieces of cloth. Though we couldn't know it at the time, the state lab's scientists would find microscopic paint particles on the cloth, and those particles would become key specks of evidence.

Although some on the team that processed the site worried about collecting enough of the body to allow for quick identification, the medical examiner knew immediately that he was dealing with a woman in our missing persons category. From one of our dental charts, he recognized a crown unearthed along with a jawbone.

Although no single victim was typical in a way that suggests they were all the same, the details of the Estes case can give you a good idea of the kinds of challenges we faced. The Green River killer was attacking women who were involved in criminal activities and therefore determined to hide from the view of the police and straight society. And while most would have been defiant if someone suggested that what they were doing was wrong, their shame led them to hide from their own families as well. They moved frequently, disguised themselves with makeup, wigs, and hair dye, and changed their names almost as often as they changed their clothes.

When she disappeared in September 1982, Debra Estes was a fifteen-year-old girl who had already spent three years running wild in the streets. Her parents described her as a twelve-year-old in a twenty-year-old's body and said that before she was a teenager, she would sometimes disappear for days and refuse to say where she had been.

Tom and Carol Estes knew their daughter ran with an older crowd and certainly suspected she was using drugs and engaging in sexual activity. What they didn't know for some time was that she was working as a prostitute under the name Betty Jones, and that as Betty, she often picked up dates while working out of a motel directly across the street from her family's trucking company on Pacific Highway South. Betty Jones was known to the local police, because she had been arrested several times. According to the information she gave police back in 1982, she was nineteen years old.

Tom and Carol Estes had last seen their daughter in July of that year, when she stole a couple of hundred dollars from them and left without saying good-bye. They were the ones who figured out that their daughter and Betty Jones were one and the same, and when they did, they criticized the task force for failing to make the connection. We were already looking for "Betty" because people on the street told us she had disappeared. But this fact didn't comfort Tom and Carol, who were worried that precious time had been lost in the confusion. In their anguish, they would frequently call and complain to me, and sometimes conversations with Tom would become quite heated.

Fortunately, the lines of communication between the Estes family and me never completely broke down. Despite their expressions of anger, they also relied on me in all sorts of situations. Sometimes I'd get called to mediate family disputes, often involving something almost trivial. I knew the argument was really about something deeper. We just tried to patch things up.

"You've got to remember you're going through a tough time right now," I would say as I tried to make peace. "You're very emotional. Debra's disappearance is the sort of thing that causes all kinds of stress within the family. You have to support each other through this."

When their daughter's body was recovered and identified, Carol and Tom asked me to serve as a pallbearer at her funeral. I wasn't sure I should do it, but I asked the command staff and they thought I should honor the request.

I got the sense that the service was helpful to Tom and Carol. Knowing that their daughter was not out there suffering seemed to bring them a little peace. They had found her, and although she was dead, the truth would allow them to grieve. It was an honor to carry her casket. But as I performed this duty, I also felt anger and grief over the tragedy of Debra's murder.

The grief of the families was a powerful motivator for those of us who remained on the scaled-back task force. My family never forgot them either. At night the children prayed, "Keep

Dad safe, help him find the man he's looking for, and protect the other girls out there."

Although my wife and children were forced to accommodate the demands of the Green River case on my time and my energy, over the years I developed a better ability to separate my work and home life. One thing that helped a great deal was volunteering to coach my daughters' soccer team. With two or three practices per week plus games, I was able to establish a routine that brought us together at predictable times. Even if I had to go back to work afterward, the time I had with them on the field was a complete break from the Green River grind.

On weekends I would try to get involved with the kids as much as possible, even if we were just doing chores. We had a big vegetable garden — a little corn, a lot of tomatoes, squash, peppers, and lettuce — and Julie, Tabitha, Angela, and Daniel all worked there with me. I could be a little obsessive about getting every single weed out, but the longer we stayed in the garden, the more time we had to chat and bond.

One year, when I left a section of the garden unplanted, ten-year-old Daniel and a couple of his buddies announced that they were going to dig a big hole and make a swimming pool. I had to admire their ambition, so I agreed to supply them with some plastic sheeting to use as a liner, but only if they signed a contract binding them to refill the hole at the end of the day. Soon he and his friends were jumping around in several feet of water.

The happiness I felt at home watching the kids grow up was a wonderful distraction from the problems with the investigation. I couldn't help but imagine the gruesome satisfaction that the killer was feeling as days, weeks, months, and years passed without our finding him. This was a case of the bad guy winning, if only in the short run, and I had a hard time accepting it.

We had to hope that someone would come forward with new information to get us closer to an arrest. But we were hearing from surprisingly few new sources. And we almost never received information from outside the local area, even though it was possible that the killer had struck elsewhere. It was also possible that someone who knew something had moved away from the Northwest and needed to be reminded of the case.

National magazines and television programs practically ignored the case. As a result, even though the Green River serial killer had become the worst in American history — he was responsible for at least forty-eight murders — our investigation was almost unknown outside the Northwest. I doubt this was because writers and producers were consciously influenced by the status of the victims, but I do think that subconsciously they placed less value on the lives of women who worked the street. The case was also easier to ignore because Seattle was not a media center like New York or Los Angeles. Though it's a big and prosperous place, the city is still stuck on the upper-left-hand corner of the map, about as far from the centers of power as you can get while still being in the lower forty-eight.

Because we wanted to shake up the public, we began making ourselves more available to the media. One of the first interview requests we received came from an unlikely place, the *Sally Jesse Raphael* show. This was in the era before television talk shows had become out-and-out freak shows with daily brawls and half-naked guests. I thought that the Oprah/Donahue style of interviewing was still the norm, so, with Sheriff Montgomery's encouragement, I agreed to fly east with Mertie Winston, whose nineteen-year-old daughter Tracy Ann, a bright and vivacious young woman with curly brown hair, was found dead near the Green River in March of 1986.

Mertie was one of the more outspoken parents of the Green River victims. She was smart and articulate. She also represented the kind of average American family person whom viewers would identify with. Mertie and her husband both worked at Boeing, and they had established a good, secure home for their family. While others may have used this kind of statement as an excuse, their daughter really did fall in with the wrong crowd and was drawn away from the values she had been taught as a child.

The Winstons had become friends of the task force. Mertie often came to the task force office with homemade cookies as well as a list of questions and suggestions. I was glad that the trip east could give her a little break from everyday life, a chance to see someplace different.

We enjoyed the flight out together and checked into a nice hotel the night before the taping. At the studio we were asked to wait in the greenroom, where guests wait before they are called onstage. While we were there, Sally Jesse Raphael, the host of the show, came in to offer us some instructions.

"You're the detective?" she asked me.

"Yes."

"Well, please do your best to talk like a human being and not a cop."

"Excuse me?" I said.

She then told me that cops aren't very sensitive and tend to be too blunt and speak in a language all their own.

I wanted to explain to her that I wasn't some sort of TV character who always talked tough, but she had already bustled off to speak to someone else about how she should engage with the audience and speak in a way that made people sympathetic.

Besides Mertie and me, the panel on the show included relatives of women who had been murdered in other parts of the country. Everything went all right for a while, until they brought in a guy who was supposed to be some kind of expert. He began yelling at a family from Michigan, saying things like "What did you do wrong to have your kid wind up on the street in the first place?"

When Sally cut to a commercial, the so-called expert kept right on criticizing the mother from Michigan, who had the presence of mind to snap back at him. After the break, Sally did some sort of wrap-up that was intended to smooth everything out. It didn't. As the audience applauded the end of the show and Sally came to shake hands, I pulled her close to me.

"I will never come back to your show again," I said into her ear. "That was complete bullshit."

Mertie and I made a quick getaway from the *Sally Jesse Raphael* circus. I was glad that she had not been attacked like the others onstage, but I could see she was shaken. To put the experience behind us, we did a little sightseeing, including a visit to Central Park.

We walked together, and then we stopped and I took a picture of Mertie. We sat down and noticed an older woman feeding some pigeons. She had an enormous bag of bread cubes, and the birds were flocking all around her. I went over to talk to her while Mertie sat there thinking, no doubt, "There goes Dave again."

The pigeon lady asked where we were from and was curious about why we were in New York. Then, out of the blue, she asked us to come to her room for dinner. I turned her down — we had to catch our plane home — but as I left, she took my hand and said, "You have a kind heart." Those words had a powerful effect on me, as if they had been spoken by an angel. I walked away feeling restored and energized.

The talk show experience soured me and other task force members on daytime TV, but we didn't abandon the press idea entirely. Sometime after the *Sally Jesse Raphael* program aired, we got a call from a TV producer who was interested in doing a special on the Green River murders. We didn't make a commitment, but we kept listening as he called every few weeks to ask what we thought about one option or another. Finally he came back with a proposal to do a documentary for a series called *Manhunt Live,* which would re-enact some elements of the Green River case and invite viewers to call a toll-free number to volunteer information. As an added inducement, the program would offer a $100,000 reward for information leading to the killer's arrest.

The best thing about the *Manhunt Live* proposal was that it granted us control over what would be presented. There would be no surprise experts popping up to berate us, and we could tailor the material according to our own theories and advice from profilers. The producers decided to use me as a central figure, and the show would end with me issuing a challenge to the killer to call the hotline and speak with me directly.

When the producers asked me to go to Hollywood to help them sell the idea to a national network, I used the free airline ticket to visit San Diego also to consult on a serial killer case there. One theory in our case had the Green River killer leaving town in 1985 or 1986. In 1987, the cops in San Diego began dealing with a series of homicides similar to ours;

most of the victims there were prostitutes who were strangled and then dumped in sparsely settled parts of the county. It would help us if we could discover whether the same killer was at work, and the San Diego cops might also benefit from our counsel as experienced investigators.

When we got together, I could see that the San Diego detectives were as determined and motivated as we were in King County. After a helicopter tour of the region, where I was shown both the dump sites and the main prostitution area of El Cajon Boulevard, other similarities became obvious. Their killer was picking up women on El Cajon, killing them, and then depositing them within just a few miles. He used Interstates 80 and 395 the way the Green River killer relied on I-5 and I-90 to get quick access to dumping grounds. And he crossed a lot of jurisdictional lines — city to county to city — which complicated the investigation.

Although the pattern of victims and methods matched the Green River MO, no one piece of evidence established a definitive link. But my meeting with the San Diego authorities began an alliance that would last for years as they developed their own task force and conducted a methodical investigation similar to ours. I went home feeling that I had made progress on two fronts. We were allied with the police in San Diego and well on our way toward the TV special. I allowed myself to get a little excited about the broadcast. Besides being a worthwhile experiment, it was going to be a new experience and a break from the routine.

While I was on my way home from California, some of the people in the task force decorated our office with gold-colored cardboard footsteps and fake movie props to make it look like a walk of fame. The idea was to raise morale by teasing me with something silly. When Lieutenant Dan

Nolan saw it, he became livid and ordered it all torn down. Then, when I walked in, he started criticizing me for being "arrogant and pompous and not following directions like everyone else."

Nolan's real problem, as far as I could see, was that the TV producers had bypassed the task force managers in selecting me to go to Hollywood. He was jealous. It was a petty reaction, and certainly no one in the office deserved the outburst he subjected us to. But I chalked it up to a clash of personalities. Nolan, inexperienced in murder investigations, was the kind of supervisor whose authority was based on rank rather than leadership skills. We were bound to have our share of conflicts.

Nothing anyone said changed the fact that *Manhunt Live* had the potential to jump-start the investigation at a time when it seemed stalled. Several of us were involved in preparing for the show. I even donated an old pickup truck I owned, which was painted with primer to look like the vehicle several witnesses had described. We found a big empty space at Boeing field to equip with both a thirty-line phone bank as well as cameras and sets for the TV program.

The narrator for *Manhunt Live* was Patrick Duffy, who was known as a star of the hit television show *Dallas*. Somehow the producers also managed to line up Attorney General Dick Thornburgh to introduce the program. Then they devoted two hours to the problem of serial murder in general and the facts pertaining to the Green River case. Every few minutes Duffy would remind people to call if they had any information at all relating to our investigation, or to any other crimes.

The response was astounding. Within minutes we received literally hundreds of calls. The detectives in the room wrote notes as fast as they could and moved quickly to open up the lines. Meanwhile the producers showed clips from our investigation, interviewed experts such as John Douglas, and spoke with members of our team. Fae spoke for all of us when she said, "They're all our daughters in a way, because we've gotten to know some of these girls better than their families through our investigation."

Lieutenant Nolan asked people to consider whether they knew someone with an unusual collection of secondhand women's jewelry or other items that could be souvenirs from serial murders. Other investigators talked about the approach the killer made toward women. "He's either a professional, clean-cut guy," said one, "or a mild, pudgy, overweight guy grateful for the attention" a prostitute provided in exchange for her pay. Either way, the killer wouldn't appear to be a monster at all.

The *Manhunt Live* program offered viewers a remarkable education. In two hours they learned about the killer's methods, his likely profile, his area of operation, and his place in history as the worst of the worst. But nothing in the program was more powerful and affecting than the voices of the mothers and the pictures of the killer's victims as little girls and teenagers. The innocence, vulnerability, and youth of the women who had been killed were just as plain as the pain in their mothers' voices.

"Mary was very free-spirited as a child, very lovable," said Mary Bello's mother as pictures of her beautiful daughter flashed on the screen. "She always told me: Don't worry, I can handle it. She couldn't." Mary Bello's body was found where it was dumped off Highway 410 on October 12, 1984.

As the producers showed elementary school photos of Kimi Pistor, dead at age sixteen, her mother said, "Oh! She was cute. She didn't walk. She danced. She was the little girl next door. She was everybody's sweetheart. When things get out of hand and I can't handle it, that's the way I think of her. I would like to have met the woman she would have been. She would have been somebody."

Near the end of the program, I appeared on the set with John Douglas, the FBI profiler, who provided a short course in the psychology of serial killers. "He's a very sane, very, very intelligent individual who definitely knows right from wrong," said John. The killer had likely been "abused and neglected as a child" and grew into an adult with "extreme anger and frustration." In his late twenties, this man began to "go on the hunt" in order to "manipulate, dominate, humiliate."

John's comments about the killer's likely personality satisfied the public's curiosity about what makes a serial killer and might motivate someone who lived with a man with this background to take a closer look at him. But the most helpful information he offered had to do with the killer's probable behavior after he committed his crimes.

"The subject becomes obsessed with the investigation," said Douglas. He told viewers to take note if someone they knew started collecting newspaper clippings about the Green River murders, or became fascinated with places where the killings occurred or bodies were dumped. "He may even take the significant woman in his life to the crime scene and have sex with her, or go to one of the disposal sites and act very, very odd."

As Douglas spoke, it was easy for me to imagine a woman watching at home — perhaps while her husband or boyfriend worked the night shift — and gradually putting the pieces together. Her man was always talking about the Green River case. He had gotten very interested in driving past the places where the cops had recovered bodies, or in having sex outdoors.

If we were lucky, someone would make a call about a man he or she knew well. There was also a long-shot chance that the killer himself might be enticed to contact us. After John finished, it was up to me to deliver a carefully scripted statement that might push him to pick up the phone.

The idea was to establish a more direct connection with the killer — he probably knew I was chasing him already — and invite him to make contact. To do this, we suggested that we understood he had problems (even though we really couldn't care less about them), and we connected that with a warning that things would go better for him if he turned himself in.

I took this assignment seriously. I was certain that the evil monster was watching me as I spoke. I knew he was wondering if a friend, neighbor, or family member was going to get suspicious. I wanted him to see that I was a person of strength, determination, and focus. I didn't want him to have the slightest doubt that I was going to catch him. I stared straight into the camera, and the focus tightened as I spoke.

"I've worked this case for over six years now, and I feel very confident that someone will be leading us to you," I said slowly and clearly. "When we get this information, nobody will care anything about you or your problems. All everyone will want is for you to be punished. Many investigators believe you enjoy the killings. But several of us believe you are haunted by this, that this experience for you has been a nightmare. However, this nightmare will not end. It still haunts you during every waking hour. You must contact me soon, before someone calls and leads us to you. If we identify you first, no one will care what you think or feel. It will be too late. Please call me. It's time for us to talk."

As I ended my statement, the very first call that came in

was from a man who insisted on speaking with me because he was the killer. I was called to the line, and when I said hello, I heard someone say in a soft voice, "I'm the guy you're looking for."

I was excited at first. But as the conversation went on, I began to feel uneasy. The man on the phone chose his words carefully and spoke in vague generalities. I thought that if he was the killer, he had decided to toy with us. Then I asked him for specifics about certain victims. He didn't respond to my questions, but I got him to promise to write to me before he hung up the phone. (I never received a letter.) I didn't believe I had heard from the killer. John Douglas agreed, noting that there would be no point in the killer calling if he didn't make sure we understood he was the real deal.

Nevertheless, the program was a success when it came to generating tips. Thousands of pieces of information were phoned in. Many related to the Green River case, and others were concerned with violent crimes around the nation. We had clearly elevated the public's understanding of the challenges police face investigating such crimes, and we had shown how the public could play a role in solving them.

If there was any price paid by those who participated, it was probably in the pain they felt reliving the horror. When I got home that night, I learned that my fourteen-year-old daughter, Angela, had been deeply affected by viewing the show. Like almost everyone else who watched, she was taken in by the drama and felt moved by the tragedy suffered by young women not much older than her. Then she saw her father appear on the screen and speak directly to the killer in the most serious terms. The sight and sound of me playing this role were too much for her. She had burst into tears.

FOURTEEN

A ROCKET RIDE

MANHUNT LIVE was like drift-net fishing. That's the method some so-called factory ships used in the 1980s, dragging enormous nets that were miles wide through the ocean to catch everything that swims or floats. It's a great way to winch up tons of sea life, but an appalling percentage of the stuff that hits the deck of the ship is discarded as trash.

Among the ten thousand tips we received the night of the broadcast and in the weeks that followed were calls from people who hated their neighbors and from victims of crimes committed in other time zones. We could perform a sort of triage using computers to isolate the most promising tidbits, but, even then, we found that most of the information was not very good.

I would include in this pile the many letters I received from men serving time for murder. One, Manuel Cortez, wrote me about a dozen times from a prison in Oregon. In tiny script, he speculated on the supposed "ritual" enacted by the killer in each murder, paying close attention to the more sexual elements. Like many others, he suggested that the man we were chasing needed to commit murder in order to feel powerful and in control.

Although most of what Manny had to say was unoriginal, he did come up with a few interesting points. One came from a fellow inmate whom Manny questioned about the sites where he had killed women and the places where he had disposed of the bodies. The answers provided a rare look inside the feverish moments before and after this man murdered his victims: "After killing her, he didn't want to leave her body at the kill site, because of tire tracks, footprints, and other evidence at the scene. Yet, as he drove around looking for dump sites, he became increasingly paranoid and concerned that while stopping he might stumble across campers while he dumped his victim. [This despite the fact that the possibility of nearby campers had *not* been a concern earlier during the killing episode.] As it turned out, he drove out of the mountains and some eighty or ninety miles back to his hometown, where he ended up dumping the body in a dark lot within blocks of his own residence."

The picture painted by Manny's interview subject was disturbing to consider: a man driving for hours with a corpse in his vehicle. Of course, the Green River killer faced the same grotesque challenge of disposing of bodies. This is an awfully hard thing to do, and the consequences of getting caught are enormous. It therefore made sense that he would end up dumping the bodies close to home, in spots where he knew he wouldn't be noticed.

The letters from Manuel Cortez offered bits of interesting speculation, but the best of the concrete leads from *Manhunt Live* coalesced around a man who reportedly disguised himself as a Seattle-area police officer and had been convicted of burglary. Much about William Stevens fit the profile of the Green River killer. He had been a military police officer, and he was smart enough to earn a doctorate in psychology. He had also lived for a while in a house that was located less than a mile from the spot in Tigard, Oregon, where two Green River bodies had been found.

Thanks to a couple of callers, we located Stevens in Spokane, and the authorities there worked with our detective Tom Jensen to arrest him on an old warrant related to his escape from a prison work program. In his home were dozens of guns, a goodly amount of pornography, and a lot of surplus police gear.

If Stevens had talked freely in the beginning, we might have been able to clear him quickly. Instead, he wanted to have our questions filtered through his lawyer, a method that would stymie our efforts. For this reason and others, we were required to dig deeper into his background — a probe that produced no definitive evidence but added greatly to our suspicions. Sources told us that Stevens talked about the Green River murders and repeatedly claimed to be involved in law enforcement. One well-acquainted contact of Stevens's described his fascination with prostitutes.

Even though we had serious doubts about Stevens's standing as a suspect, the press eventually uncovered court papers that identified him. Once local reporters made his name public, the national press picked up the story and ran with it. (I guess *Manhunt Live* really did put Green River on its agenda.)

The media's rush to all but convict William Stevens came as a shock to us. Having been burned by publicity on Melvyn Foster and Bill McLean, we had been careful to avoid inflating the circumstantial evidence we had collected and had refused to speculate about Stevens.

In the end, William Stevens was cleared, but not before millions of people were told he could be a serial killer. In a strange twist, he said that he hoped to publish his own book, written from the perspective of someone who was briefly made infamous by a brush with the Green River case.

While the media tempest swirled around William Stevens, the members of the Green River Task Force had been dealing with many other issues, including the most basic questions about the future of the investigation. Doubts were once again being aired over the value of the task force itself. By 1988, more than $15 million had been spent. About thirty-seven thousand tips had been pursued, and we had logged more than nine thousand items of evidence. We could argue that our efforts had forced the killer to stop. But critics who said we had failed in our most basic mission, to catch him, were right.

On a more personal level, we all reflected on our own direct involvement with the investigation. There were heavy costs associated with this duty. While colleagues were making arrests and closing cases that would help their reputations grow, Green River detectives were confined in a professional state of suspended animation. At the same time, Green River investigators had to deal with how the case affected them psychologically and in their relationships with others.

More than one member of the task force would seek a transfer in order to avoid psychological problems or to save a marriage. Randy Mullinax left voluntarily, in part because the work was putting a strain on his family life. Years later, Randy would realize that the experience on the task force was even more difficult than he recognized at the time. "You get to be like a sponge, absorbing all the emotions expressed by the families and the tragedy you see," he told me. "At the same time, you don't get the reward of making any good arrests. You need that to happen if you are a detective — you need at least *some* success."

I understood Randy's departure, but he was such a good detective and friend that I felt the loss. I was also sad to see Fae Brooks transfer back to the sex crimes unit and then become a patrol sergeant. Neither Fae not Randy ever fully relinquished their interest in Green River. For the rest of their careers, they would keep an eye out for pickup trucks with primer spots and middle-aged guys who pulled to the side of the road to talk to young women. It was a habit they refused to break.

Another key team member who left about this time was Detective Matt Haney. Of all the task force members, Matt was the one I found it easiest to relax around. We were both alpha males, and every time we went out together to a site or an interview, we pretended to fight over who was going to drive the car. And once, when things were very slow and we both had countless unused vacation days, we decided to take the day off and go skiing together at Snoqualmie. It was a wonderful respite from the pressures of the case.

As the task force dwindled to just a handful of detectives, I tried to delay a decision about my own future. No one was more closely identified with the pursuit of the Green River killer than I was. I had promised too many mothers and fathers that I would do everything possible to bring them justice. I was reminded of this commitment in the fall of 1989, when one more body was discovered.

Just nineteen years old, Andrea Childers had disappeared in the spring of 1983, during the period when so many young women went missing. Her body was found close to

The Strip, in the same general area as the remains of Gisele Lovvorn, Constance Naon, Kelly Ware, and Mary Meehan. It's hard to imagine how such a heavily trafficked area could hide so many murder victims. But with so many little hideaways and abandoned lots, it apparently suited the Green River killer perfectly.

Once again we marked off the area around the spot where the body had been buried and combed it for evidence. Using garden tools and scrapers, we carefully pushed aside the dirt and exposed first the skull and then the rest of the skeleton. I could tell that this body had been there for years. The medical examiner estimated that the murder occurred in 1983.

Eight more women who disappeared in the mid-1980s remained on our list of probable Green River victims. In the years to come, the sheriff's office would recover four bodies that had the hallmarks of our serial killer and several more that were quite similar. We would also be notified of at least two dozen additional cases in which prostitutes or street kids vanished from the Seattle area.

Nevertheless, as early as 1989 it was clear to everyone that the big push to find the Green River killer was over. Detective Tom Jensen, who was familiar with how our computer system ran and knew the data inside out, was going to remain focused on the case. He would continue to look for connections and patterns in the interviews and evidence and handle anything new that came in. But all the other detectives would have to find other assignments, or the command staff would find assignments for them.

It was a good thing that I ultimately had no choice but to move on. For more than eight years I had been consumed by the case. In that time, my hair had turned gray and my kids had become adolescents. My wife, Julie, had endured my moods and absences without complaint, but there was no doubt that she had missed the love and attention I hadn't been able to give.

As a first step toward a new post, I took the sergeant's exam and passed. I would be transferred to the night shift in the Burien precinct, which included the Green River area and The Strip. On the morning of April 1, 1990, my last day as the lead detective on the Green River case, my family accompanied me to the courthouse downtown for a promotion ceremony.

I hadn't worn a uniform in years, so it felt a little strange to walk through the courthouse with my new sergeant's stripes. When Fae Brooks saw me and started laughing, I first thought she was just amused to see me in such a formal getup. Then she reached over and tapped on my name badge and told me it was on the wrong side of my uniform shirt. I had pinned it on the left, under my badge. It goes on the right.

Five sergeants and a lieutenant got their promotions that day. The sheriff presented us with certificates, and we restated the oath of office that we had all taken upon becoming deputies. It called on us to uphold the laws of King County and the state of Washington and to abide by the rules and regulations of the sheriff's office. Julie and the kids applauded at the end, along with the relatives of the others who got promotions, and we went out to lunch to celebrate.

My responsibilities for the afternoon included trading my unmarked car for a patrol car outfitted with the sheriff's decals and lights. I also had to clean out my desk in the task force office. I was already feeling emotional as I rode up in the elevator, so it was probably a good thing that the place was almost deserted. The only other person in the room was Tom Jensen, who would be on the case for the indefinite future.

I refused to accept that I had failed. Others might have looked at the results that day and concluded that I was fooling myself. The killer was not in custody. The victims' families had not received justice. And the task force was shutting down. While this was all true, I did not feel like a failure, because I knew the game wasn't over. Tom Jensen was going to continue working the data, and there was a very good possibility that a breakthrough would be made. In the meantime, I looked forward to patrolling the killing ground in the Burien precinct, always looking for the devil disguised as an ordinary man.

The contents of my desk filled four boxes, one more than would fit on the little handcart I had commandeered to take the stuff down to my new patrol car. Tom volunteered to carry the extra one down, and after politely refusing his offer, I accepted. But even then I lingered a bit. The room was full of powerful memories of the people who had worked there, the women who were killed or missing, and the people who loved them. For years the work we did together had pulled on me like the force of gravity. Now I was floating free, and it was a very strange feeling.

I was the first one to take on the Green River case, and I had stayed until it was officially put into mothballs. In that time, I had ridden a number of big waves, from the excitement we felt over Melvyn Foster to the disastrous move against Bill McLean. Many times I saw people come in with an attitude that said, "Reichert's missing something, we're gonna solve this." And whether it was Bob Keppel, the FBI, or someone else, none of those experts were ever right. In the end, I had done the job as well as anyone could, and that made me proud.

In the process, I had learned more than I could possibly catalog here. In general, I can say that I became a true expert in managing outdoor crime scenes and recovering bodies. This expertise was recognized by law enforcement around the country, and I was often asked to teach my methods to other departments. I also came to know more than a cop should know about how bodies decompose, the telltale signs of strangulation, and the inner workings of the sex trade. In the same vein, I acquired a thorough knowledge of the various perverse sexual activities that people practice behind closed doors, from bestiality to bondage.

Down in the police parking garage Tom helped me load the boxes into the trunk of a patrol car. We shook hands, and he said, "Good luck." I said the same and added, "Let's keep in touch." He nodded his head. I started the car and drove away. As I descended the ramp to the exit, going around and around, I felt like I was spinning down to street level for the last time, leaving behind one of the most challenging and important murder investigations in American history. Now I was going back to the precinct and back on patrol to chase burned-out taillights and U-turn violators.

On my first day at the Burien precinct — actually my first *night,* since I worked the graveyard shift — Fae Brooks met me just inside the door. Fae had become the first female lieutenant in the sheriff's office, which put her a rank above me. I didn't need the extra challenge to my ego that would come from working for a person I had trained and led as a detective.

"Fae," I said, "this is only going to work one way."

"Yes," she said.

"It will only work if we are partners, not if you see yourself as my boss."

She agreed immediately, and we became real allies in the precinct. In fact, we both used our positions to make sure the Green River murders continued to receive some attention. Every patrol officer knew that he or she might just come across the killer in the process of abducting a woman or dumping a body. We made sure that old dump sites were checked frequently, and the officers who worked The Strip continued to warn women about the dangers they might encounter in the guise of a mild-mannered john.

I was just getting accustomed to my new job and learning to appreciate the renewed contact with the local community when a stroke of terrible luck interrupted my transition. One night when I was driving to work at about 8:30 p.m., I reached the crest of a hill and saw a car speeding right at me. A young man had moved into my lane to pass someone in a no-passing zone. There was nothing I could do to avoid a crash. However, I did manage to steer away from direct collision, so that our cars met on an angle with the passenger side of each vehicle taking the brunt of the impact.

In the moments after the crash, I didn't feel any pain, so I jumped out and went to check on the other driver and his passenger, who was his girlfriend. She was injured and would need an ambulance, but I felt fine and requested a ride to the precinct from one of the cops who had responded to the report of the accident.

When I got there, people thought I was crazy to go on duty. In a few hours I started to agree with them. A dull ache became a throbbing pain in my back, and eventually I couldn't move. A deputy drove me to the nearest hospital, where doctors discovered I had two ruptured disks that would require surgery.

It took me six months to recover and return to work. Then, on my very first night back, I responded with several other cops to a domestic violence call. A man had beaten his wife and then run from their home. A couple of cops with dogs tracked him to some woods along the freeway. I was the nearest, so I drove down the freeway and parked where I could see an officer with a flashlight. I climbed a chain-link fence and scrambled down the hill. The suspect was screaming so loudly that I could tell that the dog had him. When I got close, the canine officer called off the dog. I jumped on the guy and rolled him down on the ground, only to discover that the dog had, literally, scared the crap out of him. If only I had taken one more day to rehab my back.

Exciting as patrol could be, given encounters with dogs and suspects with loose bowels, the first time I heard about an opening for a sergeant in homicide, I decided to go for it. My career ambition had been to follow in the footsteps of my friend Sam Hicks, who held that position at the time that he died in the line of duty. As far as I knew, there was no other applicant with my level of experience in murder investigations. Certainly none would have more expertise in managing crime scenes and employing more creative investigative techniques.

I am competitive by nature, so it was hard for me to wait out the weeks that the administration required to make their decision on the homicide job. Finally I got a call from Chief Nickle at home. After a little bit of small talk, he said, "Dave, you're not going to get it."

My silence signaled the chief that I wasn't taking this

news well, so he rushed to explain. "Homicide is something you've already done. We want you to gain other experience in the organization, because we believe you can be promoted and promoted again to become a member of upper management staff."

Was I supposed to believe that after so many conflicts with command staff over Green River, and after years of ribbing from so many colleagues about the lack of progress on the case, I was recognized as a rising star? This was hard to accept. To me it was far more likely that Nickle was trying to mollify me with a promise of future rewards so that he could end a very uncomfortable conversation.

I was wrong. After two months I was asked to go downtown and work in the sheriff's main office as administrative sergeant for Frank Adamson, who had risen to the rank of chief, which was just below the sheriff himself. This was the same Frank Adamson who had been captain of the task force and led us to join with the FBI to go after McLean. To his credit, he was a fair man who was able to overlook our past disagreements, and he welcomed me to work with him.

In Adamson's office I got a close look at the politics that govern the administration of justice at the highest levels in the county. I could see how the sheriff was forced to play two roles, politician and cop. All too often, it seemed to me, the cop lost out because the sheriff owed his job to the county executive, who appointed him. For that reason, the executive was the one who set the priorities. As long as the sheriff lacked his own power base, which would exist only if he held an elected office, he could always be second-guessed.

After a couple of years in the administrative office, I was promoted to lieutenant and assigned to special operations, which included, among other groups, the SWAT (Special Weapons and Tactics) team, the bomb unit, and hostage negotiations. Special operations got involved in a lot of very difficult situations. One of my toughest nights came on the very last day of my probation as a lieutenant.

We were working a major drug case and had been issued a warrant to search the house of a man we believed was a crack dealer. The team was going to use a battering ram — we call it a "door knocker" — to break down the door and then race in before anyone could hide evidence or escape. I was supposed to drive by the south side of the house, get to the backyard, and watch a dining room window.

When we were all in position, the entry team hit the front door and I saw people inside scurry toward the dining room window. A guy looked outside and saw me, and then gunfire erupted. I ducked behind the car, making sure to keep the engine block between me and the guys doing the shooting. We all survived the firefight and I got through my probation period, but sadly, one of our officers wound up shooting and killing one of the young men who had been inside the house.

My time in special operations was brief, as the upper-level command staff continued to move me from one good post to another. It really did seem like I was being prepared for a leadership position. I had one unhappy stretch as a captain back at the Burien precinct, where I came under the thumb of a major who was a rigid manager. I was put on a tight twelve-hours-per-day schedule, handling a lot of paperwork and supervision. As fate would have it, I wouldn't have to stay there too long before I got a call from Sheriff Montgomery, the man from Boise. I was promoted to major. My command would be the Kenmore precinct, in the northern part of the county.

The rapid pace of my advancement was as startling to

Julie and me as it was to everyone in the sheriff's office. A longtime friend even asked me, half joking, "Who strapped a rocket to your ass, Reichert?" Julie and I trusted in our faith and knew that God had a plan and we were his servants.

Meanwhile, my advancement was taken as good news by the families of the Green River victims. Many of their mothers, fathers, sisters, and brothers continued to call me. The higher I rose in law enforcement, the more they hoped I could do something to restore the investigation. In fact, Tom Jensen was doing a good job of following the tips that still trickled in — some came to me personally — and it was hard to say what more could be done. But the case, like the forty-eight women known to be the serial killer's victims, was never far from my mind.

I was just getting comfortable in my role as a major in Kenmore when King County voters made a dramatic change in their government, approving a referendum that would bring back an old office — the elected sheriff. No longer would the county executive have the power to appoint the top law enforcement officer. Instead, candidates would have to campaign to persuade people that they were qualified, and the sheriff would answer to the voters and not some political boss.

Jim Montgomery wasn't interested in running election campaigns, and he made it very clear that he wasn't going to stick around as sheriff. By the end of December 1996 he was on his way out, and half a dozen people started to lobby then–County Executive Ron Sims to get the post for the time period leading up to the November election. Everyone assumed that the man or woman who wore the sheriff's uniform prior to the election would enjoy a tremendous campaign advantage.

One person who thought he understood the way things

were going to work was Mike Patrick, a retired Seattle police officer and president of the Washington State Police Officers Association. Patrick was a former state legislator, and he seemed to know everyone in county political circles. He quickly captured the support of some people in our guild, because they believed that he would promote them into key positions. Although he was a Republican and Executive Sims was a Democrat, Patrick was banking on two things — the fact that there were no strong Democrats available and the fact that the county council, which had to approve the appointment, had a GOP majority.

I didn't pay much attention to all the jockeying, because no matter what happened, I had a secure position as a major and I enjoyed my job. Besides, while all this was going on, I had a little health crisis that required some fairly intense attention. It began when my right foot became weak and I quickly lost the ability to move it. Doctors determined that particles from my ruptured disk had lodged against certain nerves. Without immediate surgery, I faced permanent paralysis of my foot and leg. I had the surgery and was forced to take a month off to recover.

On a Friday morning in early March, I called one of the chiefs, Larry Mayes, to remind him that I was spending the day at the state capitol in Olympia at a meeting on regional police issues. Chief Mayes asked me, out of the blue, "Did *you* ever consider becoming sheriff?" At first I thought he was kidding, but he made it clear that he wasn't. "Dave, if we don't find someone from inside to take the lead on this, we could get someone who doesn't know anything about the sheriff's office, how it works, and what the priorities are."

I told Mayes that I was just trying to run my precinct the best I could, and that if I had any career plan at all, it involved an attempt to get a chief's post before I retired.

"How about I just run your name up the flagpole?" he asked. "I'll just talk to people in the courthouse and see what they think."

After agreeing to let Larry float my name, I drove down to Olympia, wondering what might happen next. At the meeting, Mike Patrick shook my hand and said, "Great to see you, Dave. I've got great news. I just got a call last night and was told I'm going to be appointed sheriff on Wednesday. I'm going to be your new sheriff, and I plan to run for election in November."

Politically naive as I was, I assumed Mike was telling the truth, and I wondered why Larry Mayes didn't know about this.

Before we sat down to work, when people were still socializing, Mike took me around and introduced me as someone who was going to be one of his precinct commanders when he became sheriff. Everyone was congratulating him like it was a done deal.

The session proceeded predictably enough. The assembled cops and politicians and bureaucrats agreed that we should all cooperate more — despite intramural jealousies and competitiveness — and we considered ways we might actually put this concept into action. As the meeting broke up, I got paged to call Larry Mayes. I asked the lieutenant governor if I could use his phone, and he pointed to one in his office.

Considering what I had heard from Mike Patrick, the first thing out of Larry's mouth shocked me. "Dave, whether you like it or not, whether you want to or not, you're gonna be sheriff."

With so many political types around, including Mike Patrick, I whispered my reply. "What are you talking about?

Mike Patrick is here, saying he's going to get it. It's all wrapped up."

"Bullshit," said Larry. "Ron Sims wants to interview you Monday. If it goes well, you've got it."

That weekend the phone at my house rang off the hook. Many people inside the sheriff's office called to urge me to take the job, but I also heard from those who thought I would be making a big mistake if I accepted the appointment. The one who made this point most loudly was Mike Patrick himself. His main argument was that even if I got the appointment, he was going to win the election nine months later. "I have a campaign organization put together, three hundred thousand in the bank, and I'm going to stomp all over you," he said.

This was not the way to get me to back down, and I made sure that Patrick knew I wasn't impressed by his argument. Soon after I hung up, the phone rang again. It was a guild leader named Charlie Love. "Boy, Dave, it would be a big mistake for you to take it," he said. "Mike Patrick was going to make you the undersheriff. He just hasn't gotten around to asking you yet."

I noted that I had been with Patrick all day Friday, and he hadn't said a word. Then I said, "Thank you so much for the phone call." As I put the receiver back on the hook, I looked at Julie and said, "Well, you know what I'm going to do."

As I sat in the waiting area at the county executive's office on Monday, I looked down and noticed that my suit coat and pants didn't match. I chuckled inside and then reminded myself that I wasn't being asked to perform as a male model.

In the interview, we ran over some basic background, and

a few of the county executive's key people asked some questions. When the room went silent, Ron Sims finally spoke up. "What major issues and concerns do you see facing the sheriff in the next three to five years? What tools and philosophies will you use to address them? And why do you think you are the person to do it?"

There I was, being interviewed for one of the biggest jobs in law enforcement in the country, a job I never dreamed I would have, and a funny thought raced through my mind. I could look at my watch and say, "Uh-oh, I'm out of time. Gotta go. See ya!"

But in fact, I had answers for him. I had been involved for years on a strategic planning team. One hundred people from across the organization had participated in defining the mission, vision, and goals of the sheriff's office. We had realized that the development of new local police departments — to serve newly incorporated municipalities — was a major concern, and we needed to make sure we were identified as a valuable resource that they could draw from.

Considering this issue, our group had decided that in the future the sheriff should be the provider of police services in metropolitan King County. I told Sims we should work to be *the* provider so that we wouldn't disappear as new cities were incorporated. Citizens would benefit from this approach because the county could provide a large-scale, co-ordinated police service. At the same time, I said, we should approach our jobs with a sense of service that emphasized building the public's trust.

I guess that satisfied him, because Sims arranged for us to meet again the following night for dinner in the north end of the county. Then on Wednesday, I stood with Sims as he announced my appointment. In one press account on the appointment, a reporter asked Bob Keppel for his reaction. He predicted that I would revisit the Green River murders as soon as it was practical.

By the time the election came around, Mike Patrick had changed his mind about running for the office, and he wound up supporting me. I was endorsed by both the Democratic and Republican parties and faced a little-known opponent who had been with the Seattle police department. When 77 percent of the voters elected me, it was a sign of their support for a professionally run sheriff's office.

FIFTEEN

UNFINISHED BUSINESS

THE KING COUNTY SHERIFF heads a law enforcement agency that is charged with a remarkable range of responsibilities and duties. We serve densely populated urban centers and wide-open rural areas. Our cops conduct routine patrols and mount sophisticated investigations, like the Green River Task Force did. Small police departments in the county call on us for support, and we must be expert in every police specialty — from hostage negotiation to high-tech surveillance. At the same time, the community expects us to be compassionate when it's called for but decisive and tough when it's necessary.

Fortunately the path I had followed from the academy to the sheriff's office prepared me well for the role of sheriff. If I hadn't actually performed every conceivable duty that our cops were expected to handle, I had at least been directly involved with those who did. I had also spent more than enough time in and around top managers to see how the command staff organized and deployed a force that included nearly seven hundred uniformed personnel and four hundred civilians.

I retained several of Sheriff Montgomery's best people, including his executive assistant Sue Foy, who would become one of the most important people in my life. A dynamic person with a disarming sense of humor, Sue was also a very keen student of office politics and county affairs. She brought me up to speed on issues that would have taken me months to figure out on my own.

My leadership team would include three chiefs. I held on to Larry Mayes, who had only recently become a chief, and added Rebecca Norton and Jackson Beard. Jack had worked on the Green River Task Force, and in his new post, he would have direct involvement with Tom Jensen, who remained on the case.

A police department wins public support by handling both everyday concerns and emergencies with as much openness as possible. Whenever we had cases in which cops overstepped their bounds, I responded swiftly and publicly. And whenever we faced emergencies, I tried to act in a way that reassured law-abiding citizens that they would be kept safe.

The most visible crisis to affect King County in my early years as sheriff arose when thousands came to Seattle in 1999 to protest a meeting of the World Trade Organization. On the morning when the WTO meeting was set to open, tens of thousands of protesters jammed the streets downtown, overwhelming the 450 officers whom the City of Seattle Police Department had sent to maintain control. With the pressure mounting, I joined city, state, and federal officials at a crisis meeting to produce a plan for restoring order. We developed and then implemented a plan that called for hundreds of state troopers, King County sheriff's deputies, local police departments, and National Guard troops to deploy in the city. A fifty-block area was declared a no-protest zone, and teams of police cleared out protesters one by one. We also set a 7:00 p.m. curfew that covered most of downtown.

Fortunately, our action against the violent element among the protesters worked quite well. President Clinton kept to his schedule, arriving at Boeing Field and then attending the WTO meeting to sign an agreement against child labor practices. When all the damage was added up, it totaled $20 million in broken glass, theft, graffiti, and lost business revenue. More than six hundred people had been arrested, and the Seattle area's reputation as a safe place to visit had been tarnished. But the cops got high marks from the average citizen. In a poll conducted two weeks after the WTO left town, 68 percent of the people approved of the way we handled things.

All of the public safety people who managed the WTO crisis felt some satisfaction when it was over. I certainly considered it a high point for the King County Sheriff's Office. And overall, I was comfortable in the job. I had a good team in place, and every year we seemed to become more professional and efficient. We had the usual conflicts with the county council and county executive over budgets and priorities, but our experience showed that the voters were right to make the office an elected one. With a base of voter support, we were much better positioned to argue for the best policing practices, instead of doing what politicians thought would be expedient.

But as rewarding as the job was, I never forgot that an enormous piece of unfinished business overshadowed whatever I might accomplish. As far as I knew, the Green River killer was still alive, and given the powerful urges that drove him and all serial killers, he remained a terrible threat.

With no new reported murders, and the press turning its

attention elsewhere, the public's concern about the Green River killer had seemed to disappear. The newspapers mentioned the case when Bob Keppel retired, and they brought it up again when the medical examiner Donald Reay left office. But in general, people just stopped talking about the Green River killer — and stopped remembering the families he had hurt so deeply.

Ironically, this forgetting happened at a time when serial killers were a source of entertainment for millions of people who munched popcorn as they watched *Silence of the Lambs* and devoured bestselling books about these monsters. For a while it almost seemed that America regarded serial killers as pop icons. It was an interest that would appeal only to those who had never lived with the anguish these monsters cause.

Knowing that the Green River killer was still free to cruise The Strip made me angry and frustrated. I was not accustomed to losing at anything, and I still refused to accept that the contest between us was over. Ten years after I emptied my desk at the task force office, I still went out of my way to drive past the places where we found bodies and the streets where women disappeared.

We had interviewed scores of suspects. Most had been ruled out with just a brief investigation. Others had required more attention, either because they couldn't provide us with solid alibis or because their records included notes about violent behavior or crimes. These men had become our primary suspects, and none of them was more interesting to us than Gary Ridgway.

Ridgway had been visited in May 1983 by the Des Moines police in their investigation of Marie Malvar's disappearance. Randy Mullinax had also questioned him in February 1985 after prostitute Rebecca Guay told us about a john who had attacked her. And then in 1987, we had followed up on Paige Miley's account of her friend Kim Nelson's disappearance by searching Ridgway's home and vehicle and taking hair and saliva samples from him.

There had been plenty of leads tying Ridgway to the victims, but time and again we had come up against the lack of decisive evidence against him. The thought that he could well be our killer but we lacked the evidence to arrest him weighed heavily on all of us.

I wasn't the only one who found it impossible to let go completely. Whenever I saw others who had worked on the task force, we invariably discussed the case. And every once in a while I still heard from people like Mertie Winston, the Estes family, and others who had suffered because of the Green River killer. The passage of time may have made their grief a little less intense, but their hunger for justice had not been satisfied. However, they were afraid that the time to catch the killer had come and gone. One sign that they may have been right appeared in early 2001, when a documentary of the case was aired on national TV — by the History Channel.

No one who worked even a day on the Green River murders considered it a matter of history. This was doubly true for the family and friends of those who had been killed. So even though the media tried to push the case into the past, I frequently heard from people who wanted to know if any progress was being made.

People assume that chief executives can make things happen. After all, you're the boss. You can allocate manpower and other resources according to your priorities, and you can issue orders to every person in the chain of command. With so much power, you'd think any mission could be accomplished. If only it were so.

In reality, a boss can move an organization only so far. If the goal is out of reach, no amount of time, money, or barking commands is going to produce the result you want. This was true for me when it came to Green River. When I became sheriff, the victims' families and others hoped that I would do something to solve the mystery. I hoped I could make some progress, too, but I knew it wouldn't be easy.

To start, I made sure that detectives Tom Jensen and Jim Doyon knew they would have all the support they needed, and I named one of the best people on my command staff, Jackson Beard, to be their immediate supervisor. I also assigned a small team of detectives to review and submit to the lab for analysis every piece of physical evidence that might yield a fingerprint.

But I could do nothing to create new evidence or new avenues of investigation. Whenever I received information from longtime sources, I passed it along to Tom. And we periodically spoke, just to make sure I was kept current on his efforts. However, the real progress in our case was taking place in various laboratories around the world.

Day by day, scientists were slowly advancing their technology and techniques for extracting human DNA from difficult samples and constructing enough of a person's genetic code to provide definitive identification. In my office, Scott Sotebeer was following the progress of this science with the help of a consultant named Tim Shelberg. At the same time, Tom Jensen and Sergeant Ray Green were in close contact with the state lab, which was trying to keep abreast of every new development.

In early 2001, it seemed that the time had come. The

Washington State crime lab finally had the equipment and training to extract usable DNA from some of the old samples we had collected from suspects in the Green River murders and compare it with semen taken from the bodies of two victims. The new method was called STR, for short tandem repeats. It meant that even a tiny sample would be adequate to produce a valid report.

At a gathering of Green River veterans held in late spring 2001, Tom announced that the testing was under way. About three dozen of us had come together to discuss the tips and pieces of physical evidence that seemed most important. We had hair and fibers that were found on some of the bodies, and paint flecks from pieces of clothing found at Debra Estes's grave site in 1988. But we knew that the most valuable items in our possession were the semen samples taken from Marcia Chapman and Opal Mills, whose bodies were found on the very first day of the Green River killer investigation. And when Tom said the DNA testing had begun, our hopes started to rise.

The analysis would take a few months. Fortunately, cops are trained to endure long waits. We wait for suspects to make mistakes, for prosecutors to build cases, for juries to deliver verdicts. I put the testing out of my mind and stayed busy with the demands of my office. With so many personnel out there on so many challenging duties, the sheriff of King County never has a slow day.

On September 10, 2001, Tom Jensen called to ask if we could meet. He didn't say what he wanted to talk about, but since he made a formal appointment instead of just dropping by, I had a feeling he had some important news. When he arrived, I was sitting at the conference table in my office with Chief Fae Brooks and Sergeant D. B. Gates of major crimes.

Tom is a very reserved guy. He has a dry sense of humor and a calm temperament. But even he seemed a little keyed up as he entered the room with a folder. He came over to me and laid three sheets of paper facedown on the table. As he turned them over one by one, he told me what they were.

"This is the DNA profile taken from Chapman."

He paused and let me study it.

"This is the one taken from Mills."

I could see they were identical graphs.

"And this is the DNA profile taken from one of our suspects."

Tom pushed the paper toward me. I asked him if this meant we had a suspect. "Turn it over," he said.

I turned over the piece of paper. On the top were the words "Green River Killer." Below was a graph that was an exact match with the previous two.

"And this," said Tom, handing me an envelope, "is the name that goes with that profile."

I took the envelope in my left hand and hesitated. "I don't have to open it."

"What do you mean?" he asked.

"I *know* it's Gary Ridgway."

He smiled, and so did Fae and Sergeant Gates as I opened the envelope and read Ridgway's name. Tears began to flood my eyes, and my throat closed a bit with emotion. I could see that Tom was on the brink of tears, too. As much as we always expected to solve the case, neither of us was quite prepared. Now we knew we could charge Ridgway with the murders of all three victims found at the river on August 15, 1982.

What did we feel at that moment? Certainly we felt a tremendous flush of victory. We had at last won the most challenging competition anyone could imagine, a battle with enormous stakes and life-or-death implications. But we also felt an overwhelming sense of relief. For nearly two decades we had lived with all kinds of pressure. This included the expectations of victims' families and the general public, and the silent pleading of all the dead and missing women who deserved real justice. Finally, there was the pressure we had put on ourselves. Every day I had silently reaffirmed my belief that we would solve the case, and I had always said that I would stay on the case one way or another until it was finished.

But there was more than just a feeling of victory and a sense of relief. My mind was flooded with memories — of recoveries, interviews, meetings with parents, and long days and nights in task force offices. I thought of Julie and my children and all they had seen, heard, and experienced. I thought of all the lives that were cut short, all the grief and pain. I also recalled the critics who had attacked us in the newspapers, marched in the streets, and invaded the task force offices. They didn't believe that we were committed, competent, and caring. They were wrong.

As the images, sounds, and feelings coalesced, I realized something profound. We had done it right. We hadn't been perfect. We had even made some mistakes. But in the end, we had been thorough enough to find and preserve samples of fluids from some of our very early victims. And we had been smart enough to hand Gary Ridgway a piece of gauze, which he chewed and we then saved.

Along the way, we had refined the processing of outdoor crime scenes to the degree that it was practically a scientific discipline. We had also devised improved methods of case management and the use of computers to identify suspects from various sets of records. These advances could be adopted and taken further by other teams investigating other murders. Finally, we had shown that it was possible to solve stranger-on-stranger murders with the least bit of evidence. This had to give hope to others facing the same kind of challenge.

The urge to shout about Gary Ridgway was almost too strong to resist. But of course we knew we would have to keep the results of the DNA tests secret for a few months as we prepared to arrest him. Civilians are often surprised to learn that we don't just race out and grab a suspect when we have solid evidence; in fact, we must take the time to construct a solid case for the prosecutor before moving in. That way, a suspect is confronted with so many facts that he and his lawyers may realize that it would be futile to even contest the charges.

To limit the possibility of leaks, we decided to gather just a few key investigators, including members of a recently appointed Green River evidence review team, at Fae Brooks's house. The calls went out on September 11, 2001, as the entire nation was reeling from the terrorist attacks in New York and Washington, DC.

On that day, police departments around the country were scrambling to make sure that terrorists weren't on the loose in their jurisdictions. Randy Mullinax, who had become a detective in our intelligence unit, had teamed up with an FBI agent to investigate a report from a hotel maid who found flight manuals in a room occupied by foreign nationals. The books turned out to be the property of some Chinese pilots in town for training at Boeing, but for a moment Randy was a frontline soldier in the national response to the terrorism crisis.

When I reached him by cell phone, Randy had just resolved the tip about the Chinese pilots. I told him I had big news — a break in the Green River case. "We have DNA," I added. "And you are well aware of who it is. In fact, you worked the guy."

Randy knew better than to say Ridgway's name out loud, but he knew who I was talking about. I'm sure he got a knot in his stomach as he thought about leaving a relatively comfortable assignment to return to the stress of Green River. But he also understood that few people knew the facts of the case and Ridgway's history as well as he did.

"DNA is not a silver bullet," he said.

"That's why I need you," I answered.

A few days later, Randy showed up at Fae's house, joining about a half dozen key players. We were all excited about the idea of wrapping up the investigation. We knew the arrest would be national and maybe even international news and that a great many people would celebrate the solving of the terrible mystery.

I began the meeting by restating the need for secrecy. In the past, some members of the task force, whom we never identified for certain, had leaked information to the press at the worst moments. I made it clear that this wasn't going to happen again, and everyone agreed.

We then went over the tasks that had to be accomplished prior to the arrest. First we would have to dust off the files on key cases, including the Chapman and Mills murders, and help the prosecutors write up their charges. We would also need to locate Ridgway and establish surveillance to make sure that he didn't kill anyone else. Some of the team would have to contact former witnesses, to make sure they were alive and would testify. And we had to prepare to question Ridgway effectively once we got him in custody.

Although an arrest, prosecution, and conviction were our paramount goals, Ridgway could potentially give us a great deal more. If you added up all his known victims, other murders he may have committed, and missing women who fit the victim profile, the total was more then seventy. We knew the fates of only forty-eight. Dozens of families would benefit if he decided to tell us the truth about what happened to the others.

Along with learning the locations of more bodies, we also hoped that Ridgway would supply more details about what happened to each of his victims, as well as insights into his own bizarre thinking. These last two categories of information interested me the least. It was difficult for me even to say that I cared about what a serial killer thought. But I understood that some criminologists and psychologists would find some value in it. Perhaps it might help future experts identify potential serial killers as youngsters and allow them to intervene.

A domestic violence unit at the county's Regional Justice Center in Kent was moved to another location in order to give the Ridgway team space to work. This raised a few eyebrows. And the resentment only grew as the Ridgway group began its work under a blanket of secrecy. Access to their space was restricted. They papered over the windows and changed the pass codes on the locks. Their refusal to discuss their work with anyone was interpreted, quite naturally, as a supercilious attitude.

While the Green River detectives were pulling everything together for Ridgway's arrest, the Washington State crime lab was able to process another DNA sample, one taken from the body of Carol Christensen, and confirm that it was from Ridgway, too. This match made four murders that we could pin on one man. There would be no doubt that he was the Green River killer.

This was very good news for Senior Deputy Prosecutor Jeff Baird, who was preparing the warrants that would allow us to take Ridgway into custody and search his vehicles, homes, and workplace. Baird was the perfect choice for this assignment. Not only was he an expert in cases involving DNA, but he also was the former head of the Most Dangerous Offender Project, a program that prosecuted only the most violent suspects. He knew how to manage a case against the likes of Ridgway so that every move met the letter of the law.

Baird, who would work closely with a colleague named Patricia Eakes, estimated that their job would be done and we could swing into action on December 7, 2001. We were working toward this date when, on the night of Friday, November 15, Gary Ridgway didn't come home after work. Instead, our surveillance group saw his wife go out late and return with him around midnight.

The next day, we were all very concerned about the fact that we had lost track of Ridgway for most of an evening. Randy Mullinax was so worried about this problem that he left a bookstore where he was shopping with his family to call another detective on the phone. While they were talking, Gary Ridgway actually drove into the parking lot and walked into the bookstore. "Well, we know where he is now," said Randy. He quickly retrieved his wife and son and left before he was recognized.

From that point on, we maintained constant surveillance of Ridgway. We also set up a little sting operation to see if he was out picking up prostitutes. On an afternoon when we knew Gary would be likely to drive along The Strip on his way home, we had a prostitute/informer stand by the road-side. We instructed her to act like she was looking for johns, but under no circumstances was she to get into Ridgway's truck. With lots of cops watching from unmarked cars, Ridg-way appeared on schedule and rode by without even turning his head. For the moment, at least, he was not looking for more victims.

Everything was coming together smoothly for December 7 when Randy went to a sheriff's office computer to check for records on Ridgway's recently deceased mother. The first name that came up under the surname Ridgway was Gary's, and it showed that he had been arrested on November 15 for soliciting a prostitute. (We call it "offering and agreeing.")

Suddenly we knew where he had been on the night that his wife brought him home so late. He was being booked and then released. We also realized that we had been wrong about his discontinued interest in prostitutes. Obviously he was out trolling again. We would have to pick him up as soon as possible. The task force team worked day and night to allow us to grab him ahead of schedule, which we did on November 30.

SIXTEEN

ONE IN CUSTODY

I BARELY SLEPT the night before the arrest. I tossed and turned and at various points gave up trying to sleep and instead ran through the plan we would follow in the morning. In a smaller jurisdiction, the sheriff would be in on any arrest of this magnitude, but in King County it would have looked like grandstanding for me to be at the scene. So as much as I wanted the satisfaction of seeing Gary Ridgway's face as he was taken into custody, my main duties would be to stand by at the command post, inform the public, and deal with the media, taking special care to avoid saying anything that might damage the prosecutor's case. We didn't want to give a judge any reason to move the trial out of King County or to throw out any of the charges.

At dawn I took time for a short workout, showered, dressed, and said good-bye to Julie. She was one of the few people in the world who knew what was about to happen (I had trusted her with the news about Ridgway weeks earlier), and I realized that it was a very important moment for her, too. This investigation had dominated both of our lives for so long that it was hard to believe we were nearing the end. We talked about how she would alert Daniel, Angela, and Tabitha to watch for the news on TV. She wished me good luck. I hugged her, and then I left.

My first stop was at the King County Regional Justice Center in Kent. I asked to see the rookie deputy who had nabbed Ridgway as a john earlier in the month. I thought it would be a nice touch to let her in on the big secret.

"You know that guy you arrested a couple of weeks ago on the offering and agreeing charge? That guy Ridgway?" I asked.

"Yes sir," she answered, a little surprised to be questioned directly by the sheriff.

"Well, we're going to arrest him this afternoon for the murder of four women in the Green River case."

She stood there for a moment, speechless.

"Really, we're going to arrest him this afternoon," I said again.

"Wow!" she finally answered. "This is huge!"

It was huge, but it was still secret, and as much as I wanted to stay in the command center we had established in Kent, I needed to act like nothing was happening. So I went to my office in Seattle and pretended that it was a day like any other. This was made a little easier by the fact that a few of the staff, including my assistant Sue Foy and spokesman Sergeant John Urquhart, knew what was about to happen and we were able to talk about it in private.

While I waited in my downtown office, detectives in unmarked cars went to the Kenworth truck plant, where Ridgway worked. At eleven o'clock, while several detectives waited outside in their vehicles, Sue Peters and Jon Mattsen went inside, not to take Ridgway into custody but to see if they could get him to make false statements that might be used against him later. (Almost twenty years earlier, Sue had been the rookie cop assigned to patrol the Green River area, and we had worked together on recovering the bodies of Chapman, Mills, and Hinds.)

The ruse that Sue and Jon presented was that they were sex crime detectives investigating the rape of Carol Christensen. At first Ridgway was reluctant to talk, but Sue and Jon acted as if they were just seeking his help, and he eventually warmed to them. After taking a second look at some photos, he said he did recognize Christensen's picture but he had never had a sexual relationship with her. The officers knew this was a lie, since he had left his DNA in her body.

Sue and Jon then showed Ridgway photos of Christensen's body, as it had been left, with the fish and meat and the wine bottle. Unaware of what the two detectives were really up to, Ridgway acted like he was being helpful. He even played detective, pretending to guess about the meaning behind the way the scene had been staged. Maybe the killer left that stuff to attract animals to the body, he suggested. The detectives thanked him and left. Ridgway went back to work. He didn't know that we had undercover officers inside Kenworth, watching him finish his last shift on the job.

I left my Seattle office a little after lunchtime to attend a meeting involving hundreds of officers who had protected the city during the World Trade Organization meeting and riots. This was an event that had been scheduled for months, and I was expected to make some remarks. Mainly I wanted to thank the officers for the great job they had done and remind them that the community was grateful. They were a very enthusiastic bunch, brothers and sisters in law enforcement, and it was all I could do to keep my mouth shut about

Ridgway. As I left, I knew that they would still be meeting when the news broke, and I smiled as I imagined how they would react.

With the arrest a little more than an hour away, I drove south to the task force office in Kent. When I got there, about a half dozen people were gathered in the command center. A radio crackled with the sound of the officers communicating in the field. I heard someone say "He's coming out" and then there was silence.

At Kenworth, Jim Doyon and Randy Mullinax had been watching the employee exit from inside a big silver Chevy Suburban. Mike Brown of our intelligence division was behind the wheel. As Ridgway stepped out into the sunlight, Mike hit the gas, and the Suburban roared up to where our suspect stood. Both Randy and Jim got out.

"Gary, we're detectives from the King County Sheriff's Office," said Randy, "and you are under arrest for the murder of several women in King County."

"Okay" was all Ridgway said.

Randy opened the rear door of the Suburban. Ridgway handed him his lunchbox and then climbed inside.

Because we wanted to keep things as cool as possible and we were certain Ridgway would cooperate — he was, after all, a cowardly monster — the detectives didn't pat him down on the scene or place him in handcuffs. The idea was to get him moving as quickly as possible. We knew our men could keep him under control, and they did.

Once Ridgway was in the locked Suburban, Mike Brown got on the radio and broke the silence.

"One in custody, en route to the RJC."

These were the words we had all been waiting to hear. A small cheer went up in the command center. The celebration was short and fairly subdued. We all knew that there was much work left to do. But if the satisfaction we all felt in our hearts could have been heard, the sound would have echoed off Mount Rainier.

I wanted to stay at the Kent Regional Justice Center to see our detectives bring in Ridgway, and I even thought about interviewing him myself. In my imagination I heard him confess to everything, providing the families and the authorities with a true resolution to the entire Green River tragedy. But my duty was to the people of the county, who needed to hear the news from an authoritative source before rumors and misinformation began to spread.

Sergeant Urquhart had already warned the press that a big announcement would be made at 4:30 p.m. To the few skeptics he had added, "You do not want to miss this."

Because John had done his job well, I returned to my office in Seattle to find it jammed with people, cameras, lights, and microphones. I went into another office to compose myself and to give the local stations and CNN the time they needed to be ready for a live broadcast.

Although I had looked forward to this day for almost twenty years, nothing could have prepared me for the emotion I felt. Like others on the task force, I had been frustrated and angry over our past failures. Now those feelings had disappeared. They were replaced with a deep sense of satisfaction and hope that with Ridgway's capture we had stopped the killing and might begin to get answers. I thought about the terrible last minutes of all those women whose bodies we recovered — and those not yet found — and I thought about their families. A great many people were going to feel an enormous sense of relief.

At 4:30 I had to pick my way through the crowd to reach

my desk. All the people and the lights had made the room very stuffy and hot. I sat down and glanced at the prepared remarks I had brought with me. For a moment, the enormity of what I was about to announce hit me, and I felt a lump in my throat.

"We, uh, thank you all for crowding into this small facility to hear some words we've been waiting to say for a long, long time," I said, my voice wavering when I said the words "long, long." I paused to gain control of my emotions.

"I'm going to read a prepared statement and then I'll answer some questions."

Today at approximately 3 p.m., detectives from the King County Sheriff's Office arrested a 52-year-old man for investigation of homicide. Detectives have probable cause to believe he is responsible for the deaths of four women. The women killed are Opal Mills, Marcia Chapman, and Cynthia Hinds, all of whom were found in the Green River on August 15th of 1982.

In addition, we believe that he is responsible for the death of Carol Christensen, whose body was found on May 8th 1983 in the woods near Southeast 242nd Street and 248th Avenue Southeast in Maple Valley.

The man arrested is Gary Leon Ridgway. He lives in the Auburn area. He was arrested in the city of Renton. He is employed by the Kenworth Truck Company, a job he has held for the last 30 years.

The break in this case came when detectives from the sheriff's office, working with forensic scientists of the Washington State crime lab, were able to conclusively link Ridgway's DNA to three of the four victims.

We believe he is responsible for the fourth victim's death due to certain factors that tie him to the two others found in the river.

The reporters in the room couldn't have been surprised. Many had guessed why they were called to my office. Even so, I could see the power of my words in their faces. Although they were supposed to be objective, even dispassionate, I could see that they were truly excited and relieved. As much as I had resented much of what had been published and broadcast about Green River, the press had eventually gotten it right. They had backed off the criticism, portrayed the victims as real and worthy human beings, and recognized the challenges the detectives faced. Now, it seemed, they truly appreciated the magnitude of what we had accomplished.

The rest of my statement provided the press with background on the case against Ridgway. I explained that he had been arrested twice in the past. In 1982 he was picked up for soliciting a decoy in a sting operation against johns on The Strip. Then, just two weeks ago, he was again picked up for soliciting.

I knew that people would have great interest in the evidence and background of the arrest, so I explained that Ridgway had been a suspect since the mid-1980s. "A number of circumstantial things . . . drew us to him and gave us probable cause for search warrants, which did not result in us finding any evidence," I recalled. "However, those warrants did permit us to collect a saliva sample from Ridgway, which we did by having him chew on a piece of gauze."

That little wad of cotton had been preserved for more than a decade while DNA technology improved. When the science got to the point where we were confident that that sample could be analyzed, we had the lab check it against the DNA in the semen found in the victims. The match, I explained to the press, was exact.

When I invited questions, many of the reporters tried to get me to say that Ridgway was the Green River killer and responsible for all the deaths and disappearances under investigation. I knew this was in all likelihood the case, but for legal reasons I couldn't say it.

"As we dig deeper into Mr. Ridgway's life, there are a lot of things we're going to find," I answered. "But at this stage we have four victims that are connected with this individual, and we have a lot of work to do to investigate these other cases to be sure we have a person who's responsible for those bodies."

A few of the reporters had followed the Green River case from the beginning. They were interested in my experience, how it felt to be making an announcement that some people thought would never come.

"This is one of the most exciting days in my entire career," I said. "It's hard to put into words." Again I felt that lump in my throat and paused. "Certainly a cheer went up in the office when we heard he was in custody."

I gave credit to the science that allowed us to arrest Ridgway. And I told the story about the day when Tom Jensen came into my office with the printouts on the DNA samples. "Tom flipped over the last sheet of paper and said, 'Sheriff, here's the DNA of the Green River killer.' We were pretty damn excited, to tell you the truth."

It felt good to tell this story, but I wanted to make sure the public understood that solid investigation had led us to Ridgway, even as our task force was being ridiculed. "This vindicates our efforts during that period of time," I said. "There was a lot of negative press around our efforts. There were cartoons that portrayed the task force as the 'task farce.' But we identified this suspect as one of the top five in nineteen eighty-four. He was worked heavily for three years, and for a number of reasons we were not able to charge him. But the majority of the detectives then had him as number one on the list. We did our job in nineteen eighty-four."

"Did you ever worry this day wasn't going to come?" asked one of the reporters.

"No," I answered without hesitation.

"Why not?"

"I happen to be a positive-thinking guy," I said. "You can never give up hope, because the victims' families never give up hope. We were their lifeline to a solution, to closure. All of us who worked the case became close to a number of the families. I still get calls, cards, and letters. I was a pallbearer at one of the young ladies' funerals. This is going to be great news for them."

Again I was stopped by my emotions. My voice cracked.

"For me it's extra satisfaction to be the sheriff when this happens. It's a great satisfaction."

At that moment I thought about the friends and families of the victims, all the law enforcement people who had worked the case, and about my own family. Julie and I had made sure that everyone knew to be near their television sets. Only later would I find out that my children were deeply affected by what they saw.

Julie, Daniel, Tabitha, and Angela were on the phone with one another as they watched, alternately cheering and crying. Julie, who had gone through so much with me, was overwhelmed with feelings of relief. Angela would later tell me that she broke down in front of the TV. She called one of her aunts and they screamed and cried together. Tabitha said she felt a tremendous sense of relief, knowing that I had fulfilled my promise to all the families of the victims. "You had put so much pressure on yourself," she said. "I was just so glad it was over." Daniel said he felt mostly pride, and vindication. Like me, he had never lost confidence and had believed it was just a matter of time before we would solve the case.

Many of my family and friends were shocked to see the mild, weak-looking person who was Gary Ridgway. But I doubt that any of the detectives and deputies who had contact with him on the day he was arrested were surprised by his demeanor. This was a guy who had passed for normal while he killed probably more than fifty women. He had held the same job for thirty years. He was very good at blending in and seeming unremarkable.

On the day of his arrest, Ridgway was passive, almost uninterested in his own fate. On the ride to the Regional Justice Center, he didn't ask about the charges he faced. He didn't ask for a lawyer or for a chance to call his wife and son. His only question was "What's going to happen to my truck?" He was reassured that it would be safe.

At the justice center, the detectives pulled into a secure parking bay and took Ridgway to a room that we had filled with files and binders marked RIDGWAY, GREEN RIVER. We wanted him to know, in no uncertain terms, that we had an enormous amount of information on his murderous life, and that he had no hope of ever being free again.

Of course we hoped that Ridgway would talk without a lawyer. Any statement he made could be used against him, and there was at least a long-shot chance that in the heat of the moment, he would make it easy on everyone and confess.

He was read his rights, and when he didn't immediately stop the conversation to ask for an attorney, Randy and Jim Doyon continued talking. Watching from a two-way mirror were Tom Jensen and a transcriber, who wrote down everything that was said. (Washington State law requires both parties to agree to tape recording, and since we didn't want to make Ridgway too wary of us, we decided to rely on transcription instead.)

For more than an hour, Randy and Jim told Ridgway about the evidence that had been amassed against him. They showed him a thick binder that contained a timeline indicating where he had been and what he had done during his most active killing years. It included time reports from his job, credit-card receipts, bank records, and surveillance reports.

Intrigued by this record, Ridgway took it from the detectives and began flipping through its pages. He looked intently at the period when Marie Malvar and Carol Christensen disappeared. Randy imagined that Ridgway was recalling the visit made to his house by the Des Moines police department and how close he had come to getting caught. For a moment it even seemed like he was going to talk. But he didn't. He announced that he definitely wanted a lawyer, and that was the end of the interview.

Ridgway didn't know any lawyers, but he recalled that a member of his family had used one once. He thought he might be able to pick the name out of the Yellow Pages. He was given a phone book, and he began slowly reading the pages listing attorneys. After a good half hour of this, Tom Jensen walked in with the phone number for the public defender's office written on a piece of paper. They had already called to volunteer their services. Ridgway used Randy's cell phone and called them.

Once that was done, the questioning ceased. Ridgway was given a white jumpsuit. With his consent, Randy pulled some hair from his head. (Ridgway took care of the pubic hair sample himself.) A technician came in to draw some blood.

I wanted a look at Ridgway in custody. It wouldn't have been appropriate for me to confront him or interrogate him, but I just wanted the satisfaction of seeing him as a prisoner.

After the press conference, I went back to the Kent Regional Justice Center and heard that Ridgway was in conference with the legal aid lawyers. Tom Jensen, Jim Doyon, and Randy Mullinax were waiting to take him to the jail for booking. We waited for an hour and a half. I knew my men were tired and that there would be plenty of time for Ridgway and his counsel to confer. I finally opened the door and said, "These detectives have been waiting long enough. It's time to go."

Now it was time to treat Gary Ridgway like the violent criminal he was. Randy took out a pair of handcuffs and bound Ridgway's hands, and Jim and Randy led him out of the room. As he passed me, I couldn't resist making a comment in the kind of language he would understand. "We gotcha, asshole," I said.

Most of the people on duty that day came out to watch Randy, Tom, and Jim lead Ridgway out. They put him in Randy's silver Ford Explorer, locked the doors, and departed.

Night had fallen, and as they drove north on I-5 to the jail, Ridgway must have known he faced a future of never-ending darkness. He would either be killed by a judge's order or sentenced to life in prison among the most dangerous inmates he could imagine.

In the Explorer, the detectives finally allowed themselves

to poke at the beast they had captured. They told him that his home, including his property, was being torn apart by cops searching for evidence. Ridgway seemed bothered by this. "I just landscaped that place," he complained. "They better not ruin it."

Trampled flowers and shrubs were the least of Ridgway's problems. The detectives told him that he had made a big mistake when he was interviewed in the morning about Christensen. "You really fucked up, Gary," said Randy. "That's a nice little lie statement you gave us to use."

Later Randy would tell me that he took some pleasure in annoying Ridgway, but his mind was also occupied with thoughts of the women who had died, the families who had suffered, and all the effort that had gone into stopping this killer. Ridgway had affected the lives of thousands of people. We had all seen the anguish of the families and felt it ourselves. Nothing that anyone could do to him would soothe that pain.

Normally, two corrections officers meet officers who bring a prisoner to the jail after 10:00 p.m. When Jim, Tom, and Randy got to the jail with Gary Ridgway, more than a dozen officers were milling around, trying to get a look at our catch.

In a holding room, the detectives ran into two Seattle Police Department officers and a young man they had just arrested on some minor charge. When this young man saw Tom, Randy, and Jim with Ridgway, he asked, "Who's that guy?"

"Remember this, kid," said Jim. "You're getting booked beside the Green River killer."

After the jail took custody of their prisoner, Randy took back the handcuffs, and all three detectives returned to Kent together. I doubt any of them got much sleep that night. I know for sure that Randy was restless. He was already focused on the work that we would do in the coming months. And he had in mind a little errand he wanted to run as soon as possible.

The errand had to do with the handcuffs that had secured Gary Ridgway on the day we stopped the Green River killer for good. They had belonged to Detective Paul Smith, a task force member who died of leukemia in 1985. The cuffs would never be used again. Instead, Randy would give them to Paul's widow, to acknowledge her husband's contribution to the investigation and affirm the respect we all had felt for him.

SEVENTEEN

DEFINING JUSTICE

IN 1997, GARY RIDGWAY moved from his residence off Military Road in Des Moines to a house in the suburb of Auburn. The family who occupied the old place, where Ridgway had lived during his peak killing years, was shocked when a sheriff's team showed up to conduct a thorough search of their property.

When I visited, I couldn't help but empathize with those people. We had dogs sniffing every inch of the place, a backhoe digging in the yard, and detectives prying at the baseboards. Even though we assured them that we would repair the damage, they had to deal with the creepy fact that they were living in a serial killer's former home, a place we called the PKH, for primary kill house.

Two other residences, one that once housed Ridgway's parents and his current home in Auburn, were given the same treatment. This work produced bagfuls of potential evidence, but in the end we could find nothing significant. However, the searches did provide a focal point, and lots of photos, for the media's coverage of events in the days after Ridgway's arrest.

The press pursued all the obvious angles and produced the kinds of reports you might expect. Ridgway's family, friends, and neighbors generally described him as quiet and neat. One neighbor told the press that Ridgway's current wife, the former Judith Lynch, had been good for him. "They adore each other," said the neighbor.

But others talked about a man who was a little rooster with an overinflated ego and a streak of vanity that kept him in front of a mirror, combing his hair and mustache many times a day. "He was out-of-the-way friendly," one coworker told the *Seattle Times*. "Creepy friendly, just goofy." Almost everyone who worked with him at Kenworth knew that Ridgway had been a suspect in the Green River case in the 1980s. Behind his back they called him "Green River Gary."

In one of the oddest reports published in the days after the arrest, a member of Opal Mills's extended family revealed that she had worked at Kenworth and attended company picnics with Gary Ridgway. In another article, Opal's mother, Kathy, said she would try to follow her religious beliefs and find a way to forgive her daughter's killer. "I hope if I ever see him face-to-face, I can say, 'I forgive you,'" she said. "I know it won't be easy."

Kathy Mills struck the same spiritual tone when I spoke with her, and the strength of her conviction impressed me. She really was searching for a way to forgive him. Other survivors of Green River victims expressed their feelings with similar power, but some did not share Kathy's merciful impulse. Once they understood the evidence we had against him, some said they wanted Gary Ridgway to die in the most painful way possible.

The trucker Tom Estes, whose daughter Debbie was just fifteen years old when she was killed, clearly wanted his child's killer put to death. Tom was pleased when King County prosecutor Norm Maleng quickly announced that he would not allow Ridgway to bargain his way out of the death penalty. Norm also promised that he would not allow the expected cost of a death penalty prosecution, which would require the county to spend as much as $10 million, to affect the death penalty decision. "There is never a price tag put on justice," he said.

Not surprisingly, some of those who lost loved ones to the Green River killer were a bit ambivalent about the prospect of a trial. One was Debbie Bonner's mother, whom I had once visited with the news that her daughter was dead. She greeted me like an old friend when I went to talk to her after Ridgway was arrested, but her happiness was mixed with apprehension. She said she was relieved that justice was at hand but dreaded the prospect of reliving the events around her daughter's death. At the ripe old age of seventy-two, she said she only hoped she would live long enough to see the prosecution conclude with a conviction.

Mrs. Bonner understood the process could be lengthy. Others were impatient. In some of our conversations with relatives and friends of the murdered women, we had to remind them that we faced a long and expensive journey to Ridgway's ultimate conviction. He was, after all, innocent until proven guilty. His defense lawyers were already making requests for enormous amounts of information, which they were entitled to obtain. This process of discovery and preparation was expected to last about two years.

Although the requests for documents would go through the court, the job of locating and reproducing documents would ultimately fall to the prosecutor and the sheriff's office, and this chore would require the investment of substantial resources. We would keep our team operating at the

Regional Justice Center in Kent and hire a local law firm, at a cost of more than $1 million, to help them. When I told Mertie Wilson about all the work we faced, she responded with typical energy and spirit.

"Is this the guy who killed Tracy?" she asked.

"You know, Mertie, I have to be careful," I answered. "We only have him charged with the four murders. But yes, I personally think he's the Green River killer."

"Then how about I come down to volunteer at the office? I can help you get everything together."

I could understand why she volunteered. What parent wouldn't offer to do anything to help convict and then execute a child's killer? But there was no place for Mertie in the work we needed to accomplish, and when I declined her offer, she said that she understood.

Like almost everyone I spoke with in the days after Ridgway was caught, Mertie wanted to know what I thought about him.

"He's a human being," I said, "but he's a monstrous human being. When he killed, he did it without remorse and with cold efficiency, like a machine that produced dead bodies and would continue to run until you unplugged it."

We couldn't guarantee Gary Ridgway's safety in the general population at the jail, so he spent nearly all of his time isolated in an eight-by-ten cell. Like every other prisoner, he was allowed visits — his wife and two brothers showed up occasionally — and he could make collect phone calls. In the first month or two of his incarceration, he met almost daily with his attorneys, a group led by Anthony Savage, one of King County's older and more experienced defense lawyers.

I wasn't surprised when I heard Tony Savage claim that Ridgway was innocent. What else was he going to say? And

I could understand why he frequently filed motions to delay depositions and hearings. Delay is considered the best defense strategy in cases like Ridgway's. In fact, it is reasonable to assume that legal maneuvering can keep alive for a good ten or fifteen years any killer sentenced to die.

Any irritation we might have felt about justice delayed was soothed by the fact that as we dug deeper into the evidence, we were building a better case against our monster. With a little time and effort we were able to confirm that paint used at the Kenworth plant matched flecks recovered from the bodies of Cynthia Hinds and Wendy Coffield and from the clothing of Debbie Estes. This find allowed Norm Maleng to charge Ridgway with their murders, too. Then, given the timing of her death and the location of her body, Debra Bonner's murder was also added to the charges. The total came to seven.

Each month the judge assigned to the case, Richard Jones, held a so-called status conference to allow each side to make requests and apprise the other of their progress toward a trial. Gradually it became clear that Tony Savage and the other defense lawyers lacked real confidence. One sign was their hiring of a nationally known expert to delve deep into Ridgway's background for a "mitigation report" that would be used to argue against the death penalty in the event of a conviction. Why would they begin this work so early in the pretrial period if they weren't worried about losing?

Tony Savage's defense team could read the evidence as well as anyone, and they must have known that Ridgway was lying when he said he was innocent. In April, one of his lawyers enlisted Ridgway's older brother Greg in a scheme to bring some reality to their position. Together they made it clear to Gary that his family would prefer him to plead guilty if that meant his life would be spared.

As difficult as it is to believe, Gary Ridgway had some loving feelings for certain members of his family, especially Greg. In their childhood, Greg had been a protector of sorts and a role model. When he heard that Greg was desperate for any arrangement that would spare his brother's life, Gary dropped his claim of innocence. If a deal could be made, he told his lawyers, he would sign it, for the benefit of his brother.

When Ridgway's team requested a meeting with county prosecutors Jeff Baird and Patricia Eakes, the Green River group at the Regional Justice Center began to speculate on the agenda. No one suggested with any seriousness that the defense team would try to bargain their way out of the death penalty. After all, Norm Maleng had made a big public display of his commitment to executing Ridgway. And it was hard to imagine anyone who might deserve execution more.

At that first bargaining session, the defense promised that Ridgway would clear up twenty-eight unsolved murders and that he would help us find bodies that were still scattered around the county. Our side reminded them that Norm Maleng was firmly against a deal. This was not just because Ridgway was almost uniquely evil. It was also because he didn't want to set a bad precedent. If you bargain with a Ridgway, won't attorneys for run-of-the-mill murderers insist you bargain with them, too?

After hearing Baird and Eakes resist their idea, Ridgway's lawyers went back to their client and he upped the ante. What if he could help them solve fifty murders in addition to the seven he was charged with now? Wouldn't there be some value in this for the cops, the courts, and the families who would learn the truth about their loved ones and, at last, have a body to bury?

If Ridgway was willing to own up to fifty-seven murders, that meant that we could resolve even more than the number of killings on the official Green River list. The possibility of his answering a few questions had obvious value for fifty grieving families. Even if you believed Ridgway deserved the worst, it was hard to discount the needs of those who loved his victims. Justice required that we consider the anguish they endured every day because they didn't even know if their loved ones were dead or alive.

When Jeff and Patricia presented the defense team's proposal to their boss, Norm's immediate answer was clear. He said no.

Norm understood that every serial killer tries to play the card Ridgway had offered. The killer knows that grieving families want to recover their loved ones and lay them to rest. And he knows that police departments want to close cases so they can move on to investigate other crimes. These are powerful factors.

But on the other side of the ledger were some very basic tenets of American justice. The majority of our country's population favors the use of the death penalty as both a deterrent and a weapon of justice. It is considered especially appropriate in cases involving the most heinous crimes. Few of us like the idea of using tax dollars to keep the likes of Gary Ridgway alive. Fewer still can imagine showing mercy to a man who showed no mercy himself as he hunted and killed dozens of innocent young women.

Norm's philosophy as a prosecutor is broader than a simple eye-for-an-eye approach. His definition of justice includes the search for truth to benefit the victims and their community. And he realized that if the best investigators had failed to crack those cases in twenty years of trying,

Ridgway was probably the only one who would ever know what happened to the missing.

If Norm Maleng had been worried about his popularity and the political fallout, he would have stuck to his earlier pledge. He would have continued to reject the proposal and made the majority happy by pushing the court to kill Gary Ridgway.

He certainly would have won praise from many of the detectives who had tried to persuade him to stick with the death penalty choice. I attended several meetings where Norm listened as these cops made their case. In those sessions, and in private meetings where I urged him to make a deal that would get vital information out of Ridgway, I could see that Norm was struggling with the decision. He prayed and thought about his choice, and in the end, he came down in favor of justice and mercy for those families who still ached for the truth. As he would later say, "We have all suffered this trauma known as the Green River murders. We deserve to know the truth and move on."

At one time, my own thinking about the death penalty was more black and white. When Sam Hicks was killed, I wanted to see his murderer put to death. But as time passed and I heard about how much he suffered in prison, I started to wonder if the death penalty would have been too easy. Perhaps it was better to force a killer to rot in jail year after year, knowing that he will never again experience all the wonders of life as a free man.

Where Ridgway was concerned, I had similar feelings. As a rapist and serial killer, he would occupy the lowest rung in prison society. He would not only suffer from incarceration, but he was likely to be punished in very brutal ways by other inmates. He deserved this fate.

In the Green River case, we also had the extra element of the missing women and unrecovered bodies. The families deserved whatever information Ridgway could give. But he would never cooperate if we went for the death penalty.

In the end, I believe that Norm made the right choice. He risked political fallout by changing his position for the sake of the families. And when it was revealed to the cops assigned to follow up the case, no one disagreed with his decision.

Once the basic principle was established — full disclosure by Ridgway in exchange for life in prison — weeks of effort went into drafting an agreement that would bind him tighter than handcuffs. First, the defense had to help us confirm that Ridgway had the mental capacity to aid us in finding bodies and reconstructing crimes. We had to know what kind of information he would offer, and we wanted assurances that he would produce whatever physical evidence was available, including jewelry, clothing, photographs, maps, and anything else connected to his victims.

In the end, Ridgway promised to do everything that was asked, and that included confessing to fifty-three murders and helping us locate between ten and fourteen sets of remains. He agreed to be moved out of the jail and into a secret location where he would provide whatever help we needed for as long as we needed it. And if he lied to us, which we expected he would, we would have the right to pull the plug on the deal, and he would face trial on the original seven counts.

Ridgway agreed to the terms in early June 2003. On the thirteenth of the month, he was taken out of the King County jail. We announced that he was going to be evaluated by mental health experts, and many, including the local press, assumed he was being sent to a state psychiatric hospital. Instead, he was secreted in a task force office that had been set up near the King County International Airport.

For five and a half months, Gary Ridgway would live in a room that was empty save for a mattress on the floor. By day he would submit to grueling interviews and accompany us on field trips to look for sites where he had dumped bodies. By night he would stare at the four walls and at windows that had been papered over to prevent him from looking out and others from looking in. He would lose his visiting privileges and his access to television, newspapers, and magazines. But if he cooperated fully, he would escape execution and gain the right to live like a rat in a cage at the state prison in Walla Walla for the rest of his natural life.

EIGHTEEN

THE MONSTER SPEAKS

THE FIRST THING that strikes you about Gary Ridgway is that he's a weasel of a man. Small, with narrow shoulders, a scraggly mustache, and beady eyes, he looks like a rodent. And when he talks, he squeals, squeaks, and hesitates. You can hear the sound of deception in his voice. He's so involved in second-guessing and manipulation that he chokes on half his words, and those that do come out sound strained and raspy.

To get some idea of how difficult it was to question this man and obtain anything that made sense, consider the struggle that Detective Tom Jensen had as he tried to get an idea, early in the interrogation process, of the time frame surrounding one of Ridgway's killings.

JENSEN: You get up at what time?

RIDGWAY: Six o'clock in the morning.

JENSEN: You do?

RIDGWAY: Or not. Five . . . five and four.

JENSEN: Yeah, you get up way —

RIDGWAY: And this one.

JENSEN: — you get up way earlier than six.

RIDGWAY: And if it was on a weekend, we'd try to sleep in. But let's say four o'clock. So if she was killed at midnight, Judith and me, you know. You, you know the time frame she was killed. A couple hours.

JENSEN: Couple hours?

RIDGWAY: Uh, you know, within the, if she, you know . . .

JENSEN: Tell me.

RIDGWAY: I, uh . . .

JENSEN: Tell me when you think she was killed.

RIDGWAY: She was killed at night, according to what I heard in the news. She was killed at night, uh, as far as I know.

In the space of about one minute, Ridgway says he got up at six o'clock, five o'clock, and four o'clock. Instead of talking about how he recalls the killing, he quotes media reports. And he also provides completely unnecessary information about how he and his wife liked to sleep in on weekends.

If reading just a little sample of a transcript gives you a headache, imagine what it was like trying to discuss dozens of complex murder cases with this man. With every response to every question, Ridgway mixed lies and truth, deceit and honest information. In many instances he said he couldn't remember important details, such as his victims' names, their faces, or how they had been dressed. Most of the time, these statements were lies.

Given the fact that Ridgway was some kind of psycho, we had to consider the possibility that he was so cold and so detached from other human beings that he really didn't recall details that would make the victims seem like real individuals. We also wondered if he was so accustomed to deceiving everyone, including himself, that he no longer knew the difference between the truth and a lie.

But then we recalled how he had responded to photos of Carol Christensen during the interview on the morning before his arrest. He remembered her by name and even recalled where she had held a job for just two days. Gary Ridgway had excellent recall, when he chose to use it, and he was capable of telling the truth.

And yet, day after day, Ridgway woke up in the morning, sat down in front of our detectives and a video camera, and wove strange stories filled with factual gaps and omissions he blamed on his faulty memory. Even when he announced that he was coming clean about something, he delivered incorrect information.

After denying that he kept souvenirs of his kills, he confessed to stashing jewelry at a site where days of searching turned up nothing. Next he directed us to a place where he claimed to have dumped a body by the guardrail on a stretch of county highway.

Armed with Ridgway's information, our people spent a long weekend chopping down trees, clearing brush, and digging holes in ninety-degree heat. When they came up with nothing, we decided to shake up our subject. We would tell him he was going to go out on a field trip, to a supposed body site to help us find some bones. Once he got excited about the prospect of getting out, we would cancel the trip and confront him with his deceptions.

The detective chosen for the task was Raphael Crenshaw, a large man with a talent for making himself seem quite menacing. Preserved on videotape, his confrontation with Ridgway took place in the hallway outside his locked room, just as Gary was supposed to walk to a sheriff's van.

"What's this bullshit about there being jewelry on One Hundred Eighty-eighth Street?" shouted Raphael as he leaned in on Ridgway. "That's bullshit. I spent a whole day out there digging fifty-one holes and found nothing!"

In the video, Ridgway looks shocked. He tries to stand up straight, but his body buckles a bit, like he's facing a hurricane-force wind.

"Then I spent last weekend on Kent–Des Moines Road out in ninety-degree weather, chopping down trees and clearing brush. Why? Because of another one of your bullshit stories! There's no fucking body out there. You know what we found?"

"What?" answered Gary.

"We found the skeleton of an opossum, a little-bitty possum. Why? Because you're bullshitting us!"

Before he was finished, Raphael made sure that Ridgway understood that we considered him a liar. He even accused him of cheating on the crossword puzzles we allowed him to work on in his room at night. "You can't even do those without cheating!" he shouted.

Finally, with Ridgway gulping and gasping, Raphael canceled the field trip. "You're not going anywhere," he shouted. Then he turned to other detectives who stood nearby and muttered, "Take his ass back to the fucking cell until he's ready to start telling the truth."

Field trips were precious to Ridgway because he knew that once we were finished with him and he was sent to prison, he would never again get a chance to ride the highways of the outside world. In canceling one of those outings, we meant to pressure him to be more truthful. But this was not the only way we could exercise a little leverage. The document

Ridgway had signed to save his life gave us the option to declare him to be in breach, scrap the deal, and go to trial, seeking to execute him. He needed to reflect on this a bit.

Dr. Robert Wheeler, a psychologist with a kinder, gentler approach, worked hard to make Ridgway understand that his lies were going to lead him to an execution if he wasn't careful. In order to do this, Wheeler offered Ridgway a few excuses — suggestions for why he might have lied — so that he would have a way out of the stories he had told. Among the possibilities that Ridgway seemed to endorse were the following:

- He lied because he subconsciously wanted to be executed. At several points he admitted, "I deserve the death penalty."
- He lied to make himself appear like less of a monster, so that true-crime writers would portray him more positively.
- He lied to build himself up, to make himself seem more powerful.
- He lied to maintain control over the bodies of his victims, which were prized possessions.

Most of this information arose as Ridgway speculated about why someone else, a different serial killer, might lie. "Maybe they don't know the difference between tellin' the truth and tellin' a lie," he said.

In the end, as Dr. Wheeler pointed out, it was important for Gary to understand why he was lying only if it helped him to stop it. Otherwise, he was going to blow his deal and be put to death.

Soon afterward, we saw signs of Ridgway attempting to be more honest. We achieved a breakthrough when Tom

Jensen pressed him on the reasons for the murders he had committed. For weeks Ridgway had insisted that all sorts of outside factors affected him. He blamed money problems and nasty female coworkers. He said he killed prostitutes who had refused to pretend to enjoy having sex, and that sometimes the noise of passing airplanes pushed him over the edge. But then, in one of those rare moments when he was truly candid, he admitted that his murderous career was not anyone's fault but his own, and it was not caused by anything other than his own personal desires. He said he killed dozens of women simply because he "wanted to."

Of course, taking responsibility for his crimes didn't mean that Ridgway wasn't the product of a very strange set of life circumstances. Eventually we were able to tease out enough detail to give experts on serial killers a very close look at a monster in the making. If anyone ever cared to write it, Ridgway's biography might begin with him as a six- or seven-year-old, waking up in a bed soaked with urine.

According to Ridgway, as a child he was a chronic bed wetter whose mother just happened to be a clean freak of the first order. She would haul him out of bed, parade him in front of his brothers, and then stand him up naked in the tub for a cold bath. The way he tells it, she wasn't always fully dressed for these ritualized cleansings, and she paid so much attention to his genitals that he must have thought they were the dirtiest objects on earth.

Ridgway said little about his father. He was such a meek man that once when his wife broke a plate on his head, he didn't even respond. However, at the dinner table his dad spoke at length about his brief stint as an employee of a mortuary. Those tales included an elaborate description of a man he supposedly witnessed having sex with a female corpse. This scene became a subject for his son's teenage sexual fantasies. He liked the idea of "having sex with someone that is dead, because you wouldn't get caught," he explained. "No feelings. She wouldn't feel it."

In contrast with his portrait of a sniveling father, Ridgway's mother comes across as an aggressive, sexually provocative woman who dressed like a prostitute and applied her makeup with a trowel. She liked to talk about measuring men who bought trousers at the department store where she worked. She talked about how certain men got erections and about the scents she detected as she kneeled in front of them.

As Gary Ridgway described it, his mother's parenting style was a blend of titillation, humiliation, and threats. He loved to watch her sunbathe, and he imagined having sex with her. But when he had trouble at school — he was a very poor reader — she began talking about putting him in a state institution for the retarded. It was at about this time — early adolescence — that Ridgway added violence to his fantasies about having sex with her. He thought he might slit her throat with a kitchen knife.

"That would be the ultimate," he said, "to, to scar her for life." This would relieve his frustration over "not being able to learn and to be like a normal person."

(Ridgway's concept of "normal" and how it contrasted with his own behavior illustrated one of the major problems we had with him. In many interviews his lies were the result of his efforts to imagine what a normal person might say and do, and he offered that to us instead of the truth. He had obviously done this his entire life, studying how a normal man would act and presenting that image to others while he secretly pursued an obscenely violent existence.)

While little Gary Ridgway lived in the shadow of his

larger-than-life mother and seethed with rage, he began his own experiments with crimes of control at a very early age. While still in grade school, he developed a taste for killing animals, especially birds. Once he seized a cat that was a family pet and shut it inside an old metal ice chest. He then hid the cooler where no one would hear the animal cry. The next day he opened the lid to find the cat dead. (It was telling that Ridgway couldn't recall the name of the cat, or where he had disposed of it after it died.)

As he grew older, Gary Ridgway set fires and became obsessed with true-crime stories, reading whatever he could find on dangerous men. In one interview he said that he believed he had actually drowned a little boy who was swimming near him in a lake near Seattle. He recalled wrapping his legs around the boy and pulling him underwater until he died. He pulled the body under a dock and just left it there.

As he told this story, Ridgway seemed more confused than usual. He said, "I don't remember, um, if I did this, or if it's like I said, a dream." Ridgway said that if it happened, it was during his adolescent years in the early 1960s. Public records show that in 1964 a toddler and a teenager both drowned in that lake. We would never resolve whether either of them was Ridgway's victim.

We were able to confirm Ridgway's other tale of early violence against a child. This incident occurred when Ridgway was about sixteen. In a wooded area near his family's home, he came upon a much younger boy decked out in a cowboy outfit, including a pair of make-believe six-shooters. Ridgway led Jimmy Davis deeper into the woods and stabbed him with a knife.

As blood ran down the little boy's abdomen, Gary Ridgway laughed at him and then wiped the blade on his victim's shirt. "I always wanted to know what it felt like to kill somebody," he said before running away. Little Jimmy managed to make his way home. He was hospitalized for weeks, and he recovered after an operation to repair a wound in his liver. The budding psychopath who stabbed him was never arrested for the crime.

While he was successfully killing animals and knifing a little boy, Gary Ridgway was an utter failure in the rest of his life. He was such a poor student that he didn't graduate high school until he was twenty years old. The girls he desired would never date him, so he spent a lot of time stalking them around his neighborhood.

After high school, Ridgway quickly married a young woman named Claudia Kraig and then joined the navy. He was sent to Subic Bay in the Philippines, where he claims to have begun a fixation with prostitutes that would last a lifetime. When he came home, he discovered that his wife had betrayed him with another man, and that ended their marriage. She was, in his mind, a whore.

Ridgway claimed that his first choking victim was his second wife, Marcia Winslow, and it happened when she refused to talk to him during an argument. "I don't like hitting women," he explained. So instead, he got behind her, wrapped his right arm around her neck, and began squeezing. Not surprisingly, this marriage didn't last long either.

Years later, Marcia would say that Gary's sexual appetites were extreme. He involved her in bondage and liked to take her to secluded places — like the banks of the Green River — to have sex in the outdoors. And for a man who seemed to hate being controlled by women, Marcia noted, he sure ceded a lot of power to his dear old mom. When Gary was twenty-five years old, and well established as a truck painter at Kenworth, his mother's name was still on his bank account, and he spent most weekends at her house, even after Marcia gave birth to their son, Matthew, in 1975.

With Matthew's arrival, Gary Ridgway entered a religious phase, joining one church after another and reading the Bible almost every day. The religious obsession ended when he and Marcia got divorced in 1980. He was so angry with her, and so resentful about the monthly support payments he was required to send for Matthew, that he thought about killing her.

All through the 1970s and into the 1980s, Gary Ridgway spent much of his spare cash and a great deal of time on prostitutes who worked the Sea-Tac strip and downtown Seattle. Although he vaguely recalled killing a prostitute in the 1970s, he didn't embark on his career as a serial killer until after the second divorce.

A combination of threats from the likes of Raphael Crenshaw and constant contact with detectives Tom Jensen, Sue Peters, Jon Mattsen, and Randy Mullinax induced in Ridgway a bit of Stockholm syndrome — the well-documented phenomenon of captives befriending their captors. By mid-July he was relating well to both Randy and Tom, who covered both their anger and their disgust so well that he seemed to consider them his friends.

Ridgway said that in the beginning his hatred of the prostitutes who serviced him for a fee boiled over into murder when he felt that they regarded him with disgust and disdain. In the moments after climax, usually while behind a woman, he would reach around her neck and start choking her. But soon he wouldn't need any slights, real or perceived, to motivate him to kill. He just went hunting for women to murder. And the killing became far more important to him than the sex.

Over time, Ridgway refined his technique. Realizing that he was disturbed by the sight of a victim's face, he made sure that he always stayed behind the women he killed so he wouldn't have the image of their pain and pleading eyes in his mind. It was hard enough for him to forget the things some of them said as they begged for their lives. Some talked about their children. Nothing any of them said worked.

If a victim struggled, Ridgway placed the weight of his body on her back, or squeezed with his legs to push air out of her lungs. If he got tired, he might relax for a moment, recover his strength, and then continue before she could regain hers. In other cases, he would use a piece of clothing — anything from socks to a bathrobe tie — to create a ligature, which he sometimes pulled so tightly that it became embedded and impossible to remove when the killing was over.

Some of the murders happened out of doors, in the empty lots and isolated areas where he took women to have sex. A few occurred in his truck. But the vast majority of the murders took place in his home. He would pick up a woman from The Strip. At his place he would show her his son's room. He knew she would think that a family man could never be a killer. Then he would ask her to use the toilet. (One woman had wet the bed after she died. Given his history with bed wetting, Ridgway did whatever he could to prevent this from happening again.)

Just as it happened the first time, the sexual encounters would end with Ridgway behind the woman, attacking her. But he no longer found sexual release with a live person. That happened only after death, when he raped the still-warm corpse. Finally satisfied, he would then get up, clean himself off, and set about the business of covering up his crime.

He would wrap the body in plastic sheeting or a piece of

carpet, place her in his truck, and take her out to a dump site. (Before dumping the bodies, he cut the fingernails of those women who may have scratched him, so that police wouldn't find skin cells that might be used to determine his blood type.)

With many of his victims, Ridgway wasn't finished after they were dead and disposed of. He would go back to rape their bodies, brushing away maggots if necessary. As he left, he would douse himself with a homemade antiseptic — part rubbing alcohol, part Aqua Velva aftershave — which he believed would kill germs and cover any odor. It must have felt as cold as the water his mother used on him whenever he wet the bed as a boy.

As gruesome as these general descriptions may be, Gary Ridgway's more detailed stories about specific killings made us all feel even more compassion for his victims. He spoke of bringing eighteen-year-old Marie Malvar to his home in 1983. He had her follow his pre-sex ritual — using the toilet, washing — and then, once they had finished having sex, he wrapped his right arm around her throat. This time, however, his prey fought back, hard.

As Gary Ridgway choked her, Marie gouged at his legs and arms, making long, deep scratches, the scars of which remain visible to this day. She struggled to get out of his grasp as he pulled harder on her throat and screamed at her to stop resisting.

"I'll let you go if you stop scratching me and rolling in the bed!" he recalled telling Marie.

But she wouldn't give up, so Ridgway, nearly exhausted, gathered his strength and concentrated it all on his aching arms. She flailed and scratched some more, but he could feel her losing strength.

"Finally she was just out of energy," said Ridgway. "I was just, like, thank God she was dead and she wasn't fighting anymore." (Those of us who heard this confession while watching it on video would say a different prayer — in praise of Marie's spirit and asking God to grant her the safety her soul deserves.)

Exhausted and enraged, Ridgway poured battery acid on his arm to disguise the wounds made by his victim's finger-nails, and then bandaged himself. He then hauled Marie's body out to his truck and went to a new dumping site, off 297th Street. This seemed odd, since he had established an-other site on Star Lake Road, where he had safely deposited a number of bodies. The detectives noticed this change in his routine and pressed him on it.

"She wasn't going to go with the other women?" asked Randy. "I mean, she didn't deserve to be with those others because they didn't fight?"

At first Ridgway's answer seemed to indicate that he had been angry because Marie had hurt him. He wouldn't leave her with the others because he wanted to punish her. But after a great deal of additional questioning, he confessed that he didn't dump her with the others because she was "special." In his halting way of speaking, he made it clear that he actually admired her because she had shown such spirit.

"She was aggressive and more a fighter. And I had to, um, get her under control. And, or, I was, I was the boss. . . . She was a fighter," he continued. "More harder to get her into, into my power of control, and so she was s-special in that way."

As it turned out, Marie's fighting probably spared her body the type of assault Ridgway visited upon so many of the corpses he considered his sexual property. Gary had been agitated and emotional when he dumped her body. When he later went looking for her, to rape her, he became disoriented and couldn't find her. She would lie, undisturbed, until we used the information gained in the interview to recover her skeleton. The Malvar family would be one of those that benefited from the plea bargain. They were able to give their daughter a proper burial because of it.

On the morning when Gary Ridgway excitedly told the story of Marie Malvar's death, he seemed especially open to the detectives. Although they felt tremendous revulsion, they also recognized the opportunity. They could press him to discuss his fantasies and perhaps gain more insight into the mind of a serial killer.

While I watched him work via a video hookup, Randy started by asking a question about one of the most gruesome acts he could imagine, dismemberment of a corpse. (We already knew Ridgway had moved bones and skulls.)

"Did you ever consider cutting them up?"

In a roundabout way, Gary denied that he considered hacking up bodies. But he got Randy's drift. The detectives wanted to peer into the darker corners of his mind. "I had thoughts . . . of being . . . you know, posing them, or to a point there, I was killing so many of them that I thought about sticking one on a pole."

"Why?"

"There were . . . just had a thought of showing 'em off, or decorating them."

At this point, Randy was trying to act nonchalant, even accepting. But he couldn't have been prepared for what Ridgway said next.

"Stick 'em on a pole. Torturing them like that."

He wasn't talking about putting a corpse on a pole. He had wanted to put a *live* woman in that position and watch her suffer. He imagined it taking place in a very isolated wooded area. He would gag a woman to keep her silent, impale her on a pole, plant the pole in the ground, and watch her suffer until she was exhausted. Then he would take her down and choke her.

Ridgway became excited as he talked about this fantasy. "It was the arousal of watching, if I did it, it was the arousal of watching her in pain, dying. You live by . . . having guys put dicks in you, now you have a pole up you and you're gonna die that way. But I didn't do it. I thought about it. That would have been the ultimate if I was that crazy."

While Gary insisted this scenario was just a fantasy, Randy wondered aloud about why he didn't act on it. After all, he was killing all these women. Dead was dead. What difference would it have made if he had indulged this fantasy for his own pleasure?

"There was a limit to what I was going to do with 'em," he finally explained. "I can kill 'em and have sex with 'em and bury 'em and hide 'em, but there was a limit with where I was gonna go."

"Whose limit?"

"I set the limit myself."

"And what was that limit?"

"Screw 'em, kill 'em, bury 'em, and maybe have sex with them a few times afterwards."

Remarkable as it might seem, Gary Ridgway had limits. He was actually repulsed by some of his own fantasies and behaviors. He claimed that he began placing bodies farther and farther from his home so that it would be difficult for him to practice necrophilia. "It kinda scared me so I   . I put 'em a lot farther out."

But it wasn't the fantasy of torture that disturbed Ridgway the most. In one of his rare moments of candor, Ridgway admitted that he began to fight the killing impulse — a desire he likened to drug addiction — when his thoughts turned to cannibalism. We never found out whether Ridgway actually did it, but it was clear that he had thought about it, a lot.

At the beginning of our time with Gary Ridgway, it was very hard to imagine how a man with so little apparent intelligence could have fooled so many women and eluded the Green River Task Force over such a long period of time. I mean, the guy had trouble stringing together coherent sentence. How was he able to plot his crimes so carefully?

As the weeks passed, however, Ridgway revealed himself to be gifted in the ways of a killer. When it came to acquiring and then mastering the skills needed to persuade, slay, and then hide his victims, he was like an idiot savant.

The first thing Ridgway did right, if you can call it that, involved his choice of victims. He readily admitted that he chose the most vulnerable, powerless, and invisible women around. Then, over time, he perfected a series of ruses he would employ to disguise his true purpose. Indeed, he was so good at posing as a harmless wimp that women who had resisted his assaults — we knew of at least two who got away — didn't realize he was the Green River killer.

Ridgway was shameless in his charades. When his son, Matthew, was an infant, he would ride around with him in his truck or car and then pull over to chat with prostitutes on the street. They would coo over his baby while he arranged to meet up later for sex. When Matthew wasn't available in person, Ridgway flashed his baby pictures. If that wasn't enough, he'd promise to buy a woman food or help her to find a job. Everything he did was calculated to put the women at ease and make them think he was just a lonesome middle-aged regular Joe.

As I had always suspected, some of the women feared that Ridgway was the Green River killer and refused to go with him to the isolated places he proposed for "dates." Others wouldn't get out of his truck to perform sex, so they escaped being killed because Ridgway couldn't approach them from behind in the truck.

Of course, the victims were not the only ones Gary had to fool. During most of the killing years, when he was hiring scores of prostitutes and killing many of them, he lived with his fourth wife, Judith. To keep track of all the women he "dated" but avoid being found out, he devised a coded system for recording names, telephone numbers, and other key information.

He used notebooks that also held grocery lists and key bits of information about his job at Kenworth. A prostitute's name, Carol, for example, would be accompanied by a man's name, so that she appeared to be part of a couple. This would ensure that Judith wouldn't suspect he had women friends. Phone numbers would be disguised as notes about paint colors used at Kenworth or prices for various items. He might write on one page "paint color 555." On another he'd write, "clutch adjustment, $20.75." Carol's phone number, when the two were put together, would be 555-2075.

Ridgway needed to make notes because he was involved with so many women that he couldn't keep them straight.

He was also terrified of saying the wrong thing and being found out. This was a special risk when he was "dating" girls of sixteen or seventeen and needed to phone their homes to make arrangements. He decided to put the code word "maid" next to some of their names. He would then call their homes, and if an adult answered, he would explain that he was the manager of a hotel and he was calling because the girl had applied for a maid's job.

If a woman was African American, Ridgway would write a note such as "black car." To remind himself of a location where a woman might be found, he'd jot down something about a nearby landmark, such as a McDonald's restaurant or the name of a highway. A circle around a woman's name meant that Ridgway wanted to contact her again for sex. And of course, after he murdered a woman, her name got crossed out.

All this information would be sprinkled in with to-do lists, receipts, and other notes. Anyone who might see it — Judith, for example — would find it impossible to decipher.

Along with the coded ledger and the ruses he used to ensnare women, Ridgway employed certain strategies to avoid detection and divert attention. If he killed a prostitute who worked with a pimp, he might call the man the next morning to say he was interested in meeting her again. Whenever he did this, he referred to himself by his favorite alias, Steve. The pimp would assume that Steve was okay, because, as he explained, "Steve kept on calling and wanted to date her."

When he was especially frightened, Ridgway would take a further step. He would call a pimp literally minutes after he killed a woman. After begging for a date, he would promise to wait for her at a restaurant where he would sit and drink coffee. He'd make sure to collect a receipt, "so that gives me an alibi, that I was waiting for her, if something ever comes up." Sometimes he would even make up a complaint about the food he was served so that the manager of the restaurant would recall his presence.

Others who might have identified Gary Ridgway as a suspect included his neighbors on the cul-de-sac where the primary kill house was located. However, he was extremely careful in the way that he brought women into his house. He "dated" mostly at night, and he always parked near the front door, which was hidden by shrubbery. This meant that the women he brought home would be visible to a person on the street only as they walked the ten feet from the driveway to the house.

Like most people, Ridgway had some nosy neighbors, including a firefighter who lived across the street. When he had to dispose of a body, he would back his car or truck up to the door and use the vehicle to shield himself from view. Once, when he wanted to dispose of a small body while his neighbors were out and about, he placed it in a small trunk that belonged to his son and put the trunk in the back of his truck. Later, when it was dark, he went back, rolled the body out, put the trunk back in the house, and drove off to dispose of his victim.

Gradually Ridgway got so good at concealing his activities that he knew that none of his neighbors suspected a thing. "I don't know if anybody ever saw me bring in a woman, and she never walked out on her own," he said proudly.

He was equally proud of the way he manipulated the Green River Task Force. As we suspected, he shifted skeletons and one woman's skull to Oregon in order to complicate our investigation. And we had sometimes suspected he actually wanted to bring the FBI into the case because he believed they would make things harder for the task force. In the end, he had been right about that.

Ridgway defied the stereotype about serial killers in a significant way: He managed to slow and then stop his killing for long stretches of time. In our interviews, he explained that he feared getting caught by the task force and believed that his twin compulsions — murder and necrophilia — were controlling him the way drugs control an addict. For these reasons, he willed himself to stop killing. And when he could resist no longer, he dropped the bodies farther from home. The distance, he explained, would make it harder for him to go back and rape the bodies.

One other success Ridgway could claim came when we took him into custody and searched his house in 1987. He denied training to take the lie detector test, which he passed. Instead, he explained, he just tried to stay calm and "act normal" in the way that he had throughout his entire life. Being a sociopath who felt no guilt or remorse made it easy for him to fool the polygraph. His heart rate didn't go up, and he didn't start to sweat, because he was perfectly capable of forgetting his victims and believing, if only for the moment, in the false front he had constructed for the world to see.

A big part of Ridgway's self-image was tied up in his desire to be the world's worst serial killer. This is why he sometimes claimed to have killed forty-eight women, then fifty-two, and then more than seventy. He had an eye on other notorious murderers, like Ted Bundy, who took twenty-five lives, and John Wayne Gacy, who killed thirty-three people.

Ridgway's total may have exceeded seventy, but we were

not interested in helping him confirm a record. We only wanted to find bodies that had not been discovered and to confirm those deaths that could be linked to him definitively.

On these counts, we made real progress. In mid-August 2003, Ridgway accompanied detectives to a spot near Highway 410 in Enumclaw, where they found the body of Pammy Avent, who had been missing for almost two decades. Two weeks later, the body of April Buttram was found where Ridgway said it would be off Interstate 90. At the end of September, Marie Malvar was found after an extensive search of a ravine in Auburn. A fourth body discovered with Ridgway's cooperation had not been identified as late as summer 2004.

In addition to the four new finds, Ridgway confirmed his role in the deaths of forty-four more women. The total might well go up, because he provided enough information to keep us searching various sites for months and perhaps years. In the meantime, advances in DNA analysis and other techniques for identifying bodies may also help us attach names to bones.

There was no doubt in my mind as we approached the end of the interrogation process with Ridgway that the plea bargain had worked. I was also convinced that our patient approach to the interviews had been effective. Because we wanted to hear every detail, including those that would lead us to bodies, we all put up with Gary Ridgway's self-serving attitude. We grilled him hard when it came to important facts. But we tried to hold our tongues as he rationalized and made excuses. No one challenged him even when he claimed to have killed according to a "code of ethics."

The Ridgway code, he explained, required that he concentrate his murderous energy on prostitutes. "I wanna be put down in history as killin' prostitutes," he added, because they were people society rejected. "Money was the thing they wanted," he added. "Money was their downfall."

Ridgway talked about how the victims deserved to die and how he had achieved a place in history when a psychologist came to talk with him near the end of his stay in our offices. It was yet another expression of Ridgway's twisted view of himself, and it made many of us angry. After all the talking, he still didn't understand that he was a coward who didn't deserve to share the air we all breathe.

I had this in mind on the morning of November 13, 2003, as I was going to meet with Ridgway to conduct our final interview. I had been the first detective to chase the Green River killer, and now, more than twenty years later, he would have to deal with me on the day before he would be sent away for life. I would give him one last chance to continue talking with the detectives, but only if he gave them valuable information. I didn't expect him to take the offer. And this meant I would be free to deal with him as I chose.

After saying hello, Ridgway immediately tried to convince me that he had cooperated fully, meeting the requirements of our deal. I was there to give him a chance to confess to more, and to let him know that we understood all the games he had played.

In his six months with us, Ridgway had occasionally cried during questioning. The tears were always shed for himself. He cried about how he was treated as a child and about how he had been unable to stop killing. He also tried to convince himself that he was changing. He was starting to develop human feelings, he claimed, and this newfound sense of humanity was behind his efforts to tell the truth and help the families of his victims.

He said he wrote the Fred letter to the *Post-Intelligencer* to help the authorities catch him. Of course, I pointed out, he didn't offer anything in that letter that would have implicated him in the murders. In fact, the letter suggested that the task force should focus on police officers as suspects.

Thwarted by that argument, Gary decided to tell me that he was better than Ted Bundy because he claimed only the murders he had committed and didn't try to run up his score. He wanted credit for telling us the truth, after that first month of lies, and he wanted me to know he felt bad about a few of the murders. He named Connie Naon, because she was so beautiful; sixteen-year-old Colleen Brockman, because he killed her on Christmas Eve; and Debbie Abernathy, because he killed her on his son Matthew's birthday. In each of these cases, he claimed, the victim had become more real to him than the others.

But while Ridgway wanted to impress me with his emotional sensitivity, almost every remark was about how his crimes affected him. He was dreading an upcoming hearing, where families would be allowed to speak, because they were bound to express their anger and he hated confrontation. And he resented those who had written letters that described him as the devil.

"What do you think about that?" I asked Gary.

"I think it's . . . I think it's true. Yeah . . . it is," he said, his voice filled with self-pity.

Swinging back to his narcissism and grandiosity, Ridgway said he expected the families at the hearing would ask him questions, which he would then answer in order to make them feel better. When I told him the hearing wouldn't work this way, and that no one really cared about what he had to say, he had trouble accepting it. I couldn't help but turn sarcastic.

"Well, what if someone killed your son?" I asked.

"I'd be ornery and mad about it."

"Would it matter what they said to you, explaining why?"

"It'd matter a little bit, but you know —"

Here I interrupted him and pretended to be a killer in the courtroom: "I killed your son because I'm evil."

"Evil, bad," said Ridgway.

"So please understand that," I added, my voice full of disdain. "Thank you very much."

Our talk turned to the questions left unanswered, and Ridgway made it clear that he was finished helping us. He continued to deny that he had stashed souvenirs of his crimes — jewelry, clothes, and so forth. Since every serial killer in history has kept mementos, I refused to believe him. That made Ridgway agitated, even angry.

"I'm, I'm a hundred percent, a hundred percent sure that you're not gonna find anything."

I saw to it that Ridgway would be 100 percent sure about the harsh conditions he would face in prison. We discussed the fact that he would be in solitary confinement, because so many inmates would want to kill him. And when he said that perhaps his twenty-eight-year-old son, Matthew, might come to visit and relieve the loneliness, I reminded him of a statement he had made that would be released to the press and public.

Ridgway had once gone into the woods and killed a woman while his young son waited behind in his truck. Our detectives had gotten him to confess that if Matthew had left the vehicle and witnessed the murder, Ridgway would have killed him, too.

"What do you think he's gonna do when he sees that?" I asked.

"Uh . . . I think he's going to be upset."

"Do you think he's comin' to visit ya?"

This took Ridgway aback. He stammered some protests, but I could see the point had been made. Soon he was talking about how he would suffer in prison. More self-pity. I couldn't help but mock him.

"You killed 'em all, Ridgway. You killed 'em all."

"Yes, I did."

"And you think you're gonna suffer by sitting in a cell?"

"I'm not gonna suffer as much as the women that I killed, no."

Just to make sure Ridgway understood what his status would be in prison, I explained that he was not just a killer. He was also a rapist. And rapists occupy the lowest rung in every prison. He fought me on this point, insisting that he had paid the women he killed for the sex they provided. We argued a bit. Then I managed to convince him that when he took his money back from his victims after they died, the sex became rape.

"I guess," he finally agreed. "I'll be a rapist-murderer."

This admission didn't seem sincere to me, but then again, I didn't come to see Ridgway expecting sincerity. To be honest, I came, in large measure, to make sure he knew what I thought of him. Later, when I viewed a videotape of the meeting, I realized that I had leaned into him, going nose-to-nose. And I had expressed a fairly significant amount of anger and outrage. I expressed it best in a little exchange we had about the excessive force he had used, which left his makeshift ligatures embedded in the flesh of his victims, and his reluctance to practice his evil face-to-face.

"You're a coward," I said. "You choked 'em from behind. You choked young, innocent women from behind. Sixteen-year-old girls. You got behind them, you choked them. You're an evil, murdering, monstrous, cowardly man."

For a moment, Ridgway was silent. He stared at me, with all the evil and cowardice I knew was present in his soul, and then he spoke the three words that let me know I had gotten through.

"Yeah," he said, "I am."

NINETEEN

Families First, and Last

No record of the serial murder case that we worked for nearly twenty years should end with the killer getting the last word, even if it is an admission of guilt. Gary Ridgway does not deserve that honor, because, in the end, the important figures in this story are those who died and the loved ones they left behind.

From the day I stood on the bank of the Green River and contemplated three young lives ended with brute force, it was my contact with the families of those who were murdered that kept me going. They had depended on me to bring the killer to justice and had given me, in exchange, their trust, kindness, and support. In the years that followed, none of us really gave up hope. And we grew closer than I would have first imagined possible.

I had these families in mind as the interviews with Ridgway were winding down and we approached two important court dates. The first would be November 5, 2003, when Ridgway would enter his plea. The second would come about six weeks later, when the judge would welcome families to speak before he imposed a life sentence on Ridgway.

We had been able to keep the plea bargain secret, but we knew that there would be a strong reaction once word got out, especially among the survivors of Ridgway's victims. For this reason, Norm Maleng and I decided that they should be told ahead of time. The county rented a hotel suite south of Seattle, and we made appointments with every family that wanted to come in. I accepted the responsibility of staying there for three days straight — 8:00 a.m. to 8:00 p.m. — to explain the decision that had been made, to answer questions, and, if necessary, to offer comfort or simply serve as a target for any anger that might arise.

The schedule allowed for about one half hour per family. Some didn't want to be there that long. Other family groups were so large — parents, grandparents, sisters, and brothers — that they needed more time to have all their questions answered. Fortunately everyone tried to be flexible, and we managed to get all the visits in.

Once I explained the reasons behind the plea deal, most families accepted that it had brought us as close to justice as possible. But this view was not shared by all. Members of at least three families were outraged to hear that Gary Ridgway would be allowed to live out his years, while their daughters and sisters were gone forever.

Tom Estes, for one, was livid. He said that Ridgway deserved to die and that there could be no other acceptable punishment. He went on to say that we had bungled the investigation all along, and that we could have prevented many of the killings from taking place. "You didn't try hard enough," he said. He was disgusted with the sheriff's office and no longer respected me or my team of detectives and deputies.

After all I had been through with the Estes family, Tom's words were hard to understand. No one knew better than

Tom the depth of my commitment. I recalled that when we solved Debbie's case, we shared tears and hugs and Tom had told me, "You kept your promise." Now he was destroying years of support and a relationship I thought was unbreakable.

I got another shock from the family of Connie Naon. The deal we made with Ridgway had produced a wealth of information about Connie Naon's death. But instead of being grateful, her family chose to rail at me and other members of the task force because they thought that the police had targeted their family over the years. They believed that traffic officers had stopped members of their family without good cause, and that teens in the family had been unjustly regarded as troublemakers by deputies in their local precinct. Supposedly that's why their daughter was out on the street.

Fortunately, almost all of the other families I met in those three days were able to understand the choice that had been made, and they recognized the wisdom in it. And when a few noted, "You're a victim too, Sheriff," I understood that they recognized me for something more than the role I had played. They saw me as a human being, a human being who had joined with them in a desperate and grief-filled cause.

One week before Christmas I joined families and friends of Gary Ridgway's victims in a hearing room at the King County Courthouse in Seattle. In the moments before the judge arrived, Tony Savage and a few sheriff's deputies led the killer to the defense table. He was dressed in jail-issued white cotton trousers and a white pullover, with a red T-shirt underneath. His face was pasty pale from the long days he had spent without sunlight.

Ridgway stared down at the floor as he walked. Once he

was seated, he focused on a stack of papers that had been placed on the table. A hush fell over the room, and it stayed quiet until Judge Richard Jones entered and delivered his instructions.

"We are here today for the sentencing of Gary Leon Ridgway," began Judge Jones. He went on to explain that time constraints would limit those who addressed the court to ten minutes each. And he assured them that he understood this was not adequate for family members to express "the extent and depth of your grief or the feelings you have about Gary Ridgway."

Next the prosecutors read the charges against Ridgway — all forty-eight — noting the names of those victims who had been identified and informing the court that Ridgway's plea of guilty, on each count, required a sentence of "mandatory life in prison without the possibility of early release or parole."

Judge Jones's decision to have all the names read, and to attach a sentence to each murder, required us to listen for a long time. But this was not a boring exercise. It had a powerful effect on the courtroom, concentrating our minds on the fact that we were there, at least in part, to honor forty-eight lives and to come to grips with the utter evil that Gary Ridgway represented.

Once the record of charges was read, dozens of people took their turns talking about the women who had been lost, the way the murders had affected their families, and the fate of the man responsible. Many made sure to remind us that the women who were killed were not the caricatures — street people and prostitutes — sometimes presented by the media. They were vibrant young people with hopes and dreams. They had been loved during the time they lived, and they were deeply mourned in their deaths.

As I expected, a few speakers criticized the plea bargain, and one, Connie Naon's mother, laced her remarks with bitter asides about the task force and its investigation. "Had the investigations gone right in the last twenty years," said Helen Dexter, "many of us would not be in this court today." She also issued harsh words for the media and for prosecutor Norm Maleng. She said they had "sold" the interest of the families.

At several points, Helen Dexter referred to the ongoing victimization of her family. And I think this feeling may be one reason for the anger she aimed at me and at others who had done their best to solve the Green River killings. She seemed to feel that her family was under a never-ending attack, so she had to lash out in every direction.

Others who spoke at the sentencing hearing showed they were at different points in the recovery process. Sure, almost all of them heaped venom upon Gary Ridgway. They said he was "trash," an "animal," a "terrorist," a "coward," and worse. And they said that death would be too easy for him. He should, instead, suffer every day of his life and then spend an eternity in hell. But when they eventually began to talk about themselves, and the loved ones who had been lost, one speaker after another offered insight, grace, intelligence, and courage.

Kathy Mills, mother of victim Opal Mills, displayed a level of spiritual depth and Christian commitment that was nothing short of amazing. "I want to thank Mr. Ridgway for there being no trial," she said, adjusting her granny-style glasses and glancing over at the man who killed her daughter. "That would be really hard to take. This is enough.

"Even if you may say you're sorry, Mr. Ridgway, it would not bring back Opal. You have held us in bondage for all these years, because we have hated you and we wanted to see you die. But it's all going to be over now, that is, prov ding we can forgive you.

"Gary Leon Ridgway, I forgive you. I forgive you."

Across the room at the defense table, Ridgway had turned to face Mrs. Mills, and he began nodding his head.

"You can't hold me anymore," continued Mrs. Mills. "I'm through with you. I have a peace that's beyond human understanding. My life today is lived to one day being with little Opal . . .

"I want to say good-bye, Gary Leon Ridgway."

With those words, Kathy Mills turned away from Ridgway and yielded the microphone to her son, Opal's older brother, Garrett. It was a testament to their relationship that Garrett announced he felt free to publicly disagree with his mom. He apologized to her as he said he couldn't give Ridgway forgiveness. She looked at him with love in her eyes and encouraged him to go on. Garrett then read a passage from his journal. It was written on a day when he visited places where he and Opal had once spent time — schools, playgrounds and former homes, as well as the banks of the Green River.

"I went to the school where we played and thought of her little chubby face and her Care Bear lunch box," he said. "I left a rose at the same swing set where we sat and dreamed about our future." Opal's dreams, he explained, included "having children, being rich enough to take care of our mother, and having a son and daughter who would be named Garrett and Opal. We'd all live together in a huge house, which she would buy, and watch cartoons and stay up as late as we wanted to."

To see this large, dignified young man and hear his tender words and loving memories of his sister was a moving experience. He said she was a tough "little peanut." She always stood up for him, he said, telling bullies, "That's my brother and you better shut your mouth or you'll get a knuckle sandwich."

I could easily picture the scene as Garrett described revisiting his old junior high school, where he and Opal sometimes danced to the cafeteria jukebox when no one else was around. "I ate the biggest doughnut I could find," he said with a smile, "in honor of her constant concern about her weight."

Garrett's journal entry ended with him sitting on a bench near the spot where his sister's body was found. He hadn't gone near the Green River in twenty years. A couple of fishermen stood on the bank, casting their lines. A couple of young lovers walked by. "I sat on that bench," said Garrett, "and cried."

Others shared their memories of little girls who loved horses, rode bikes, and played softball. Virginia Graham made it clear that one victim, her sister Debbie Estes, was not to blame for the circumstances that brought her into contact with Ridgway. She had taken to the streets as a teenager to escape "the first monster in her life," someone who was abusing her.

Like many others, Virginia said she welcomed the fact that Ridgway would suffer the pain of imprisonment and looked forward to his eventual death. "You are going to die of something," she said. "It is then that I will have closure in my life, not because you are dead but because the evil that you chose to become will have left this earth and gone to hell from where it came."

The grief and anger expressed by the women who addressed the court did not have any apparent effect on Gary Ridgway. He turned to face those who spoke, but he stared past them with unblinking eyes. He was lying once again, acting the way he thought that a normal person would act. But unlike any normal person, he was unmoved by the suffering of those whose lives he had ripped apart.

But when the men spoke, Ridgway seemed to react more. He shuddered as Charles Winston said, "I begged the sheriff to let me talk to you personally." He left no doubt that he had wanted to kill Ridgway, and he also made it clear that the desire continued to burn. "If you understand what that means, you need to be nervous," he added.

Chuck's son Kevin spoke for many of us when he said, "I hope you do go into the general population in prison. Don't go into protective custody like some sissy. It's easy to kill women. Let's see how you do against the other prisoners in the general population. Hopefully you won't last long."

Kevin plainly captured Gary Ridgway's attention, but the only man who moved Ridgway to shake, cry, and turn away was Robert Rule, whose wavy-haired daughter Linda disappeared in September 1982 at the age of sixteen. Dressed in suspenders and a tie, Mr. Rule was a large man with white hair and a white beard that came in handy when he played Santa Claus every Christmas. His face, even at this time and place, looked calm and kindly.

"Mr. Ridgway, there are people here that hate you," he began. "I'm not one of them. I forgive you for what you've done. You've made it difficult to live up to what I believe, and that is what God says to do, and that's to forgive, and He doesn't say to forgive just certain people. He says to forgive all. So you are forgiven, sir."

The tears that Ridgway cried after hearing these words were obviously in response to the amazing grace in Mr. Rule's statement. This meant that Ridgway's tears were a reflection of the sense of relief he felt from being forgiven. He was crying for himself, and not for any of the scores of women he had killed and the hundreds of people who had been stricken with grief.

Ridgway cried one other time, when he was invited to make his own statement. He walked up to stand before the judge and spoke in the same lying, raspy voice we had heard during six months of interviews.

"I'm sorry for killing all those young ladies. I have tried to remember as much as I could to help the detectives find and recover the ladies. I'm sorry for the scare I put into the community . . .

"I know the horrible things my acts were. I have tried for a long time to get these things out of my mind. I've tried for a long time to keep from killing any ladies.

"I'm sorry that I put my wife, my son, my brothers, and my family through this hell. I hope that they can find a way to forgive me. I'm very sorry for the ladies that were not found. May they rest in peace. They need a better place than where I gave them."

Before he read the names of the victims and announced Ridgway would serve a life sentence for each of their murders, Judge Jones had some words of advice for the families gathered in the courtroom. He suggested they honor the memories of their loved ones by investing time in the lives of other young people who needed help. He warned them to avoid thoughts of hatred and revenge, calling them "wasted emotions."

Then he turned to Gary Ridgway and said, "The remarkable things about you are your Teflon-coated emotions and complete absence of compassion. It comes as no surprise that you had such disregard for the lives of your victims. You violated the sanctity of every relationship in your life, including the one with your own son. When he was of a tender age, you used his existence and his presence to gain the confidence of your victims. You used your family to create the facade of an average hardworking family man."

The judge ordered Ridgway to turn around and look at the people in the hearing room. Ridgway did. And then Judge Jones said, "As you spend the balance of your life in a cell in prison, I hope the last thought you have of your time in the free world is of their faces. If you have one bit of emotion, you will be haunted for the rest of your life."

In the hours, days, and weeks after the hearing, many people who had seen bits of it on television asked me what I thought of Gary Ridgway. We all want to know how a child born on this planet can grow up to become a serial killer. We want to know the circumstances that lead to the development of such a human being, and whether he is human at all.

I can summarize what many of the experts about serial killers say. They believe that upbringing plays a role. Many, if not all of these killers were abused one way or another. But they also suspect that these people suffer from mental illness, brain damage, or a combination of the two. And they know for certain that the signs of trouble arise in childhood. Almost every serial killer was a bed wetter, a fire starter, and an animal abuser.

By the time he was an adolescent, Gary Ridgway exhibited the hallmarks of a serial killer. But even so, we have to remember that he still had freedom of choice. Other people suffer similar problems and worse in childhood but manage to do well in life. And mental illness is never an excuse for murder. In fact, psychiatrists will tell you that people with serious mental disorders almost never commit murder. They are far more likely to hurt themselves.

Ridgway never looked for a path to sanity. He never asked for help as a boy, and he practically ran from anyone who noticed something amiss when he was an adult. He didn't try to educate himself or advance in his work. Instead, he posed as a meek little family man while devoting enormous amounts of energy to the practice of murder.

How was it that he avoided feelings of guilt and shame? I have to believe that his mind was never wired for genuine emotions in the first place. Then he further shielded himself by rationalizing his deeds and pushing them into the deepest recesses of his mind. Lie built upon lie. The denial grew deeper and wider. Eventually, using what amounted to self-hypnosis, he mastered the trick of convenient forgetting.

With no emotions, no memory of his most grotesque acts, and no genuine relationships, could Gary Ridgway be considered a member of the human family? I have my doubts. To me, he is a machine who looks like a human being but possesses none of the higher qualities God gave to His creation.

But Ridgway is not an ordinary machine. By his acts and his attitudes, we know that as he abandoned his humanity, he also became truly evil. I believe there is evil in this world as well as good. And I also believe there is a hell. Whether God chooses hell for Ridgway is something I cannot begin to speculate about. But I have to wonder, if Gary Ridgway isn't a candidate for eternal damnation, who would be?

EPILOGUE

In God's Hands

WHEN ALL THE WORK was done and Gary Ridgway had pled guilty, I had one last chance to see him, man to man. On New Year's Eve 2003, the last day before he would go to state prison, I left my office and walked one short block to the King County jail. Each step was filled with a mix of emotion and memories I had never experienced before.

For years I had imagined confronting this sadistic, craven being, America's worst serial killer, with all the rage and loathing I felt inside. But on the previous Sunday, I had gone to church and heard my pastor talk about forgiveness and Gary Ridgway in the same breath. Other people were present — some would tell me they were shocked by the sermon — but it felt like he was talking to me directly.

"If there's no forgiveness for a Ridgway," the pastor had said, "can there be forgiveness for anyone?"

Three days later, the words rang in my ears as I entered the jail, passed through security, and walked toward the day room where he waited.

*　　*　　*

It's a cliché to say that serial killers look like ordinary men, but in Ridgway's case it is true. Medium height. Medium build. Thinning brown hair. Droopy mustache. Dull, steel-blue eyes behind clunky glasses. There is nothing powerful or distinctive about him. In fact, when I got to the room where he sat on a chair with his hands and feet in chains, he looked weak and pathetic.

Even as he said hello, Ridgway tried to ingratiate himself, telling me how much he appreciated the way he had been treated by my deputies and detectives. We were the last people who would ever treat him well. At state prison he would face hell on earth. I think he understood this.

"You were straight with me," he said.

I asked him again to tell me where he had hidden his souvenirs from the murders. Again Ridgway denied he had a collection. But in the middle of the denial, he slipped, saying, "You'll never find anything." By the tone of his voice I knew that there was something out there.

He was not going to cooperate anymore. He was not going to help me. I could feel my sense of reserve and restraint slipping way.

"You're a murderer," I said, surprised by the strength in my own voice. "You're a murderer, a rapist, a thief, and a coward. You're the worst kind of monster, Gary, a devil."

"I'm not a rapist," he insisted once again. "I paid those girls."

"Then you took the money back after you killed them!"

"I'm not a rapist!"

I changed the subject, asking Ridgway about his faith. A Bible reader in the past, he had recently declared that he had found God again.

"You know that story in Matthew where the woman is possessed and Jesus drove the demon out?" he asked.

"Yeah."

"I kind of think that I was possessed, that maybe that's what happened."

He was trying to hold on to his denial, to keep the guilt at bay. My pastor had preached forgiveness, but it will take time for me. I told him that I don't want anyone to go to hell. "Not even you," I said. "But that's where you're headed if you don't understand forgiveness. Unless you are forgiven, it's an eternity of unimaginable suffering."

Suddenly the man who had never felt the suffering of the women he killed or the families he crushed seemed to imagine his own soul's endless suffering. He began to shake, and tears streamed down his face. In the next half hour, he asked me about salvation. I told him that the key lay in his heart, in his own ability to sincerely accept his own guilt and beg for God's mercy. "And if you pray, and perhaps your memory is refreshed and you want to help some of these families, you call me."

He asked for my phone number and address, and I left them with him.

On my way out of the jail, I suddenly felt an almost dizzying sense of freedom, as if a crushing weight had been taken off my heart. I knew I faced a period of emotional turmoil. And in fact, I had already realized that all of my feelings — happiness, sadness, anger, joy — were much closer to the surface than they used to be. All of the pent-up emotions that I had never had time to express — grief, anger, frustration, and more — were ready to come out, and in due time they would. But in the meantime, I was going to enjoy the sense of relief.

For twenty years I had been held hostage by the Green River case, imprisoned by my own obsession with catching a killer and bringing justice to his victims. In those years, Ridgway had set a macabre record, murdering more people than anyone in U.S. history. I was finally walking away from the daily nightmare that was the Green River murders case. A terrible price had been paid, but in the end we had caught a man who many people believed would never be apprehended.

As I finish writing this book, I think about how we are all in God's hands. I have faith that He will take care of us all, including Gary Ridgway. And I notice, as I look out on a Seattle landscape that everyone associates with clouds and rain, that the sun is shining.

Acknowledgments

IN MOST BOOKS, this is the place where an author recognizes the many people who helped bring his work to print. Certainly I thank my editor, Reagan Arthur, and friends such as Sue Foy, Scott Sotebeer, and John Urquhart for this kind of assistance. They have all been enormously helpful with shaping the manuscript, offering suggestions, and keeping me from losing my way.

But this book is no ordinary work of nonfiction. It is an account of a twenty-year struggle against evil that required commitment and patience beyond imagination. For this reason, my thanks go mainly to the people who shared the fight with me and became a community of concern that supplied support, wisdom, and talent in ways I doubt I will ever see again.

At the top of the list is my wife, Julie, who knew she was signing up to be a cop's wife but was never told that her life would include helping me through the Green River case. As strong as she is beautiful, Julie made up for my necessary absences at home and put up with the times when I was both emotionally and physically drained. I could never express in words my love and gratitude in a way that reflects what I truly feel, but I intend to show her for the rest of our lives.

Similarly, my children, Angela, Tabitha, and Daniel, were patient, playful, kind, and understanding whenever I needed them to be. As youngsters, they didn't know that their childhoods were unusual. Today, as adults, they understand and are even glad to have been raised in a family where service to the community was a part of everyday life. Throughout the Green River struggle, they were always bright examples of the goodness in the world that I was struggling to protect.

During the long years of the Green River investigation, the team that chased the devil grew and shrank several times. Scores of people were involved, too many for me to offer adequate credit for their achievements. However, a few deserve to be singled out for their special roles in the investigation.

Fae Brooks, Randy Mullinax, Jim Doyon, Sue Peters, and Sheriff Vern Thomas stand out for their commitment, intelligence, and varied skills. I worked closely with them and felt a kinship with them as cops and human beings that will never fade away. Even when they were not assigned to the task force, Fae, Randy, and Jim checked in with me on a regular basis, offered analysis and advice, and expressed their concern for the victims and their families. Each of them also paid an emotional price for their involvement in the investigation, but none of them ever voiced a word of complaint.

I gratefully offer the same observations about Detective Tom Jensen and still cannot thank him adequately. Once he joined the task force in 1984, Tom never left the Green River case. Even when the investigation wound down in 1992, he stayed on as the sole investigator. His job involved following up active tips, accepting new information, and managing a collection of case files and evidence that could fill a supermarket.

Sometimes I compare a crime task force to a football team. The best group includes people with many different skills. In the case of the Green River Task Force, though, a better analogy might be a relay team. Tom was the last man to receive the baton, and he had to finish the race. He stayed on course, refused to give up, and in the end finished in first place. The entire Northwest will forever be grateful for his effort, especially those who ran their own legs of the race. I include here a list of people who were involved — with apologies to those I may have overlooked — so that they may be honored by name.

GREEN RIVER TASK FORCE, 1982–2003

Frank Adamson	GRTF Captain
Bob Agnew	FBI
Jerry Alexander	Port of Seattle PD Detective
Cheri Allen	Civilian Support Staff
Terry Allman	KCSO Major
Barry Anderson	KCSO Deputy
Bob Andrews	KCSO Sergeant
Frank Atchley	Detective Sergeant
Jeff Baird	Lead Prosecutor
Robert Bardsley	KCSO Detective
Richard Battle	KCSO Detective
Jackson Beard	Detective Sergeant
Brent Beden	KCSO Detective
Donna Blades	Civilian Support Staff
John Blake	KCSO Detective
Pat Bowen	KCSO Detective
Greg Boyle	KCSO Major
Rich Brenner	KCSO MPO
Fabienne Brooks	KCSO Public Information Officer and Detective
Malcolm Chang	KCSO Detective

Connie Chinn	Civilian Support Staff
Rick Chubb	KCSO Detective
Marc Church	Evidence Specialist
Robin Clark	Seattle PD Detective
Ben Colwell	KCSO Detective
Raphael Crenshaw	KCSO Detective
Wayne Cross	KCSO Deputy
James Doyon	KCSO Detective
Gerry Drake	KCSO Deputy
Elizabeth Druin	KCSO Deputy
Patricia Eakes	Prosecutor
Nate Elledge	KCSO Detective Sergeant
Bob Evans	KCSO Detective Sergeant
Pat Ferguson	KCSO Detective
Bill Frost	KCSO Special Ops
Robert Gebo	Office of Attorney General
Ian Goodhew	Prosecutor
James Graddon	KCSO GRTF Captain
Linda Grass	KCSO Latent Lab
Ray Green	KCSO Detective Sergeant
Carolyn Griffin	KCSO Detective
Paul Griffith	KCSO Detective
Larry Gross	KCSO Detective
Lisa Gross	Paralegal
Matt Haney	KCSO Detective
Derek Haining	KCSO GRTF Staff
Ed Hanson	WSP Detective
Mike Hatch	KCSO Detective
Sheila Hatch	Civilian Support Staff
Joe Higgins	Seattle PD Detective
Ralph Hope	FBI
Ty Hughes	Port of Seattle PD
Bob Hutchinson	KCSO Sergeant
Linda Jackson	Civilian Support Staff
Rick Jackson	VISS

Tom Jensen	KCSO Detective
Gene Kahn	KCSO Detective
Bruce Kalin	GRTF Captain
Rob Kellams	City of Kent PD
Bob Keppel	WA State Attorney General's Chief Investigator
Bob LaMoria	Office of Attorney General
Kathleen Larson	Public Information Office and Detective
Rupe Lettich	KCSO Civil Sergeant
Alice Lipp	KCSO Civilian Staff
Charlie Love	KCSO Detective
John Luer	KCSO Deputy
Cheri Luxa	KCSO Detective
Kirsten Maitland	Evidence Specialist
Graydon Matheson	KCSO Detective
Jon Mattsen	KCSO Detective
Larry Mayes	KCSO Lieutenant
Nancy McAllister	Port of Seattle PD
Ralf McAllister	KCSO Detective
Brian McDonald	Prosecutor
Henry McLauchlin	KCSO Detective
Tony McNabb	KCSO Detective
Bill Metro	KCSO GRFT Civilian Staff
Bill Michaels	KCSO Detective
Grace Mitchell	Civilian Support Staff
Jim Montgomery	Sheriff, 1988–1997
Ted Moser	KCSO Detective
Randy Mullinax	KCSO Detective
Lisa Murphy	Paralegal
Spencer Nelson	KCSO IIU Detective
James Nickle	Interim Sheriff
Dan Nolan	KCSO GRTF Administrative Lieutenant
Ross Nooney	KCSO CIS Detective

Sean O'Donnell	Prosecutor
Kevin O'Keefe	Seattle PD Detective
Elycia Organ	Database Manager
David Parks	Evidence Specialist
Jake Pavlovich	KCSO Detective
Susan Peters	KCSO Detective
Bruce Peterson	KCSO Detective
J. K. Pewitt	KCSO Detective
Tom Pike	Seattle PD Detective
James Pompey	KCSO GRTF Commander
Bill Ramm	KCSO Sergeant
Cecil Ray	KCSO GRTF Detective
Kelly Rosa	Paralegal
Erin Sanders	Paralegal
Ed Schoemaker	KCSO Deputy
Bob Seager	KCSO Detective
Paul Smith	KCSO Detective
Ivind Sondergaard	GRFT Volunteer
Frank Spence	KCSO Detective
Mick Stewart	KCSO CIS Detective
Bob Stockham	KCSO GRTF Detective
Walt Stout	Pierce County SO Detective
Ed Streidinger	Seattle PD Detective
Vern Thomas	King County Sheriff
John Tolton	KCSO CIS Detective
Charlene Underhill	Civilian Support Staff
David Walker	KCSO Detective
Chuck Winters	KCSO Detective
Tonya Yzaguirre	KCSO Latent Lab

In Memory

* Wendy Lee Coffield, disappeared July 8, 1982
* Gisele A. Lovvorn, disappeared July 17, 1982
* Debra Lynn Bonner, disappeared July 25, 1982
* Marcia Faye Chapman, disappeared August 1, 1982
* Cynthia Jean Hinds, disappeared August 11, 1982
* Opal Charmaine Mills, disappeared August 12, 1982
* Terry Renee Milligan, disappeared August 29, 1982
* Mary Bridgett Meehan, disappeared September 15, 1982
* Debra Lorraine Estes, disappeared September 20, 1982
* Linda Rule, disappeared September 26, 1982
* Shawnda Leea Summers, disappeared October 2, 1982
* Denise Darcel Bush, disappeared October 8, 1982
* Shirley Marie Sherrill, disappeared November 1982
* Colleen Renee Brockman, disappeared December 28, 1982
* Delores Lavern Williams, disappeared March 1983
* Alma Ann Smith, disappeared March 3, 1983
* Gail Matthews, disappeared April 10, 1983
* Andrea M. Childers, disappeared April 14, 1983
* Sandra K. Gabbert, disappeared April 17, 1983
* Kimi Kai Pitsor, disappeared April 17, 1983
* Marie Malvar, disappeared April 30, 1983
* Carol Ann Christensen, disappeared May 3, 1983

* Carrie Ann Rois, disappeared May 13, 1983
* Martina T. Authorlee, disappeared May 22, 1983
* Cheryl Lee Wims, disappeared May 23, 1983
* Yvonne Shelly Antosh, disappeared May 31, 1983
* Constance Naon, disappeared June 8, 1983
* Kelly Ware, disappeared July 17, 1983
* Tina Marie Thompson, disappeared July 25, 1983
* April Buttram, disappeared August 18, 1983
* Debbie May Abernathy, disappeared September 5, 1983
* Tracy Winston, disappeared September 12, 1983
* Maureen Sue Feeney, disappeared September 23, 1983
* Pammy Avent, disappeared October 26, 1983
* Mary Sue Bello, disappeared October 11, 1983
* Delise Louise Plager, disappeared October 30, 1983
* Kimberly Nelson, disappeared November 1, 1983
* Lisa L. Yates, disappeared December 23, 1983
* Mary Exzetta West, disappeared February 6, 1984
* Cindy Ann Smith, disappeared March 21, 1984
* Patricia Barczak, disappeared October 11, 1986
* Roberta Hays, disappeared February 1987
* Marta Reeves, disappeared March 5, 1990
* Patricia Yellowrobe, disappeared August 1998
* Human remains #10, located at S 146th ST/16th Ave S
* Human remains #16, located at Mountain View Cemetery
* Human remains #17, located at Mountain View Cemetery
* Human remains #20, located at the Kent–Des Moines
  Rd/Reith Rd

Four victims' remains have not yet been found. They are: Kassee
Ann Lee, Becky Marrero, Kelly Kay McGinnis, and Patricia Ann
Osborn. These cases remain uncharged. There are five victims
whose remains have been located but no identity established.
Ridgway is charged in four of those murders.